'Phyl?' The girl met her eyes. 'What happened to me?'

Phyl hesitated, but she knew she had to deliver the truth. 'It wasn't just a dream. You did fall. Down a rocky ravine. Fortunately your fall was halted by the undergrowth. There were a lot of bushes. They saved you.'

The girl looked down, puzzled. 'Maybe that's what I remember then, the falling . . . I've been thinking about things, trying to remember. And I can. I mean, I can remember things about San Francisco – buildings and the bridge. But I don't remember where I live. I remember the taste of frozen yogurt and that I don't like ice cream. I remember I like the colour red, but not whether I have a red dress. I remember the scent of mimosa . . .'

About the author

Elizabeth Adler was born in Yorkshire. She is married to an American lawyer and has one daughter. They have lived in Brazil, the USA, England, France, Canada and Ireland.

The Secret of the Villa Mimosa

Elizabeth Adler

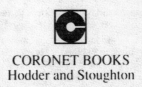

CORONET BOOKS
Hodder and Stoughton

First published in Great Britain in 1994
by Hodder and Stoughton
A division of Hodder Headline PLC

First published in paperback in 1995
by Hodder and Stoughton

A Coronet Paperback

10 9 8 7 6 5 4 3 2

British Library Cataloguing in Publication Data

Adler, Elizabeth
Secret of the Villa Mimosa
I. Title
823.914 [F]

ISBN 0 340 62867 7

Typeset by Keyboard Services, Luton, Beds

Printed and bound in Great Britain by
Cox and Wyman Ltd, Reading, Berks

Hodder and Stoughton
A division of Hodder Headline PLC
338 Euston Road
London NW1 3BH

For my sisters
Dorothy and Irene
and my brother-in-law
Peter

and for my father and Ken
with love

Heaven from all creatures hides the book of Fate.

Alexander Pope (*The Dunciad*)

Surely there are in everyone's life certain connections, twists and turns which pass awhile under the category of Chance, but at the last, well examined, prove to be the very Hand of God.

Sir Thomas Browne (*Religio Medici*)

PROLOGUE

The man was blond, tall, and definitely handsome, with the kind of well-muscled body that looked as good in clothes as you knew it would out of them. He parked the rented automobile – a white Lincoln Town Car, not the Ferrari or even the sporty Jeep Cherokee you might have expected from his cool, slightly arrogant attitude – at the arrivals exit of San Francisco airport then glanced impatiently at his watch. The evening flight from Honolulu was late and parking for more than a few minutes was risky. He might be noticed, moved on by the traffic cop, given a ticket. He strode quickly into the arrivals hall and checked the flight information screen. The plane had landed five minutes ago.

Outside again, he leaned against the car, hands thrust into his pockets watching the doors. He smiled when at last he saw her. Her soft, dark-copper hair swished around her shoulders as she headed for the taxi-rank clutching her green canvas bag. She didn't even notice him, didn't hear his soft footsteps as he came on her from behind. He heard her gasp as she felt the quick prick of the needle in her arm. Her terrified brown eyes recognised him and he smiled at her. With scarcely an 'oh' of shock and fear, she slumped into his arms and was bundled easily into the back seat of the waiting automobile.

He quickly flung a rug over her, slipped into the driver's

seat and pulled into the line of traffic crawling endlessly towards the city. He shrugged and lit a cigarette. What the hell, he had plenty of time. Plenty. He had time to kill.

Forty minutes later, he parked the car on Battery, stepped out, opened the back door and looked at the girl. He checked her pulse and lifted her eyelids. She was out for the count. No trouble from her. He pushed her onto the floor, covered her with the blanket, and locked the car. Then he lit a cigarette and strolled casually round the corner into Il Fornaio.

The brasserie was crowded. The noise bounced from the walls as he pushed his way through to a seat at the counter, ordered a Carta Blanca and small pizza with mozzarella, anchovies, olives and capers, checking the basketball scores in the *Examiner* while he waited. He had another beer while he devoured the pizza, then, because he never could deny his sweet tooth, he ordered the tiramisu.

'That's about as close to heaven as a dessert can get.' The girl sitting next to him smiled. 'I can never resist it myself,' she admitted.

She took a sip of her Margarita, half-smiling at him. Her hair was red and shoulder length, and she was about the same age as the girl he had just left, drugged and unconscious in his automobile. He shrugged and called for his check. 'Once in a while is okay.'

She had given him the opening and he could sense her waiting, but he turned indifferently away, heading for the cash register by the door. He felt her curious eyes on him, heard her laugh, sensing the so-who-cares shrug of the shoulders that accompanied it. She was young and pretty and she wasn't used to rejection. It was just that tonight she had picked on the wrong guy.

He unlocked the car, lifted the rug covering the girl and checked her again. She was still out and he climbed into the

2

driver's seat and eased the car out of the tight parking space into the traffic on Embarcadero. He knew exactly the spot he was heading for, but it was still too early. Still too much traffic, too many people, too many lights.

He cruised slowly through town, looping back on himself several times, finally heading north through the sub-divisions, past an area of elegant homes standing in their own grounds, past a golf course, up to where the road ran along the edge of a steep, wooded ravine.

He stopped the car and pulled the girl from the floor. She lolled against him and he cursed her dead weight as he half-carried, half-dragged her through the trees until he stood in a small clearing on the edge of the ravine. The fog had disappeared and a three-quarter moon illuminated the rocks and scrubby trees, and, far below, the tumbling stream that wound its way along the bottom. He hesitated, thinking longingly of the gun in his pocket. But it had to look like an accident. This was the only way.

He lifted the girl to her feet. He held her in his arms for a second until he got his balance. Then, with all his weight behind her, he thrust her over the edge into the abyss.

She made no sound. She didn't even know what happened.

The moon went behind the clouds and the fog rolled back, winding ghostly tendrils around him as he strained his ears for the sound of her fall. With a pleased whoosh of expelled breath he turned and felt his way through the trees to the car. Then he drove slowly through the dense fog, back to the sumptuous anonymity of his suite at the city's finest hotel.

CHAPTER 1

Homicide Detective Franco Mahoney of the San Francisco
Police Department watched impassively as the men from
the Fire Department Rescue Services clambered down
Mitchell's Ravine towards the girl's body. Not that you
could see much of her, just her foot in a red sandal and her
arm sticking up through the underbrush that had stopped
her fall but failed to save her life. Now she would be just
another statistic on the unsolved homicide list. He had seen
it all before, endlessly, and he turned away. He had a job to
do. Find her killer.

He glanced at his watch. It was eight a.m. His shift
would just be finishing and he thought longingly of the
other, luckier, guys, heading wearily for home, or for
breakfast together at the diner on Brannan, talking over
the night's mayhem or maybe just talking dirty, letting
off steam. It had been a long night: the usual drug killing
in an alley; a cutting in a squalid tenement room with
more blood from the tiny Chinese victim than had ever
been seen in a butcher's shop; and a body tossed out
onto the highway and run over several times before he
was discovered and found to have been shot. The call
about the girl in Mitchell's Ravine had come at 7.34. It
was his turn, his bad luck at the tail end of the shift.
Some nights he wondered if he had done the right thing,
becoming a cop.

He sighed feelingly as he surveyed the clearing at the edge of the ravine. It was crowded with guys from the Fire Service and the Public Health Department, as well as the paramedics, the Medical Examiner, the lab technicians taking photos and the TV news-crews, plus all their equipment: cables, winches, ladders, stretchers, oxygen tanks, drips and cameras. The damp grassy clearing was now just a sea of mud.

There had been just enough time to look around and assess that there was no sign of a struggle before the rescue services arrived and by now any vital clues had disappeared, churned into the mud.

Several uniformed cops, their eyes fixed on the ground, were sifting through the undergrowth, but Mahoney knew in his gut they were not going to find anything. There would be no torn off buttons today, no threads caught on a branch, no spent bullet casings, no perfect clue.

As a murder crime scene it was a dead loss. He grinned, excusing himself the pun. Agatha Christie would have had just one perfect footprint, he thought longingly. Me, I'm left with just a body.

And once the rescue services had arrived, that body had taken precedence. Everything must wait until it had been retrieved, even if it meant trampling on the evidence. The woman in the ravine still had her rights as a person, though probably for the last time. Then she would become just another toe-tagged waxen Jane Doe in the chilly steel drawer in the city morgue. Until the Public Medical Examiner finally got around to carving her up in search of physical evidence. Or until some distraught parent, or grieving – though maybe not – relative recalled that aunty Flo or sister Joleen or cousin Peggy Sue hadn't been seen around in a while and came inquiring.

He turned reluctantly to face the TV news cameras and

told them briefly what he knew. That the body of a woman had been discovered early that morning by a man out walking his dogs. No, the man was not a suspect. And no, he had no other suspect as of that minute. Thank you and goodbye.

Franco Mahoney had been a cop for fourteen years, seven of them as a detective on the Homicide Squad. He was said to be one of the best, a meticulous sifter of information and a finisher. He was known as a cop who never let go of a case. Years might pass, but Mahoney never forgot an unsolved murder. The facts and evidence re-rolled themselves in his head in bed at night and sometimes something clicked. He'd gotten convictions on a number of homicides that had been pushed to the back of the filing cabinet, labelled 'unsolved', by sheer persistence, hard work and intuition.

He had a 'nose' for a killer. 'It's like I can smell them. They are like bad meat, guys. That's all there is to it,' he would tell the news reporters whose favourite he was because he always kept his sense of humour and always gave them a good story, and besides he looked good on TV. The perfect macho cop.

'She's coming up,' the chief of the rescue squad yelled.

Franco stared at the girl as the sling-stretcher was winched carefully upwards. He had seen more murder victims than he cared to remember. Like any cop, he knew the only way to keep his sanity was to keep a mental distance between him and the victim. When that victim was a child, it was humanly impossible; and when it was a young girl, like this one, it was tough.

She was maybe twenty-four; her face was grotesquely swollen, a mass of purple bruises with livid red patches where the skin had been scraped away in her fall. There was dried blood on her nose and ears, indicating a fractured skull, and her copper hair was a mat of dark congealed blood. Maybe she had been pretty, he thought bitterly. Fun loving, free. Until last night when some cheap bastard decided not to let her live.

He stepped back to let the paramedics take over as she was winched over the edge. Clearing his throat, he began to take notes: 'Female caucasian. Probable age twenty-four. Estimated height five-seven. Weight a hundred and fifteen. Hair red . . .'

'Jesus man, there's a pulse. She's still alive!'

The paramedics were kneeling over the stretcher frantically inserting a drip into her arm, feeding her oxygen through a mask, wedging her broken skull with sandbags. They quickly eased pressure pants over her legs, inflating them to constrict the blood flow, forcing the blood pressure into her upper torso and head, then enveloped her in shiny aluminium shock foil.

'Wait a minute.' Franco stared at the double row of puncture wounds along her right forearm. 'What's that?'

The paramedic looked closely at the punctures. 'Damn me, Mahoney, those are teeth marks. A dog bite, I'd say. And a biggie.'

Mahoney followed them back through the woods as they rushed the girl back to the waiting ambulance and loaded her quickly in. 'Think she'll make it?' he asked.

The paramedic shrugged. 'I don't even know if we can stabilise her to get her as far as Trauma.'

Mahoney sighed as he assigned a uniformed cop to the San Francisco General Trauma Unit. 'Stay outside the operating theatre,' he ordered. 'Let me know if she wakes up.' It was no longer his business to care. He was a homicide detective. He needed a body before he could do his job.

'No need for us yet, Mahoney,' the Medical Examiner,

Pete Preston, said, climbing into his car. Like the detective, his job came after death.

'Not yet, Pete,' Mahoney said. 'But I have a feeling in my bones, this one's gonna be murder.' He sighed, shrugging off the early morning's events. 'How about I buy you a cup of coffee?'

CHAPTER 2

That morning, Phyl Forster woke, as usual at 7.30 a.m., in the Pacific Heights apartment where she lived alone. There was no need to turn off the alarm because she didn't need one; she always woke at the same hour. It went along with medical training: you learned to catnap when you had a spare ten minutes and to wake up by sheer instinct.

Thirty-seven today, she thought, striding towards the bathroom. Surprise, surprise, how it creeps up on a girl, and funny how I still feel only thirty-six. She paused and looked round her glamorous apartment, the symbol of her success. At the huge windows with their view of San Francisco Bay, at the shelves of books, the interesting paintings and pieces of sculpture by young American artists. At the old silk rugs with a burnished sheen scattered across pale wooden floors, and the hi-tech bathrooms and kitchen, all steel and halogen, white, grey and black.

Some people considered her home soulless, with its deliberate lack of colour, but Phyl thought the rugs and artworks and books were what made it live. All the rest was just background, the accoutrements of living: there to serve and not for show. 'Plain but good', as somebody's grandmother would surely have said approvingly. And all bought and paid for by herself.

She dressed in the same spare style. Monochrome understated chic by Japanese designers. With her shiny black hair sleeked into a chignon, her pale skin, red lip-stick and her startled-looking deep-blue eyes, she was a familiar figure on television and at book signings across the country. Because, as well as her successful psychiatric practice, she had also earned a fortune from her popular problems-solved-style books that sold in their millions. *Dr Phyl Focuses on: Matrimony*. *Dr Phyl Focuses on: Menopause*. *Sibling Rivalry*. *Divorce*. *Drugs, Alcohol, Domestic Violence*. Any trauma you could name, Dr Phyl could explain it in simple terms, and tell you how to cope, or how to overcome it. Oprah loved her.

She showered, thinking of the day ahead: a morning clinic at the San Francisco General where she gave her services free. Then the afternoon at the University of California Medical Center where she acted as a consultant; then private patients from four-thirty to seven-thirty. Try to beat the traffic on her way home. Shower, then a glass of red wine.

Afterwards, wrapped in a white terry robe, with her black hair tumbling free from its tight chignon, her face clean of makeup and artifice, she would have supper. Alone. Again.

But now she was towelling her hair dry as she watched the early morning newscast on TV. Political scandals; traffic; weather ... plus some news just in. Another homicide. An impassive-faced, macho-looking detective told them that the victim was a young woman discovered in a ravine by a man out walking his dogs.

Phyl watched, fascinated as the cameras zoomed in on the rescue services clambering down the ravine to the girl's body, half-hidden amongst the foliage of a large bush. They got her into a sling and began to haul her up. She caught a glimpse of coppery-red hair, a pale outflung arm, a foot with a red leather sandal still dangling from the toe.

She shuddered and pushed the off-button, horrified at her own voyeurism. She had surely seen enough dead bodies in her years as a hospital intern and then as a resident, but this was obscene. The girl looked so vulnerable, her final moments exploited by prying TV cameras. And she looked young, with her red hair and the jaunty red sandal. Last night she had been alive, perhaps out with her friends; walking, talking, maybe having dinner, dancing ... poor, poor little girl. Because Phyl knew she had to be somebody's 'little girl'. And no doubt today that mother would be told the dreadful final truth. That she didn't have a little girl anymore.

'Goddamn,' Phyl said savagely. She switched on the hairdryer and glared at herself in the bathroom mirror. Life could be rotten, as many of her patients could testify, but it was better than what had happened to that poor girl.

She dried her hair then swept it back so tightly her scalp hurt, twisting it into a knot at the nape of her neck. She dressed quickly; in minimalist silk underwear – she was lean and her curves had no need of underwires and Lycra – and besides, the silk was her touch of luxury, her secret beneath the façade of severe black and white she presented to the world. Sometimes she shared that secret, but not often these days. She shrugged as she buttoned the jacket of her black pantsuit. What the hell, work ruled. And besides, celibacy was fashionable.

Leaning into the mirror, she applied the Paloma red lipstick carefully. Her mouth was too wide, full and gentle. Without the bright lipstick it had looked soft and vulnerable. Coloured a vivid velvety red, it made a statement. She was a woman to be reckoned with. A woman at the top of her profession. A woman who knew what she was doing every minute of her day. Even if sometimes, she thought with a pang, her nights seemed a bit lonely.

She clipped gold and onyx studs in her ears, no other jewellery, just a man-size watch, big enough for her to tell the time without lifting her arm to check. So her patients wouldn't think that she was keeping her eye on the clock.

She picked up her black suede purse and her keys and checked her appearance one last time. Her working uniform. And no perfume; she never wore it to the hospital; it might disturb the patients.

Grabbing the big black bag containing the files she needed for the day, she took the elevator down, collected her car, a Lexus, black and compact and as designer understated as herself, and drove to the real world. The San Francisco General Hospital on Potrero Hill.

As usual, the hospital was busy, though it was still only 8.20 a.m. Her first appointment wasn't until nine and she headed for the cafeteria and the cup of coffee she hadn't been able to stomach earlier, after seeing the dead girl on television. Halfway along the corridor, she changed her mind. The Italian deli down the street made a more powerful coffee – and a wickeder Danish.

Outside, she heard the scream of an ambulance. She turned to watch. The paramedics were out in a flash, and a second later they had the stretcher on a gurney and were running with it, one holding the drip leading into the patient's arm, towards the waiting group of doctors and nurses. The patient's body was swathed in shiny aluminium shock foil, her head was strapped to the stretcher and supported by sandbags on either side. Phyl just caught a glimpse of a bruised ashen face, tightly shut eyes, blood-matted copper hair. *The girl from the ravine*.

'She's not dead after all,' she said surprised. And then, remembering her waxen colour, she added grimly, 'Not yet.'

Somehow, the Danish didn't seem as enticing as it had before. She turned on her heel and walked back into the hospital, her head down, thinking about the girl; about the parents who would be summoned to her bedside, about her chances of survival. Even from just the glimpse she had caught, it was clear she had serious head injuries, and lord knew what other damage, internal as well as external. 'Poor, poor little girl,' she said sadly, again.

Shaking her head to clear it, she grabbed a cup of coffee from the machine and strode down the shiny corridors to her office to begin her day.

By twelve-thirty she had seen eight patients and she was starving. Gathering together her notes and her files and putting them in the black bag, she thought hungrily of tomato, chicken and fresh basil on foccachia. Halfway to the door, she hesitated, glancing undecided at the telephone. She still hadn't been able to get the sight of the girl from the ravine out of her mind. Right through all her interviews this morning, she had kept superimposing herself on her thoughts: the foot with the jaunty red sandal dangling from its toe; the battered face as colourless as moonstones, the bloody head. A shudder ran through her and she strode quickly out the door and down the corridors to the Trauma Unit.

The nurse on duty smiled, recognising her. 'You mean the Jane Doe brought in at 8.22 this morning,' she said briskly. 'They assumed she was dead when they saw her down there in the ravine, but when they got her up she still had a pulse. And broken ribs, possible internal bleeding, and a couple of holes in her skull, left temporal area. They rushed her right into theatre and she's not out yet.' She glanced up from her notes. 'I guess they're doing their damnedest for her,' she said encouragingly. Then suddenly alert, 'You know her then?'

Phyl shook her head. 'I saw it on the early news. Somehow she just stuck in my mind.'

'I can imagine,' the nurse said feelingly. 'It's a pity you don't know her though, because we have no identification. The cops are still searching the ravine for maybe her purse, and clues I guess. But as far as I know, she's still just plain Jane Doe.'

'Maybe they'll run her picture in the newspapers,' Phyl suggested, still thinking of the mother, not knowing her girl was near to death. Surely a mother's touch, the sound of her voice, just her presence in the same room by the bedside would help. Suddenly it seemed terribly important to find her, to bring her here.

'There won't be any pictures,' the nurse said. 'Not the way she looks. Even her own mother wouldn't recognise her.'

Phyl sighed regretfully as she thanked her and turned away. It was foolish to become so involved, she didn't even know the girl. But still, she hoped she made it through. Forgetting all about the foccachia sandwich, she drove slowly through the traffic to the Medical Center at UCSF.

After the Medical Center, she saw her private patients, and for once she found herself losing her concentration. She was relieved when her last patient failed to show at seven, and it wasn't until she was driving home that she remembered she hadn't eaten a thing all day.

'No wonder you were losing it,' she admonished herself, because she felt guilty that she hadn't given her usual all to her patients. She swung the car impatiently onto Sansome, turned onto Embarcadero and found a parking spot right in front of Il Fornaio.

As usual, the restaurant was jammed. 'I could seat you at the bar, Doc,' the hostess said. Phyl often dropped in after work when she was too tired to think of fixing supper at home, and they knew her well. 'There's a quiet corner where no one will bother you.'

The hostess showed her to a seat at the far end of the bar and handed her a menu. Phyl ordered a glass of red wine. A copy of the *Chronicle* was lying on the counter. They had run a picture of the rescue scene at Mitchell's Ravine on the front page. GIRL'S BODY FOUND IN RAVINE, was the headline. She read it, surprised, but then remembered that at first they had thought the girl was dead. Probably tomorrow, unless something more important than poor little Jane Doe took over the news, they would reinstate her in the land of the living. Unless, by then, she *was* dead.

She toyed with her pasta, thinking about going home to her empty apartment, remembering it was her thirty-seventh birthday. On an impulse she ordered a glass of champagne and then almost instantly regretted it. A birthday was not a proper birthday celebrated alone.

She flicked through the newspaper, stopping at an enticing travel article about Paris. 'Paris.' The very word sounded full of promise: springtime and chestnuts in blossom, café tables under the trees, and walks by the Seine. A handsome man in your bed, sharing cups of hot, strong coffee the next morning . . . The stuff of dreams on a rainy San Francisco night.

She sighed wistfully again. She recalled vaguely there was to be a psychiatric conference in Paris later in the year. Maybe she would find time to attend after all. Feeling better, she called for her check, powdered her nose and added a flash of Paloma red to her lips.

The girl sitting next to her turned and smiled as she got up to leave. Her red hair swung round her shoulders, and Phyl thought with a pang of sorrow of the poor red-haired girl hovering between life and death in intensive care at the San Francisco General. With no one who knew her to hold her hand, no friend to whisper words of comfort, no mother to stroke back the red hair and tell her to hold on, she would be all right.

She called the hospital from the car. The neurosurgery had been successful, but the girl was in a coma. They were still not sure about brain damage. It might be a while before they knew, one way or the other.

Tears spilled down Phyl's cheeks, splashing down onto her jacket as she drove slowly home. Remembering things she did not want to remember, things that, as a good psychiatrist she had tried to put behind her. The fear and the guilt and the grief . . . And now, because of a young, brutalised red-headed girl lying in a hospital it had all come flooding back again.

'Fool,' she told herself severely. 'You're a damn fool, Phyl Forster.'

CHAPTER 3

The girl was hurtling through a dark tunnel, faster, faster towards a speck of light. She needed that light, needed it urgently, yet, no matter how fast she catapulted towards it, it was always the same distance away. But she knew she must not let it go, she had to catch up with it: it was where she belonged. Faster, she told herself, faster, fly towards it . . . and then she was falling, oh God she was falling, drifting downwards, arms outstretched. The sound of the wind was in her ears as she fell into an abyss from which she knew she would never return.

'No,' she screamed. 'No, no, no . . .'

'It's all right, honey, you're okay. Just don't worry about a thing.'

The girl tried to open her eyes but her lids seemed to have weights on them. And she couldn't move, couldn't feel. There was no use flying down the tunnel towards the spot of light. She was dead after all. 'I don't want to be dead,' she cried, anguished, 'I don't want to be . . .'

'You're not dead, honey,' the nurse said soothingly. 'You're right here in hospital. You had an accident, but you're going to be okay. Don't you worry about a thing.'

The girl did not trust her. She knew the abyss was waiting. 'Then why can't I open my eyes,' she whispered hoarsely.

'You will, honey. You will. Just give yourself time. Lie quietly now. Rest. The doctor is on his way.'

The girl lay still, taking in the sounds around her: the low hum of machinery and electronic bleeps, the rustle of starched cotton and the pad of rubber-soled feet across the room. She could smell things too: hospital smells of disinfectant and soap. And something sweet; a gentle floral scent that was hauntingly familiar. So delicate, so pretty, so . . . familiar. But still she just couldn't recall exactly what it was.

She tossed her head frustratedly on the pillow, then gasped as a pain like a hot knife shot from the base of her skull and exploded somewhere in her brain.

'Lie still, honey.' The nurse pressed her back against the pillows. 'Here comes the doctor now,' she added, sounding relieved.

There was the sound of brisk footsteps; then a cool hand on hers, and gentle fingers on her pulse. 'Well, young lady, we're certainly glad to have you back with us again.' The doctor's voice was crisp, deliberately cheerful, encouraging.

'Why?' she asked in her new, strangely hoarse voice. 'Did you think I was going to die?'

He laughed, a nice easy sound and she felt her own mouth stretch into a smile. 'We try hard not to let the pretty patients die on us,' he joked.

'Sexist,' she whispered, and heard him laugh again.

'The truth,' she begged. 'Please. Tell me the truth.'

She could feel him hesitate. Then, 'There was an accident. You were injured. Broken ribs, damage to the spleen – we had to remove that . . .'

'My head,' she insisted. 'What happened to my head?'

'Depressed fractures of the skull, in two places. We operated, fixed you up. Good as new.'

'Then why,' she asked plaintively, 'can I not open my eyes?'

He lifted her left lid and shone a light into it. It bounced somewhere in the back of her brain triggering memories of daylight and sunshine. Maybe she had come out of the dark tunnel after all. 'Are you real?' she whispered, still not believing.

He took her hands in both his. They felt strong, comforting, human. 'You are in the San Francisco General Hospital. You've been in a coma for almost three weeks. You're alive all right. Now all you have to do is get better. And don't worry about opening your eyes. Soon enough they will open and then you can check us out for yourself. Meanwhile get some rest. Maybe later, we can talk again. Then you can tell us who you are.'

'Who I am?'

'Later,' he said. 'Don't worry about it now.'

She heard his departing footsteps crossing the floor, a whispered conversation with the nurse, the closing of the door. From the deepening silence she knew she was alone.

An accident, he had said. Three weeks in a coma. In San Francisco. Was San Francisco her home then? She thought about it for a minute: vague images of Telegraph Hill, the TransAm building, the Golden Gate Bridge flipped through her mind. She told herself triumphantly, you do know it. But she did not know this hospital, she didn't know where it was, or what had happened that had put her in here.

An accident. She pondered on the word, visualising a car crash, the harsh screech of metal against metal, the sharp crescendo of breaking glass, the burn of brakes and rubber … but it was like a film without characters, it meant nothing to her. She did not remember it. She shivered. *Maybe it was better she didn't.*

21

The doctor had said head injuries, a brain operation . . . the pain zigzagged upwards again as she turned her head restlessly and she moaned. And then it came to her. She couldn't open her eyes because her face was smashed. They were keeping her sedated so she couldn't see the terrible faceless mess she was . . .

She tried to lift her hand, she wanted to feel it, trace the damage with her fingers, but her arm was anchored by needles and tapes and drip bottles and machinery.

Tears of despair trickled from her closed eyelids, coursing a hot salty path down her cheeks, into her ears. Like a child, she thought; in bed, crying in the dark, calling for her mommy . . . except there was no mommy.

'Mom?' she said tentatively, out loud. But she knew her mother was not there. She tried to bring a picture of her into her mind, but nothing came. That's odd, she thought, puzzled. I can remember how the TransAm building looks, and the Golden Gate Bridge, but I can't remember my own mother's face. I can't even remember her name.'

My name. She searched the blackness inside her head for an answer. There was none. There was just nothingness, and the tunnel threatening to drag her back again, away from the light, away from remembering. Away from life.

'You're going to be fine now, honey,' the nurse's voice had a smile in it. 'Maybe tomorrow we can unhitch you from some of these drips and machines. And maybe, if you're good, you can have a little ice cream for your supper.'

'I don't like ice cream,' she replied automatically.

'Well, frozen yogurt then. You like that don't you?'

Did she? She couldn't remember, yet she had just remembered she didn't like ice cream.

Panic forced her eyelids open. They lifted slowly, like a theatre curtain on a dim set, but still it dazzled her.

Gradually the room swam into focus. Someone was bending over her, the light behind her head like a halo.

It was a madonna's face. Pale skin, dark hair, red lips parted in a welcoming smile. She felt a cool hand on her brow as the madonna said, 'Hi there. Glad to see you're finally awake. I'm Phyl Forster.'

The girl gripped her hand as though it were a lifeline. 'Phyl,' she whispered, 'you must know me. *Tell me, who am I?*'

CHAPTER 4

Mahoney leaned back in his swivel chair in the squad room on the fourth floor of the Hall of Justice, concentrating on what he had just read about the Jane Doe found in Mitchell's Ravine. It wasn't much, that was for sure. Multiple injuries, in particular two depressed skull fractures that might have been caused by a blunt instrument. Or, on the other hand, they might have happened when she bounced from the rocks.

Then there were the dog bites. Obviously she had raised her right arm to protect herself from an attack. The dog was big, no doubt about it. 'We're talking your Rottweiler, Doberman-type dog,' the experts had told him. 'Not your Pit Bull though. They have a different grip. And a Pit Bull would never have let go.'

Had a stray Rottweiler attacked her? Chased her to the edge of the ravine? Maybe she had stepped back, unthinkingly, into the abyss? He shook his head, he didn't think so. Where there was a dog like that, there was a man. Had he set the dog on her? Had he planned to rape then kill her? He shrugged wearily. The world was full of crazies. Anything was possible.

He went over the girl's details yet again. They still had no identification. There was a round-the-clock uniformed cop waiting at the SF General, and since he hadn't heard anything from him today, he guessed she was still in a coma. It was still a 'will she or won't she make it' situation.

He thought about suicide and decided there was no chance. If you wanted to throw yourself off something in San Francisco, it wasn't Mitchell's Ravine.

No, this was an attempted homicide all right, and if it wasn't for the miracle that the undergrowth caught and held her, and the marvel of modern neurosurgery, then it would have been 'homicide' three weeks ago, instead of just 'attempted'. And God knows there was nothing harder to prove than 'attempted' murder; he knew only too well that it was likely to be downgraded to 'aggravated assault'. Either way, the poor girl was the loser. She either lost her life, or lost the satisfaction of sending her assailant away for a lot of years.

He pushed back his chair and strode to the coffee machine. He took it black with no sugar and as he tasted it he wished it were stronger, then he decided that with the amount he drank in a day he'd probably be a shaking caffeine wreck if it were.

He was a big man, thirty-nine years old, tall, and a fitness fanatic who spent what spare time he had working out at the Y or running in the hills. A San Francisco Marathon runner twice over, he had plans for the New York event, maybe next year, if he could make enough time to train up to it. And get off the coffee habit. Still, that was better than the Italian half of his family, on his mother's side, who drank more red wine and grappa than anyone he knew and still stayed standing. And the Irish half, on his father's side, who could put away the Paddys with the best and still sing 'Galway Bay' at the end of a long night without tripping over the words.

He leaned his bulk against the wall, sipping the coffee, watching the early Friday evening turmoil: a dozen phones ringing; an early drunk yelling obscenities in the holding tank; a blank-eyed man being interviewed; a desperate-looking couple demanding help finding their teenage son; an arson suspect; a youth accused of a stabbing. He thought you needed the patience of a saint to be a cop – and that was something they didn't tell you at cop school. That, and never to assume anything. He couldn't tell you how many times he'd proven that one right. Because, folks, he thought, wending his way back to his desk to pick up his ringing phone, in the real world virtually nothing was the way it seemed.

'Yeah?' He leaned back, his feet on his desk, the phone clamped between his shoulder and his ear, sipping his coffee. 'Doctor who d'ya say? She's here now? Okay, tell her I'll be right with her.'

He checked his notes again. A Dr Forster had been appointed by the neurosurgeon to help in the rehabilitation of Jane Doe. He hadn't known she was a woman doctor though. He sighed, suddenly realising who she was. Female and famous. Great. Just what he needed on a busy Friday night with a virtually clueless attempted homicide. He guessed he must be one of the few who had never seen her on TV or read one of her books. And he didn't see how she was gonna be of much help now. He knew if the girl came out of the coma, Dr Phyl Forster would want to protect her from his questioning. And he knew he had a job to do. He would want to question her as soon as possible, before she forgot what she remembered.

He decided to let Dr Forster wait a while. Give the lady psychiatrist a little character test. See if she could keep her cool, or whether she would play Miss High and Mighty Famous Doctor with the poor dumb cop.

Phyl had driven straight from the hospital to the precinct.

The neurosurgeon had told her that Mahoney was anxious to interview the girl as soon as she came out of her coma, and she wanted to explain personally that he must not. At least, not yet. She paced the corridors, peering impatiently through the glass doors at the organised chaos inside. She thought it was a bit like the hospital; a sudden slice of real life that jolted her out of the safety of her own carefully planned and controlled environment.

She glanced impatiently at her watch. Goddamnit, where was the man! She had been waiting ten minutes, and she was exhausted. Maybe it was reaction to seeing the girl come back to life, like a swimmer surfacing deep water. God, the relief of it. Then the flutter of apprehension when she realised the girl didn't even remember her name. Anyhow, she just thanked the lord she was alive, that her motor senses were functioning properly, and that she was rational, if understandably distressed.

'Ms Forster?'

She swung round and met Franco Mahoney's Irish blue eyes. *Unsmiling* eyes she noticed. She offered her hand. 'I hope I'm not interrupting, but I wanted to talk to you about your Jane Doe. The girl in the ravine.'

His eyes hardened. 'Is she awake? I asked to be told the moment she came out of it . . .'

'And I came here to tell you exactly that news, Mr Mahoney.'

'Detective,' he corrected her.

'*Detective* Mahoney.' She sighed. She could tell he was going to be difficult. He was handsome too, if you liked big and brawny with half a day's growth of beard. Six-four or thereabouts, broad in the shoulders, narrow at the hips and with that macho gun in his holster. He had thick black hair with a wave in it, worn combed straight back, a strong Italian nose, a firm Irish jaw, a wide, easy-going mouth, and his sea-blue eyes had upward crinkles at the corners, as though he smiled a lot. Though you'd never believe it now. If this wasn't a head-to-head confrontation, then she had never seen one.

She said, 'The girl regained consciousness just over an hour ago. I've spoken to the neurosurgeon, and he agrees that it is too soon yet to start asking her questions. She is still very ill. And she is distressed.'

Mahoney heaved an exasperated sigh. 'Miss Forster . . .'

'Doctor Forster.'

His blue eyes grinned mockingly at her. 'Doctor Forster. You understand we have an attempted homicide here. My job is to catch the perpetrator of the crime. The assassin.'

'The girl is not dead.'

'Would-be assassin,' he amended impatiently.

'And *my* job is to help return the girl to health. *Mental* health, Detective Mahoney. Apart from her considerable physical injuries, she has suffered severe mental trauma. If, as you suggest, it wasn't an accident after all, and someone really did try to kill her, you can only imagine what she is going through. Trying to remember.'

'*Trying* to remember?'

'Right now, Detective, your Jane Doe cannot even remember her own name.'

'Jesus.'

He slumped back in his chair, staring at the ceiling, ignoring her. She stared stonily at him. She thought he was as big a chauvinist as she had ever met.

Leaning across the desk, she gave him her most feminine pleading smile. 'I'm sorry, Detective Mahoney, but it's for the girl's own good. Imagine if she were *your* wife, or *your* daughter. You wouldn't want them to be forced to confront the facts about what happened, before they were well enough to withstand the shock.' She shrugged sadly. 'The girl is suffering from retrograde amnesia, a loss of memory for events preceding the trauma. Caused obviously by the injuries to the skull, but I feel certain also by the mental trauma of the assault. Often in these cases the memory returns involuntarily. Maybe by tomorrow she will have remembered, maybe she'll be eager to talk about it, anxious to get to the truth, finally. If not, then I shall try to help her. Meanwhile, bear with us. Please.'

He sighed. 'Okay. If you say so.'

Times might change, she thought exasperatedly, but not men. At least, not all of them.

'I guess you're right,' he admitted, grudgingly. 'But you'll understand I'm just as concerned as you are, Dr Forster. Somebody tried to kill her. If she dies then it's my job to bring that person to justice, and in order to do it I'm gonna need her help.'

'So what do you know about her? Besides her probable age and what she looks like?'

'I can tell you in two words. Not much. When she was found she was wearing Levis and a white Gap T-shirt. A blue cashmere sweater was found nearby. And sandals.'

Phyl remembered the red sandal dangling forlornly from the girl's toe. She shivered. 'No jewellery? A watch, a wedding ring?'

'Only pearl earrings.'

'Good pearls?'

He nodded. 'Small but good, they tell me. Still, she could have bought them anywhere. Same with the jeans and the T-shirt. The cashmere sweater had no label, and the sandals were French. Expensive, like the earrings and the sweater, but you can purchase them in good stores across the country. Or even in France, I guess. No purse. We searched that ravine thoroughly. There was nothing else. There's no missing person matching her description. No

30

fingerprints on record. No one has come forward claiming to know her.'

'So tell me, Mahoney, what makes you think someone tried to kill her?'

He gave her a long exasperated look and then said slowly and deliberately, as though he were explaining to a child, 'The ravine is far enough out to need a car to get there. No car was found near the scene. She did not live in the area, so she wasn't out walking her dogs and just happened to slip down. She had to have been taken there and then dumped. Or, more likely, pushed over the edge.'

'She wasn't raped.' Phyl knew that from the medical reports.

He shrugged. 'Maybe she wouldn't come across and the guy got mad. It happens. More often than you think,' he added grimly.

'So there are no clues?'

'None, other than the dog bite. And what the girl can tell us.'

'And that brings us back to the reason I'm here.' She gave him the smile again, and a little feminine shrug of the shoulders.

'So it does,' he said abruptly, standing up, dismissing her. 'You've got forty-eight hours. Then we'll have to reassess.'

He walked with her to the door. 'Thanks,' she said sarcastically as he opened it. 'For your cooperation.'

He watched her walk down the corridor, noting her long slender legs and the swing of the hips under the black suit. 'Hey, Forster,' he called after her. She hesitated, then turned slowly round.

'It's *Doctor*,' she said icily.

'Yeah. *Doc*. There's a nice little Italian restaurant round the corner from the General. Maybe after I've interviewed the girl, you and I could go there. Have a bite? Compare notes?'

She laughed at his Irish chauvinist cheek. 'Why, thank you for the invitation, Detective Mahoney,' she retorted sweetly. 'I'll have to think about it, and "reassess".'

Phyl was back at the hospital, bearing flowers, at nine the next morning. She had puzzled all night over what might have happened to the girl, and about who she might be, worrying why no one had come forward to claim her. No mother had come in search of her lost daughter; no lover; no husband. Not even a work associate or a girl friend. She was like the invisible woman – there, but no one could really see her.

She was there all right this Saturday morning though. In person, sitting up and taking nourishment. It was a shock, seeing her shaven head with the livid scars running across the scalp, and the still bruised and swollen but undeniably pretty face.

'Well, well,' Phyl said, smiling with genuine pleasure. 'Aren't you the lively one today.' She leaned forward and kissed her on the cheek, depositing the big bunch of flowers on her lap. 'For you.'

The girl's eyes widened with pleasure. She picked them up and buried her nose in them. 'Mimosa,' she whispered. 'Such a heavenly scent. I smelled them when I first woke up. It must have been you who brought them?'

Phyl noted that she recognised the flowers but she made no comment. She took a seat next to the bed and accepted the offer of a cup of tea from the nurse. 'How's your patient doing?' she asked, smiling her thanks.

'Better than we expected last night, Doctor. You can see for yourself, she's on the mend.'

'Last night I was in a tunnel.' The girl looked at Phyl

despairingly. 'I thought maybe I was dead. It was so dark, terrifying, I couldn't escape. And then I was falling, just falling and falling into an abyss, and I knew I would never come back . . .'

'Well, now you are back so you see, it was all just a bad dream.'

'Phyl?' The girl met her eyes. 'What happened to me?'

Phyl hesitated, but she knew she had to deliver the truth. 'It wasn't just a dream. You did fall. Down a rocky ravine. Fortunately your fall was halted by the undergrowth. There were a lot of bushes. They saved you.'

The girl looked down, puzzled. 'Maybe that's what I remember then, the falling . . . I've been thinking about things, trying to remember. And I can. I mean, I can remember things about San Francisco – buildings and the bridge. But I don't remember where I live. I remember the taste of frozen yogurt and that I don't like ice cream. I remember I like the colour red, but not whether I have a red dress. I remember the scent of mimosa, but not where I've smelled it before. I remember you, from last night, and the nurses and the doctors, but I cannot recall a single person from my past. She lifted huge frightened brown eyes to her and said, 'What ever am I going to do?'

Phyl patted her hand encouragingly. 'Okay, now you listen to me. You are just a few hours out of a coma, only three weeks away from a major trauma and surgery. There's no need for you to remember one damn thing right now, so stop worrying about it. Soon enough you'll remember. Until then, concentrate on smaller things: think about books you might have read, music you enjoy, favourite paintings, the kind of clothes you like to wear.'

'I like what you are wearing.'

Phyl laughed. It was Saturday and she was in her off-duty

33

uniform: black jeans, black suede loafers, white shirt and black leather jacket.

'Especially the belt. Is it from Tucson?'

Phyl stared at her surprised. The belt was American Indian, black leather with a silver and turquoise buckle. 'Santa Fe,' she said, pleased. 'You recognised it.'

'I suppose I did.' The girl looked surprised and she laughed.

'See, your memory is coming back already,' Phyl said comfortingly.

'It just seems to be there,' the girl said. 'Things pop out. Like the mimosa, and the belt.'

'That's the way it goes. And speaking of going, I must be on my way. I don't want to tire you out and undo all the good work.'

'Phyl?'

Phyl glanced inquiringly at her.

'Why did you come to see me? If you don't know me?'

Phyl hesitated. She didn't want to tell her about seeing her on television. But there was also another reason. One she didn't choose to talk about to anyone. She said, 'I was at the hospital when they brought you in. I was concerned about you. I'm a psychiatrist, and I work here, at the General, three days a week.'

The girl smiled wryly. 'A psychiatrist. Then I guess I'm in the right hands. You've got yourself another nutcase to straighten out, Doctor.' Her eyes widened in astonishment. 'Dr Phyl Focuses . . ,' she said. 'It's you. You're famous.'

'Well, look at that. You remembered.'

'I did too,' the girl replied, pleased with herself. 'And there's something else I'm sure I'll never forget. The sight of your lovely face, smiling at me when I came out of that tunnel of despair.'

Gratitude shone from her eyes and Phyl gulped back her emotion. 'Glad I was there,' she said quietly. 'See you later, young lady.'

'Phyl?' The girl called her back as she was halfway out of the door. 'Just one thing. Do you have a mirror? I want to see what I look like. I still can't get out of bed, and nobody seems to possess a hand-mirror in this hospital.'

Phyl hesitated; she knew it was dangerous. First, because the girl was only a few hours out of the coma. Second because she looked like hell, all bruised and battered, and the swollen face and naked shaven head with its livid red scars would be a terrible blow. And third, because she might suddenly recognise herself and remember what had happened. And it was too soon. Too much of a shock.

'Maybe tomorrow,' she promised, waving goodbye, 'I'll bring one.'

CHAPTER 5

'You're young,' Dr Niedman told the girl later the next morning. 'Strong as a horse. It would take more than a broken skull to kill you.'

'But they *shoot* horses to kill them, don't they?' she wailed irrationally. 'And I got pushed over the cliff.'

Niedman sighed. Detective Mahoney had called him and insisted on interviewing the girl earlier that morning. That's why she was so upset.

'Don't believe everything you hear from the cops,' he said with a cheerful grin. 'Maybe you were just out walking and fell. After all, who would want to harm a nice girl like you?'

'I don't know,' she said simply. 'But then I don't know who I am either. Maybe if I knew that, I would know why someone wanted to kill me.'

There was a knock at the door and Phyl Forster came in. Her blazing blue eyes met Niedman's. 'I heard Mahoney was here,' she said angrily. 'Did he ask your permission to interview the patient?'

'Unfortunately, he did. He said you had given him twenty-four hours and that every hour that passed made his job more difficult. Now that the patient was awake and sitting up and taking notice, he suggested we might be thought to be obstructing the course of justice. I had to agree, though I didn't approve.'

Phyl snorted angrily. She thrust a Saks bag at the girl, and deposited a kiss on her cheek. 'For you,' she said. 'To perk you up for the unveiling.' She turned back to Niedman. 'Today's the day she gets to see your handiwork.'

Niedman laughed as he stood up to go. 'Sorry about the haircut,' he said to the girl, 'but I'm the best stapler in the business. A few months and you won't even remember you had to be patched up.'

'Oh I hope I will,' she said, looking alarmed, and they laughed.

'First though, we have to get you out of that hospital nightshirt and into something a bit more flattering,' Phyl said. 'The nurse will help you change, and I'll be back in a minute.'

The girl stared wonderingly after her, then she opened the bag and unwrapped the layers of white tissue paper, smiling with pleasure as she saw the pale pink silk and lace. 'How pretty,' she said, running her hand across its cool smoothness. 'How lovely.'

Phyl was on the payphone in the hall, calling the precinct, tapping her foot impatiently as she waited for Franco Mahoney to pick up the call. 'You jumped the gun, Mahoney,' she said when he finally responded. 'By seven hours, not to mention the period of "reassessment" we talked about.'

'I talked it over with the surgeon in charge,' he replied coolly. 'He gave me the go-ahead. Naturally if he hadn't, I wouldn't have done it.'

Phyl gritted her teeth; he was an arrogant interfering bastard and he might have done untold harm to her patient. 'Goddamn it, man, what did you ask her? Why didn't you let me be there at least?'

'Hey, hey, I'm no ogre. I was gentle. I didn't insist, for

God's sakes. I asked her what she knew and she said, "Nothing." I asked her her name and she said she didn't know. I couldn't decide whether she was telling the truth or just stalling. You're the expert, you tell me?'

Phyl almost stamped her foot, she was so angry. 'Of course she's not stalling, you idiot! The girl has been traumatised. She can't remember because subconsciously she doesn't want to remember. She has pushed it all away from her, to some recess in her mind with a Do Not Disturb sign on it. And it's my belief she's not going to remember voluntarily. Not until something happens that brings it all back to her.'

'And what then?'

'What then?' Phyl thought about it. 'Why, someone had better be there to pick up the pieces, that's all.' And she knew as she said it, that it would be her.

She put the phone down on Mahoney and walked slowly back to the girl's room.

She was sitting up, smiling, wearing the new pink nightdress. She watched Phyl come back in, searching her face for a reaction.

'Now you look better,' Phyl said approvingly. 'I thought this might be the only time in your life you could wear pink.' She grinned. 'When your hair grows in, you'll be back in blue.'

'It's beautiful. Thank you. But you didn't have to ... I mean, I'm nothing to you.'

'Sure you are. You're something to all of us here. You came to us broken, and we put you back together again. And speaking of that, are you ready for the unveiling?' The girl's apprehensive eyes met hers.

'Is it really bad?' she whispered, suddenly afraid.

'It's not wonderful,' Phyl admitted. 'The truth is your face is swollen and badly bruised but it's not seriously

39

damaged. You still have the same nose you were born with, your eyes are in the same place, you didn't lose any teeth. In other words, there's nothing that time, and a new crop of hair, won't fix. Just prepare yourself for the sight of the scars on your scalp. And the . . . the *nakedness* of it.'

She held the mirror for her and the girl took a long look at herself. Tears spurted from her eyes. They ran down her face, dripping onto the new pink silk nightdress.

'Take it easy,' Phyl said gently.

'But I don't know her,' she whispered anguished. 'I don't know that girl.'

Phyl took a Kleenex and mopped the tears. 'You will, one day soon. I'll help you to find yourself again. I promise. And anyhow, you don't look exactly like you right now.' It was like talking to a child, she thought. And then she suddenly wanted to cry too.

'Why are you so good to me?' the girl said, pressing her head against Phyl's cool hand. 'I'm no one. Nothing. A meaningless non-person. You don't have to be nice to me; you're busy, successful, famous. *Why* are you bothering with me?'

'It's my heart of gold,' Phyl said lightly.

'No, it's not. It's more than that, isn't it?'

Phyl nodded.

'Won't you tell me?'

The girl was holding *her* hand now, reversing their roles. Phyl's chest felt tight and the muscles at the back of her neck were rigid with tension.

Her voice shook as she said, 'Perhaps one day. When you are better.'

She pulled herself together and said briskly, 'I'm forgetting the rules. You are the patient. And I'm the famous analyst, here to help you. Not the other way round.'

They looked at each other. Phyl sniffed back her tears,

reaching for the Kleenex. 'If you are still prepared to let me be your doctor, I think maybe you are crazy after all.'

'Your mascara is running,' the girl said gently.

'So much for tearproof!'

They grinned at each other and then Phyl reached out and hugged her. 'I just felt you needed someone around,' she said. 'Why not me?'

'I can't think of anyone better.'

Their eyes met again. 'Except maybe my mom,' the girl added wistfully.

CHAPTER 6

It was strange being anonymous, the girl thought, staring at her face in the mirror a week later. Strange but somehow peaceful. After all, if no one knew who she was, then no one would try to kill her. And why would anyone want to kill her anyway? What had she done to create such anger, such violence in a person?

She stared down at the row of red scars on her arm where they said a dog had bitten her. Surely she should remember that. It was a big dog, Detective Mahoney had told her. A Rottweiler or a Doberman. Did she know anybody with such a dog, he had asked? All she could do was shake her head, and then she had gasped with pain and put up her hands.

'I'm sorry,' Mahoney had said, and she could read the sympathy in his warm blue eyes. 'I really don't want to hurt you. But between us, the Doc and I have to sort you out. I have to figure out your past, and she's working on your future. All we need is a little input from you.'

'I'm trying,' she had said, desperately casting round in the blank that was her mind for any stray memories. 'All I can think is that you don't look a bit like I thought a detective should look.'

His eyes had crinkled at the corners as he grinned at her. 'The leather jacket's just a disguise to fool the felons, make them think I'm one of them.'

'They'll never believe it,' she smiled back. 'You look too nice to be a criminal.'

'You'd be surprised how "nice" a lot of criminals can seem. That's how they persuade lovely girls, like you for instance, into letting them take you home. Or out on a date.'

She knew he was angling for a response and she only wished she could give it to him.

'Maybe I wasn't the sort of girl who got picked up in a bar and let a guy take her home,' she said doubtfully. 'Do you really think I was that dumb?'

'No I don't. But you sure as hell are pretty. Who knows, somebody might have followed you.'

He was getting nowhere and she saw him sigh as he looked down at the yellow pad with only a few brief notes scribbled on it.

'I'm sorry,' she said. 'I really want to help. I want to know who I am. Maybe I'm not remembering because I feel safer. If nobody knows who I am, nobody will want to kill me.'

He shrugged as he stood up to go. 'Run that one by Dr Phyl,' he said. 'It's more her line of work than mine. One more thing though. When we found you you were wearing light clothing – too light for San Francisco in early March. And the rest of the country was under ice, apart from a couple of hot spots. Maybe you had just arrived from a warmer climate. Mexico? Florida maybe? Or Hawaii? The Far East? I've checked the airlines but you'd never believe how many women travel alone to these vacation resorts, and how many flights there are each day. We're checking them all, individually, but if you happen to dream you are on a flight tonight, just let me know which one it is. It'll save a hell of a lot of time.'

He winked cheerily as he went out the door and she laughed even though it made her head hurt.

But she still did not recognise her face in the mirror. And she could not recall getting on a plane. And she had not recognised her clothes when he had shown them to her.

She had flinched in horror from the bloodstained T-shirt and sweater, but she had touched the red leather sandal and read the label inside it. *Stephan Kelian, Paris*. She had felt Mahoney's eyes riveted on her as she had hesitated, running her finger along the label.

'Paris?' she had said wonderingly, searching her empty brain for the answer to the tingle of emotion she was feeling. But there was nothing and she had burst into tears.

Phyl had arrived then and she had practically shoved Mahoney out of the room.

'Brute,' she had called after him down the shiny hospital corridor.

'Give me a break, Doc,' he had cried, backing away, arms outstretched pleadingly. 'I'm just a guy doing his job.'

'*Ohhh!*' Phyl had been speechless and the girl's tears had turned to laughter at her outraged face. That was when Phyl had suggested hypnotising her.

'We've taken every test, tried everything,' Phyl said, 'and frankly, we're getting nowhere. Retrograde amnesia such as yours often responds to hypnosis. But do you think you are ready for it?'

'Ready to know the truth, you mean? For better, for worse?'

Phyl nodded sympathetically. 'For better, for worse. Either way I want you to know you can count on me for support. Whatever happens.'

'I know.' The bond between them had grown into friendship over the few weeks they had known each other. One woman looking to absolve her past; the other seeking it. She had nodded her agreement and today was the day of the experiment.

Phyl breezed through the door carrying a huge bunch of mimosa. 'It's the first thing that really triggered a memory,' she said, setting the flowers on the table. 'Maybe it will help.'

She drew the curtains and sat opposite her in the darkened room. 'Are you nervous?' she asked, patting her hand comfortingly. The girl nodded. 'No need to be. Just relax. Empty your mind and listen to my voice.'

The girl did as she asked: Phyl's voice was low, soothing, rhythmic. Her eyes closed on command and she was taken back in time, such a long way, such a long time ago . . .

'Where are you now?' Phyl asked gently.

The girl drew in an amazed breath. 'Oh, it's a lovely place, so beautiful. It's the place I love most in all the world.' Her voice was light, childlike.

'And where is that?'

'A long long way. Oh yes, it's a long way away. It's so peaceful . . .'

'Do you know where it is?'

Her voice faltered. 'Where? I don't . . . I'm not sure . . .'

Phyl saw she was disoriented and said quickly, 'Tell me what you see in this lovely place.'

'A child, sitting on the steps of a wonderful pink villa. I hear the sound of a hundred songbirds. I feel the coolness of the marble against my legs, and the warmth of the sun on my face. And ohh . . . I can smell the mimosa . . . there's just the sound of the birds, and the rustle of the tall trees in the breeze . . . and . . . and something else . . .'

Phyl leaned closer. The girl's expression had changed from innocent happiness to frozen fear. 'What is it?' she said urgently. 'You can tell me, you can trust me with your secret . . .'

'Footsteps on the gravel. Someone is coming up the driveway. Getting closer, closer ... a great dark cloud is looming over me, stifling me, shutting out the lovely pink villa and the light ... there's only the scent of the mimosa...'

Tears flowed down her cheeks and Phyl watched her quietly for a moment. 'Poor child,' she whispered. 'Do you know *who* it is coming up the drive?'

The girl shook her head, crying silently.

'Is the child you?'

She shook her head again. 'I don't know. I just don't know who it is.'

'Do you know how old the child is?'

'*Non, je ne sais pas.*'

Phyl blinked in surprise. 'You answered me in French. Do you speak that language fluently?'

'*Oui. C'est pareil pour moi, Français ou Anglais.*'

'And can you tell me where you learned to speak French so well?'

'I ... I don't know.'

She was distressed again and Phyl asked her one last question. 'Do you have a French name?'

'My name? I have no name ... I don't know ...'

'It's all right. Don't distress yourself. But I want you to remember everything you have told me about the pink villa. You can wake up now. Come, open your eyes. Look at me.'

The girl's eyes flew open. She put up her hand to touch the wetness on her cheeks. 'Tears?' she said wonderingly. 'Why was I crying?'

'*Peut-être vos mémoires sont tristes?*'

'*Tristes?*' She stared astonished at Phyl, then she said. 'My God, I spoke to you in French. What *does* it mean, Phyl?' She stared pleadingly at her. 'Please tell me.'

Phyl went over what she had recalled about the villa. 'Do you remember anything like that happening to you?'

The girl shook her head angrily, 'Oh God, I wish I did.'

'Don't be upset. It's progress. Quite a breakthrough I'd say.'

'Really? You mean that?' The girl looked pathetically pleased at the small ray of hope Phyl offered. 'Did I tell you my name?'

Phyl laughed. 'No, not yet. But we can't go on calling you Jane Doe for ever. Why don't you just go ahead and choose a name? Any name you please. Think of all the famous redheads throughout history.'

'Beatrice,' the girl said thoughtfully after a while. 'You know, Dante and Beatrice. She's famous enough. Besides, I don't feel like a Rita Hayworth or a Queen Elizabeth the First.'

'Mmm, Beatrice . . . Bea. Sounds good. And how about "French", since it's the first thing you have remembered?'

'Bea French. It sounds great.' The girl laughed, pleased, pushing her terror of not knowing who she was temporarily away from her. 'Now maybe I'll be a somebody again, instead of an anonymous nobody.'

CHAPTER 7

It was seven p.m. two weeks later and Mahoney had just finished his shift. Three hours late as usual.

'You know y'only do it just to make the rest of us guys look bad,' complained Detective Valentino Benedetti. 'Why can't you finish a shift promptly like the rest of us?'

He was a tall man with a red face, a beer belly and flat feet that were the bane of his life and the butt of every cop joke in the squad room. He was also known for working the fewest hours God sent to any detective – and he somehow got away with it. Unless it was legitimate paid overtime of course.

They were sitting up at the bar in Hanran's, drowning their sorrows and attempting to solve the day's problems over a beer.

'Why d'ya only drink that light crap instead of real beer, like Bud? What kinda cop are you anyways, Mahoney?'

'A tired cop, Benedetti, that's what I am. I've just spent four hours hanging around the court, trying to get an ignorant felon put away for robbing his grandmother and then tying her to the bedpost with her stockings. Surprise, surprise, she died. He pleaded not guilty. He only meant to tie her up for a joke, he said, oh so sadly. The fact that the stockings were tied around her neck and she choked to death probably in front of his eyes meant nothing. He put on the performance of his life. Said he's only nineteen, he

49

loved the old lady, she had been a mother to him. It was just spur of the moment, kid stuff, he was a good boy really. And he had a stack of witnesses to prove it. As shameless a bunch of liars as you're ever likely to meet, even in Court No 3. He got two years suspended sentence, and fifty hours community work. Jesus, Benedetti! D'ya ever wonder why you're a cop?'

They downed their beers in silence, contemplating the inequities of the American judicial system. Benedetti ordered two more and the barman slid them down the counter, along with a bowl of pretzels.

'Y'ever hear what happened to the girl in Mitchell's Ravine?' Benedetti asked, taking a deep swallow of Budweiser. 'I mean, I know she didn't die and technically it's not your problem. I just wondered if the assailant had ever surfaced. Y'know, if he'd come back to try again in case she remembered who he was and told the cops?'

Mahoney shook his head. 'I've been tied up for the last couple of weeks. We got nowhere on the airlines check, nowhere on missing persons and nowhere on fingerprints. Nobody came forward looking for her, and as far as I know she's still recovering from the head wounds in the General. The interesting thing about the wounds, though, was the dog bite.

'There are a lot of big houses in that area and most of them have guard dogs. I had them checked, but suddenly they are all sweet family pets. All of them were in their nice homes being fed Alpo and steak and affection the night of the attack. At least that's what their owners claim and there's no way to prove otherwise. And they are all solid citizens, families of wealth and standing, pillars of society.'

He grinned mockingly. 'But you and I know all about pillars of society, don't we, Benedetti? We know never trust a man by the cut of his clothes and the amount of money in his bank account. Because underneath, he's just a man.'

'Like you and me,' Benedetti replied gloomily, ordering up another couple of beers. 'Only without the big bank account.'

Mahoney put up his hand. 'No more for me, pal. I'm going to call the hospital and see if I can pay my young Jane Doe a visit, before they shut for the night. Thanks for the beer.'

He strode through the crowded bar to the payphone, dialled the hospital, identified himself and asked to be put through to her ward.

'The patient is sleeping, Detective Mahoney,' the ward sister told him. 'But Dr Niedman has just finished his rounds. Would you care to speak with him?'

'Sure. And thanks, Sister.'

Niedman came on the phone, sounding harassed.

'I won't keep you, sir,' Mahoney said quickly. 'I just wondered if you could bring me up to date on the progress of the Jane Doe from Mitchell's Ravine.'

'Ah, you mean Bea French,' Niedman said tiredly.

'Excuse me? *Bea French?*' Mahoney almost yelled at Niedman. Nobody had bothered to contact him and tell him she had remembered who she was. 'Is that her name then?'

'Not exactly. She and Phyl Forster invented it. After Dr Forster hypnotised her and found she spoke fluent French. They seemed to think it appropriate.'

Mahoney felt his blood pressure rising like sap in his veins. Goddamn it, good old Doc Forster had gone ahead and hypnotised the girl without so much as telling him. God knows what else she had revealed besides the fact that she spoke French. He was exploding with anger. It was the first real clue they had and he was the last to know.

He thanked Niedman, hung up the phone and checked his watch. It was almost eight-thirty.

He stalked to the parking lot, automatically eyeballing the kids littering the sidewalk. They quickly melted into the night as something in his black-leather-jacketed presence breathed 'cop' to them. He knew a couple of the faces and he guessed they were up to no good, hanging around in the rain, but he was off-duty and in a hurry. Tonight they had gotten themselves a break.

His '69 glossy black Mustang convertible started at the first touch and he took a couple of seconds to enjoy its finely-tuned growl before taking off in a shriek of rubber and adrenaline.

Phyl Forster lived on a very smart street in a very smart building in Pacific Heights. Mahoney parked on the double yellow and surveyed the canopied entrance, the uniformed doorman, the immaculately maintained façade. He whistled. Doc Forster was doing all right.

Sticking his hands in the pockets of his jeans, he sauntered towards the entrance. The doorman stared suspiciously at him, until he flashed him his badge, then hurriedly let him in. Mahoney took in the marble lobby covered in about an acre of oriental rug, the huge gilt-framed mirrors reflecting crystal vases filled with fresh flowers, and the antique consoles and deeply-cushioned chairs. He wondered what the doctor's monthly maintenance bill was.

He waited while the doorman telephoned to see if Dr Forster would see him. 'You can go on up,' he finally told Mahoney reluctantly. He wasn't used to police in his quiet, affluent building. 'Apartment 10B.'

Mahoney strode carefully across the oriental rug into the wood-panelled elevator, checking his appearance in the mirror as it zoomed noiselessly upwards. He smoothed back his hair, brushed the rain off his leather jacket and thought about what he wanted to say to the Doc about Bea French. He was still simmering with anger.

The door to apartment 10B stood open and he walked in. Phyl was wearing an oversize white terry robe, no makeup and her black hair hung loosely around her shoulders. She was curled up on a black couch and she looked drained and exhausted. She stared at him but she didn't get up.

'To what do I owe the honour, Mahoney,' she asked wearily. 'Isn't it a bit late for the cops to come calling?'

He stared back at her unsmiling, bristling with anger. 'Why the hell didn't you tell me you were going to hypnotise the girl? Why didn't you let me know the result? How the hell is it that I'm the last person to get to know what's going on with Bea French?'

Her sapphire eyes darkened to jet with sudden anger. 'How dare you shout at me,' she yelled back. 'Didn't you tell me she was no longer your concern? Unless she died of course. Then you could have had a field day. The clever, macho cop, the darling of the media, solving yet another homicide. Well, I'm sorry to disappoint you, Mahoney, but she didn't die. She's very much alive and now she's in my charge. Not yours.'

He stood over her, his hands in his pockets. His eyes met hers as he said quietly, 'And what do you think our murderer will do when he finds out Bea is still alive? That he didn't kill her after all? You're the clever one, Doc. You tell me. Whoever he is, he wanted her dead. How does the old saying go? "*If at first you don't succeed, try, try again?*" Take it from me, Doc, he will.'

She stared back at him, shocked into silence. He thought she looked suddenly vulnerable, her face pinched and drained of colour.

He turned away, glancing round the sumptuously-simple immaculate apartment. Everything gleaming, everything carefully arranged, everything in its place. He took off his black leather jacket and flung it onto the Eames chair that looked as though no one had ever sat on it, and walked through to the pristine steel, granite and halogened kitchen.

He opened the refrigerator, checked the contents and began taking things out of the cupboards.

'What the hell do you think you're doing?' Her voice shook with indignation and fatigue.

'What does it look like I'm doing? I'm cooking dinner. Since you don't look as though you have the energy.'

'You're cooking dinner! I didn't ask you to dinner. I didn't even ask you round for a drink!'

He threw her a mocking grin. 'Y'know what's wrong with you, Forster? You sit on your butt all day. Or maybe it's all that lying on the couch that does it. You should be working out, training, running. Getting all those endorphines working for you. Sharpening up your braincells.'

'Like yours I suppose.' She flung herself from the sofa and leaned angrily across the expanse of black granite counter that separated her from the kitchen, her eyes shooting blue venom at him.

He glanced up from chopping tomatoes. 'You think I'm just an ignorant backstreet boy, don't you? A guy who made it up to detective the hard way? Well, y'know what? You're right. And it was tough.' He shrugged his wide shoulders expressively. 'A scholarship to Berkeley, working every job I could get so I could eat as well. Graduated Magna with an honours degree in English literature. My thesis was on the effect of the European Romantic Poets on the American approach to human relationships today. I was in my second year as a grad student at Stanford when I decided I wanted to be a cop instead of a professor.' His eyes met hers coolly. 'Just so you know who I am, Doc.'

She stared silently at him, his shirt sleeves rolled up, chopping tomatoes in her kitchen, softly whistling an aria from *Traviata* whose title she couldn't remember. Then she sank into a chair and put her head in her hands, ashamed.

'I'm sorry,' she said. 'I'm just so goddamn tired. It's been a long day. A long week, month, year... And anyhow, you're wrong. I'm the one up from the streets.'

He flung the vegetables into a pan with a slug of olive oil, then folded his arms, leaning against the counter, waiting gravely for her to tell her story; but her pale face looked suddenly closed and tight with a remembered pain she was not going to admit to him. Not yet, anyway.

'I'm so busy taking care of everyone else's problems, there's just no time left,' she said finally, shaking her head in bewilderment. 'No time for myself. I bring my work home with me.'

He glanced round the cool, perfect, beautiful room. 'Yeah. I can see that. It looks as though you forgot to live here.'

He took a bottle of red wine from the rack and checked the label. 'Good stuff,' he said approvingly, pouring her a hefty glass. 'My Italian mamma used to tell me a glass of red wine brought a blush of colour to a girl's cheeks and a glow to her heart. I've always hoped it was true.'

She smiled as she took a sip, staring tiredly into her glass.

He walked across and studied her CD collection and soon the pure sound of Callas singing an aria from *Norma* wafted through the lofty silent rooms like a refreshing breeze.

Fifteen minutes later she was sitting opposite him at the kitchen table with a fragrant bowl of pasta and fresh tomato sauce in front of her.

'Sorry, I couldn't find any bread,' he said, pouring wine into their glasses. 'Except for a wizened crust that must have been there for about a week. I guess you're not much of a bread eater. Always thinking about your weight huh?'

'I am not,' she retorted indignantly. 'I love foccachia, *and* olive bread, *and* sourdough. And I'm not always thinking about my figure. Thank God, I don't have to. Yet.'

He grinned at her as she wound a forkful of pasta and tasted it, and she realised too late he was baiting her.

'It's just that I don't eat home that often,' she said, needing to explain. 'It's usually late and I'll just grab a bite on my way home.'

'So why didn't you do that tonight?'

'I was too tired to even care,' she said honestly.

'Or too lonely,' he said, sipping his wine and watching her eat.

She glanced at him for a moment, but said nothing. He got up to change the record and she watched him walk across the room. She thought he walked like an athlete, on the balls of his feet. Lithe, like a panther. Only this panther stalked the jungle of the city streets. Then she remembered what he had said about the killer and she was suddenly afraid for Bea.

He came back and sat opposite her, his elbows on the table, sipping wine, watching her eat.

She finished the pasta and sighed with satisfaction. 'That was wonderful. It's also the first home-cooked food I've eaten in about a year.'

She sat back and they looked at each other. 'What do you want from life, Mahoney?' she asked, suddenly curious.

He laughed off her question. 'Oh, to be Police Commissioner one day. Or maybe run for Mayor. Just like any other red-blooded cop. And?'

'And what?'

'And what do you want from life, Doc?'

She flung her arms wide, indicating the beautiful apartment, the priceless rugs, the artworks. 'What more can any woman want,' she said defensively. 'I've got it all.'

'It sure looks like it, Doc,' he said, standing up abruptly and putting on his jacket.

She glared at him. He didn't say it but she knew what he was thinking. *Maybe she wanted a man who loved her; children; a happy, bustling home; maybe a dog or two . . .*

Damnit what was she doing, letting this macho-chauvinist, poetic, opera-loving, fitness-freak cop put her life on the line? She had it all organised, everything in its place. Didn't she?

'You're tired,' he said, offering his hand. 'Thanks for the dinner. And the company. Let me know what happens with Bea.'

It seemed odd to hear the girl's new name on Mahoney's lips, as though his saying it brought her to life again.

A resurrection, she thought, as she closed the door behind him.

Dr Niedman was waiting for her at the General the next morning.

'Our patient is doing well, Dr Forster,' he said. 'In fact well enough to be dismissed.' He glanced up from his notes. 'The question is, of course, dismissed to where? I understand from Detective Mahoney that his investigations have led nowhere, and as you too seem to have drawn a blank, I'm at a loss to know what to do about her. I don't want to put her into a psychiatric ward since there is nothing mentally wrong with her, other than the loss of memory. On the other hand, how can she cope if we simply turn her over to welfare?'

Phyl thought about Bea with her shorn head and her terrible scars, knowing nothing about herself, not even what had happened to her. She thought of her out on her own, on the streets again, and she remembered what Mahoney had said the previous night. That if the killer knew she was alive, he might try again. Perhaps he already knew it from the newspapers? Maybe he was just waiting for her to get out of hospital . . . ?

'Bea can stay with me,' she said quickly. 'After all, I'm the one responsible for her rehabilitation.'

Niedman's bushy eyebrows raised over his spectacles in surprise. 'Isn't that a bit over and above the call of duty, Dr Forster?'

'I like her,' Phyl said defensively. 'We have become friends, as well as doctor and patient.'

'I see. Well, she is a nice girl and I for one am glad of your offer. It surely helps resolve my dilemma. I reckon next weekend, if that's all right with you?'

Phyl went to tell Bea the good news. 'It's been six weeks,' she said. 'You must be sick and tired of gazing at these four walls, so you can come and gaze at mine for a change. At least the view is better, though I can't guarantee the food.' She thought of Mahoney's delicious pasta and smiled.

Bea laughed delightedly. 'Believe me, *anything* is better than hospital food. But are you sure, Phyl? I mean, it's a terrible imposition, taking in a perfect stranger . . .'

'Hey, hey, what do you mean? A perfect stranger? Let's not forget that right now I know you better than anyone else. Besides, I like you. And it'll be fun having a room mate. I haven't had that pleasure since college.' She laughed, looking round the bare hospital room. 'At least we won't be fighting over closet space.'

That night Mahoney came by again, surprising her. And this time with a gift. A charming cream and chocolate

Siamese kitten. It looked minute in his big hands, purring confidently, quite certain it would be loved.

'I thought the apartment was too lonely,' he explained. 'A cat will keep you busy, keep you from getting introverted. Think of her as therapy. And make no mistake, this kind of cat thinks it's human. You do as she tells you. She wants to play, you play. She wants to eat, you serve her food. She wants to hug, baby you get hugs. So tell me right now, Doc, if you're not prepared for all that, and I'll take her back to the breeder.'

'Who is the breeder?' The tiny cat's wide blue eyes stared into her own.

'My Aunt Sophia, down in Sacramento.'

'You drove all the way to Sacramento to get this kitten for me?'

He looked nonchalant. 'I thought you needed something to care for. It takes you out of yourself y'know, having to think of someone besides yourself. Even a little cat.'

She looked accusingly at him. 'You wanted to make me more "human".'

He grinned. 'I guess you could say that. Anyhow, her name's Coco. Kinda chic, I thought. Like you.'

'This is a very personal gift, Mahoney,' Phyl said warily. The kitten was crawling up her shoulder, burying its soft damp nose in her neck, tangling its paws in her hair. She laughed. 'But your Aunt Sophia certainly knows what she's doing.'

'Then you want to keep her?' He looked anxious. 'Remember, she needs love and affection.'

She glanced sceptically at him. 'I guess I have enough of that to give, despite what you think. And what can I give you in return?'

'Buy me dinner sometime?'

She laughed, hugging the kitten to her breast. 'You drive

a hard bargain, Detective Mahoney. By the way, I'm getting a room mate.'

'I know. I spoke with Niedman. When?'

'At the weekend. I thought maybe if she were here with me, I could work with her. I also remembered what you said about the killer, and I thought she would be safe. Until she remembers who she is, that is. Besides, she has no money, though for all we know she might be an heiress.'

'A chance in several million, but I learned the hard way a long time ago, never to discount *any* possibility. That little cat needs a litter tray, if you don't mind me speaking frankly, Doc. Better fix it real fast so she knows where to go. Then you'll never have any problem with her.'

'Spoken like an expert.'

'Yeah, well I have three of my own. That and opera and cooking keep me from being too introspective. Well, I'd better go. I'm due in court in half an hour. See ya, Doc.' He paused at the door. 'By the way, I'm following up the French connection with the passport and immigration authorities. If Bea is really French, we'll soon know who she is.'

CHAPTER 8

Bea felt like an amateur in the game of life. She knew how to do everyday things, even what music she liked, and how to cook. Nothing fancy, but she was capable enough, and she remembered recipes, many of them French. She remembered the familiar faces of TV personalities, the names of authors whose books she enjoyed, movies she had liked. But she didn't know where she had seen those faces before, or where she had read those books or what cinemas in what towns she had seen the movies.

'Don't worry about it,' Phyl told her. 'It will come to you, bit by bit. Remember you are on R & R leave here. Rest and Recuperation. I just want you to get strong again and enjoy life.'

But even though Phyl sounded confident, Bea wasn't at all sure that her memory would return, because every time she tried to cast her thoughts back she came up against the same blankness. It was as though her mind were covered by the same black cloud as the child on the steps of the pink villa she had dreamed about. Because she was convinced it was only a dream. If that villa had ever existed, she would have remembered it. And if the child were her, she would have known who she was.

She had not told Phyl that. Phyl still thought it was a breakthrough. And certainly the fact that she spoke French as easily as she spoke English was a remarkable find. And it was good Parisian-French the experts had deduced from her accent, though she didn't recall ever being in Paris. It was the only definite thing from her past. Unless it was not a true memory but just a second-nature reaction. Something locked into the computer part of her brain that never disappeared, like knowing how to cook.

Phyl had said thoughtfully, that it was an asset that might prove useful later, though she refused to say why. And anyhow, Bea did not want to think about later. She didn't want to think beyond this moment.

She had been at Phyl's a month and had rarely left the apartment, but this evening Phyl said she was taking her shopping. Bea didn't know whether she was looking forward to it or not. The idea of the crowded stores and people staring at her cropped head, of making choices, walking in the street, eating in a restaurant, terrified her. *Real life terrified her.* She liked it here, in Phyl's beautiful apartment. It was big, light, uncluttered. *Safe*.

Mahoney rang from downstairs to announce his arrival. He had gotten into the habit of dropping by from time to time. 'To check on the cat,' he said.

'To visit *Phyl*, you mean,' Bea said, teasing him. She laughed at his embarrassment. 'Come on, Detective Mahoney, admit it. I can't blame you, she is gorgeous. And wonderful. And generous.'

'And an occasional pain in the ass.' Mahoney grinned, letting the kitten clamber up his leg, claws clinging to his jeans. He scooped her up and sat her in the palm of his big hand and she stared arrogantly round, claiming her victory.

'And anyway, how do you know I'm not working undercover, pretending I'm here to see Coco when in reality I'm checking on you? Seeing if you're holding out on me and have remembered everything?'

'I'm not holding out,' Bea said seriously. 'I really can't remember a single thing about the past. Not even,' she hesitated and a flash of fear crossed her face. 'Not even who tried to kill me.'

The door slammed as Phyl breezed in, home early to take Bea shopping. Since Bea had moved in Phyl's whole life had changed. Here she was, the dedicated loner who kept her emotions to herself and valued her privacy and independence above all, sharing her home with the victim of a murder attempt and a Siamese cat. And you know what, she liked it. She liked having someone yell hello when she came home, and the appetising smells of cooking coming from the kitchen and Coco scampering eagerly to greet her, claws skittering on the polished boards. She didn't even mind the cat hairs on her black jacket.

Somehow in these weeks together they had helped each other. Phyl the smart psychiatrist who locked away her own emotions and her past by burying herself in her work: and Bea, the girl with no past and a threat hanging over her future.

Phyl yelled 'Hi' as she flung her raincoat onto the sofa instead of hanging it neatly in the closet as she would certainly have done a few weeks ago. Today, she was going to begin Bea's rehabilitation. She had plans for her. And over dinner, after the shopping expedition, she was going to reveal what those plans were.

She sighed as she saw Mahoney with Bea.

'Not you again, Mahoney,' she said scathingly. 'How ever are they managing at the Hall of Justice without you? Or are you just on your way to solve the crime of the century and finally make it to Mayor?'

Mahoney sighed exaggeratedly and Bea grinned, watching them spar. He folded his arms wide and quoted in a melodious voice:

> '*Or if thy mistress some rich anger shows,*
> *Emprison her soft hand and let her rave,*
> *And feed deep, deep upon her peerless eyes...*'

Then he said solemnly, 'Doc, someone should tell you that aggression does not suit you. Seems to me Swinburne had the right answer.'

'I'm not your "mistress" so don't quote European poets to me, Mahoney. And if you're here to collect on that dinner I owe you, I'm sorry but I already have a date.'

Mahoney grinned. 'Yeah. Bea told me. Shopping and dinner. Sorry I can't join you. I just came by to make sure you're treating Coco right. And to tell you that we've drawn a blank at Passport and Immigration. Every French woman in Bea's age group entering the country prior to her ... to the incident ... has been accounted for. Meanwhile, I'm still working on the thousands of names on the airlines' lists of women travelling to San Francisco in the week prior to that. Every name is being checked against its real-life owner. We've also inquired about private aircraft. There were plenty that night. From Mexico, from Baja, Palm Desert, and Hawaii. All piloted by their owners and none carrying a female passenger.'

Bea looked downcast; she'd had high hopes that he would find her name on the airlines' lists.

Mahoney patted Bea's shoulder comfortingly and said, 'I have to go, or I'll be late solving that crime of the century and miss my chance at being Mayor!'

Phyl was holding the kitten and he stopped to tickle it

behind the ears. 'You're looking good, Doc,' he said with an approving grin.

'Oh thanks, Mahoney,' she said sarcastically again. 'But I'm not sure I need your back-handed compliments.'

He laughed as he walked to the door. She turned her head as she felt his eyes on her.

'I don't know though,' he said consideringly. 'Maybe it's all that sitting I warned you about, or maybe it's the home-cooked food, but I'd say your butt looks bigger.'

'Oaf,' she yelled after him as he slammed the door, laughing. 'Beast. Asshole.'

The door opened again and he poked his head round, looking shocked. 'Doc, Doc, really. Resorting to bad language. You must ask yourself what that means . . .'

'Ohh you . . . you cop,' she yelled as he disappeared again, still laughing.

Bea was laughing too and despite herself Phyl joined in. 'Why do I like him?' she asked half to herself. 'The man is a conceited chauvinist.'

But he had made Bea laugh and she liked that. Her protégée was ready for her first outing and she inspected her, pleased with what she saw.

Bea's soft copper hair was growing in, finally hiding the hideous scars. Now it feathered softly around her face, making her look like a young Audrey Hepburn. Her big copper-brown velvety eyes were two shades lighter than her hair, and her skin was no longer the colour of moonstones but of fresh cream. She was still too thin, of course. The bones were too close to the surface showing every bump in her spine, the sinews of her long neck, her wrist and ankle bones prominent. But compared with only a month ago, she looked wonderful.

She was wearing jeans and a shirt Phyl had bought for her, and Phyl knew she would be a joy to dress. And she was right. Anything looked good on Bea's tall, slender frame.

They covered the designer departments in the stores and the younger boutiques and despite Bea's protests Phyl insisted on equipping her for every possible occasion, from casual to cocktail.

'But where am I going to wear all these lovely clothes?' Bea demanded as they struggled back to the car burdened with yet more carrier-bags.

'That's what I'm going to tell you over dinner,' Phyl said briskly. 'And if ever two women deserved a good dinner, we do. We have battled the stores bravely, particularly you, and emerged with the trophies of victory. Now let's celebrate.'

She had booked a table at Stars and Bea slipped the supple new bronze suede jacket over her T-shirt and jeans. She put on the dangling amber earrings Phyl had insisted on buying and a touch of the Prescriptives Havana lipstick the salesgirl had recommended.

'Well, look at you,' Phyl marvelled as they took their seats in the restaurant. 'You look fantastic, Bea. You're turning every head in the place.'

'I thought they were staring at you.' Bea glanced cautiously round. 'This is wonderful,' she said, pleased. 'But I wish you hadn't spent all that money on me, Phyl. I promise I'll pay you back though. One day. When I get a job.'

'Speaking of a job, that's what I wanted to talk to you about.'

Bea stared at Phyl, astonished, as she ordered a bottle of wine and studied the menu.

'Here's to you, darling Bea,' Phyl said raising her glass. 'To your recovery, to your health, and to thank you for your friendship.'

'It's I who must thank you. For everything. For giving me a roof over my head, for the lovely clothes.' She looked gratefully at Phyl and added softly, 'For my sanity.'

'It's time for phase two of the recovery,' Phyl said. 'You may find this idea a little frightening, but it will achieve two things. Both of which are important to you.'

Bea stared anxiously at her. She didn't want anything to change, she just wanted life to go on as it was now.

Phyl said, 'I have this friend, Millie Fenwick. She's as rich as Rockefeller and mad as a hatter and she's the most upbeat person I know. She lives in New York and she's looking for a social secretary. Someone to keep up with her appointments, make calls for her, act as a travelling companion.' She laughed, remembering. 'A general dogsbody is more like it, knowing Millie. She's an old dragon, but it's all on the surface. Anyhow, she's planning a trip to Paris. And since you speak French and Millie cannot utter a word to save her life, who better for the job than you?'

Bea's stomach clenched in sudden fear at the thought. She didn't want to go to New York; she was afraid to go to Paris.

'I know Millie well,' Phyl said. 'I've helped her through a couple of personal traumas and her guilt at having so much money and indulging herself. Though you can take it from me, she gives away as much as she spends. There's no more generous and charitable woman on earth than Millie Fenwick. But I'm warning you. She's an original. A oneoff. They don't make them like Millie any more.

'I want you to go alone to New York to meet her. Make the quantum leap all by yourself. If you're ever going to get back into the world again, then this is the time to go for it.' She looked eagerly at Bea. 'So? What do you say?'

Despite her fears Bea knew Phyl was right. She smiled, a little sadly. 'So that's what all the smart clothes were for?'

'Millie is a clothes horse and she frequents only the best places; the best restaurants, the best hotels and the best resorts. It can't be bad now, Bea, can it?'

They laughed together and then Bea said, 'You mentioned there were two reasons my working for Millie was a good idea. What's the other?'

Their eyes met across the table. 'I want you out of San Francisco. Away from the danger.'

Bea's eyes darkened with fear. 'You mean, you think he might come back for me? He might try again?' It was a thought that had gone through her own mind many times.

'You'll be safe with Millie,' Phyl reassured her. 'No one will know you, or what happened. Soon you'll be in Paris. And that's another thing. I thought maybe in France you might start to remember.'

'And what then?' Bea whispered, terrified. 'What if I remember who I am? And who tried to kill me?'

'All you have to do is call and I'll be there,' Phyl promised. 'You can count on me. Anyway, I've been invited to attend a medical conference in Paris next month. That's not too long to wait. And it gives me something to look forward to. Seeing Paris, and you and Millie.'

She told Bea she had booked her on a flight to New York on Thursday. Only two days away. 'So there's no time to change our minds,' she said firmly, because she knew Bea didn't want to go. And she knew too, how empty her apartment would seem without her. She hated to lose her, even though she knew she was doing the right thing.

She took a photograph of Bea before she left, looking tall and elegant in her new mint-green pantsuit, clutching the kitten under her chin with both hands, like a little girl. She was smiling tentatively and there was a worried look in her eyes, but nevertheless Phyl thought she looked dazzlingly pretty. And she bought a silver frame and placed the picture on the table by her bed. As though it were a picture of her own daughter.

'Don't take Millie on face value or you'll never stick it a day,' were her final words as she put Bea on the plane to New York. And Bea soon found out why.

CHAPTER 9

Manhattan had ground to a halt in a torrential downpour aggravated by hurricane force winds. Buses and cars stacked up at the broken traffic lights and taxis were an impossibility. Bea was forced to walk the ten blocks to her future employer's Fifth Avenue apartment building opposite Central Park. Nevertheless, soaked and windblown, she managed to arrive exactly on time.

The Fenwick apartment took up an entire floor and as Bea stepped from the elevator, Millie herself flung open the door.

'What kept you?' she demanded, sweeping impatiently from the lofty gilded hall into a gold-brocaded drawing room. She waved an imperious arm for Bea to follow. 'You're late. I hope this isn't a regular occurrence with you? The blasted butler just quit and the housekeeper ran off last week with some of my best jewellery and there's a new Filipina in the kitchen who can barely understand English. I declare, I'm just about to go out of my mind.'

She was small and plump with girlish golden curls, an elaborately ruffled cerise dress and high heels. Her wide mouth was generously lipsticked, her mascara was lavishly applied and her arthritic hands glistened with large rings in every colour gemstone. She was a cloudburst of colour, and the style was entirely her own.

Phyl had warned Bea that Millie Fenwick was a rich,

spoiled woman of uncertain years. She said the only thing certain in her life story was that there were more years than she laid claim to. The details of her past varied to suit the moment and her audience: from orphaned heiress of a grand old family to shrewd businesswoman; from lucky gambler to poor little rich girl.

Millie's shrewd blue eyes that were older than her face took in Bea for the space of a minute. 'Well,' she said in her gravelly voice, 'if ever I saw anyone who needed a job, it's you. You look as though you could use a good meal.' She shook a Marlboro from a crumpled pack. Ignoring the elaborate gold lighter on the table next to her, she took a book of dimestore matches from her pocket and lit it. She waved out the match, inhaling with the ardour of a true nicotine addict.

She examined the soaking girl dripping onto her Chinese silk rug. After a flurry of coughing, she said sarcastically, 'What's Phyl into these days besides psychiatry? The Animal Rescue Service?'

Sticking her chin in the air Bea turned and squelched indignantly back to the door. 'I think I had better go.'

'Oh, for God's sakes!' Millie flicked ash exasperatedly into a large crystal ashtray already overflowing with lipstick-rimmed butts smoked down to the filter. 'You can't live with me and be touchy. Take off your coat and those ghastly wet shoes and sit down. Here. By the fire. Come, tell me about yourself.'

She flung Bea a smile of such genuine warmth and roguish charm, half-apologetic, half-mischievous, that Bea found herself doing as she was told, even though a minute ago she could have killed her. Millicent Fenwick was that kind of person, she was soon to discover. One minute you adored her, the next you couldn't stand her. One minute she was good, the next she was horrid. Just like the little girl with the curl in the middle of her forehead in the childish poem.

She slipped off her soggy shoes and her wet coat obediently and put them on the marble hall floor where they wouldn't ruin anything. Then she returned to the drawing room and sat cautiously on the edge of a gold brocade sofa.

Millicent's curious eyes, dark as blackcurrants, met hers. 'Well?' she said expectantly. 'Phyl told me the bare bones of the story, but not all of it.'

'There's not much to tell. There was an accident. Although the police think maybe it wasn't. They think someone tried to kill me.' Bea lifted her wet hair from her brow to show the scar running into her scalp as she told Millie the story.

'I'm fine now,' she said reassuringly, anxious for the job. 'The only thing is . . . I don't remember any of it. And I don't remember who I am.'

'And the police didn't help?'

'No one of my description had been reported missing. No one came looking for me. No one seemed to care whether I lived or died,' she said with a frightened shiver for the girl she used to be, whom nobody cared about. 'Except Phyl. And Detective Mahoney, of course.'

Millie dragged thoughtfully on the last of her cigarette, then stubbed it out amid the heap of butts in the crystal ashtray. 'Well, well, a girl with no past.' She stared at Bea and then smiled and said cryptically, 'The perfect companion for the woman with no future.

'You can start immediately by fetching me another pack of ciggies from my room. And then we shall have some tea. Tell the Filipina in the kitchen, Earl Grey for two. And not too strong this time or I'll kill her. And sandwiches. Smoked salmon and egg salad. Finger sandwiches, no

73

crusts, she knows the way I like them. And then get on the 'phone and order me up a new butler. I don't like answering my own doorbell.'

She glanced at her enormous diamond-studded watch. 'And after that it'll almost be time for the first glass of champagne.' She rolled her eyes heavenwards and grimaced. 'God, why at my age do I think a glass of bubbly taken before the sun is over the yardarm is the first step on the path to decadence? When I don't give a damn about decadence. And anyway, it's not alcohol that'll kill me, it's these blasted ciggies . . .'

Bea moved into the grand fourteen-room apartment overlooking Central Park. Her pretty blue and white room was next to Millie's palatial suite. 'Near enough to yell if I need you,' Millie told her cheerfully. She was sitting on Bea's bed, watching her unpack, passing critical comments on each garment as she hung it in her closet.

'Mmmn, not one for colour are you dear girl?' she said witheringly, eyeing yet another neutral-toned linen dress. 'How do you hope ever to get yourself noticed in beige? I can see Phyl's influence at work. You know I've never seen that women in anything but black and white? I can tell you it would drive me nuts.'

She smiled, wafting away cigarette smoke and added smugly, 'I've always found the best way to catch a man's eye is to wear a bright colour. Pink preferably. And a few good diamonds of course. But then, I guess after what you've just been through, you don't want to be noticed right now.' She patted Bea's hand sympathetically. 'Don't worry, dear girl. You'll be safe with Millie.'

Bea smiled gratefully. She could see that life with Millie was going to be a series of ups and downs, but she knew she really was kind under that bullying façade.

'Who needs men anyway?' Millie demanded, holding up

a copper-coloured sweater that almost matched Bea's hair and shaking her head disapprovingly. 'I've been married three times, dear girl. First to a polo player. Then – in my racing phase – to a jockey. And last to an international playboy. And let me tell you there is nobody less *fun* than *a playboy*. After him I figured three times was enough. Marriage was not for me. Not that I haven't had the odd little flutter,' her blue eyes twinkled with mischief, 'but at least I didn't marry them.'

Bea laughed with her and then Millie said impatiently, 'Hurry and get changed, dear girl. We're off to lunch at Le Cirque. Put on the smartest of those ghastly beige suits and a big smile and prepare to enjoy some of the best food in New York. And make sure you order all the most fattening dishes, you could use a bit of flesh on your bones. And then tonight, there's a fund-raising dinner at the Waldorf. Our President is speaking you know. I thought it might be interesting, and I bought a table so there will be lots of people to introduce you to.'

Bea's heart sank at the thought and Millie caught her apprehensive glance. She said briskly, 'Of course you'll cope. I'll just tell them all you had an accident and that your memory is a bit hazy.' She yelped with laughter as she added, 'Other than that you are a perfectly normal girl.'

Bea found herself whirled into two frantic weeks of lunches, fund-raising dinners and charity balls. She even got used to Millie complaining all the time about her simple taste in clothes, her minimal use of make-up and her unwillingness to eat a good breakfast.

'You're as bad as my mother,' Bea retorted one day, as she turned down dessert at yet another smart lunch.

'Even your mother would not have turned down dessert at Lutece.' Millie glanced overly-casually at her as she added, 'By the way, what was your mother like?'

Panic fizzled up Bea's spine. She stared blankly at her. 'I just said that, didn't I? About my mother. And yet now, when I'm trying to visualise her, trying to think of her voice saying, "Eat your breakfast or you won't grow up big and strong," all I get is that same blank wall in my mind. There's just nothing there.'

Her voice had risen in panic and Millie patted her hand soothingly. Phyl had asked her to watch out for any signs of returning memory but she hadn't realised quite how upset Bea would get.

'Poor child,' she said in a quiet voice, unlike her usual boisterous high-pitched chatter. 'You must feel desperately lonely. And I can tell you I know a thing or two about loneliness myself. We shall just have to cheer each other up, won't we? After all, we're off to Paris next week, and there's nothing like France to put a glow in a girl's heart.'

Bea surely hoped she was right.

CHAPTER 10

Mahoney telephoned Phyl a few days later. 'I'm calling in my marker,' he said confidently. 'Remember? You promised me dinner?'

'In exchange for Coco. I remember. And since I'm a woman who always pays her debts, Mahoney, you can name your time and place.'

He could sense she was smiling. 'Tomorrow,' he said. 'And anywhere as long as it's not McDonald's.'

She laughed. 'Tomorrow,' she agreed. 'Pick me up at seven-thirty.'

'Seven-thirty,' he said uncrossing his fingers, marvelling at his good luck because he hadn't really believed she would say yes.

'And Mahoney . . . it won't be McDonald's, so try and look decent for once will you?'

He laughed out loud as he put down the phone.

He rang her doorbell promptly at seven-thirty the next evening. She opened it and stood silently, taking in his smart dark suit, the white shirt and flamboyant red-flowered silk tie. His dark hair was still wet from the shower with track marks from the comb showing, and she could have seen her face in the shine of his shoes. He was clutching a bunch of flowers in one hand and a small brown paper bag in the other.

'You look like a cop pretending to be a solid citizen,' she said, amused.

'Yeah. Well you're softening up a little yourself,' he replied, grinning as he saw her blush. Her dark hair was loose tonight instead of the usual tight knot. She was wearing black as always, but this time it was a gauzy low-cut dress with a slinky skirt, and she smelled of lilies and gardenias.

His eyes admired her as he handed her the bouquet. 'You smell better than nature's roses,' he said.

'It's Bellodgia,' she replied coolly. 'A bit old-fashioned but it suited my mood tonight. And thank you for the beautiful roses.'

They were pink with a hint of cream, and their velvet petals were just beginning to unfurl.

'They're called Oceana,' he said. 'I thought they were like garden roses, a bit old-fashioned. Like your perfume. Seems I got the mood right for the night.'

He gave the paper bag to the cat who was wrapping itself round his legs, purring. 'And this is for young Coco. To keep her busy while the Doc is out.'

They laughed as the kitten swiftly tore out the catnip mouse and tossed it into the air, pouncing after it.

Phyl offered him a glass of champagne.

'A wonderful choice,' he said, tasting it appreciatively. 'And not obvious. Laurent-Perrier is a fine old house and their Grand Siècle ranks with the best.'

Phyl stared astonished at him. 'Is there no end to your surprises, Mahoney?' she demanded. 'I would not have recognised Grand Siècle in a blind tasting. How on earth did you?'

He shrugged nonchalantly. 'Just one of those things they teach you at cop school.' He grinned teasingly. 'No, I didn't mean it. I spent a year in France, after college. Part of it in

Épernay picking grapes. Every bar and café sells champagne as a matter of course so I got to taste all the small growers. I liked it so much I made a point of visiting all the Grand Houses. I have a reasonable palate and I knew what I liked, and this happened to be one of them.' He shrugged again, 'So you see. No mystery. Just a lucky shot on your part that you picked on my favourite.'

'I almost wish you were doing the cooking,' she said wistfully. 'You'd be hard to beat.'

'Any time you say, Doc. Just whistle and I'll be there, trying out my Italian specialities on you. Marcella Hazan's wild mushroom risotto. Roger Vergé's *Petits Niçoises farcies* and *pistou* soup, my mama's old-fashioned vegetarian lasagna. And the best desserts this side of Rome.'

'Tiramisu?' she asked jokingly. It was one of her favourites.

'Hate the stuff, but if you like it, Doc, you shall have it.'

'Not tonight,' she said, collecting her jacket. 'And it's getting late.'

Mahoney's eyebrows rose when he saw the long black limousine waiting at the kerb. He glanced, astonished, at her as the driver held open the door and she threw him a mocking grin. 'You didn't think I was going to let you drink and drive did you? After all I wouldn't want to be responsible for you not making Mayor.'

He glanced apprehensively over his shoulder before getting in next to her. 'At least it's black,' he said nervously. 'If any of the guys spot me I hope they'll think I'm on my way back from a funeral and not that I have a sideline as a pimp. Doc, limos were not in the deal. A simple dinner was all I asked.'

'And that's what you'll get,' she replied serenely. 'The best simple dinner you've had in a while, I'll bet. Though maybe not,' she added, remembering his spaghetti. 'And would you mind, just for this evening, calling me Phyl instead of Doc? Somehow it suits the occasion better.'

He nodded solemnly as they drove north out of the city into Marin County. 'You've got it, Phyl.' He shook her hand. 'Meet Franco. And you know what? A guy could get very used to this kind of life. Beautiful women, limos, great meals ... Maybe I've died and gone to paradise.'

'Don't bet on it, Franco,' she warned. 'You're still dealing with Dr Forster even though tonight she's called Phyl.'

It was an unusually warm May evening and the windows of the Lark Creek Inn stood open to the balmy air. The candles on the table flickered in the soft breeze as they sipped a bountiful California merlot. 'Edgy but beautiful,' Mahoney said. 'Like you.'

'Thanks, Franco. Tell me why is there always something back-handed in your compliments?'

He sighed exaggeratedly. 'I don't know, Phyl. I guess you'll just have to analyse me to find out what's wrong with my psyche.'

'There's nothing wrong with your psyche,' she retorted. 'It's your head that's the problem. It's swollen from all that media attention.' She leaned closer, interested. 'Tell me how do you do it? Solve all those unsolvable crimes?'

'Hard work. Intuition. Painstaking searches through the facts. Good eyesight – you need it inspecting the crime scenes. And a bad memory for the daily horrors of it all.' He grimaced. 'There's no glamour about being a homicide cop, Doc. Except that created by the media.'

'Then why did you choose it? Instead of the English professor?'

'My Irish great-grandfather was a cop, and so was my

Italian grandfather and my father. Seems I couldn't beat the genes.'

'Or you wanted to do some good,' she suggested softly. 'To help your fellow-men.'

He laughed. 'Sure. I'll accept that. Saint Franco. That'll go down well in the squad room. Phyl, the truth is I'm just a hard-working cop who, for some reason I've yet to figure out, finds it satisfying to catch murderers and crazies who feel they can play god and kill other guys just for a fix. Or for five bucks. Or for merely looking at them the wrong way. And rapists who shoot their victims so they can't tell on them. And kids who tie their grandmother's stockings round her throat and watch her choke to death, in return for her meagre life savings. A hundred and fifty bucks hidden under her ancient mattress. And what does he want it for? A pair of Nike airs and a cheap leather jacket so he can act flash to his friend's girl, maybe buy her some coke and then maybe she'll fuck him.'

Franco's handsome face was grim and Phyl stared horrified at him. 'I'm sorry,' he said quietly, 'but you asked.'

'I understand.'

He looked admiringly at her. The breeze fluttered the candles, casting the light upwards onto her face. Her shoulders and the swell of her breasts looked like fresh cream against the soft black chiffon. 'You should wear red,' he said lightly, changing the conversation and the mood. 'It would look great with your colouring.'

She looked down, embarrassed, the conversation was becoming suddenly personal. 'Red is for Las Vegas hookers,' she said coolly. 'Or overdressed old ladies on cruise ships.'

'Is that so?' His eyes mocked her. 'Some of us think it is

the colour of roses and valentines. Now I wonder what a good psychiatrist would make of that?'

'She would probably say that at your age, you are still a foolish romantic, Franco Mahoney.'

They both laughed and he thought how much he liked her cool independence. They talked, striking sparks off each other, as they ate simple roast chicken that he swore must have been bred by a chicken connoisseur and cooked by a real grandmother who knew her stuff.

'I couldn't have done better myself,' he said, with a satisfied sigh. 'This was a very wise choice, Dr Phyl. You know me better than I thought.'

'That's my job,' she said with a mischievous smile. 'But I insist you taste the bread and butter pudding. It's simply the best.'

'If you say so, Ma'am. You see, I'm just putty in your hands.' He laughed, enjoying himself hugely. 'I could get used to this toy boy role, limos, wine, dinners, a beautiful companion who is paying for it all. Though it does seem a tad extravagant in return for a kitten.'

'Not just any kitten.' She took his hand across the table and he looked at her, surprised. 'You were right, of course that night. You analysed my silly selfish compartmentalised life accurately. I would never have dared be so truthful with myself. I might never have stopped thinking about the past and got on with the present. But because of you, and Coco and Bea, my whole life has changed.'

He looked searchingly at her. 'You want to tell me about that past?'

She glanced down, tracing the pattern on her knife with her finger. Her voice was so low he had to lean closer as she said hesitantly, 'I was married, once. We were too young, of course. We were both doing our internship at Chicago General. It may be the busiest hospital in the country, especially weekends. The Saturday Night Special, they called it, though Friday was just as bad. People out drinking, fighting, slaughtering each other. We met there, in the emergency room over a multiple stab wound. He was Stanford and I was Yale. We hated each other on sight, and so of course, we fell in love.'

She smiled sadly, remembering the sweetness of youth and love. 'He was the old-fashioned type, he wanted marriage. And children. And a wife who stayed home to look after her family. The child came along almost immediately. A girl. So pretty, so sweet.' She glanced up at him, her face suddenly alight with love for her child. 'Oh Franco, you know how most babies always seem to be crying? Well, not this one. She was a dream baby, right from day one.

'My husband's family were well-to-do; they were financing their son through med school. It was different for me. I was abandoned when I was just a kid. I never really knew my own mother and there wasn't any father around. When she took off I was taken into court and then fostered out. I had seven different sets of foster parents between the ages of three and seventeen. And boy, how I missed my mother all those years. Even now . . . it's hard to adjust to not being wanted.

'So you see, I was determined that wouldn't happen to my little girl. I gave up my ambitions and settled down to become a full-time mom in a pretty little house in Dearborn. My husband worked eighteen-hour days, he was exhausted. I understood; after all, I had been there. I said we must go on holiday. Just the two of us.' There was an endless pause as Phyl stared silently down at the table. Franco waited, afraid to speak.

Finally she said in a hoarse emotion-choked whisper, 'We dropped the baby off with the grandparents in San

Diego and kissed her goodbye. She waved her plump little arm at us and blew kisses as we went off to Mexico. Blue skies, the sea, perfect peace, just for a week or two.'

Franco saw the raw wound in her soul as she looked up at him with blank blue eyes. He reached out to her, taking both her hands in his. He wanted to enfold her in his arms, hold her to him, tell her it was okay . . .

'We had been there two days when we got the phone call. She was sick. They suspected meningitis. There was no flight out until the next morning. There was no charter available for hours . . .'

'Don't tell me,' Franco said, gripping her cold hands. 'It's too painful. I understand.'

Phyl didn't seem to hear him. Her eyes were brilliant with unshed tears. 'She died before we could get there. She was just two years old. And all I could think of was that she must have been calling for me, Mommy Mommy . . . And I wasn't there. *Her mommy wasn't there.*'

'Oh God,' Franco said, sharing her anguish.

He could see her fighting for control as she said shakily, 'It took years for me to be able to cope with it. Sometimes I wonder if it made me better at my job? Going through the pain. I try not to think about it, but somehow, when I saw Bea on television and they thought she was dead, it brought it all back again. And I thought about her mother not being there, about her being told . . . her daughter was dead . . .'

'Thank you for telling me,' Franco said simply.

Phyl nodded. 'It was just as bad for my husband. He thought we should have another child right away, but I couldn't bear it. I went back to med school, back to the hospital grind . . . we divorced a couple of years later. He's a successful internist now, in San Diego. Married with four kids. And I am Dr Phyl, focusing on almost anything but myself.'

'And maybe now that's just what you should be doing. Thinking more about yourself . . . as well as Bea. Life is for living, Phyl, and you are a woman with a lot to give. Give yourself a break, love yourself more.'

'And then maybe someone else can love me?' She managed a grin. 'Remember me? The ice maiden? Oh, I don't think so, Franco. I've chosen my course.'

He stared at her, seeing how beautiful she was with the tears still glistening on her long black lashes and her soft mouth tremulous with the pain of her love, and the guilt she could never allow herself to lose. He thought that beneath that invincible façade Phyl Forster was the most vulnerable woman he knew. And one of the bravest and most lonely. She shouldered her own agony along with her patients', and one day he knew she had to crack.

He gripped her hands tighter and bent to kiss her fingers. Somehow he hoped he would be around when that happened, and it would be him she would turn to.

'Well, now you know the real me, and that's enough of the past,' she said, blinking away her tears and giving him a brilliant smile. 'Let's talk about Bea.'

She took her hand away from his and smoothed back her hair. 'Let's order that bread and butter pudding,' she said brightly, and again he admired her courage, and deplored her foolishness.

She told him that Millie demanded all Bea's time, and that suited Bea just fine because she still wasn't sure who, or what, she was.

'There's such an enormous gap in her life, you see,' Phyl said, 'and that's what terrifies her. The background to her existence just isn't there. All those details that go to make up a person: the parents, the sisters, brothers, cousins. The schools and college, cheerleaders and football games. She doesn't know what her life was like. She says it's driving her crazy, and so mostly I think she is pushing it away and living for the moment. And tomorrow they are off to Paris.'

'Sounds good to me. Better than moping around your apartment waiting for her memory to return. Or the murderer to try again.'

Phyl's eyes widened. She sounded frightened as she said, 'You don't really think he will?'

'What can I tell you?' Mahoney lifted his hands, palms up, helplessly. 'Except we've drawn a blank on all our inquiries and the case is now officially "on hold". Stashed in the "unsolved mystery" file. The consensus is that it was a random killer on the loose. They figure anyone would have suited him. It just happened to be Bea.'

'And is that what you think?'

Phyl looked so scared Mahoney wanted to put his arm round her, tell her it was all right, that he would find the killer, he would work it all out and she need never be afraid again. But he couldn't promise any of those things.

He said, 'No I don't agree. I think this was a purposeful and knowing murder attempt. The guy knew Bea and for some reason he wanted her out of the way. What I have to find out is why? And unless Bea regains her memory, I'm afraid there's not much hope.

'Detective work is fifty per cent slog and fifty per cent intuition,' he added bitterly. 'You get so you can feel who the villains are, even when they are cloaked in normality. Straight decent-seeming folks, just like you and me. But the famous Dr Forster must know better than anyone what goes on in people's minds. In those deep, dark recesses. Things that are hidden behind good-looks and charm and expensive clothes. The wife-beaters, the child-abusers, the murderers. They are all just folk, like you and me.'

'Speak for yourself,' she retorted. 'And let me know

what nice good-looking charming young man tried to kill Bea. And why!'

'I'm not giving up,' he said, 'I can promise you that.'

Mist was wreathing ghostly tendrils down the road as they drove home. Phyl closed her eyes, leaning tiredly back against the cushions. 'Now tell me the limo wasn't a good idea, Mahoney,' she murmured.

'It wasn't a good idea, Doc,' he obliged, and she groaned.

'I'm still waiting for it,' she added.

'What's that?' She rested her head against his shoulder and he smiled tenderly, staring straight ahead at the lighted towers of the city.

'The poetry quote of course. I've never known you miss an opportunity. Nor be lost for words.'

'You're right.' He thought for a minute and then said, 'How about this:

> *She walks in beauty, like the night*
> *Of cloudless climes and starry skies;*
> *And all that's best of dark and bright*
> *Meet in her aspect and her eyes.*

'Byron,' he said.

'I know.' She had opened her eyes and was looking at him.

'Corny, maybe, but appropriate. It was meant as a compliment to my hostess who is as beautiful as the night.'

Her eyes were smiling at him in the dark. 'Thank you, Mahoney,' she whispered.

'Franco, please.' He read the meaning in her eyes and he patted her hand tenderly.

The limo drew up in front of her apartment building and Mahoney jumped out and raced round to open the door for her before the chauffeur had a chance. He looked at her, lying back against the cushions. There were violet smudges under her eyes and her lipstick had worn off. He thought she looked like a tired young girl. He took her hand and walked her up the steps to the door. 'Go get some sleep.'

He bent his head and kissed her lightly on the cheek, breathing in the scent of her. 'Thanks, Doc, for a memorable evening. It was fun.'

She nodded. 'You make me laugh, Mahoney. I like that.'

He grinned. 'It goes with the job, ma'am. We are only here to serve.'

'Then you can serve me dinner. Next time.'

'Yes, Ma'am. You've got it, Doc. Any time you say.'

She watched him walk to the car. He turned and looked back at her and she said quietly, 'And thank you, Mahoney, for listening to me. And for all you have done for Bea. I know if anyone can find the murderer, you can.'

He made a mock salute as he quoted:

> *'And therefore, since I cannot prove a lover,*
> *To entertain these fair well-spoken days,*
> *I am determined to prove a villain,*
> *And hate the idle pleasures of these days...*

'Shakespeare, *Richard the Third*.'

She rolled her eyes heavenwards in mock-despair as she waved goodbye, but he saw she was smiling again as he closed the door.

The limo driver flinched when Mahoney told him to drop him at the old City Jail.

'Just wanted to see if you were awake,' Mahoney said grinning. 'Make it the Hall of Justice.'

'Same building, isn't it?'

'It might even be the same place!'

He just wanted to check Bea's file one more time. He was sure there must be something in there that held a clue to the secret.

CHAPTER 11

Millie and Bea were staying in the Chanel suite at the Paris Ritz and had spent the previous days at the couturiers on the Avenue Montaigne, ordering Millie's fall wardrobe, as well as in the Left Bank antique shops generally buying up a storm. Millie simply bought anything she fancied on the spur of the moment and usually regretted it later.

'The truth is, dear girl, that my father manufactured plumbing fixtures in Pittsburgh, as his father did before him,' she said. They were sitting in the Ritz bar a few nights later, enjoying a drink before dinner while Millie checked out the patrons to see who she knew.

'That's how I can afford all this,' Millie confessed. 'Daddy made himself a tidy fortune, before the accident at the plant that killed him. He was still a young man and he left my mother an even younger widow, with a four-year-old daughter and a great deal of money. Mamma was a shy woman, without many friends and it was a solitary life for a child.' She sighed, reflectively, sipping her Campari and soda. 'Maybe you're better off not recalling your childhood, Bea. It might turn out to have been as disappointing as mine.'

'I don't think so,' Bea said. 'I don't get bad feelings about the past.' She had become used to Millie's sudden clumsy probing questions. She knew she was only following Phyl's instructions and trying to help. But so far without any luck.

Except she felt completely at home in Paris. The language was her own, just as much as English, and she spoke it so fluently the Parisians paid her the biggest compliment of all by assuming that she was one of them.

Millie waved at an acquaintance across the room. She seemed to know people everywhere they went. She said, 'Perhaps it's because of my provincial Victorian-style upbringing that I've always craved change and excitement. I always adored people and parties and clothes and jewellery. You know how I like tinsel and flash. Well, when I was a girl I yearned for red silk instead of burgundy plush, I wanted rubies instead of garnets, diamonds instead of opals. I liked the grand hotels where my mamma occasionally took me for holidays, with their sparkling chandeliers and sparkling wines fizzing in saucer-shaped glasses. Even when I was very young I wanted orchids and not tea-roses, shiny gold bracelets instead of demure ivory bangles.

'I still remember Mamma saying, "You must eat up all your potatoes and vegetables, Millicent, before you can have dessert."' Millie snorted disparagingly, 'Is it any wonder I was plump as a pumpkin, as well as being short. And you know what, Bea,' she leaned closer and said in a loud confidential whisper, 'I never wore silk next to my skin until I was eighteen years old. After my mother died.

'I had no family, except for a remote cousin in Ohio who never contacted me again after writing to express his regrets, so there was no one to consider except myself.' She signalled the waiter for the check and signed it with a flourish. 'But I wasn't afraid to take the reins of life and gallop the horses myself. No sir. Not Millie Fenwick.

'I inherited the lot, y'know,' she continued in the chauffered car on the way to Robauchon. 'The big house in Pittsburgh that I hated, and all its ghastly Turkey-carpeted, silver-candelabrad splendour. Plus the fifty million dollars that went with it. And let me tell you, Bea, fifty million was a lot of money in the 1930s. Especially for a young girl. I was an heiress. A catch.'

She yelped with laughter at the thought. 'I moved out of the house, out of Pittsburgh into Manhattan. Took a suite at the Plaza, hired someone who knew about these things to take me shopping and bought myself an entire new wardrobe. Head to toe. Everything from the skin outwards.' She sighed luxuriously, remembering. 'And it had to be silk, though satin was nice too. And I wanted everything in bright colours.

'I had Mamma's old diamonds reset at Buccelatti and bought myself a whole slew of shiny new stones in every colour; earrings, necklaces, bracelets, rings, watches. Then I took myself off to the hairdresser and emerged four hours later, a platinum blonde, like Jean Harlow. She was all the rage then, dear girl.'

She patted Bea's knee affectionately. 'I've never told anyone this for years you know. Except Phyl. She said it was good for me to talk it out, so now I tell anyone who's foolish enough to listen, the truth about myself.' She tilted her bright blonde head consideringly to one side. 'Well, approximately the truth anyway,' she amended.

'But then, dear girl, I began to look around for companionship. And I found it amongst the polo-playing set in Palm Beach. I bought myself a wonderful Adizon Mizner gem of a Moorish castle and married a handsome man twice my age, the captain of the visiting Argentinian team. Of course I didn't need Phyl to tell me I must have been looking for my daddy. Anyways, he didn't last long. *No good in bed, dear girl*,' she said in another loud confidential whisper, making Bea giggle. 'Not that I was any good myself, being a novice filly at the time, but I knew it had to be better than this. Or why were so many people doing it?'

They had arrived at the restaurant and she wafted confidently inside, shaking hands with the maître d' and greeting waiters by name.

'I didn't realise you came to Paris so often,' Bea said amazed. 'Every place we go, they know you.'

'It's not just my baby blues, dear girl, I'm also a phenomenal tipper,' Millie replied shrewdly. 'I can afford it and it smooths life's path and makes other people happy, so why not?'

'Money really means nothing to you, does it?' Bea said amazed.

'Don't you believe it, dear girl. Money means everything to me. It has bought me a lot of pleasure, and I like to think I've been able to share it around.'

'Phyl said you were a champion of good causes.'

'Did she now? Then she was talking out of turn. Everyone knows I'm just a frivolous rich old biddy who fritters her time and money on selfish pursuits. And that's why we are here tonight,' she said, ordering for both of them because she knew best.

Bea laughed, as she looked around the exclusive restaurant. Millie had told her it was one of the best in Paris, and as she tasted each dish, she knew Millie was right. Though how Millie managed to eat and talk non-stop at the same time amazed her.

'After Palm Beach, I moved on to Saratoga and the horse-racing set,' Millie continued. 'I was very partial to a flutter on the races. Still am. And that's where the second husband came from.'

She chewed the stuffed seabass, remembering. 'He was a small man, of course, had to be in his profession. Though he wasn't small in the department that mattered. He certainly taught me a thing or two in bed, I can tell you, dear girl. Even if he did treat me a bit like a horse. I always felt he wanted to tack me up; y'know the saddle and stirrups and the whip, and then afterwards take me out into the stableyard and hose me down; the curry comb and a sack of oats, that sort of thing. Of course it couldn't last, but then I never expected it to. I wasn't into "lasting". After all I was only twenty-two, and I was still learning my way around life and men.

'Next came the playboy. He had a title, it was *almost* phoney but not quite. He was the third son and his elder brother was actually the Count. But he was the best-looking man I'd ever seen. French, and he had a nice line in a romantic turn of phrase. And he was the perfect party animal, he had been to every major event in the previous twenty years. I thought he was the perfect match for me because at that time I was determined to be known as the party girl of the decade. Very Scott Fitzgerald you know. And speaking of Fitzgerald, of course I met him, down at the Cap, with that crazy wife, and Chanel. And Picasso, that naughty man, and Cocteau.'

She sighed, recalling gay times on the Côte d'Azur. 'It was all just tiny fishing villages then, dear girl, and endless sunny days, and the Hôtel du Cap was small but still the chicest place on the coast.

'Anyway, surprise surprise, the aging playboy lost his playboy ways when he married the young heiress. Suddenly he didn't want to party anymore. He wanted to be the country squire in a huge château with liveried servants. He even started thinking about entering politics. I was out of there so fast he never even saw my dust.'

She exploded into laughter at the memory. 'Then I went back to the States, bought the Fifth Avenue apartment, kept on the Palm Beach place, though I rarely used it. I could never stay in just one place; the grass was always greener somewhere else and I was always travelling, crossing the oceans on liners and cruise ships, and the skies in Flying Boats and Pan Am Clippers. Those were the days,' she said reminiscently, over dessert and coffee. 'Now it's boring old 747s and Concorde and private Gulfstream jets. So now you see, Bea, why everyone knows me at all the great hotels around the world.

'They greet me with open arms and, I hope, genuine affection, because I've known some of them since we were all young, forty years or so. I'm always generous and they seem to find me amusing, and they put up with my eccentricities and my demanding ways. Like you, dear girl,' she added, giving Bea's cheek an affectionate pat.

Bea beamed happily at her. 'Of course they do,' she said loyally. 'And thank you for telling me your life story.'

'There's a catch to it,' Millie warned, cheerfully ignoring Paris's restaurant no smoking laws and lighting up a Marlboro. 'I expect to hear yours in return, one day soon.'

Bea promised, smiling, to do her best to remember it. She thought Millie Fenwick was okay. And she understood that her millions had bought her fleeting happiness and a great deal of loneliness, wandering the grand hotels of the world, hoping the warm welcome of the hotel managers and staff were not just because she spent a fortune and tipped well, but because they were genuinely glad to see her.

'It's probably all due to my father getting killed like that when I was nothing but a kid,' Millie said, suddenly moist-eyed. 'I guess I've been missing him all my life.

'And talking about the Côte d'Azur has made me nostalgic for the place.' She dusted away her tears, and looked at Bea, her eyes sparkling with a sudden idea. 'Why not let's go there tomorrow?'

'But Phyl is coming to Paris in a couple of weeks,' she protested.

'And no doubt she'll be tied up all day and half the night with the shrinks' conference. She can fly down and join us afterwards, at the Hôtel du Cap. They know me there. They'll look after me like the prodigal daughter.'

Bea knew by now there was no use arguing. When Millie made up her mind, it stayed made up. The Hôtel du Cap it was. And tomorrow.

CHAPTER 12

It was early June and the Côte d'Azur was living up to its name; all blue skies, calm azure sea and brilliant sunshine. As Millie had forecast, the staff at the Hôtel du Cap welcomed her like an old friend and she filled her afternoons contentedly playing bridge with a host of new acquaintances, while Bea lazed by the pool overlooking the Mediterranean, acquiring a light golden tan.

Inspecting herself in the mirror a week later, Bea thought she looked different. 'Like a new woman,' she said, shaking her head to fluff out her hair until it resembled a shaggy copper chrysanthemum. It was long enough now to flop into her eyes and form a little ducktail at the nape of her neck, but she decided she wasn't going to cut it yet. She laughed, admiring it. She was just so glad to have hair she might never cut it again.

While Millie still slumbered in her lavish suite, Bea spent the early mornings wandering through the street markets of Antibes and Nice, admiring the stalls, heady with the scent of roses and lilies, and gleaming with morning-fresh peaches and apricots, aubergines and olives. She joined the chic women browsing through the bargain-priced linen jackets and skirts with Paris labels, and the inexpensive jewellery and strings of brilliantly coloured glass beads.

Then she sat on a café terrace, shedding her worries like dust-motes in the sunshine, happily watching the world go by over a *grand café crème* and a buttery croissant. And the hospital and the broken skull and the man who wanted to murder her seemed about a million miles away. Only the dark terror of not knowing the past remained to haunt her, dragging her sweat-soaked from sleep and the nightmare of falling endlessly down the black tunnel, falling and falling...

She would still leap shaking from the bed and run to the open window, looking out at the midnight blue sky, like a gauzy theatre curtain sparkled with stars, feeling the cool air on her fevered skin, waiting for her heart to stop its pounding and things to become normal again. Or as normal as they could for a girl who did not know who she was. But there were still many nights when the beauty and stillness failed to do their work. They did not soothe her. And those nights despair took her over, and she sobbed and wailed her lostness and terror into her tear-wet pillow until the dawn, and then, exhausted, she finally slept. But she never spoke to Millie about those awful despairing nights, she did not want to burden her with her problems. And if Millie noticed her pallor and swollen eyes, she passed no comment.

Bea was reluctant to worry Phyl too. She decided her new friends had done enough for her; she could not go on being a burden to them. It was up to her to manage her own life now.

Millie had hired a white Mercedes convertible and with Bea at the wheel, they explored the coast and the hills behind. Millie was full of memories of the way it used to be, 'in the old days', when she was just a girl, kicking over the traces, dining and dancing and flirting and gambling.

'It was still unspoiled, dear girl,' she said, filled with nostalgia. 'You should have seen it then, Bea, when this string of towns and high rises along the coast were just tiny fishing villages. There are some compensations to getting old, I suppose. The things one has seen and done, the memories. You never lose them you know.'

Millie flung herself into the hectic social life of the Riviera, looking up old acquaintances and making new ones, attending openings and galas and dinners and concerts, and enjoying herself thoroughly. And being a woman who could afford to indulge her whims and fancies, she suddenly announced that she intended to buy a house somewhere along the coast that she loved best.

Bea did her best to talk her out of it, saying it was just another whim she would live to regret, but Millie was adamant. She had made up her mind she wanted to spend her summers on the Riviera. 'Just like in the old days.'

They were going house-hunting that very morning and Millie had dressed for the occasion. She looked like a plump tropical bird in a floating lime green and pink dress with her blonde curls hidden under a shady pink straw hat.

She threw a critical glance at Bea, cool in navy silk shorts and white T-shirt.

'You should always wear a hat, Bea,' she told her severely. 'Believe me, if you don't you'll regret it when you're forty. You'll have skin like a bit of old leather.' She laughed as Bea obligingly pulled on a Yankees baseball cap. 'That's not quite what I meant, dear girl. But on you it looks good.'

Bea drove to the smart real estate office in Cannes and Millie told the smooth buttoned-down, blazered agent she wanted 'something with a touch of class'. Like in the old days.

'Don't bother showing me any of those white plaster boxes all tricked up with marble and sliding glass doors on lots the size of a postage stamp,' she warned him. 'I want terraces and balustrades and proper french doors and arches and columns. And a view of the Mediterranean. *Class*, my dear man. That is what I want.' And the agent raised a supercilious eyebrow and informed her that they only dealt in the best.

But a few days and several dozen houses later both she and the agent were exhausted and beginning to lose their patience. 'I'll leave it to you,' she told Bea, retreating to the comforts of the hotel and the bridge table. 'You know exactly what I want, dear girl. Find us something nice.'

Bea spent the next few days happily zigzagging along the coast inspecting properties, but still found nothing that was quite right. She was up in the hills near Vence when she noticed the thunderclouds stacking ominously over the mountains. The temperature and humidity were soaring; it was so hot she thought she would melt and she stopped for a cool drink at a café.

The small village square was deserted and the only other customer on the café terrace was a young man at the table opposite, busy writing.

She sipped her cold drink, watching him, wondering what he was writing that kept him so absorbed. He was *almost* good-looking, she conceded. Not too tall, with rumpled curly brown hair that looked as though he had run his hands through it once too often. And he had an interesting bony face and a generous-looking mouth that she thought would have been described in romantic novels as 'finely-chiselled'. She guessed he was in his early thirties and decided he must be a writer, wondering if he was famous and if maybe she should know him.

She jumped as lightning suddenly forked through the blackened sky followed by a peal of thunder and the spatter of raindrops. A wind gusted from nowhere, scattering his papers, and she ran to help pick them up before they were soaked. He thanked her in French but she could tell from his accent he was English.

There was another flash and the rain began to come down in torrents as they ran together into the café. 'Better sit out the storm in here,' he said, smiling at her. 'Let me buy you a drink. To say thank you for saving my priceless manuscript.'

They sat at the small scarred, wooden bar, sipping a glass of rosé wine and he told her his name was Nick Lascelles, then he asked where she was from.

Bea stared blankly at him. It was such a casual question, so easy. For anyone else. 'San Francisco, I guess,' she said finally.

He looked quizzically at her. 'You don't sound too sure.'

'Oh I am,' she said quickly, embarrassed. 'Of course I am.'

'You're on holiday I suppose.'

'Sort of. I'm supposed to be working but it seems more like a holiday.' She told him about Millie, playing endless games of bridge at the Hôtel du Cap, and said that Millie wanted to buy a villa and she was supposed to be out looking for one to match up to her requirements.

'And what are you doing here?' she asked finally.

'I'm researching my book. About crime on the Riviera, from the turn of the century, to the present day. Crimes of passion, violence, grand theft, and murder. Solved and unsolved.' He grinned. 'You'd be surprised how many there are.'

Thunder rumbled ominously around the hills and he glanced at his watch, then looked hopefully at her. 'The storm will be around for a while. Won't you join me for lunch?'

The café had filled up and they squeezed round a little table by the window. Bea watched the rain bouncing from the cobblestones in the square, and realised suddenly that she was enjoying herself. Nick Lascelles was nice, he was young, and attractive, and he talked non-stop throughout the generous seventy-five franc meal-of-the-day.

Over the soup, he told her that his mother was French and his father English. 'From one of those "good" families with an old name and not much money,' he said with a grin. 'I was the poorest boy at the "rich boys" school they sent me to in Switzerland. No helicopters whisking me off for weekends on the yacht like most of the other boys; no private planes sent to take me home for the holidays.'

As he ate the omelette, he told her that all that was left of the once-vast family fortunes was the old manor house and a few acres in Gloucestershire that his brother had inherited. And an old run-down vineyard near Bordeaux with the prettiest little château, that he had inherited and was attempting to up-date into the twentieth century.

'But what I really am, is a writer,' he said finally, over the *steak-frites*. 'I began on a local paper and after years of slaving, writing up village flower shows and the church fêtes, I graduated to one of the national dailies. Then I branched out and wrote my first book about wine; then a guide book to France; articles about European life for the American glossies. That sort of thing.'

There was so much food, Bea couldn't manage the cheese and salad, and she watched astonished as he wolfed his down and told her that he would make a decent living, if only he didn't keep funding it all to 'The Charity' – that was what he called his vineyard – for new roofs and modern steel fermenting vats, and new equipment.

'Then why do you do it?' Bea asked curiously. 'Why bother trying to save an old vineyard when you'd be much better off financially without it?'

His nice grey eyes met hers seriously. 'I feel an obligation.

After all, it's been in the family for almost two hundred years. I've got to get it into shape for the next generation, so there will be something for them to inherit.' He laughed as he added, 'Of course the roof is collapsing and floor-boards are rotting and for all I know there's death-watch beetle in the beams as well. And the thirty hectares of vines have been neglected for a couple of decades. But it's my ambition to restore it to its former glory. I want to produce a Grand Cru wine with an *appellation contrôlée* and then live out my remaining years in serious splendour.'

He laughed, unconcerned, as he added, 'I expect it to keep me broke for the next twenty years or so. That's why I call it Château Charity; because I give it all my money.'

Bea laughed with him, liking him. He was so cheerful and so positive about what he wanted, and something in her yearned towards that kind of strength.

They had finished their coffee and she saw it was getting late, but she invited him to come by the hotel that evening for a drink. 'Come and meet Millie,' she said, 'I think you'll like each other.'

She was waiting for him promptly at seven-thirty, wearing her prettiest dress, a short amber linen sheath whose colour blended with her golden-tanned skin. Her soft copper hair hung in soft bangs and her anxious brown eyes lit up when she saw him striding confidently towards her.

Nick's curly hair was neatly combed for the occasion and he wore a rumpled cream linen jacket, a white shirt and jeans. Bea thought he looked great, though she noticed Millie eyeing him critically as she ordered him to tell her all about himself.

'Nick didn't bring his cv, Millie,' Bea protested. 'He only came for a drink. Can't we talk about the weather or something?'

'I never talk about the weather,' Millie said impatiently. 'The weather is either good or bad and then the conversation is finished. It's *people* I'm interested in. Bea told me about your book, dear boy. And I have a terrible feeling you might be writing about some of my old friends. They were all rogues, you know. There's something so fascinating about crime,' she added with a delighted shiver. 'Though poor darling Bea doesn't think so.'

Bea shot her a warning glance: she didn't want Nick Lascelles to know what had happened to her. At least, not yet.

But Millie seemed to find Nick so entertaining she decided he was staying for dinner. 'It's so nice for Bea to have a young friend,' she said, making Bea roll her eyes in embarrassment.

But Millie meant it. She watched them approvingly, thinking how animated and pretty Bea looked tonight, in the simple amber linen with the string of green and silver beads, picked up, she knew, for a few francs in Antibes market, wrapped around her long neck. A girl like Bea didn't need flamboyant clothes: she gave anything she wore that instinctive touch of elegance.

'Invite Nick again, dear girl,' she boomed as she said goodnight to him later. 'I like having him around.'

Bea made a wry face at Nick. 'I'm afraid you've got your orders,' she told him mischievously as she walked him to his car.

'Suits me,' he said pleased. They stopped and looked uncertainly at each other, then he leaned forward and kissed her lightly on either cheek, 'Same time tomorrow night?'

She nodded, waving as he climbed into his little red Alfa Spyder and drove away. It had been a good day, she thought. The best since her accident.

* * *

The next day the real estate agent told her of another villa, old and run-down, and unlived in for years. 'But it has everything Madame Fenwick wants,' he said. 'It has character, elegance – and a view of the sea. It has been owned by one family since it was built around 1920. No one has lived there for decades, but they've only just put it on the market. It's a gem, off on its own on a hillside. But I warn you it will need work.' He glanced superciliously at her and added, 'Naturally, the price will reflect that. You can tell Madame Fenwick the villa is a bargain.'

He showed Bea on the map how to get there and told her there was a *gardien* on the property who would show her around.

The morning air felt fresh and sweet after the previous day's storms. Bea put down the top of the Mercedes and drove along the coast road, then up into the hills, enjoying herself, thinking more about Nick Lascelles than the house she was going to see. No doubt it would be another wild-goose chase. She just didn't understand why Millie was so insistent on buying a villa anyway, and she almost wished it wouldn't be suitable so they could call it a day. It was just another whim Millie would be sure to regret later.

She drove along the dusty white lane to the top of the hill, past a peeling pink stucco wall tumbling with roses and bougainvillaea. She stopped the car at the big iron gates and pulled the old bronze bell set in a stone niche. She listened to it ringing, staring up the drive curving into the distance between the trees.

No one came so she pulled the bell again, waiting in the hot silence. There was no one around, no human noises of cars and machines. She leaned against the pink stucco wall, waiting. It felt warm against her back and she closed her eyes, listening to the chirrup of the crickets and the sigh of the wind in the tops of the tall old cedars and the endless drone of bees in the blossoms. The sun was hot on her bare arms and the scent of wild rosemary hovered in her nostrils . . . it was so wild and quiet, so secret . . . she felt like the last person on this beautiful earth . . .

'Mademoiselle. I was told to expect you.'

Her eyes shot open and she stared at the *gardien*. He was old and frail, in bright blue work overalls. The sleeves of his blue shirt were rolled back, revealing the sinewy arms and the hands gnarled from decades of physical labour. His face was deeply lined, and the blue eyes looking back at her had the faded innocence of another more peaceful era. He removed his battered straw hat and bowed politely.

'It is a pleasure to see a visitor here again, M'mselle,' he told her as they walked up the drive together. He looked pleased when she answered him in French. 'It has been a long time since anyone came here. Too long.' He sighed deeply. 'A lifetime it seems.'

Their footsteps crunched on the gravel as they turned the curve in the drive and then the house came into sight.

Bea stopped dead in her tracks. Her legs refused to walk and her eyes to believe what she was seeing, and her heart suddenly pounded so hard it hurt. She stared at the beautiful pink villa. At the tall windows with their faded green shutters, at the big double doors standing open with a glimpse of the shadowy hall beyond, and the columned portico with wide marble steps.

The light sunny day receded and she felt herself tremble. *The ghostly scent of mimosa was in her nostrils, though it was the wrong season and none was in bloom. The sound of songbirds filled her ears, though none were there. Was it just déjà vu? A combination of all the villas she had seen over the past weeks and her own imagination and longing? Or was she really looking at the house of her dreams?*

'*Et voilà*. The Villa Mimosa,' the old man told her proudly. He glanced, concerned at her. 'Are you ill, M'mselle? Please, please, come inside. The sun is hotter than you think. It is unwise to be without a hat . . .' He hurried off to fetch a glass of water.

She was alone in the hall. The hair at the nape of her neck prickled and goosebumps rose on her arms. *She knew this house. She knew exactly how the rooms were arranged: dining to the left, grand salon to the right, and at the back of the house the long room with its many windows leading onto the arched terrace overlooking the sea. The floors were a cool pink-veined marble and in front of her rose a graceful curving staircase, leading up to a wide gallery.*

'The staircase is made from a very rare wood,' the *gardien* said, handing her the glass of water. 'From the tropics somewhere. It was built specially.' He was eager for her to like it. 'Everything is of the best, M'mselle, as you can see.'

Bea walked slowly through the villa, feeling as though she had stepped into her dream. Even though the plaster was flaking and the old wallpapers were stained and peeling, it was just as beautiful as she had known it would be. She shivered, asking herself *why* she should know? What trick of fate had brought her here? Could it have been the *future* she had seen in her dream?

'I have worked here since I was just a boy, a gardener's lad,' the old *gardien* said. 'For Madame Leconte. She married the Foreigner soon after, and then they went to live abroad.' He hesitated, trying to recall, but he was old and his memories were vague. 'When Madame returned,' he said finally, 'she was pregnant. She wanted the child to be born here, in France, in this house that she loved so much. And that was her undoing.'

He sighed deeply, remembering. 'Her husband doted on her, I never saw a man behave like that. He treated her like a precious piece of Limoges porcelain. And all for nothing. Two weeks after the baby was born, she was dead.'

A thrill of horror ran down Bea's spine. 'Dead? How?'

'She fell, M'mselle. Down the precious staircase he had built specially to please her. Her husband, the Foreigner, left immediately after the funeral. He never lived here again.'

Bea shuddered, looking at the fatal staircase. It was graceful, curving, with wide easy steps and she imagined the woman crashing down it onto the marble floor below.

And yet, despite its tragic history, as she walked through the lovely rooms, she did not find the house frightening. It was like an enchanted villa in a fairy story, protected by its high walls and tall cedars and pines, its thickets of thorny damask roses and the mimosas that gave it its name. She thought that it was like a sleeping castle, waiting to be discovered by the prince who would bring it back to life.

She walked outside and sat on the marble steps, closing her eyes, trying to recapture her dream, imagining she was that child again ... *the marble steps were cool against her bare legs ... the sky darkened ominously and she held her breath, waiting for the sinister sound of footsteps on the gravel.*

But when she opened her eyes it was just that the sun had gone behind a cloud as another storm approached. She glanced up startled as a flock of gulls flew, mewling, overhead, and she then remembered the song of a hundred birds in her dream. She turned anxiously to the old caretaker. 'M'sieur, where are the songbirds?'

He looked at her, astonished. 'Why, M'mselle, how do you know about that? There have been no songbirds here since the 1930s when the aviary was destroyed.'

Bea's velvet brown eyes darkened with fear. '*Then if there are no songbirds*,' she whispered anxiously, '*how can I remember them?*'

CHAPTER 13

'Of course it's just coincidence,' Millie said, peering anxiously at Bea. They were sitting in the gardens of the hotel, and Bea had just poured out the whole story of finding the Villa Mimosa. The villa of her dream.

'You've looked at so many houses, dear child, they've all blurred together in your mind. I sometimes get that *déjà vu* feeling myself, and I admit, it's eerie, feeling as though you know a place when you know you've never been there before.'

Bea looked at her, scared. 'Perhaps I have been there before, Millie. What if I lived there before ... before my accident?'

'Don't be ridiculous, Bea. The agent told you no one has lived there for decades. And you saw the evidence for yourself, the neglect, the peeling wallpaper, the antique plumbing ...' she shuddered, imagining it. 'But yet you say it has charm,' she added thoughtfully.

'It is the most beautiful villa I've ever seen,' Bea said sincerely. 'It's like a secret house, waiting to be discovered by someone who will love it and lavish their time and care on it.'

'And money,' Millie added.

Bea nodded regretfully. 'A lot of money I'm afraid.'

They fell silent, contemplating the Mediterranean, rippling like molten pewter under the newly gathering storm clouds.

'Maybe it was the future you were seeing and not the past,' Millie said after a while. 'Perhaps that was it, Bea. That's why you thought you recognised it. My astrologer – she's the famous one you read about in the newspapers, the one who counsels the movie-stars and presidents – told me it can happen like that sometimes. And she's always right.'

Bea glanced hopefully at her. Somehow Millie made it all sound logical. She decided to call Phyl and tell her what had happened. Phyl was flying to Paris tomorrow and she would be in Nice a few days later. Then she would take her to the villa and tell her about her strange experience, she would ask her whether it was all just longing and wishful thinking on her part. *Or something more sinister*.

Nick picked Bea up that night just as the storm broke. They parked the car behind the old quay in Cannes and ran, laughing, hand in hand into a deserted café. They sat at a table in the window, watching the rain bounce from the cobbles and the lightning flash. He grinned and said, 'It's *déjà vu*. I have the feeling we have done this before.'

Bea threw him a startled glance. 'That's the second time today it's happened to me,' she said. 'Only this time I know it's real.' She looked wistfully at him, thinking how different his life was from hers. Nick knew who he was and where he was going, and how he was going to achieve it. He did not know that behind the carefree façade of the person called Bea French lay an unknown quantity. A girl who faced the nightly terrors of the dark tunnel. And a faceless killer.

He looked so straight ahead, so sympathetic, somehow so tuned in to the girl he knew as Bea, she wished she could go on pretending to be that girl for ever. But she knew she could not. One day the terror of the past would come to claim her, she just knew it. And she felt like she was deceiving him.

Suddenly she was telling him about what had happened to her in San Francisco; how the police suspected someone had tried to kill her, about her loss of memory and the dream she had had under hypnosis. And how today that dream had seemed to come true when she had seen the Villa Mimosa.

'Millie thinks maybe I saw the future,' she said tremulously, afraid he would think she was crazy. 'But what about the songbirds? How else could I have known about them if I had never been there?'

'Poor Bea,' Nick consoled her. 'What a dreadful time you've had. But don't worry, I'm sure it's all going to work out, and soon you'll remember everything.'

She shook her head miserably. She didn't think so. 'I'll call Phyl tonight,' she said, a touch of hope creeping into her voice as she thought of Phyl's steadying presence. 'Phyl will know what to do.'

Nick was intrigued by the story the *gardien* had told her about Madame Leconte's fatal accident. 'It's exactly up my alley,' he said thoughtfully. 'Tragic death in a grand Riviera villa. It must have made the headlines when it happened. Tell you what, Bea, I'll go through the newspaper archives tomorrow and see what I can come up with. If I find more information about the house, maybe it will help you to remember.'

Nick found what he was looking for the next morning, in the archives of the *Nice-Matin*. The newspaper, dated 5 October 1929, carried the story of Madame Leconte's fatal fall on its front page. It said that she came from a well-known Marseilles family and that she had lived at the Villa Mimosa for several years. She had given birth only two weeks previously and it was thought that a faint or a dizzy spell had caused her to fall from the top of the stairs onto the marble floor of the hall below. There was no mention of any inquest and no mention of her husband. It merely stated that the funeral had taken place that afternoon.

At two-thirty Nick went to meet Millie and Bea in Antibes. They were going to inspect the Villa Mimosa, but then Millie suddenly said she felt 'too tired' to go with them.

'I would prefer a quiet game of bridge, dear girl,' she said wearily to Bea. 'But you must go. Show the Villa Mimosa to Nick. If he likes it too, tell them we'll buy it.'

Bea shook her head, shocked, at her. 'You can't do that, Millie. You might hate the place. You must at least see it first.'

'I've learned to trust your taste by now,' Millie said carelessly. 'And besides, there's all that good antique furniture I bought in Paris urgently awaiting a home. Get a good decorator to put it in shape, dear girl. And tell him I want it ready yesterday. Or else he's fired. Understand?'

'You know you're just acting on impulse again, Millie,' Bea warned. 'You'll regret it later, just like always.'

Millie shook her head, making her blonde curls bounce. 'Oh no, dear girl. I'll not regret this one,' she said, with a secretive little smile, waving them off as she headed serenely for the afternoon bridge table.

'Even for Millie, this is crazy,' Bea said nervously to Nick as they waited for the *gardien* to open the gate. 'I mean I know she's really rich and can afford to indulge her every whim, but . . .' she shrugged, 'not even to take a look at it first!'

'This is some expensive whim,' Nick marvelled, peering

through the gates. 'Do you have any idea how much land this place must have? And what land around here costs per hectare?'

'No. And nor does she. That's just it, Nick. Millie knows nothing about it. *Why* does she want to buy it?'

'Maybe because you're in love with it?'

Bea shook her head. 'No chance. She's buying it because she's in love with the past. She's an old lady trying to recapture her youth.'

Looking at Bea, so young and pretty with her fluff of sun-gilded hair falling into her exasperated brown eyes, Nick thought she was wrong. He thought lonely old Millie Fenwick had found in Bea the granddaughter she had never had. Maybe it was because of the terrible thing that had happened to Bea. The loss of memory had left her so alone in the world, and made her vulnerable, he would bet that Millie was trying to please Bea, and trying to help her get her memory back. And if it cost her the price of the villa, so what?

They followed the old *gardien* up the drive and when Nick finally saw the Villa Mimosa, he gave a low whistle of appreciation. Bea had not exaggerated. It was a rose-pink wedding cake of a house with colonnaded terraces and a pillared portico and marble balustraded balconies. But neglect was apparent everywhere: the faded green shutters hung askew, many windows were broken and a thousand cracks had turned the marble terraces into crazy-paving. The overgrown lawns stretched down the hillside towards the sea, and old rose bushes fought for their beautiful existence with the rampaging bougainvillaea and honey-suckle, the tamarisk and the mimosas.

A small stream tumbled musically from a grotto on the hillside above the house, and an empty stone fountain adorned with crumbling naiades and dolphins peeked forlornly from the high grasses of what was once a velvet lawn. And a grove of ancient silvery olive trees creaked and sighed eerily in the wind that sent lazy silver ripples across the azure sea beyond the peninsula, and shivers down their spines.

Nick took her hand as they stood looking at it, and the villa cast its spell over them. It was like love at first sight. He could see it in his mind's eye. The pink stucco walls glowing softly under a new coat of paint; the re-glazed windows reflecting the sunset and the old shutters flung wide to catch the breeze. He could almost smell the fresh-hay scent of newly mown grass and hear the tinkle of water in the fountains.

They walked hand in hand, into the hall and stood, looking up at the great curving staircase. Nick shook his head and said, with a puzzled frown, 'Something's wrong. You see that broad landing halfway down. And then the other half-landing, near the top. How could Madame Leconte possibly have fallen from the top to the bottom, the way the newspaper said? She would have been stopped by the curve of the landing.'

'Maybe she fell from halfway and the newspapers got it wrong. You know how it is.'

'I wonder?' Nick said thoughtfully. 'I have a feeling there is more to this than meets the eye. Let's see what the *gardien* can tell us.'

The old man was waiting outside. He had cut a rose for Bea. It was big with dark velvet petals and she smiled her thanks as she breathed its old-fashioned scent, of musk and incense. 'They were Madame Leconte's favourite,' he told her with a smile. 'She loved their perfume.'

But he knew little about the accident. 'I did not see it. M'sieur,' he said. 'Remember, I was only a boy, still in school, living in the village with my family. We were poor and I was working part-time as a gardener's lad to earn a little extra money.' He thought hard then he added, 'There was a journalist who came here. He was very young, not much older than myself. He wrote the story for the *Nice Matin*. But whether he is still alive, only *le bon Dieu* knows . . .'

The secretary at the *Nice Matin* newspaper office was very helpful. She told them that of course she knew the journalist. Everybody knew Monsieur Marquand. He had been one of their star reporters for years until his retirement. *Naturellement* he was still alive, very much so. And he could usually be found in the Café du Marin Bleu, in Antibes, where he had spent his mornings every day for the past fifteen years.

They found Monsieur Aristide Marquand sitting comfortably at his usual table on the terrace, sipping a glass of pastis. He sprang nimbly to his feet when they introduced themselves, throwing an appreciative Gallic glance at Bea. He might be old, but he was still handsome and spry, and a bit of a dandy in his Panama hat, sharply pressed white pants and dark blue linen jacket. And a Frenchman was never too old to appreciate a pretty girl.

'It's strange you should ask,' he said to Nick, accepting another drink. 'I was thinking about the Villa Mimosa the other day. Heard it was finally on the market.'

'A friend of ours is thinking of buying it,' Nick said, 'but we heard there had been a tragedy there.' He told Monsieur Marquand he had also been a journalist and about the book he was researching on crimes on the Riviera. 'So any information you can give me would be appreciated,' he said, looking hopefully at him.

'It is a strange story, what happened at the Villa Mimosa,' Monsieur Marquand said. 'Stranger than anyone knows. But enough time has gone by for it not to matter any more, and so I shall tell you.'

They leaned forward, waiting impatiently for what he would say as he slowly sipped his pastis, collecting his thoughts.

'Life was changing on the Riviera then,' he said finally. 'People were flocking down here, not just to the winter resorts of Nice and Cannes like in the old days, but to the summer beaches. It was Chanel who started the craze of course, when she came here on the Duke of Westminster's yacht, in 1922, brown as a sailorboy. Then the Americans came, Cole Porter and the Murphys and Fitzgeralds, and the society people from Paris.

'It was a whole new era, of sunbathing and beach pyjamas and floppy hats and potent drinks. There was the tiny Hôtel du Cap and the old villas here in Antibes, and then suddenly all the chic young couples brought their children and their nursemaids. They built extravagant villas and had them designed by smart people from Paris, white and blue and green with cool marble floors and black satin sofas. They put huge striped umbrellas by their new turquoise pools overlooking the sea. And they carved beautiful gardens from the rocky hillsides and planted fully-grown palms and shade trees. Everything had to be instant you see, there was no time to wait for plants and trees to grow. They wanted it all *now*.

'Ah my dear, young people,' he said reminiscently. 'You have no idea what it was like, how wild and almost pagan it was then. The sun seemed to shrivel their brains and relieve them of their inhibitions. It was an era of wild naked parties at the beach, of dancing until dawn in newly-sprung-up clubs. Of winning and losing heavily at the casinos, of drinking pale pink wine and lingering over lunch on the terrace of the Hôtel du Cap.'

Aristide Marquand's faded blue eyes held a hint of regret as he regarded them. 'Ah M'sieur,' he said softly, 'it was about lovers. And about requited passion behind green-shuttered windows on long hot summer afternoons.

'But this woman, Madame Leconte, was never part of it. Always she was on the outside. The lumpy woman of a certain age, dining alone at a table on the terrace, returning afterwards, always alone, to her villa. Maybe standing under the stars on her balcony and gazing yearningly at the moon in the midnight velvet sky, longing for love. And though they called her "Madame" Leconte, it was merely an honorary title, in consideration of her age and her financial status. But everyone knew her simply as "la Célibataire". The Spinster.'

Bea gave a shocked gasp. 'Oh, how cruel,' she whispered.

The old man nodded, 'It was. But these were superficial people living a glamorous superficial life. To qualify for their charmed circle you needed to possess looks or style or talent, or an aristocratic name. To be a writer, an artist, or composer, the latest musical comedy star, a prince or a duke. Mere money was not enough.'

Nick ordered more pastis and the old man sipped it while he told them that Madame Leconte was the daughter of a back-street Marseilles lad who through his own ingenuity and enterprise had made himself a fortune dealing in armaments. He had married later in life and when his daughter was born he had named her Marie-Antoinette because she was his own little princess. He had kept her home with governesses to educate her, and they said he adored her so much he was always afraid of losing her to some other man. His wife had died early. Then later when he too died, Marie-Antoinette was already nearing forty years old, and she was left all alone.

'She was never pretty, you understand,' Monsieur Marquand said. 'She was a stocky woman with dark hair, the kind that has no lustre. Her eyes were black with heavy brows and her face was long and narrow with incongruous dimples that rude Paris street urchins would call after her looked like "pissholes in the snow". Of course then, she didn't seem to know she wasn't pretty. She was protected you see, and her father always told her how beautiful she was, until I swear she saw another face in her mirror. She only saw the truth later, after he was dead and she was alone in the Villa Mimosa.

'Her father had built the house for her in 1922, because she loved the sunshine and fresh air, and she did not like their grand apartment in Paris. And now, she inherited everything. La Célibataire was an heiress at forty.

'I remember the first time I saw her: she had sallow colouring and a deep-breasted matronly figure, and she wore the new 1920s' flapper fashions that did not suit her.' He glanced at Nick and added with an expressive shrug, 'To tell you the truth, M'sieur, had you put her in the peasant black dress and shawl, she would have looked just like them. You would never have known she was an heiress.

'And then love walked into her life. He was American, blond, handsome and much younger than she. "A fortune hunter" everyone said, but if he was then he wasn't the usual sort. Either that, or he was a very clever young man. When he was out with her, his eyes never left her. Not even a glance towards the young beauties flaunting themselves, flinging themselves at him.

'They were seen everywhere together; at all the smartest cafés and clubs. She bought a new boat and they would speed around the bay, stopping for a swim or lunch at the little beach restaurants. He accompanied her to the salons to advise her on clothes; he had her old-fashioned jewellery reset. He took her to buy a car, an open-top Bugatti of course – that's what everyone wanted then – red with a dove-grey leather interior, and she learned how to drive it. No one ever saw him at the wheel, it was always she – so no one could ever say she had bought *him* the car. He seemed to take nothing. Except her heart.

'He returned with her to Paris and they were married, and then he took her back to wherever it was he came from. My memory fails me on that one. Anyhow, a year later she returned. Alone and obviously pregnant. Remember, she was a woman in her forties and she was considered too old to begin a family.

'Naturally there was gossip. I remember the servants said she looked pale and ill, that there was something in her eyes that reminded them of a terrified animal, like the ones they had seen unloaded from the carts and herded into the abattoir in Marseilles. *Those animals knew they were marked for death*, they said.

'I saw her once myself, coming from her doctor's office in Cannes, and it seemed to me then, being young and impressionable, that she knew it too. It was there in her big, dark empty eyes. *Death*.

'The handsome husband came back. The servants said he behaved like a saint, that he showered her with attention and kindnesses, with flowers, gifts, love. And she shunned him. She walked in the gardens alone. She took her meals in her room, alone. She slept alone. But after all, she was a pregnant woman, it was normal to be tired, distracted, a little off-balance ... especially at her age.

'The baby came. A boy. And a few weeks later she fell down the stairs. And I was proven right. Death had marked her. We both had seen it.'

Monsieur Marquand shrugged his thin shoulders re-signedly again. 'A sad tale, you say. Yes. A great sadness.' He fell silent, thoughtfully sipping his drink.

Bea heaved a sigh, close to tears. 'There's something more, isn't there,' Nick said, 'something else happened.'

Marquand nodded. 'Your journalist's instinct for a story is right. But it's all so long ago now, what harm can it do to tell you?

'I was very young then, the most junior reporter. It was late and I was alone in the office, typing up my copy – births, deaths, marriages, small local events. I hadn't yet graduated to the grand society events and scandals – not to say the news. I was just a cub, someone they sent when there was no one else to go. Then a call came through from one of the servants at the Villa Mimosa. There had been an accident. La Célibataire was dead.

'It was my big opportunity and I flung myself on my bicycle and pedalled furiously through the sleeping town, along the coast road, up the hill to the villa. Light spilled from the downstairs windows, across the lawns and ter-races. There might have been a party going on, it looked so festive. I rang the doorbell and waited. No one came. I found out later that the husband had sent all the servants to bed. The door opened under my touch. I stepped into the hall and found myself staring at the body of la Célibataire.

'She was lying face-down on the marble floor. She was some distance from the foot of the stairs and I remember thinking someone must have moved her after she fell. My heart jumped into my throat as I glimpsed the sticky mess that had been the back of her head. Then the husband appeared suddenly from the library.

He was wearing a silk dressing-gown and he lit a big cigar and stood there, staring at the body, smoking coolly, and I marvelled at his strength because you never know how a man will react to shock and grief. He was a man in charge of his emotions and I admired that.

'Then he saw me and anger flared in his eyes. "Who the hell are you?" he demanded. "Get out of here. How dare you intrude . . . no one is allowed in here but the Chief of Police." He rushed menacingly at me and I ran out, shouting apologies. "Don't you dare come back," he yelled after me. But I was a cub reporter with a hot story and I wasn't about to let go of it so fast.

'I hid myself in the bushes outside the window and waited. The Chief of Police arrived. He was driving his own car, not the official one, and had obviously dressed in a hurry. He went inside and the door shut. I peered through my window, straining to hear what was said.

'The husband welcomed the Chief genially, smiling, shaking his hand. He poured brandy generously, telling him what had happened. He had not seen the accident. He couldn't sleep, he had been in the library, reading. But he had heard her cry out and then the sounds of her fall. The injuries did seem somewhat remarkable, the gaping wound in the back of her head, but obviously there was some explanation. "Why not let's you and I go into the library and discuss it, maybe have another drink, a fine cigar . . ." he said.'

Aristide Marquand paused, and his shocked eyes met Nick's as he said, 'And then, M'sieur, he did something that made my blood run cold. I have seen many victims, and many murderers in the course of my journalistic career, but I never saw anything to match this for callousness.

'Marie's body was between him and the Chief. She was lying there with her blood and brains splattered all over the white marble floor. *And her husband stepped over her smashed head as though she were nothing but a tigerskin rug*. Take it from me, Monsieur, you watch anyone near a body; normally they will keep their distance, circle round it, keep ten feet away from it. They never, *never*, step over it. *And this was his wife*.

'I peeked through the window at them talking, smoking their cigars, sipping good brandy. They had smiles on their faces, as though this were a social visit and his wife wasn't lying dead in the hall after all. So I crept back inside and tiptoed over and looked at her again. *And then I knew she had not fallen*. There was a big hole in the back of her head. A big red hole. Made, I was certain, by a bullet.

'*Eh bien*. The Chief emerged an hour later. They shook hands on the steps. The body was whisked away to the mortuary and sealed in its coffin. There was no inquest, just the Chief's story that it was an accident. She was buried the next day and that was that. *Except I knew she had been murdered. And I thought the man who had done it was her husband*.'

Marquand shrugged as he met their stunned eyes. 'A young boy's wild imagination you might say? Then tell me how was it that the Chief, a local man who had never owned more than a modest apartment, suddenly took early retirement on the pretext of ill-health? He bought himself a grand villa near Marseilles, he had a smart new automobile in his new garage, and enough in the bank to allow him to live in luxury the rest of his life.'

Nick was full of questions. He wanted to know who the husband was, where he came from, what happened to him? And what about the baby?

The old boy shook his head. 'I never really knew. I told my chief what I'd seen and he said I was nuts, and if I ever mentioned a word, he would fire me.' He shrugged philosophically. 'So that was that. I was young, I had my career in front of me ... besides, there was nothing I could do. Nothing I could prove. And now, it's just the ramblings of an old man. But I can tell you that the husband departed the day of the funeral. And he left his son, just a few weeks old, in charge of an English nursemaid. I can still recall her name. Nanny Beale.

'They lived alone in that ghostly villa, with just the servants. They were a familiar sight along the coast, driving along in Madame Leconte's big silver Rolls to the promenade in Nice or Cannes. I remember the Nanny was very proper. She wore a grey flannel coat and black shoes in winter, and one of those funny round English hats with a brim. And in summer she always wore a crisp white apron over a blue dress, with the same style hat, only in straw, and sensible, immaculately white shoes. She never smiled, just nodded a lofty "Good day" here and there. They were a bit of a mystery, though I guess the servants must have gossiped about them, as they always do.

'But what I can tell you is that Nanny Beale came back here, years later. She had a cottage down the hill from the villa and she lived out her last years there, tending her roses. And her memories I guess. Anyhow, M'sieur, it is still there, her cottage. No one goes there. No one touches it. As far as I know it is just as she left it. Maybe there, you might find some of the answers you seek.'

CHAPTER 14

Mahoney pounded wearily up and down the hills of Marin County. He was light on his feet for a big man, but he had been keeping up a steady pace for three hours now. Sweat soaked his running shirt and his knees had turned to lumps of lead. He told himself angrily that he was out of shape; he had been too busy to keep up his training and the New York Marathon was just pie in the sky.

He sighed as he slowed to a jog, keeping up the slower pace for ten more minutes before decelerating into a walk. He mopped his brow with a big red spotted handkerchief, finally allowing himself to sink onto a convenient boulder, breathing deeply and slowly. The gigantic redwood trees in Muir Woods loomed in the distance and the hillside below him was dotted with pretty houses. Beyond that lay Sausalito and the wide sweep of the bay with the far-off orange gleam of the Golden Gate Bridge.

A plane was making its ascent over the horizon leaving a faint white trail across the blue sky, and he thought of Phyl Forster, already on her way to Paris. He told himself San Francisco would be a lonelier place without her, and then asked himself what the hell he meant by that? He hardly ever saw her.

The fact that she had called him at the precinct last night and asked if he were free, and could she come by meant nothing. He had promised to look after the cat for her and she wanted to drop it off, that's all. And then all she had wanted to talk about was Bea. Still, goddamnit, he liked the woman. He *enjoyed* her. She brought out the best and the worst in him, with her spiky verbal jousting, and her undercurrent of vulnerability. She thought she was so goddamn tough, with her cool uncluttered life. He heaved an exasperated sigh, thinking of last night; he'd just bet she would be a sucker for the wrong guy.

Mahoney lived in a seedy area near the waterfront, but the apartment had high ceilings and brick walls, wooden floors and space. It was on the top floor and a walk-up and when Phyl had buzzed, he had run down the stairs to meet her. 'Just in case you were scared,' he said with a mocking grin that showed off his good teeth.

'I'm perfectly capable of taking care of myself, Mahoney,' Phyl had retorted coolly.

'That's what they all say, Ma'am,' he countered, taking the cat basket and paraphernalia from her and following her up the stairs.

'If you make any comments about the size of my butt, Mahoney,' she said over her shoulder, 'I shall have you arrested for sexual harassment.'

'Now why would I make comments about your butt, Doc?' he asked plaintively. 'It looks great to me.'

'Mahoney!' Her eyes flashed as she swung round and then they both laughed.

'You are a fool,' she said, walking into his home.

'Yeah,' he agreed. 'Maybe you're right.'

He poured her a glass of wine – Italian and red – as she wandered interestedly around the apartment. The windows were flung open to catch the last rays of the setting sun and the breeze coming from the ocean. A Wagner opera was blasting from the speakers and three cats – two slender Siamese and a well-fed tabby that looked like a plumped-up cushion with yellow eyes – clustered on the kitchen counter, staring hostilely at the newcomer cat still in its carrying cage.

The apartment was basically one room cleverly divided by Japanese screens and he had furnished it with an eclectic mix of junk shop, Crate & Barrel and Williams Sonoma. There were some good second-hand oriental rugs and a few interesting antique pieces, and two of the walls were lined with shelves of books.

Phyl looked interestedly at them, noticing learned works on the psychology of the criminal mind, and the bound scores of most of the operas as well as the librettos. There was a huge section of poetry, and about a million cookbooks and old copies of *Gourmet*, a couple of shelves on cats and a stack of several years of *Cat Fancy Magazine*. And about every detective novel known to man.

'Everything for the well-rounded personality,' she said laughing, as she inspected the enormous cat playhouse that took up one entire corner. She admired his stereo, the best Bang & Olufsen, and she told him she thought the paintings, most of which were just stacked against the walls, were intriguing.

'Yeah, they're all by unsuccessful young artists. Quite a few of them live around here, and they're all I can afford. Which doesn't mean to say they're not good,' he added. 'Anyways, I like them. I chose each one carefully for the pleasure it gave me.'

She ran her hand over a piece of sculpture. It was honed from wood and was composed of subtle curves with a tactile smoothness that was irresistible.

'Ah, the wood sculptures,' he said bashfully. 'I confess to having created those myself.'

'There really is no end to your talents, is there, Mahoney?' she marvelled, sliding onto a stool at the kitchen counter, looking interestedly at him.

'None,' he agreed immodestly. 'And to prove it, the kitchen you are looking at so critically was designed and built by myself.'

She stared at the steel restaurant stove, the butcher's block countertops, the copper-bottomed pans hanging from a rail behind it, and at the battery of whisks and spatulas and lethal-looking knives and cleavers.

'What the hell are you doing, being a cop, Mahoney?' she demanded finally. 'You could have been a great chef. Or a cat-breeder. A sculptor. A poet. A professor. An opera-star.'

He looked at her and laughed. 'Everything but the opera star. You haven't heard me sing! But *chef* maybe. Now this is a Roger Vergé recipe – fricassee of chicken with fresh herbs – and believe me that man knows what he's cooking. I tell you, if I could, I'd swop places with him tomorrow.'

He swept the crowding cats off the table and set down their plates. 'Vergé's restaurant is right there, where you're heading. In the south of France. You should try it. Tell me how my version compares.'

'Maybe I'll do that.' She hesitated, wishing for a minute he was coming with her. 'Mahoney, Bea called me this afternoon. She said she had found the dream villa. The one she told me about when I hypnotised her.'

He listened seriously while Phyl told him about the villa, and about the woman who had died there; that it had been uninhabited for decades, and that Bea had remembered the songbirds that were no longer there.

'How do you explain that, Mahoney?' she demanded finally.

'There are only two logical ways she might know the

place. Either she *has* been there before. Or someone else told her about it.'

'That would have to be a remarkably vivid story-teller, for her to remember all the details, the smell of mimosa, the songbirds.' She looked at Mahoney and said honestly, 'I have no answers for her. And poor Bea is relying on me to help her.'

Mahoney shrugged sympathetically. 'You can only do what you can do.'

'Oh damn it, mouthing platitudes isn't going to bring back her memory,' she snapped angrily. Then she looked apologetically at him. 'I'm sorry. I just thought if you could find her attacker, we would know who she is.'

'Chicken or the egg,' he said quietly.

He got up, put on another record, poured more wine. He said, 'The National Center for the Analysis of Violent Crimes, the FBI's behavioural analysis unit, prepared a psychological profile of Bea's killer. *Would-be killer*, I mean. There wasn't much evidence for them to go on, just the method of the crime. The lack of use of a weapon indicated that he was a person who wanted to keep his hands "clean", so to speak. It had to look like an accident, not for her sake, but for his. This tells us that he is a person who cares what society thinks about him, a man with a public image. Perhaps even famous. Anyhow, he's your white-collar killer. They say he is probably in his late thirties or early forties, successful, charismatic and attractive. And that people who know him probably think he's a nice regular guy.'

'But why would he want to kill her?'

Mahoney shrugged. 'Personally, I believe she was a threat to him. He couldn't allow her to live.'

'*Bea* was a threat?'

'She knew something about him that he couldn't allow

anyone else to know. Something that threatened his existence.'

'Then you don't think it was a random murder attempt? That anyone would have done, it just happened to be Bea?'

'No. I don't think that. I think our man knew exactly what he was doing. Did you ever think about those teethmarks on her right forearm? The Doberman/Rottweiler? How about this scenario? Bea meets our man. His dog is trained to attack. He gives it the command. The dog goes for her throat and kills her. He shoots the dog, claims it turned wild. He is heartbroken about the accident.'

Mahoney's blue eyes were suddenly implacable as they met Phyl's. 'Homicide by canine. That would be a first, now wouldn't it, Doc? No guns, no mess. And absolutely unprovable.'

Phyl stared at him, stunned. 'The person you are describing is a sociopath. He would rationalise his actions. He would feel no remorse. It would all seem logical and simple to him. Something that had to be done. *But why?*'

'That's what we still don't know, Doc. That – and who Bea really is.'

Later Mahoney had driven Phyl home and she had sat silently beside him, not even throwing a dig at him about the vintage Mustang. He could tell she was brooding over what he had just told her and when they arrived at her apartment building, he looked compassionately at her. Then he leaned across and put his hand under her chin, tilting her troubled face up to him.

'Hey, hey,' he chided. 'This doesn't look like a woman on her way to Paris, glamour capital of Europe and culinary capital of the world. Look, forget what I told you. Just have a great time. And give Bea my love. Tell her I'm looking out for her. I'm not giving up.'

Phyl leaned forward and kissed him lightly on the lips.

'Thanks, Mahoney,' she said, opening the door and sliding out of the seat. 'I'll think of you in Paris.'

'You do that, Doc,' he said, smiling. 'And don't forget. Vergé. The Moulin de Mougins. Think of me when you're eating that chicken.'

'I'll try,' she said with her old mocking grin.

That had been last night, and Mahoney had spent the rest of it awake and prowling his apartment until it was time for his midnight shift, wondering what the hell he was going to do next on the Bea French case. Because there was sure as hell no evidence. Even her clothes had gone through the laser fingerprinting tests at the Bureau of Alcohol & Firearms and had come back negative. And there had been no stray fibres or hairs or scraps of any identifiable materials on them that could have been a clue.

Mahoney thought Bea French's would-be killer had got away with it. And his only chance to catch him would be if he tried again.

CHAPTER 15

Phyl was almost never late. She sat in the back of the limo taking her to San Francisco International airport, glancing nervously at her watch, fretting about the bumper-to-bumper traffic filtering slowly out to Candlestick Park. The sea of red tail-lights in front of her stretched into infinity, and she groaned. She should have left more time but she had just had to see that last patient; he had been desperate, she couldn't leave him for a week without counselling. He had needed her.

That was the trouble, she thought worriedly; they all needed her. And it was also one of the reasons she had decided on her career as a psychiatrist: she had wanted desperately to be needed again. It could never replace the need of a mother for her child, but it satisfied some bleak lost part of her own soul. And having gone through her own personal agony and mental turmoil, she empathised with her patients. It was only rarely that she let it get on top of her, when she was particularly tired, like today.

Last night when she had finished packing, she had sat wearily on her bed staring at the locked suitcases. If it had not been for the thought of Bea, with her pretty face and her anxious brown eyes, waiting for her in Nice, she might easily have picked up the telephone and cancelled the whole trip. All she really wanted to do was crawl into bed and stay there for about a week.

But of course she had not; even if Bea had not been the beloved friend she now was, she was still her patient and that was where her duty lay.

She scowled, glaring at the stuck traffic. 'How are we doing?' she asked the driver, thinking worriedly of the flight time.

'We'll be okay once we're past the Park,' he said. 'Don't worry, Doctor, I'll get you there in time.'

She sank back and closed her eyes, thinking how many times she had told people there was no point in worrying about the inevitable. The only answer was to deal with it. But that didn't apply to her and missed flights, she thought, feeling stress tensing her spine. God, she hated to be late, she hated delays, and she had never missed a flight in her life.

The driver was right; at the Candlestick Park exit the traffic divided into a tributary of red lights and the limo surged towards the airport. The driver summoned a porter and hastily unloaded her two bags while she ran to the first class check-in. 'I'm late,' she said guiltily handing over her ticket.

'The flight has already boarded, Dr Forster,' the man said. 'I'll call ahead and tell them you're on your way. They won't close the gate till you get there.' He handed her back her ticket with a smile, 'But you'd better hurry.'

'Thanks.' She grabbed her hand luggage, turned quickly and almost fell into the arms of the tall blond man standing behind her.

'Ohh,' she gasped, grabbing at him to stop from falling. As she looked up the female in her noticed quickly that he was very attractive, even as she made her apologies. 'I'm late,' she called over her shoulder as she fled down the concourse to the gate, 'I'll miss my flight.'

She heard his laughter following her as she ran and

thought irritatedly it was all right for him to be so cool; his flight probably wasn't for another hour yet. An airline agent was waiting at the gate to escort her on board and she glanced round the empty first class cabin as she sank thankfully into her seat. Good, she thought, I've got the place to myself. I'll just close my eyes and hopefully get some sleep, then maybe I'll be up for this conference after all. She shook her head, sighing impatiently at herself: a conference of international experts in her field was something she should have been looking forward to, not treating like a chore.

She glanced at her watch, surprised that the cabin doors were not yet closed; they were already ten minutes late. She asked the flight attendant what the delay was.

'We're waiting for one more passenger,' he told her. 'Meanwhile, may I offer you a glass of champagne? Or orange juice?'

She shook her head, thinking irritably she need not have bothered nearly killing herself running all that way. She heard the flight attendants greeting the tardy passenger, and then the Captain requesting that the cabin doors be closed. She glared irately up at him as he walked by. It was the blond good-looking guy whose arms she had fallen into at the check-in desk.

There was a twinkle in his eyes as he caught her glare. 'Sorry,' he said with an apologetic grimace. 'I wanted to tell you there was no need to run, but you were too quick for me. You just took off . . .'

'Like a bat out of hell . . .' she finished for him. She shook her head, laughing at herself. 'I just hate to be late.'

'I always thought that was a virtue,' he said, handing his jacket to the flight attendant and stacking his hand baggage in the locker. 'And anyhow, I'm the one who should be apologising for delaying your flight. Especially now I know

139

how much you hate to be late. Still, you don't have to worry, the tailwinds tonight will have us there on time.'

He was smiling down at her and she thought with a surge of interest that he really was attractive: tall and lean, with an angular face and light blue eyes behind gold-rimmed Armani spectacles. He had an easy rangy body and thick smooth dark-blond hair and he looked like a man very much at ease with himself. She wondered curiously what he did.

'How did you know that? About the tailwinds tonight?' she asked.

'I usually like to fly myself on these trips,' he said with a deprecating little shrug of his shoulders. 'Unfortunately tonight we had a spot of trouble in the electrical system at the last minute. And I have to be in Paris by tomorrow morning. So, that's why I'm on this flight and why you were delayed.' He laughed, a deep attractive sound as he said, 'My apologies again,' and went forward to take his seat as the plane began to taxi towards the runway.

Fatigue swept her curiosity about him away. She refused the meal, turned out her light and closed her eyes, hoping for sleep, but she only managed a fretful doze. The flight was annoyingly bumpy and the seat belt signs remained lit most of the journey. She drank cups of hot tea and took Advil to sooth her pounding head, and checked the time once more. They were five hours into the long flight and an eternity of turbulent plane ride stretched in front of her.

She stood up to retrieve her black work bag from the overhead locker and noticed that her fellow-passenger's light was on. Peering closer she saw he was writing busily in a yellow legal pad. He was, she thought mockingly, a real little bundle of energy, making the most of every moment. Just the way she always told herself she should.

She took out the paper she had prepared for the

conference, and began to go through it once again. Dawn was breaking when she next glanced up, and orange juice and breakfast were being served. Thank God, she thought, putting away her papers, they were almost there.

Paris was obscured beneath a bank of carbon-grey cloud when at last they began their descent, and when they finally landed, Phyl nodded goodbye to her handsome fellow-passenger. He was still gathering his papers together as she strode off the plane and she thought he really was a cool customer. He acted as though the world would wait for him.

And maybe it would, she thought, surveying the usual chaos of Charles de Gaulle airport. She had to wait ages for her bags and by then all the taxis had disappeared and she was left alone on the sidewalk, staring at the bouncing rain.

Her knees trembled with tension and exhaustion as she glared frustratedly at a waiting chauffeur-driven dark-blue Bentley.

'Looks as though it's not your lucky day,' an amused voice said, and she turned and looked into the laughing eyes of her handsome neighbour.

'It's my own fault, I should have had a car meet me.' She shrugged, 'I guess there'll be a taxi before too long.'

'In Paris? In the rain?' He grinned. 'No chance. But I'd be glad to offer you a lift?'

She glanced at him and then at the enormous Bentley. 'That yours?' she asked, nodding in its direction.

'It's a company car. My personal tastes run to more racy lines.'

She laughed, 'It looks wonderful to me right now. But I wouldn't want to take you out of your way. I'm at the Rafael.'

'The Rafael first please, Adams,' he told the English driver. 'Then home.'

Phyl stepped into the car and sank gratefully back into its luxurious leather cushions. She looked across at him, smiling. There seemed to be about an acre of seat between them but she was as aware of his masculine presence as though he were touching her. It must be Paris, she thought, amused.

'You look tired,' he said sympathetically and she groaned.

'You mean I look a wreck. I certainly feel it. All I want right this minute is a hot bath, a cool drink and soft bed.' Their eyes met as the car slid smoothly through the traffic. 'Perhaps we should introduce ourselves,' she said, holding her hand across the great divide between them. 'I'm Phyl Forster.'

'Brad Kane.'

His hand was hard and unexpectedly cold. 'I'm in Paris for a conference,' she added. 'Psychiatry.'

'Of course. Dr Phyl. Forgive me, I should have recognised you.'

'Not necessarily. Besides, the way I feel now I'm sure I don't resemble the photo on the book jacket.' She laughed, even though weariness was overtaking her. She liked her handsome good Samaritan.

The telephone rang and she closed her eyes as he answered it and had a quick conversation in French. 'Please excuse me,' he said to her, 'but there are some important calls I must make.'

She lay back, half-dozing, listening to the soothing murmur of his voice in the background, wondering vaguely who he was, and what he did, and if it was a woman he was talking to in that soft sexy French voice. Still, she was glad when they finally arrived at the hotel, thinking longingly of that bed waiting for her.

He took her arm as she stepped from the car, apologising

again for having been on the phone. 'I don't know what I would have done if you hadn't been there to rescue me from the rain,' she said, smiling tiredly.

He held her gaze for a long moment then he took a card with his address and phone number from his pocket and gave it to her. 'Call me, busy lady,' he said lightly, 'if you have a moment to spare in Paris.' He took her hand and raised it to his lips, and then with a quick wave and a smile, he climbed into the big car and was gone.

Like a man I met in a dream, she thought a short while later, sinking into a hot bath. The Rafael was one of those smaller Paris hotels that prides itself on luxury, service and discretion. The water was hot, the soap smelled delicious, the Evian was iced and the bed enveloped her in a flurry of soft pillows, crisp sheets and cosy blankets. She was asleep within minutes.

She awoke six hours later in a jet-lagged confusion of time and place, staring puzzled round the darkened room. Then it came back to her: she was in Paris.

The bedside clock said six-thirty p.m. She walked to the window and pulled back the curtains. The grey buildings across the street looked even greyer and the sidewalks glistened. She sighed, watching the traffic surging past. It was her first night in Paris. She was alone and it was raining.

She took a quick shower and put on her face and a little black dress. Then she added a splash of her favourite perfume and headed downstairs.

In the bar she ordered a glass of red wine, a Brouilly, nibbling moodily on tart little green olives, thinking of the long evening ahead of her. A quick survey showed almost everyone in couples, and those still alone were obviously waiting for someone. Loneliness overwhelmed her, as grey and bleak as the clouds over Paris. She felt lost without her familiar busy routine where there was no time for such self-indulgences as 'loneliness'. For the first time in years she was not happy with her own company.

She crossed her long legs, trying to look nonchalantly as though she too were waiting for a friend. She was in the most beautiful city in the world, the bastion of great food, the citadel of culture, the haven of lovers. And she was alone.

The waiter brought her wine, properly lightly chilled, and she sipped it, thinking of the card tucked temptingly inside her purse with Brad Kane's telephone number and address. She told herself that of course she couldn't call him. He probably wouldn't even remember her, and if he did, he would surely be busy. A man like that must have a dozen girlfriends, or probably just one special one. Anyway, she was sure he wasn't just sitting alone in his apartment contemplating a solitary dinner, the way she was.

She watched wistfully as the bar gradually filled up, and people greeted each other with kisses on both cheeks, feeling even lonelier as she listened to the cheerful multilingual chatter. In desperation, she fished his card from her purse and studied it.

Of course she couldn't call him. She put it on the little table in front of her, staring at it. Then she stood up quickly, smoothed down her skirt, and before she could change her mind, she hurried off in search of a phone.

She listened to it ringing with that funny beeping sound French phones have, biting her lip, nervous as a schoolgirl hoping for a first date. She tapped the card impatiently on the marble counter. After ten rings, half-exasperated, half-relieved, she was about to replace the receiver, when suddenly he answered.

'Mr Kane?' she exclaimed. *Fool*, she groaned blushing, of course it's him.

'Who is this?'

Brad Kane's tone was cool, distant, as though he had other things on his mind. Or as though someone else were in the room.

'It's Phyl Forster.' There was a long pause and she bit her lip nervously. 'We met on the plane.' She knew she was stupid to have started this but now she had to go through with it and suffer the indignity of him pretending to remember. Then telling her, with suitable French finesse, that alas he was busy tonight, perhaps some other time . . .

The pause seemed endless. At last he said with a hint of a smile creeping into his voice, 'It's very kind of you to call me. I didn't think you would.'

'You didn't?' she said doubtfully. And with a surge of anger at herself, 'Then why go to the trouble of giving me your card and asking me to telephone you?'

'Call me an optimist,' he retorted laughing. 'Besides, I liked you. I thought you were beautiful and smart, and I wanted to see you again. Make that *want* to see you. If I apologise, would you consider having dinner with me tonight? Unless you have a business function, of course,' he added smoothly, giving her an out if she wanted one.

Phyl smiled, suddenly elated. 'Well,' she said, playing the game, 'I really should be meeting a colleague . . . But it's my first night in Paris, and it's raining. Yes. I would like to have dinner with you.'

'Great. Terrific. You want to go somewhere grand? Or real bistro French? The choice is yours.'

'Oh, I'd love a real French bistro.'

'There's a place right round the corner from me. It's a favourite of mine and I think you'll enjoy it. I could pick you up at say, eight-thirty.'

She glanced at her watch. 'The traffic is hell. Why don't I just get a taxi and meet you there?'

'In that case why not come to my place first for a drink. You have the address?'

She nodded, smiling, relieved. 'Yes.'

'At eight-thirty then, Dr Phyl Forster.' He laughed, 'And remind me to ask if the Phyl is for Phyllis? Or Philomena? Or Philodendron? Or Philosophy . . .'

'Or fool,' she said to herself, smiling as she put down the receiver.

CHAPTER 16

The traffic on the Champs Elysées was backed up and it was every man for himself. The cab driver fluently cursed the weather, the other drivers, his fellow-men and the French traffic laws as he edged a wheel onto the sidewalk then sped past a dozen other trapped horn-honking drivers. He made a quick right down a side street and a series of rapid zigzags and emerged onto the equally blocked Avenue MacMahon. He surveyed the scene and shrugged resignedly.

'This will take at least twenty minutes. It's better if you walk.'

Phyl glanced down at her elegant black suede shoes and the rain-slicked sidewalks. The downpour had subsided to a fine drizzle, like mist on the wind. She sighed resignedly. What the hell, they were only shoes, even if they had cost a small fortune.

The cab driver told her how to get there and she tightened the belt of her black silk raincoat, put up her umbrella and strode to the corner of MacMahon, praying she had translated his directions correctly.

Avenue Foch was a wide, beautiful tree-lined street lined with elegant houses and apartments, but it was longer than she had thought. It was a stiff ten-minute walk and she arrived at the smart apartment building, breathless and damp and late. A uniformed concierge took her name, checked his list and then escorted her to the elevator. The brass cage whooshed her creakily upwards, and then she stepped out into an enormous duplex penthouse.

Brad Kane was waiting for her. He looked even more handsome than she had thought: tall, lean, and blond. He was wearing an elegantly cut dark-blue cashmere jacket, a blue shirt, open at the neck, well-pressed blue-jeans and expensive Western boots. She thought with a smile he looked like a guy in a Ralph Lauren ad.

His light blue eyes were half-hidden behind the gold-rimmed spectacles as he walked towards her, his hands outstretched.

'*Ma pauvre petite,*' he exclaimed, taking in her soaked appearance. 'Paris has attempted to drown you. Come, we must take care of you.'

She thought, astonished, that he must be very rich; the apartment was palatial, there seemed to be acres of polished parquet floors and enormous Aubusson rugs, massive pieces of gilded boulle furniture, beautiful Venetian mirrors and sparkling chandeliers. As she followed him through the hall, Phyl caught a glimpse of a huge Rembrandt on one wall, and surely that was a Renoir, and wasn't that a Corot?

'Come with me,' he said briskly, taking her hand as they walked through a sitting room, down another hallway. And into a bedroom.

Phyl froze at the doorway.

'Quickly, take off your shoes,' he said. 'And your stockings.'

She stared numbly at him. He walked to the bedside table and pressed a bell, then he turned to look at her and laughed. 'It's all right. I'm not going to seduce you. I'll just ask my valet to dry them. After all, you can't sit all night with wet feet.'

Phyl knew she was blushing, and knew he was laughing at her. She thought angrily she hadn't felt this foolish since she was seventeen.

He pointed out the bathroom. 'You'll find a pair of slippers and a towel in there.'

She went to the bathroom and closed the door. She pulled off her tights, smoothed back her hair and pressed a cool cloth to her burning cheeks. The terry slippers were too big for her and she grinned wryly at her ridiculous image in the mirror, in sexy black Alaia and floppy slippers. She took a deep breath, took herself in hand, and shuffled back out to find him.

'Hi,' she said, smiling hesitantly at him from the doorway. 'Sorry I was late but the traffic . . . and the rain . . .'

'No matter, now you are here.' Their eyes met. 'And just as beautiful as I remembered.'

A young white-jacketed Asian hovered behind him in the doorway, clutching her wet shoes. 'Give François your other things,' Brad said, 'he will dry them for you.'

She did as she was told and François disappeared. Brad led her to a chair and told her to sit down. Weakly, she found herself obeying his every command. She was astonished by how compliant she was; it was usually she who gave the orders, she was always the one in control. She was surprised how easy it was for her to assume the new submissive role. And how subtly pleasant. She watched silently as Brad took a towel and knelt in front of her. He removed the slippers, then he took her right foot and began gently to dry it.

He glanced up at her and smiled. 'You know it's a fact that not many women have pretty feet. Too many years of high heels and tight shoes. But yours are truly beautiful. Slender, smooth, beautiful bones. Delicate as a racehorse.'

The sight of him on his knees in front of her holding her

foot generated such a sudden erotic charge, Phyl felt herself tremble. Fool, she told herself severely again, as she quickly put on the slippers and walked with him into the enormous salon. You've only been here five minutes and that's twice you've thought he was about to seduce you.

'Sit here, my dear Dr Phyl,' he said leading her to a sumptuous brocade sofa in front of a blazing fire. 'Toast those beautiful toes while I attempt to redress the rain damage by pouring you a drink.'

Champagne waited in a silver bucket on a side table. 'To a happy coincidence,' he said raising his glass and looking deep into her eyes. 'That you and I were on the Paris flight together. And that I get to see you again.'

'You seem to spend a lot of time on planes,' she said, remembering their conversation.

'My business causes me to travel a great deal.'

She crossed her legs primly and took a cautious sip of the champagne. 'And what exactly is your business?'

'You'll be surprised when I tell you,' he grinned engagingly at her. 'I own one of the largest cattle ranches in America.'

Phyl gave an astonished laugh. 'You don't look like my idea of a real cowboy.'

'Maybe not now. But I was. Still am, when I need to be. When I was a kid I loved all that: riding the range, rounding up the cattle. Now it's all numbers and percentages, taxes, and acreage, government subsidies and lobbies, and about a million problems. But I guess I still love it. Or at least, I love the land. And the tradition. The Kanoi ranch was started in Hawaii by my grandfather. When he died my father inherited it, and now it's mine. Third generation may not make it the oldest in the US but it's one of the few still remaining in the same family.'

'That's wonderful. To love what you do. What you are.'

'And I really do love it. Passionately. You might call it my *raison d'être*.'

His eyes hardened as he looked at her. 'I would never part with Kanoi, though lord knows I've had enough offers. Enormous offers. From the Japanese especially. But I'll never let Kanoi pass out of the family. Never. I'd die first.'

'And when you do die, who will inherit?'

His look was enigmatic. 'Why, my son, of course.'

Phyl thought regretfully she might have guessed he was too good to be true: he was married. 'And how old is your son?' she asked as nonchalantly as she could, taking a sip of her champagne.

He threw back his head and laughed. 'He's no age yet. Zero. A figment of the future, yet to be born. And I have yet to find a wife. *The perfect wife*.' His eyes twinkled as he refilled her glass. His mood-change from intense and serious, to teasing and flirtatious was so sudden it took her by surprise.

'Tell me about yourself,' he commanded.

She laughed uneasily. 'I'm usually the one asking that question. Now I'm not sure I like it.'

'But surely you have nothing to hide. Do you?'

'I have found that most people have something to hide,' she said seriously. 'Maybe even you and I.'

She began to tell him about her work, and her busy life. 'I'm constantly on the run,' she admitted with a weary sigh, 'from TV studio, to hospital, to patients, to my writing, to book tours. And I confess this Paris trip is an excuse to escape it all for a week.' She laughed. 'I feel like a kid playing hookey.'

François reappeared with her shoes, miraculously dry and looking good as new. She put them on and they walked round the corner to Chez Georges.

Brad put his arm round her shoulders as they walked,

holding her close to him, sharing the umbrella. As she matched her stride to his long legs, Phyl was aware of the warmth of his body, his nearness, the touch of his hand. The gentle intimate pressure of his arm on her shoulders sent a thrill of excitement through her and she pulled away, afraid he might sense it. She told herself severely she was reacting like a high school teenager on her first visit to Paris, but then she smiled, suddenly not caring. She was enjoying herself in a way she had not in a long time; enjoying feeling young and carefree.

The bistro was crowded. Lamps cast pools of golden light over the white linen-clothed tables and there was an aroma of good food and the soft murmur of conversations in French she could not understand. It added to her feeling of isolation, of separateness, alone with Brad Kane at their small corner table.

She was giddy from jet-lag and wine; a different person from the calm, controlled, busy Dr Forster. It was as though, tonight, she had left her real world and her cares behind. She felt feminine, sensual, alive to every nuance. And, she told herself nervously, less sure of herself. But Brad Kane was attentive and charming, he was handsome and sexy. And she was footloose and fancy free in Paris. Life felt pretty good in Chez Georges that night.

Brad gave the waiter their order and then he began to tell her about his idyllic childhood on Hawaii. And about his parents: the good-looking father and the ravishingly beautiful mother; about running wild on their own private island retreat. And about the great house at Diamond Head; and the thousands of acres of ranchland on the Big Island, as well as in Texas and Wyoming.

Phyl was enchanted by the ideal world he described, it was so different from the harrowing tales of family life she was so used to hearing, and she thought how lucky he was.

'It was my father who instilled in me my deep love of Kanoi,' Brad said, and she thought, enthralled, that his voice was as deep and smooth as the red wine she was drinking. 'He taught me the history of Hawaii, he told me how the Kane family had worked hard for almost a century to carve out our heritage. He told me about the sweat and toil and anguish that had gone into making the Kanoi ranch what it is today.

'I adopted my father's wisdom like a sponge. He gave me my values. He told me that the Kane name and the Kanoi ranch and fortune were paramount in our lives. Nothing else mattered.'

He met Phyl's wide sapphire eyes frankly. 'And that's why I travel so much. I divide my time between Europe, taking care of our business interests here, and the ranch in Hawaii.'

'Tell me about your father?' Phyl asked, curious about every aspect of Brad's life. 'He sounds like a dynamic character.'

He laughed. 'That he was. Jack Kane was a hard man. And a hard drinker. He never really counted any man his friend because he could never bring himself to trust anybody. But women found him exciting. He was tall, fit, good-looking. He could ride a horse better than any cowboy. I used to watch him when I was a kid and I remember thinking he looked the picture of grace, flowing with the animal as though they were one. And he lived for Kanoi.'

'And your mother?'

Brad's eyes hardened. 'My mother was spoiled and temperamental. But you cannot imagine any woman more beautiful. She had that kind of loveliness that strikes like a poisoned dart at men's hearts. My father hated other men to look at her. And yet he was never faithful to her.'

'Did she know about it?'

'I guess she did,' he said, staring moodily into his glass. He drank the wine in a quick gulp, then as if realising he had revealed too much, he added lightly, 'I mustn't forget that I'm with a psychiatrist.' He gave her a quick sunny smile in another sudden mood-swing that left her bewildered. 'Next thing I know you'll have me on your couch and I'll discover I'm full of complexes and phobias I never suspected I had.'

Fatigue crawled subtly down Phyl's spine, her limbs were suddenly heavy and her eyelids felt as though they had weights on them. She yawned, apologising, and he said quickly it was his fault and they were both jet-lagged.

They strolled back to his apartment and picked up his car, a black Ferrari. What else would a man like Brad have? Phyl thought, leaning sleepily back against the soft leather as he drove her home.

At the hotel, he stopped the car and turned to look at her. 'I can't think when I've enjoyed an evening so much,' he said softly. 'Thank you, Dr Phyl.' She gazed into his eyes, breathless with anticipation of his lips on hers. 'We should do this again,' he said, taking her hand and kissing it instead. 'May I call you?'

Phyl said regretfully, 'I'm busy with the conference. And I'm leaving for the Riviera on Tuesday.'

'I'll remember that,' he said as she waved and he sped away into the traffic.

The next evening when she returned to the hotel from the conference there were masses of white tulips and freesia, and a note from him. 'Dinner tonight? Please say yes?'

She didn't think twice; she just cancelled the conference reception, and called him.

'I'll take you to one of Paris's oldest and finest restaurants,' he promised .

She dithered for ages over what dress to wear, finally deciding on her most feminine short black lace. She smiled as she remembered Mahoney's remark about red, and tucked a red rose into her hair and rubies and diamonds in her ears. When she looked at herself in the mirror she saw a different woman, a softer, big-eyed, tremulously alive woman. A *sexy woman*, she admitted with a long sigh that had nothing to do with fatigue or despair. And that was a woman she had not allowed to be seen for a long time.

In the bar downstairs, Brad looked admiringly at her. 'The American in me would say you look like a million dollars,' he said, kissing her hand gallantly. 'But tonight, the Frenchman in me must tell you, you look *ravissante*.'

He took her to Le Grand Vefour and Phyl thought the rococo dining room with its gilt mirrors and enormous floral displays was divine, she thought the food was delicious and the wines sublime. And Brad Kane looked after her as though she were some precious hothouse flower. She smiled as she felt herself blooming in the warmth of his subtle compliments, remembering herself telling Mahoney she was an ice maiden. Mahoney hadn't believed her, and she thought now he was being proven right. She could almost feel herself melting under Brad's warm gaze.

He was the perfect host, and the most attentive escort. He recommended dishes he thought she would like, he ordered red wine because it was her favourite and he pointed out all the celebrities who were dining there. He recounted the history of the grand old restaurant, and told her stories of Paris life and gossip. He put himself out to entertain and amuse her and he succeeded so well she was enchanted.

When the coffee came, he smiled and said quietly, 'I seem to have done all the talking. Now what about you? Tell me about your life, Phil Forster. About your fascinating work.'

She came regretfully back to reality. 'It *is* fascinating,' she admitted, 'finding out how people's minds work. You would be surprised at the apparently ordinary people who live outrageous fantasy lives. And the brilliantly successful people who tell me that their lives are full of despair and self-doubt. I treat manic depressives who can see no reason for living, and sociopaths who commit terrible sins and show no signs of remorse. I see abused children, disturbed teenagers, distraught new mothers who long to kill their babies.' She shook her head, gazing sadly into her glass of wine. 'Sometimes I go home at night wondering if anyone in this world is sane. Including myself.'

'But you have taken on the burden of their problems,' he said. 'Surely that's wrong?'

'Of course, it's wrong. And I try not to. At night, I try to relax, to forget about it. I drink a glass of wine, I listen to music, read a book. There's only one case I've allowed myself to become personally involved with, and that's because of my own needs as much as hers. It's a case of lost memory.'

'Surely it's easy to reinstate someone's memory?' he said. 'Don't relatives come looking for them? A brother or husband, or mother?'

'Not this one. This girl lost her memory as a result of an accident and so far no one has come forward to claim her.' She smiled, 'I make her sound like lost property.'

'And in a way she is.'

'I suppose that's true. Still, I haven't yet been able to bring back her memory. Now I'm trying to rehabilitate her so that she can get on with her life. I found her a job with a friend of mine. That's why I'm going to Antibes next week. To see her.'

'Checking on the progress of your experiment?' he asked, cynically, she thought.

'It's not quite that clinical,' she replied, with a touch of her old assertiveness. 'My patient is just a young girl. It means a lot to me, to be able to help her.'

'*Touché*, Doctor,' he grinned apologetically. 'I guess I just don't have time for maladies of the head. A broken leg,' he shrugged expressively, 'now that I can understand. But madness? Never.'

'My patients are not mad,' she protested. 'They are disturbed.'

He laughed and took her hand. He turned it palm up and kissed it tenderly. He said, looking at her, 'I think you are a very kind lady, Dr Phyl Forster, as well as a very beautiful one.'

Desire lurked in his light blue gaze. In an instant she forgot all about work and murders and Bea. All she could see were his eyes, all she could feel was his touch; she was suddenly breathless with matching desire.

She wafted from the restaurant on his arm, barely aware of the polite goodbyes from the staff. They drove back to Brad's apartment in silence, not touching, but alive to each other's nearness. He parked in the downstairs garage and they walked hand in hand to the elevator.

He put his arms round her as they waited. He began kissing her. Gently. Small kisses, covering her face, her eyes, her throat. The elevator pinged and a smart older couple got out. They glanced, amused, at them, wrapped in each other's arms, but Phyl didn't even notice.

Alone in the elevator Brad slid his hands under her jacket, he pulled her to him, holding her tight, as his mouth covered hers. Shivers of delight rippled through her; she did not want the kiss to end. When the elevator stopped at the penthouse, Brad swung her up in his arms and carried her into the apartment, his lips still on hers.

They sank together into the depths of the big brocade sofa, still lost in each other. Finally he stopped kissing her. He stroked back her tumbled hair and looked question-ingly into her eyes. He read the answering message of desire in them. He tilted her chin and held her mouth up to his again, drinking her like wine. A charge shivered from Phyl's lips to her breasts, from the depths of her belly to her toes and she moaned happily.

He took her by the hand and led her willingly to his bedroom. Dark-shaded lamps cast muted pools of light across the big four-poster bed and a fire glowed in the ornate limestone grate. Silky soft rugs in muted pewter and rose covered the dark parquet floor, and tall shutters closed them off from the night. They were in a world of their own, a place Phyl had not been for a long time. Maybe never before.

He turned her round and unzipped the black lace dress. She wriggled her arms free and let it slide to the floor. In a minute both of them were naked.

They stood looking at each other. Then he held out his hand. She gave him hers, trustingly. He drew her towards him and they stood, trembling naked body pressed against naked body. She threw back her head ecstatically as he began to kiss first her throat, and then her breasts, until they sank together onto the bed. He put his hands under her, lifting her body to his mouth, drinking her in until she trembled and moaned and gasped for mercy. And only then did he enter her.

He was a hard lover, demanding more from her than she had known she had to offer, and she wrapped her legs tightly around him, reaching for the almost unattainable peak of desire. Again and again.

A long time afterwards, they finally lay silent and spent, tremors like aftershocks rippling through their bodies.

He lay back on the pillows, his hands behind his head. He glanced at her and said softly, 'I haven't felt like that since I was fourteen.'

Phyl smiled at him, still lost in a sweet hot afterglow. She waited lazily for him to tell her about his first love, about some fresh high school girl and the first kiss that rocked him back on his teenage heels.

But Brad's voice was suddenly hard, as he said, 'I was fourteen and brimming with sexual curiosity, though I had absolutely no practical knowledge. One afternoon I was out riding my bicycle when I got a flat. It happened just outside the house of a friend of my father's, so I pushed my bike up the driveway, thinking to get help.

'The door was open and no one was around. I looked into the hall but it was empty. I circled the house, expecting to find him at the tennis court, or in the pool. The window of what he called his "entertaining room" stood open and I heard a sound coming from there. I stopped to listen. It was a different kind of cry; strange, eerie. Something inspired me to caution, and I tiptoed silently closer and peered in the window.

'I saw a woman lying naked on the huge golden fur rug. It was she who was making those strange sounds. Her legs were wrapped around the man's neck, his hands were underneath her buttocks, holding her high. *And he was devouring her*. She was moaning and crying out. Her eyes were shut and her face was contorted with passion.'

Brad stared silently at the ceiling and she waited, wondering what was coming next. After a moment he said, 'It was my first introduction to sex and the results were immediate. I hurried away, ashamed. But I've never forgotten that scene. It's indelibly imprinted on my memory and I swear I've never made love once in my life without thinking of it.'

'I can imagine,' Phyl said understandingly. 'Your first pornographic experience.'

'More than that.' Brad got up and walked naked to the window. He picked up a packet of Gitanes from the table, shook one out and lit it. He drew deeply on it, then exhaled the pungent smoke, staring blindly out of the window into the leafy lamplit courtyard. His voice chilled her blood like winter raindrops as he said finally, 'The man was a friend I had known all my life. And the woman he was devouring so avidly, was my mother.'

Brad's eyes had a terrifying emptiness as he looked at Phyl. She knew she was looking into his soul and she could think of no words to comfort him. There was nothing she could say to her lover. In her professional capacity, with the proper distance between patient and doctor, she would have been able to find the formula, the correct answers to lead him out of his icy bitter memories. But this was different. Lying naked in his bed, with the imprint of his lovemaking still on her, all she could say was, 'I'm sorry.'

He shrugged moodily. 'That's just the way Rebecca was. How my father put up with it all those years, I'll never know. Nor why. My father was a good-looking man, rich, successful. But my mother was beautiful, young, aristocratic. A socialite from way back. And he was just the son of a rancher.' He shrugged, 'I guess they must have suited each other. I never talked about it with him. And I have never told anyone else about what I saw.' He came over and kissed her lightly on the cheek. 'I shouldn't even have told you. Forgive me.'

She forgave him, of course, but the shock was still

rebounding. Like the mood-swings from sombre to cheerful, there was something disquieting about Brad Kane.

But, as he always seemed able to do, he quickly shrugged off his mood and took her for breakfast at the Café Flore, then shopping on the rue du Cherche-Midi and browsing amongst the book stalls on the banks of the Seine. Phyl forgot all about the conference she was in Paris to attend. Brad was handsome, he was charming, and he was amusing. And by now she was so passionately sexually crazy for him and he for her, she thought people must be able to sense the heat coming from their bodies as they paused to kiss shamelessly in shop doorways; or just to stare breathlessly deep into each other's eyes. They were in that flash heat of sexual attraction when they wanted nobody but each other. Phyl didn't even think about Bea or Millie. Or Franco Mahoney. All she thought of was Brad.

They spent long sensual afternoons in her shuttered bedroom, and romantic evenings in dimly lit bistros, and wonderful nights in his apartment. They would shed their clothes as they walked in the door; touching, kissing, devouring each other. One night Brad couldn't even wait to undress, and he took her up against the wall, lifting her onto him, driving savagely into her. She cried out with pain but he didn't stop until they slid, tangled together onto the floor, half-sobbing, half-laughing. They made love everywhere, in his bed and on the priceless Aubusson in front of the fire in the grand salon, and in the shower, slithering with soap and their own juices.

It was Monday night when Phyl finally came to her senses and remembered that she was supposed to fly to Nice the next morning. They were in Brad's apartment and they had just made love. He was standing by the bedroom window lazily smoking a Gitane when she told him.

He stared silently at her then turned and gazed out over the rooftops into the night. 'Cancel it,' he said coldly.

She looked at him, astonished. 'I can't do that. I promised.'

'And your promise means more than I do?'

Phyl had to laugh, it was such silly reasoning.

'Oh please, Brad, you're being childish. And you know it's not true. I would much rather be here with you.'

'Then why won't you cancel? Arrange to go some other time?'

Phyl shook her head, smiling at his foolishness, secretly pleased that he wanted her so much. She sat up in bed, pulling the sheet up to her chin, smoothing back her long dark hair; aware that her body was still damp with the heat and sweat of their lovemaking. 'Brad please,' she said coaxingly. 'We're talking about my patient. The girl with the lost memory. It is quite serious and I simply cannot break my promise to her.'

He looked icily at her. 'As you wish,' he said abruptly. She watched, blank-eyed with shock as he strode into the bathroom and closed the door.

She heard the shower and wondered, puzzled, why he could not accept that there was something important she must do. And that for the moment, it was more important than he was. Surely he knew she would rather be here with him. She sighed worriedly as she told herself that she had been acting just as crazy and irresponsible. Surely Brad would resign himself to her absence when she told him she would only be gone a few days.

But he did not speak as they took the elevator down to the garage and then drove to her hotel. 'I'll be back Friday,' she said as he dropped her.

His remote blue eyes sent a foreboding chill down her spine as he looked at her. She stood on the sidewalk, smiling appeasingly at him, but he turned away and drove quickly off without another word.

Tears stung her eyes as she glared after him, then she turned on her heel and walked forlornly into the hotel.

The telephone was ringing in her room. Her heart lifted as she ran to pick it up. Thinking it was him, she called a joyous 'Yes?'

'Just checking in, Doc,' Franco Mahoney said cheerfully. 'Making sure you're keeping all those smartass Frenchmen in line. And to tell you that Coco is settling in nicely here, along with her kinfolk. I'm telling you, Doc, you'd better not stay away too long or she won't want to go home again.'

Franco Mahoney's voice sounded strong, straight-ahead, real. Light years away from Paris and Brad Kane's turbulent moods. 'Thanks for looking after her for me, Franco,' she replied, suddenly wistful for him.

'No problem, Doc.' There was a long silence and he said gently, 'Say, are you all right? Don't tell me the Frogs are getting you down?'

'French not Frogs,' Phyl corrected automatically. 'No, no, I'm all right. Just tired I guess. You know, jet-lag and all that.'

'I figured you'd be seeing Bea tomorrow. Just wanted you to give her my best regards and tell her I'm still working on it. And I hope she is too. Maybe if things hot up a little, I'll hop on a plane and come over there myself,' he added half jokingly.

'I'll call and let you know, Mahoney,' she said wearily. 'Meanwhile it's late, I've got to get some sleep.'

'Yeah, that's another thing I was gonna ask you. What the hell are you doing out 'till four in the morning? Are those medicos working you to death at that conference, or what?' He had been calling every hour on the hour and he was worried.

'That's right, Mahoney,' she replied. 'Goodnight, kiss Coco for me.'

'I'll do that,' he replied laconically.

CHAPTER 17

The interior decorator summoned by Millie from Cannes was going through the Villa Mimosa, assessing the work needed to make it habitable, Bea was waiting on the front steps, staring into space, lost in her own thoughts.

She recognised Nick's little red convertible as it whizzed up the drive towards her. 'Millie told me you were here,' he said cheerfully. 'Hop in, we're off to see Nanny Beale's cottage.'

Her eyes widened, 'Really? But how do you know where it is?'

'I jogged old Monsieur Marquand's memory with another morning of pastis at the Café du Marin Bleu. He remembered it wasn't too far from the villa. Just drive down the lane, he said. There's a small turn-off near the bottom, you'll see a few houses. He said we shall know which is hers because it looks English.'

They drove along a small winding road until they spotted the cluster of houses, tucked into a fold in the hillside. The cottage was tiny with a picket fence and a patch of garden filled with roses and delphiniums and Michaelmas daisies.

'That's an English garden all right,' Nick laughed.

Even though the cottage was unoccupied, it did not look neglected. The garden was weeded, the paintwork looked fresh and the roses had been well-pruned. They peered through the sparkling clean windows and from the glimpse of the neat interior, they knew someone had to be caring for it.

Nick went off to ask a neighbour while Bea waited for him. She sat on a splintery wooden bench in the green shade of overhanging vines, imagining the old English lady tending her pretty garden, maybe sitting here in the evenings watching the changing light over the sea as the sun set. Perhaps thinking about the past, and the little boy, left for her to bring up alone.

Nick came back with the information that someone came every week to do the garden, and clean the house. The neighbour had given him the name of the agency involved and if they hurried, they would just catch them before they closed for the two-hour French lunch.

They drove quickly to the next village and Bea waited in the car for Nick. He was gone for ages and she kept glancing impatiently at her watch, but when he finally emerged, he was triumphantly waving a key.

'I used all my charm,' he said, grinning. 'But I practically had to guarantee my bank account – not to say my life, before the dragon of an agent would part with it. I also got her to tell me who pays the gardener for his labours – something called the Flora Beale Trust, managed by a bank in London. They pay quarterly and promptly and the dragon-lady was not anxious for her arrangement to be disturbed.' He grinned, 'But when I told her I was a writer and maybe she would feature in my book about life on the Riviera, she became putty in my hands. Handed the key over in a flash – and with a smile.' He laughed as they drove off. 'Ah, the awful lure of fame.'

Still they felt like trespassers when at last they opened Nanny Beale's cottage door and stood looking round. Somehow it felt as though the old lady still lived there.

It might have been an old-fashioned English movie-set.

A big old Windsor rocker stood in front of the fireplace next to a flowered cretonne couch scattered with needle-work pillows. There was a cheerful red-paisley rug and dozens of silver-framed photographs of small children arranged on the mantelshelf on the oak bureau. Nanny Beale's round tortoiseshell spectacles rested on the open pages of a copy of Dickens's *David Copperfield* – just as she must have left them. Her grey flannel coat hung in the closet alongside a few simple dresses and her sensible shoes – black for winter, white for summer were lined neatly up underneath. On the shelf were her round brimmed hats, the navy and the straw, exactly as Monsieur Marquand had described.

Bea gave a satisfied little sigh as she stared around. The cottage was simple but certainly not poor or deprived. The narrow cherrywood bed with its heavy white quilt, the plain dishes in the kitchen and the empty crystal vases were good quality, but obviously the choices of a woman who, because of her job, had always lived other peoples' lives and had little time to form her own taste. Nanny Beale's cottage gave out the message that this was a woman who had what she needed and nothing more. And that was enough for her.

Bea sat tentatively in Nanny's chair, '*Nanny Beale, Nanny Beale,*' she whispered hopefully, rocking gently back and forth. She ran her hand lightly across the pages of her book, fingering her spectacles as if touching them brought her nearer. '*I feel sure I must know you.*'

She stared intently at the faces in the photographs on the bureau, hoping to trigger a memory, but they had been taken many years ago, and were of very-English-looking children sitting in ponycarts outside grand English houses, wearing starched white dresses and stiff little sailor suits. Or scowling into the sunlight, skirts tucked into their bloomers in a seaside snapshot that captured them for posterity, paddling in the wind-ruffled ocean at places called Frinton and Margate.

Bea was reluctant to pry further into Flora Beale's private life, but Nick told her not to be so foolish. 'If anyone knew anything about la Célibataire and her husband, it was this woman,' he said, rummaging through cupboards and drawers full of plain white linen handkerchieves and lace collars, starched white aprons and pristine cotton sheets. Nanny Beale had kept everything neat, everything in its proper place. He smiled as he imagined her bossing her young charges, instilling the virtues of tidiness and cleanliness, exhorting them to brush their teeth and always to carry a fresh handkerchief in their pockets.

Bea watched hopefully as he searched, but all he found were a few old receipted bills for groceries and laundry. There was nothing of importance and he had looked everywhere, even in the old tin trunk stored in the loft.

He leaned against the bedroom door, arms folded, thinking. 'Now just where would an old lady like that keep her secrets?' he asked. Then his eyes met Bea's, and he grinned. He walked into the bedroom and lifted the mattress. He put his hand under and felt around. His fingers closed on something and he pulled it out.

'*Got it*,' he said to Bea triumphantly.

It was a large manilla envelope, stuffed with papers. They took them out and sat at the kitchen table looking at the documents and letters and a small silver key. Several of the letters had English addresses, 'Manors', and 'Halls', and they turned out to be glowing references to Miss Flora Beale's excellent temperament, her sobriety and her absolute devotion to the children and to her duty. But there were also two letters written in a firm French script. Bea and Nick looked excitedly at each other. They were from Marie-Antoinette Leconte, discussing the employment of Miss Flora Beale as nurse to her as yet unborn child.

Flora Beale had written to Madame Leconte applying for the job of nanny to the as yet unborn child.

'I would enjoy the challenge of working in a new country,' she wrote, in the careful rounded handwriting of a woman whose education, as she told Madame, 'had been limited to parochial school and had ended at the age of thirteen, when I went into service at the local manor house in Oxfordshire.

'But my experience with children covers many years, Madame Leconte,' she wrote at the end of her letter. 'And I am sure you will agree, there is no better education for looking after children than experience.'

Madame Leconte had immediately written back in English, offering her the job. She told her that the child she was expecting meant everything to her... 'More than my own life', she wrote.

Bea looked up from those sad words. 'Monsieur Marquand was right,' she said with a shiver. 'Marie Leconte knew she was marked for death.'

'I wonder,' Nick said, 'if even then she thought her husband capable of murdering her? And if so why she didn't do something about it?'

'I'll bet it was feminine pride. Remember, she was la Célibataire the dowdy plain woman always on the edge of the crowd, always alone, despite her money. She was the butt of their jokes all those years. Even the street urchins mocked her. And here was this handsome young guy, playing the loving husband for everyone to see. Maybe she just hoped she had been wrong about him after all.'

'Here's something else,' Nick said. He held up a

document bound with pink legal tape. 'Look, Nanny Beale even went to the trouble to get it notarised.'

Their heads were close together as they pored over Flora Beale's words. 'I must put this down in writing,' Nanny Beale said, 'so that one day those who need to know the facts, will know the truth.

'It is simple,' she wrote:

I knew it as soon as I saw the husband. He had married poor Marie-Antoinette Leconte for her money. Why else would a handsome, ruthless man like that want a woman like her?

Madame Leconte asked me to come to work for her three months before the child was born – to get acclimatised to my new country and its ways, she said. But in my heart I suspect it was for companionship. She was without doubt the loneliest woman I ever saw.

I knew Madame only a short while before she died, but I found her to be kind, gentle and intelligent, though she was not a well-born woman and did not possess the 'good taste' of my previous employers. But there was no doubt in my mind that the child meant everything to her. And no doubt also that Madame did not trust her husband.

Madame gave me a letter she had written to her unborn child. She asked me to keep it safely. It was to be given to the child when it was old enough to understand . . . 'If anything should happen and I die before him,' she said to me, with that bleak look in her dark eyes, for all the world as if she knew what was to happen just a few weeks later.

Madame Leconte had given me her trust, but she also gave me her most precious possession, the baby that was worth more to her than all her money. She asked me to promise that if anything happened to her, I would care for her child. Of course I gave her that promise – what woman would not?

And in return she was generous. She told me I would

never want for money. She even bought the cottage for me and set up a trust fund that provided me with an annuity for life.

I was in the nursery on the second floor when the accident happened. I heard the sound of raised voices then a loud bang like a pistol shot. I was afraid, but the baby had woken at the noise. He began to cry and it was some minutes before I ran into the upper gallery with him clutched in my arms.

I stared aghast at the terrible scene in the hall below. Madame Leconte was lying face down on the marble floor and it seemed to my horrified eyes there was blood everywhere.

Her husband came from the direction of the library. 'My God, there has been an accident,' he cried, rather theatrically, I thought. All the servants were gathering and staring at the still figure of Madame. 'Go. Go away,' he screamed at us, and the angry look in his eyes sent us all running.

The 'something dreadful' Madame Leconte had feared had finally happened. And though he said it was an accident, I knew in my heart he had killed her.

They buried poor Madame the very next day and immediately afterwards her husband departed for Paris to talk to the lawyers. He did not come back. And so I was left the effective guardian of young Master Jean Leconte, whom I always called with the greatest affection, Johnny.

I had promised Madame I would protect her son. For five years I kept that promise, and we lived in peace at the Villa Mimosa. But when the event I dreaded finally came to pass, I was no match for the enemy.

Bea knew what Nanny Beale had written next, before she even read it. She could see it in the dark recesses of her mind, she could feel it, just the way she had in her dream . . .

* * *

It was seven-thirty on a June morning. The birds had already greeted the sunrise and were quiet and there was not a ripple of breeze to stir the surface of the ornamental pools. Nothing disturbed the silence as the butler opened the front door, bowing his head deferentially to the little dark-haired boy who raced past him onto the portico, sniffing the air with the eagerness of a released puppy.

He was a small, dark, wizened-looking child, five years old and thin, with stick-like limbs and intelligent dark brown eyes. He bore no resemblance to his blond blue-eyed good-looking father, and possessed none of his robust physique. Nanny Beale, mindful of her duty to the dead mother, kept him wrapped in cottonwool, away from other children in case he got their germs. And, mindful of his wealth and his future standing in life, she dressed him in silk from head to toe, like a little Lord Fauntleroy.

Nanny was his friend and the butler, the chauffeur, the maids and gardeners, his companions. The nursery cupboards were filled with every toy and game imaginable, though he had no childish companion to share them with, and his dearest possession, his truest friend, was his woolly toy dog named Fido – because Nanny Beale said a real live dog was too dirty, had too many fleas, bred those frightening 'germs'.

They had lived this way ever since he could remember and he was a happy child, content with his life because he knew nothing else. And he was the centre of his particular little universe.

He sat on the marble steps, feeling the chill through his little blue shorts, happily surveying his domain. The morning air was as fresh as the hope in his heart that this day might be more special than the last, because his days were all the same. He stared across the lawns, past the giant cedars, to the azure sea far below. He could hear the peacocks screeching near the rose garden and smell the different scents of the flowers whose names he knew because the gardener had taught him. His favourite was the mimosa for which the villa was named, but its sweetness belonged only to the springtime.

The twitter of the yellow and blue canaries and the gay little parakeets came from the silver aviary that Nanny had told him his grandfather had built as a birthday gift for his mother long ago, and water tinkled prettily in the elaborate courtyard fountain, mingling with the rush of the fierce little stream from the grotto on the hill above.

This was his kingdom, his security, his entire world.

There was a new sound, the bronze bell at the gate. The boy lifted his head interestedly, scrunching his eyes against the sun, watching.

Footsteps crushed the gravel, a man was walking towards him. A tall, handsome man. The sun glinted on his blond hair. The man stopped at the foot of the steps and stared at him. The boy heard Nanny Beale in the hall behind him, running. That's odd, he thought, smiling up at the stranger, Nanny never runs, she thinks it's undignified.

He had been told never to speak to strangers, but he said anyhow, 'I am Johnny Leconte.' He smiled trustingly. 'Who are you, M'sieur?'

The man stared coldly at him, taking in his sallow looks, his frail physique, his prettified silk clothes. He finally said in a tone of numbing indifference, 'I am your father.' Then to Nanny Beale, 'Pack him up. I'm taking him with me.' Just as though he was a parcel.

The child turned at Nanny's horrified gasp. 'Where are we going, Nanny? Where?'

Her frightened eyes met his anxious ones. 'To the land of the heathens,' she wailed. 'To the very end of the world.'

A nameless fear engulfed the boy, and a dark cloud settled over him, cutting off the beautiful morning, the birdsong, the silken air, the sunlight. Cutting him off from his world.

I loved that child [Nanny wrote in her document]. *And I intended to keep my promise to Madame, as she had kept hers to me. My heart quailed at the thought, but there was no way in the world that my little boy was going alone with that evil man. Duty is duty. Still, I wondered* why *he wanted his son, after all these years.*

There followed the most horrible journey of my life. On the Italian liner out of Marseilles on our way to America, Johnny and I were quartered in a mean little cabin in the very lowest class, while his father lorded it in first, never even acknowledging the presence of his son. And when the liner hit a storm in mid-Atlantic, I became so sick, I was confined to my bunk, and poor little Johnny had to fend for himself. Then New York and the endless train journey across that big outlandish country, America, sleeping upright in our seats, though I knew his father was sleeping in luxury elsewhere on the train.

We arrived in San Francisco and drove to a grand hotel. Monsieur Leconte got quickly out of the motorcar, but when I made to follow him he slammed the door rudely on me and told me other arrangements had been made for us. We were to take the next boat to Honolulu. Alone.

The docks were seething with brawny evil-looking men but I could not show my fear to Johnny, who, thank heavens, was too interested in everything around him to be afraid. Our boat was old and rusty, with a villainous-looking crew of heathen Chinese who spoke not a word of English, and the journey seemed endless, with many days of storms when I felt sure the great green waves would engulf

*us. And what food there was, was foreign, heathen food,
and uneatable. Johnny and I were forced to survive on a diet
of plain boiled rice.*

*Then, when we finally arrived in Honolulu, we were put
immediately onto another, smaller boat, that was to take us
to Johnny's father's private island. To his own 'Kingdom'.*

Flora Beale's document ended abruptly with those words.
Bea and Nick looked mystified at each other, longing to
know what had happened. They looked carefully through
the other papers, but she had written nothing else.

Suddenly Bea began to cry, great silent, desperate sobs.
Nick put his arm comfortingly round her. 'Poor Bea. But
we've made progress. At least now you know what your
dream meant.' He stroked her hair back from her forehead
and said, 'Though how you knew it beats me.'

'I don't understand,' she sobbed. 'Nick, it's not just
Nanny Beale's words I'm reading. Those words are in my
own head, the boy's fear is in my heart . . . I feel it as though
what he went through happened to *me*. And I just can't
bear it, Nick. *I'm afraid.*'

CHAPTER 18

Millie's yellow curls were freshly done. She was wearing a matching yellow flowered silk dress with a smattering of yellow diamonds pinned across her bosom, and a fresh coat of bright pink lipstick. She was sitting at a table on the terrace at the Hôtel du Cap waiting for Bea and Phyl to arrive from the airport. But she wasn't thinking about her friends. She was thinking about the telephone call she had received in the early hours of that morning, from an attorney in Ohio.

'Who the hell is calling me from Ohio at two-thirty in the morning?' she had demanded groggily, reaching for her spectacles and putting them on as though she would be able to understand more clearly what he was saying. Because what he was saying was so astonishing that if it hadn't been so serious she would have thought someone was playing a hoax on her.

The attorney said that he was calling to tell her of the death of a long-unheard-of Fenwick third cousin. Tragically, the cousin and his wife had been killed in an automobile accident. Their two young children were now orphans. In his will, the cousin said that Millie was their only relative and he had appointed her their guardian.

Meanwhile, the attorney said, the children had been taken into care. If Millie declined to act as guardian they would be fostered out and he hoped they might eventually be adopted.

'Hell, no!' Millie had said shocked. 'Kinfolk is kinfolk, even if I didn't know about them until right this minute. Those poor kids need a home,' she told him. 'Get them anything they need and bill it to me. I just need a little time to work things out. Meantime, tell them their Aunt Millie loves them and she can't wait to shower them with new toys and affection.'

She had put the phone down, astonished but pleased at the idea of suddenly becoming a 'mother' at her age. But she knew in her heart she had done the right thing.

'Of course everyone will think it's just another of my whims,' she told herself hours later as she was finally drifting back to sleep. 'But as always, there is a method in my madness.'

She was still sitting on the terrace, staring dreamily out to sea when she heard her name called. She smiled at her old friend Phyl and her new friend Bea as they walked towards her.

'There you are at last, dearest Phyl,' she said clasping her arms to her cushiony bosom. 'You look wonderful, as always, even if you are still in that everlasting black. Like widow's weeds, dear girl. It's time you made a change.'

'You're not the first one to say that,' Phyl laughed, remembering Mahoney.

Millie held her at arm's length, inspecting her critically again. 'Mm,' she added, 'I'm not sure I approve of those dark circles under your eyes though. Either the shrinks' conference kept you up all night, or Someone Else did. I hope for your sake it was the "Someone Else". Do you good.'

They smiled understandingly at each other; they had no

secrets. Phyl knew all there was to know about Millie; and Millie knew all about her.

'I'm sure Bea has already told you the latest events,' Millie said sailing grandly towards 'her' table on the terrace and waving them imperiously after her. 'It seems we're getting somewhere at last, though I'm not sure I understand *exactly* where. That's your department, Phyl,' she said, ordering tea. 'Meanwhile, I have a little surprise of my own.' They looked expectantly at her and she smiled back at them, enjoying her moment of suspense. 'You'll never guess,' she teased.

'Don't tell me you've gone and bought a condo in Monte Carlo as well?' Bea asked suspiciously.

'Of course I have not. I am already the very proud owner of the Villa Mimosa. Who could want more?'

'Come on, Millie,' Phyl implored, 'don't keep us dangling.'

'I am about to become a mother.' She yelped with laughter as they stared unbelieving at her. Then she told them about the telephone call from Ohio.

'They are Scott and Julie Fenwick,' she finished her story. 'Aged nine and seven. Now don't you think those are a couple of grand names? That smug attorney asked when I'd be home so he could put them on the plane to New York, and I would have loved to have seen his face when I told him *home* was right here, on the Riviera. "They can come here and attend the local school," I told him. "If it's good enough for Princess Caroline, it's good enough for me." Besides,' she added, clutching her hand compassionately to her heart, 'I thought a change of scenery would be good for the poor little things, after what happened to them. But I told him they would have to wait a week or two. Just until the villa is finished.'

'*A week or two?*' Bea said faintly, remembering the villa,

reduced to a shell with roofers and carpenters and painters still crawling all over it. There was just a huge hole where the new swimming pool was to go and landscape gardeners were still busy cutting back the undergrowth and laying new turf.

'Well, maybe a tiny bit longer,' Millie admitted. 'But I already called that stuffy interior designer and told him to get his skates on. He has a new deadline. One month and that's it. After all,' she said glancing appealingly at Phyl, 'I can't have the poor kids arrive and have to stay in a hotel. Not after that long journey and all they've been through. They need a proper home and I am going to provide it for them.'

She looked mockingly at them. 'Imagine *me*, Millie Fenwick. A *mother* after all these years.' She yelped with laughter again at the very idea. 'And that's something none of my useless husbands could achieve. I always said it was their fault.'

The fate of Scott and Julie Fenwick was the chief subject of discussion over dinner that evening and it wasn't until later when they were alone in her room, that Bea was able to show Phyl Nanny Beale's 'document' and the letters.

Phyl told her that Mahoney believed someone must have described the villa to her. 'It's the only logical answer,' she said. 'And that same person must have told you the story of the father coming back for the child. That's why you remember it.'

'Then Phyl, *why* do I feel so strongly about it? Why do I have this awful feeling of foreboding, as though it's *me*, sitting on that doorstep waiting for my world to end?'

'Perhaps it was someone close to you?'

'Someone I loved, you mean? But how could I ever forget someone I loved that much?'

Phyl shook her head, she wished she knew. 'Bea, my advice to you is to look forward to things instead of looking back. Let the past take care of itself. One day things will pop right into your head again, just the way the scent of mimosa did that first day at the hospital, and you will remember everything. Including who you are.'

Bea's copper-brown eyes were desperate as she looked at her. Only Phyl knew the true depth of her terror at not knowing who she was, and why someone wanted to kill her. But even though she knew Phyl was right, she still needed to find out what happened to Nanny Beale and little Johnny Leconte, alone on the island with his wicked father.

Nick had noticed that Marie-Antoinette's husband was always referred to in the newspaper report of her death as 'Monsieur Leconte' and he went to find Marquand, the journalist, in the Café du Marin Bleu to ask if he knew why he used his wife's name.

'The Foreigner took Marie-Antoinette's name of course, because her father had decreed it in his will,' Marquand said. 'Her father said if Marie-Antoinette ever changed her name, she would lose her inheritance. Of course, it was just his way of trying to stop her from marrying. He hated the thought of losing his daughter, even after he was dead, and he was determined that at least she would go to her own grave bearing his name. It was all a matter of inheritance, you see,' Monsieur Marquand added. 'And I'm sure the Foreigner came back to claim his son for the same reason. The inheritance.

'You must understand, my friend, that the old Napoleonic code of succession still applies in France. Under its laws a man does not inherit the entire estate of his spouse. Their children come first. In the Lecontes' case there was only one child, Johnny, and he automatically inherited half his mother's estate. The Foreigner inherited the other half, on which he had to pay the taxes. Then there was the Leconte property. The Villa Mimosa and the flat in Paris were only a small part of her property holdings, and a lot of money would have been tied up in that. By law, the husband could not sell it immediately. He would have had to wait until the son was eighteen years old. Then it could be sold and the money divided.

'So it's my guess that when the Foreigner realised he couldn't beat the French inheritance laws, he came back to claim his financial stake in the future. His son. The man was a big spender, you know,' Marquand added thoughtfully. 'I'd bet in that five years he had gone through most of his share of Marie-Antoinette's fortune, and that it had been a lot less than he expected. He must have needed the boy's money.'

Nick called the London bank and arranged to meet with the administrators of the Flora Beale Trust, the next morning. 'Maybe now we shall find out what happened to little Johnny Leconte on that far-off island,' he said hopefully as Bea waved him goodbye at the airport.

CHAPTER 19

A few days later, when Phyl returned to Paris, her hotel room looked as though it had been invaded by a florist. There were fragrant bouquets on every table and even a Hawaiian-style *lei* of white orchids on her pillow. And there was a message. '*I miss you. Please forgive me. Brad.*'

She stripped off her clothes, took a cool shower, put the orchids round her neck and called him. 'Thanks for the extravagant welcome,' she said with a smile in her voice.

'They were also an apology. I didn't dare hope you would call. I don't deserve it. I guess I was just plain jealous.'

She shook her head, and said with a sigh, 'But Brad, you knew I wasn't going to see another man.'

'I'm jealous of anyone who takes you away from me.'

She asked, with a sudden flash of her old cool independence, 'Isn't that a little unreasonable?'

'It is. But then I'm an unreasonable man – where you are concerned.'

She laughed, touching his orchids lying against her breasts and heard him sigh with relief as she told him to come on over.

She opened the door to him half an hour later, naked but for his orchids, her long hair a smoky cloud around her pale shoulders, wondering if she would feel differently about him since she had been away and had time to reassert herself. But he was still as attractive, still as charming, and still as sure of himself as before. He looked her slowly up, then down. He shook his head in disbelief at her beauty and told her he was the luckiest man alive to have found the perfect woman. Then he picked her up in his arms and took her to bed.

The next day Phyl cancelled her flight home and cancelled all her appointments for the next week in San Francisco. She checked out of her hotel and into Brad's apartment.

They scarcely moved out of there for an entire week, emerging only to stroll round the corner to the bistro or wander along the boulevards, hands clasped, eyes meeting every now and then, telling each other private messages of desire.

Phyl thought of no one else. She told herself that she was crazy, that she was infatuated with Brad the lover, the charming companion, the attentive escort. She knew she was behaving irresponsibly, for the first time in her life, but she just couldn't help herself. After years as the 'ice maiden' she had melted to a sensual woman whose body rippled and responded to every nuance of Brad's lovemaking.

And yet there were times when she was aware that even though she knew every inch of his body intimately, she did not really know the man. Brad Kane was a stranger she had known only a few days.

There was another side to him. Sometimes she got the feeling their lovemaking was not enough for him, that he wanted to go further, into dangerous games she did not want to play. And the psychiatrist in her became uneasily aware that there were depths and undercurrents in his personality, hidden beneath the charming façade. His unreasonable jealousy about the trip had already shown her that. But she was too infatuated to care. She told herself she didn't want to analyse her lover: she only wanted to enjoy the moment.

Then one night, after they had made love and were finally exhausted and they were lying entwined in bed, Brad began to talk about his family.

He told her his grandfather, Archer Kane, was a Yankee adventurer. He had left home aged thirteen and made his way out west. 'My grandfather panned for gold, dug for coal, picked fruit, worked on a ranch. You name it, Archer had done it,' Brad said, smiling proudly. 'He ended up in San Francisco, and from there he worked his way to Hawaii on a cargo vessel, transporting horses and cattle to the Big Island. He was still only nineteen when he met his future bride.'

Phyl turned to look at him, her head propped on her hand, listening fascinated as he told her about Archer's bride.

Her name was Lahilahi. In Hawaiian it meant 'Delicate One', and she was the treasured daughter of noble Hawaiian parents. It was only when the sweet-faced seventeen-year-old had threatened to die of a broken heart that they had reluctantly agreed to allow her to marry the yellow-haired foreigner.

Brad said, 'My grandfather told us they gave them an elaborate wedding, appropriate for a girl of Lahilahi's position and wealth. There were four days of feasting and dancing, with *luaus* and dozens of pigs baking in the *imu*, many gallons of *poi*, *lomi lomi salmon*, *hupia* and much more. The bride wore a sarong of brilliant blue with many *leis* of Imperial feathers, and orchids and *maile*, with a wreath of fragrant *pakalana* flowers crowning her glossy black hair that my grandfather said fell, like a rippling waterfall to below her knees.

'Archer was a very handsome young man and he wore a

bright flowered shirt, also with many *leis*, and as a wedding gift, he gave his lovely young bride a *lei* of pearls – small, it's true, but of a beautiful colour.'

Brad laughed, breaking the spell of the story as he added cynically, 'No one could think where Archer got the money for such an expensive gift. They knew he was not one of the rich *haoles*. But they were just simple Hawaiians; they didn't know the backstreet places Archer knew about, where men could go to pledge their futures – and even their souls – for the loan of a few hundred dollars.

'Archer was smarter than they were: in return for his pearl necklace he gained an island. True, it was small, but it was off the coast of Maui, and it had been owned by the bride's family since the very beginnings with King Kamehamema. It was their wedding gift to the young couple. They hoped Archer would grow sugarcane and pineapples there and make his fortune.

'After the four days of festivities were over, the bride and groom set sail for their island in an outrigger canoe. They were accompanied part of the way by hundreds of other gaily decorated canoes, filled with wedding guests singing traditional songs of *aloha* and farewell. Grandfather said it was a tremendous sight. He truly felt like a king.' Brad laughed.

'Soon the scent of their *maile* flower *leis* was drowned by the crisp salt smell of the Pacific ocean. And when the other canoes turned and made back for home, and his bride waved a final farewell, Archer saw a tear slide down her face. He turned her impatiently round to face their island and their future. He had had enough of Hawaiian weddings and he was already counting his profits on his crops, yet to be sown.'

Brad smiled indulgently. 'That was my grandfather Archer. I guess you could call him a pragmatic man.'

'I would call him a hard man,' Phyl said, thinking of his romantic little bride, so beautiful, and so sad to be leaving her loving family behind.

'That's true,' Brad agreed. He turned to smile at her. 'Am I boring you? I've heard this story so many times. It's part of the Kane family lore, passed down from generation to generation.'

'No, no. Tell me more,' she said, curling happily into the crook of his arm and burying her face into his neck, loving the smell of him, the feel of his skin, the sound of his mellow voice.

'Then I shall tell you about our island. It's the heart of our family, our soul you might say. If we have one,' he added with an abrupt cynical laugh.

'Can't you just see Lahilahi looking eagerly at her island as its rocky outline emerged from the ocean? She saw that it was small, a mere twelve miles at its widest and maybe seventeen miles long. The north-eastern tip was rocky with fierce waves hurling themselves at the precipitous cliffs, and there were dangerous currents that could pull an unwary canoe deep under the ocean within seconds. But the tranquil south-eastern shore was rimmed with talcum-white beaches, fringed by palms and shady *milo* trees, sea grapes and flowering *koali*, morning glory.

'A series of small cone-shaped mountains, once volcanic, ran like a spine down the centre of the island, dividing east from west, catching the incoming storms from the Pacific Ocean and trapping the rainfall on the western side. And the lower slopes had gradually become covered in dense thickets of *hau*, hibiscus, and their red, yellow and orange flowers ringed the mountains. Lahilahi said she thought they were like *leis* around the neck of Pele, the goddess of volcanoes, whose spirit she was certain must live there, waiting her time to emerge once again.

187

'Beyond those mountains the western side of the island was a place of deep gulches and tumbling waterfalls, spanned by rainbows and dense with fiddlehead ferns and thick forests of trees and vines and creepers. In between were wide grassy acres interspersed with the gleaming cooled black lava that years ago had flowed from the volcanic peaks forming a river of stone all the way to the ocean.

'The gentler eastern side would have been barren if it were not for the habit of a long-ago travelling man. He was exploring the island and as he scrambled over the slopes on his wiry little pony, he scattered the seeds of the pinetrees of his native land. The seeds took root and the trees grew, holding the soil from erosion. And so the valleys were shaded from the fierceness of the sun by tall trees, and grasses and fruits grew readily in the runoff of the rainfall from the mountain slopes.

'As young Lahilahi stepped from the canoe onto her island, she clasped her handsome yellow-haired husband's hand. She gazed round at the curving white beach, at the tall palms and shady *milos*, at the bright flowers ringing the mountain slope and the bare conical volcanic peaks, like the goddess Pele's breasts surmounting her island. And she breathed a sigh of happiness.

'Ah husband,' she said softly. 'We must call it Kalani – "Heaven", for that is surely what it is.'

Tears of compassion stood in Phyl's eyes as she looked at Brad. He was lying on his back, his hands clasped behind his head, staring up at the ceiling as though he were seeing the heavenly island. 'That's the most romantic story I've ever heard,' she said, thrilled.

He threw her a sceptical glance from the corner of his eye as he got up and poured a glass of brandy. He lifted the decanter, offering her some but she shook her head.

He said mockingly, 'I didn't expect a woman of your scientific mind to be thrilled by such soap opera. The reality is that the romance was already over. Archer Kane had got what he wanted. He was consumed with pride of possession in his land. The first thing he did was organise the islanders, a shiftless mixture of Hawaiian and Chinese, to help him build a small lodge of koa wood and stones with a palm thatch roof.

'He worked hard the first year, but his crops didn't do well and he was impatient and angry. He had thought his island would be the stepping-stone on his way to a fortune, and now it was all going wrong. So he took off for Honolulu, carousing with whores on the waterfront, trying to forget his problems. And that's where he was, little more than a year later, when they came to tell him about his wife.

'The servants said Lahilahi had dressed herself in her wedding sarong. She had placed *maile leis* around her neck and threaded fragrant plumeria flowers in her hair. There was a violent storm with huge winds and towering waves. Lahilahi set sail alone, in her outrigger canoe into the stormy night.'

Brad's pale blue eyes were enigmatic as they met Phyl's horrified ones. 'She was never seen again,' he said quietly.

'Oh my God,' Phyl whispered. 'The poor young girl. She killed herself?'

Brad shrugged carelessly. 'My grandfather said he didn't know. Of course Lahilahi's family blamed him. They said he had broken her heart. Archer didn't attend the funeral feast, but he heard that the family cursed him and his offspring into eternity. He just laughed and said what was more important than their curses, was that Kalani now belonged to him.'

Brad smiled icily at Phyl, sipping his brandy. He said,

'And that's how Kalani became the cornerstone of the Kane family fortune.'

A chill ran down Phyl's spine as she watched him begin to prowl the room like a restless cat, backwards and forward, sipping the brandy. She was puzzled that he seemed to see nothing wrong in his grandfather's actions. The only thing that mattered to him, as well as Archer, was the island and its role in establishing their fortune.

'Don't you pity that poor young girl?' she exclaimed angrily.

He looked at her, surprised. 'It was all very unfortunate,' he said calmly. 'But let's put it this way, if Lahilahi had not died then my grandfather would not have gone on to achieve what he did. He might have stayed a poor sugarcane farmer all his life.'

Brad raised his glass in the air, laughing. 'And then what would have become of me?' he demanded. 'I might have been eking out a living on a tiny Hawaiian island, hitting the bottle earlier and earlier each evening out of sheer frustration, like a character in a Somerset Maugham story. Oh come on, Phyl, it was all a long time ago. I can't afford to get emotional about it.'

'And nor could your grandfather,' Phyl retorted angrily.

'Now you're being silly.' She had wrapped the sheet around her and was sitting up in bed, her arms clasped tightly around her knees. She glared at him and he sighed. 'I should never have told you. I thought you would like the story.'

Phyl remembered his description of the island and she realised how much it meant to him. 'I did enjoy it,' she admitted. 'And I know you're just being cynical. You love Kalani, don't you?'

He came to sit beside her, tenderly stroking her hair. 'It's the place I'm happiest in the world,' he admitted, brushing her lips lightly with his own. 'And one day I shall take you there, so you can see if I did it justice.'

Phyl smiled again as he put his arms round her. She nestled her face into his neck, dropping tiny butterfly kisses on his skin, feeling the roughness under her tongue. She told herself that, after all, everyone had a black sheep in their family. And in this one it just happened to be Archer Kane.

Then the very next night Brad told her a different family story. One that rocked her back on her heels.

He was talking to her about his childhood, about the holidays spent running wild on the island. The original lodge his grandfather had built had been expanded into a sprawling comfortable holiday home, with long *lanaiis* cooled by ceiling fans, and hammocks strung between the palms. He told her the greenness of the sea was matched by the deep fern-filled gorges, and the jewelled intensity of the tiny emerald salamanders, he told her about the flamboyant scarlet birds and the aquamarine undersea world, studded with bright little fishes like Christmas tree ornaments.

Brad's tone was smiling, indulgent as he remembered. Then with that same quick-as-a-flash mood change, he was suddenly tense.

'My mother hated the island,' he said abruptly. 'She never went there. She only liked Diamond Head, or San Francisco where she kept an apartment. She loved to shop and she had closets and closets full of clothes. She rarely allowed me into her room, said I got under her feet. She would shoo me away, half-laughing but I knew that she meant it. Of course, I always wanted to be with her. I loved her. She was my beautiful, scented, bejewelled adored mother, and I was only six years old.'

191

He glanced at Phyl and his voice became tender again as he said, 'She always slept late and I would creep in in the morning and steal a look at her sleeping face. There would be smudges of mascara under her eyes, traces of lipstick still on her lips, but she always looked peaceful and so innocent, as she slept.

'Sometimes I would hide in her closet, amid the tissue-wrapped clothes, waiting for her to wake so I could surprise her. I would sit on the floor gazing up at the fantasy world of rustling colour, chiffons and tulles and sequins, thinking how I would make her laugh.

'One morning I crawled quietly into the closet to hide, looking up at the ruffles of colour; the bright blues and greens and reds that she loved. And then I saw the shoes. They were big and made from a chestnut-brown leather polished to a fine gleam, and I knew they could not be my mother's shoes. They had pale shiny soles and they were dangling above me.

'My eyes travelled upwards to the socks. Jazzy red socks. I smiled. I knew only one person who wore socks like that. A man who often visited my mother, and whom I had been told to call "Uncle" Wahoe. I peered at the grey flannel trouser legs and I laughed as I emerged from my childish hiding place.

'"Uncle Wahoe," I said, "have you come to play hide and seek too?"'

Brad's voice grew harsher as he said, 'I pushed aside the rustling party dresses and stared up at him, puzzled. There was a rope around his neck. He was hanging from the rail. His head was tilted at a grotesque angle and his face was purple. His mouth hung open with the black swollen tongue sticking out and his eyes bugged like a toad's.'

Brad put his head in his hands. His whole posture was

one of despair and Phyl stared horrified at him. But she did not dare interrupt.

After a while he lifted his head. He lit a cigarette and said quietly, 'I stood for a terrified moment and then I ran to get my mother. She was sitting up in bed with her breakfast tray and her view out over the lawns to the sea. She looked impatiently at me.

'"What are you doing in here?" she asked irritably. "Didn't I tell you never to come in unless I gave you permission?"

'I stared at her. I was frightened, but even then I thought how lovely she was. Tall, but not willowy, dark-haired and almond-eyed. She had a strong body and I know now she moved with a deliberate sexiness, every swing of her slender hips calculated to show off her curves.

'"Why is Uncle Wahoe in your closet?" I demanded, clutching at her hand.

'She shook me away; she was reading a letter and scarcely seemed to hear me. "In the closet?" she said indifferently.

'I said, "He looks so funny hanging from the rail. He scared me."

'She looked up from the letter. I know now it was from him, telling her he intended to kill himself because she had finished with him. She had sent him away and he couldn't bear it. Her face turned white. She screamed and the servants came running.

'"You dreadful little boy. Whatever have you done?" she shrieked at me. "It's all your fault."'

Brad looked bleakly at Phyl. 'I was six years old. But that is why, for most of my life, I felt that somehow I was the one responsible for my Uncle Wahoe's suicide.'

He drew on his cigarette, then stubbed it out viciously. Then he took her in his arms and made love to her. If it could be called 'love'. Phyl was not even sure at that moment whether he even knew it was her in his arms. She closed her eyes, she didn't want to see his face, to witness his pain. It was over in minutes.

'I shouldn't have told you,' Brad said harshly, later. 'But there's something about you, Phyl Forster, that drags a man's secrets out of him.'

CHAPTER 20

Mahoney folded his arms and leaned against the wall of the interview room on the sixth floor of the Hall of Justice, watching his partner, Benedetti, giving it to a murder suspect they had brought in at four a.m. It was now ten in the morning and Benedetti was in his element because he was on overtime, and they had a guy he knew in his gut had killed a girl by ramming her up against a wall with his automobile.

The suspect, a weasely little guy in his early thirties with thinning hair, a receding chin and a two-inch forehead that didn't allow much room for brains, claimed he was nowhere near the alley where it happened. He was at a club in North Beach with his friends. 'Which club?' Benedetti asked again. 'What friends? Come on for Chrissakes man, give y'self a goddamn break. We know it was your car killed her. Your girlfriend was there, your car was there – and you say you were in fucking North Beach at some fucking club whose name you can't recall, with some fuckin' friends whose names you just don't remember off-hand. Some friends huh? When you don't even know their names.'

The suspect shook his head stubbornly, eyes fixed on the floor at a point to the right of his inquisitor. 'I already told ya' somebody musta took the car.'

Benedetti glanced exasperatedly at Mahoney. He had been at it for two-and-a-half hours and he was getting nowhere. The girl had been found squashed up against an alley wall with her guts hanging out and unless they could get him to confess this little shit was going to get away with it. Because they had no witnesses and because, despite his pea-sized brain, he was street-smart enough to *know* they had no witnesses. He was right: anyone could have been driving that car. Except they knew it was him.

'Why not take a break,' Mahoney suggested. 'Let me and Mr Zacharias have a little talk.'

Benedetti nodded. He pushed back his chair wearily. 'I'll leave you to it, Mahoney,' he said, walking to the door.

It was an old ploy: first the hard line approach, bludgeoning the suspect verbally, allowing him to think you'd got him so he might as well confess now and get it over with, then he can have a cup of coffee and that cigarette he's been dying for for the past few hours, ever since they hauled him from his bed at four a.m. Break him down until he either confessed or until he hung himself in a series of lies that got him deeper and deeper into the shit. But he was a toughie. He hadn't broken. So now it was Mahoney's turn: the buddy routine.

'Y'look as tired as I feel, Zacharias,' Mahoney said. 'How about we both have a cup of hot coffee?' Zacharias nodded without looking up. Mahoney went out into the hall and returned with two styrofoam cups of something that passed for coffee. At least it was steaming hot. He put one in front of Zacharias. 'Cigarette?' He offered a fresh pack of Marlboros.

Still without eye-contact, Zacharias took one and Mahoney noticed with satisfaction that his hand was shaking. He was a non-smoker but he lit up to keep his suspect company and they sat in silence for a few minutes. 'Drink your coffee while it's still hot, Mr Zacharias,' Mahoney said mildly. 'It's been a long night, hasn't it?'

Zacharias nodded dully, sipping the coffee. 'Listen, fella,' Mahoney said a few minutes later, 'I've got woman trouble myself. I know how it is. They can fuck you about till y'get crazy.' He sighed deeply. 'I had this girlfriend and boy was she great-looking. Y'know how it is with us cops, we work odd hours, shiftwork, just like in a factory. Turns out when I'm working nights, so is she. With her best friend's husband. Y'know what I mean? Y'just can't let them get away with a thing like that, can you, Zacharias? I mean it dents a man's pride pretty bad, I can tell ya.'

Zacharias said nothing and they smoked on in silence.

'Tell y'what, Zacharias,' Mahoney said easily, 'you must be starving by now. Why don't I send out for some Danish? Then you and I can talk. You can tell me all about her.' He sighed deeply, 'I'll just bet she was a bitch from hell, a looker like that. They just don't know when they've got a good man lookin' after them.'

Zacharias glanced warily at him, then nodded. 'She was a bitch all right,' he said vehemently.

Mahoney smiled sympathetically. 'She fuckin' round with someone else, man? Was that it?'

Zacharias nodded. His hands were trembling so much now he could hardly hold the cup. Mahoney sat back in his chair, watching him, waiting for him to crack. He could see it coming, he knew he had him.

The Danish came and Zacharias wolfed one down without lifting his eyes. 'Have another,' Mahoney said, 'they're almost as good as my Italian mama made.'

Zacharias took another and in between bites he began to spill out his version of the truth: how she was a bitch all right, how he'd looked after her, kept her in style, bought her clothes, food . . .

'Heroin?' Mahoney suggested, thinking of the festering sores along the girl's arms. He knew the odds were she would have been dead from an overdose or septicaemia or Aids before too long anyway. And she was all of nineteen years old. He hated the bastard in front of him so much he was surprised Zacharias couldn't feel the vibes across the table.

'She was a bad junkie,' Zacharias admitted.

'Where d'she get the money for it, friend?' Mahoney asked with a sympathetic smile.

Zacharias shrugged indifferently. 'She whored for it, like they all do.'

'Man, these women are something else,' Mahoney marvelled. 'I'll bet she didn't turn the money over to you, the way she should, did she?'

'Yeah. Right. Well the bitch pulled that once too often, didn't she,' Zacharias exclaimed, erupting with sudden rage.

'Listen, Zacharias,' Mahoney said leaning across the table, putting his face close to his and staring into his eyes. 'Maybe you had good reason for bouncing her with the auto. You think she deserved it. I'll make a deal with you, fella. You know you did it and we know you did it. Now there's no logical way we can get around that fact. But you tell me how it all happened and I'll do my damnedest to help you. Maybe we can go for a plea bargain. After all, you told me there was provocation, didn't you? I mean, she was working for you and she didn't turn over her earnings. She knew the rules; she just blew it all on heroin instead.'

'Yeah,' Zacharias agreed wearily. He sat sullenly and Mahoney could tell he was thinking it over. Out of the corner of his eye, he glimpsed Benedetti watching through the window but he made no sign. He waited for Zacharias to speak.

'Ya promise to get me off?' Zacharias said finally.

Mahoney spread his hands and said quietly, 'Zacharias,

you know I can't promise that. But if you tell us the truth, I can promise you a fair hearing, and I'll do what I can for you. See if maybe we can go for a plea bargain, a reduced sentence.'

'Yeah. Well she asked for it, didn't she?' Zacharias demanded suddenly belligerent. 'She fuckin' asked for it, man. Y'know how it is . . .'

Mahoney signalled Benedetti and a couple of minutes later he came in with a stenographer carrying her notepad. Benedetti put another cup of coffee in front of Zacharias and turned on the tape, and Mahoney pushed the packet of Marlboros across to him then read him the Miranda. 'You understand your rights, Zacharias?' he said finally. Zacharias nodded.

'Then tell us, man,' Mahoney said tiredly, 'so we can all go and get some sleep.'

In the event, he didn't get any sleep: he was due in trial court at two: the case was a typical Saturday night domestic homicide. Several months ago, the woman had shot her husband through the head as he slept drunkenly in his bed in a sleazy tenement they called home. When Mahoney got there, three kids, all under the age of seven, had been huddled in a corner of the only other room, their heads hidden under a filthy blanket so they couldn't see what had happened. They were covered in bruises and the mother was just sitting helplessly on a broken rocking chair, crying quietly, with the gun on her lap. The neighbours had called the cops and Mahoney had been first on the scene.

Her husband had knocked her kids around once too often, she had told him sombrely, and then she'd found out he'd been abusing them sexually. Her own face was a mess as she looked bleakly at him: a blackened eye, a bloody mouth, teeth missing. He had been beating her up for years but when he had started on the kids, that was the finish of her. The neighbours confirmed her story and, looking at her kids, cowering terrified with the blanket over their heads, Mahoney's sympathies were with her, and he was sure that today the jury's would be. He just hoped the judge would go easy on her. And make up for the little weasel-faced cold-blooded bastard he'd just spent his last nine hours with, who had killed the nineteen-year-old he had turned onto heroin and then sent out to work the streets for him. Mahoney would not easily forget the gory scene of that particular crime.

He hated the courts, hanging about waiting until it was his turn to be called. Then after he had given his evidence, waiting round some more until it was over. After that, he paid a visit to the ME at the city morgue, seeing if he had gotten around to cutting open the bloated body fished out of the bay last night and whether there were any bullet holes or if he had been drunk and just fallen in. Or if there was any evidence that he had been maybe hit over the head first and had been dead before he hit the water.

Afterwards, he dropped in at Hanran's bar and found the guys from the shift that had just finished, downing a beer and bitching about the day's events. He sat up at the bar and ordered a Bud light and said wearily, 'D'ya ever wonder why we do this job? Are we masochists or what?'

'The "or what" is about right,' someone replied gloomily. 'Who else but a bunch a jerks would do a job like this? My wife complains she hasn't seen me in weeks, I walk in the house and my kids look at me like they don't know me. I tell 'em, "Hey look I'm your daddy. Y'know, the guy who goes to work and brings home the bucks." "Yeah baby," my wife says, "real *big* bucks." Jeez Mahoney, I ask ya, is it worth it?'

Mahoney thought of Zacharias, safely behind bars two

blocks away and the nineteen-year-old girl avenged because he and Benedetti had done their job. He thought of the relief on the woman's face that afternoon when the judge had acknowledged the aggravation and intimidation she had suffered, and that she had been protecting her children. He had given her a year suspended and she had walked free with her children beside her. Mahoney would bet it was the first time she had been able to hold her head up in years, without fear of being smacked in the face.

'I guess it's a good job,' he said with a pleased grin. 'On the good days, that is.'

'You look as though it's been a long day, Mahoney. What y'doin' here anyway? I thought you were on the midnight shift this week.'

'Yeah. I guess I just forgot to go home.' Fatigue washed over him in a sudden wave as he allowed himself to remember he hadn't slept for twenty-four hours. He said goodbye to his buddies and drove slowly home to snatch a few hours before the next shift began.

He was standing under the power shower letting first hot then icy water spray him from every angle in an attempt to revive himself, when he heard the door-phone buzz. He stepped from the shower, wrapping a towel round his loins as he walked to the phone.

'Yeah?' he said.

'Mahoney? It's me. Phyl Forster.'

He had completely forgotten she had left a message on his answering machine that she was back from Paris and was coming round to pick up the cat. Unless he called her and said it was not convenient.

'Come on up, Doc,' he said. 'But I warn you, I'm not dressed. Think you can stand it?'

'I'll try, Mahoney,' she said acidly, and he grinned.

'I missed you,' he said as she stalked through the door,

looking as beautiful as he remembered. Maybe even more so. 'That new?' he asked admiring the red cashmere blazer she was wearing over a white T-shirt.

'I bought it in Paris.'

'I see you took my advice. About the colour.'

'How do you know it was *your* advice I took? And not someone else's?' She grinned cheekily at him and Coco came running with that loud Siamese yowl that bore no proportion to her tiny size. Phyl picked her up and hugged her.

'Watch out for the cat-hairs,' he warned, 'she's shedding like crazy.'

'I don't care. I missed her.'

'And me? Ya miss me, Doc?' He grinned, hitching up his towel.

'I see your sartorial sense hasn't improved, Mahoney,' she said scathingly. 'You still don't know how to dress for a lady.'

'You caught me on the hop, Doc. I worked late and I forgot about your message.' He swept her a low bow and waved her into the room. 'I'm so sorry, Dr Forster. Please, make yourself at home while I attempt to make myself more presentable.'

Phyl drifted across to the windows. They were wide open and the night breeze was blowing in. She leaned her elbows on the sill and gazed at the big ship, probably a liner, crossing the dark bay, its lights sparkling like extra stars. Mahoney's two enigmatic Siamese sat like bookends, each one on a corner of the window-ledge, sniffing the breeze that ruffled their fur, and the fat cushiony tabby snoozed contentedly on the back of a chair, legs dangling like a leopard up a tree after a good meal. The beautiful voice of Pavarotti singing the old Italian songs, drifted into the night, and something delicious simmered on the big steel stove. Phyl smiled as she turned to look at Mahoney. She liked it here. It felt like home.

He was wearing a pair of blue running shorts, and a T-shirt with the name, 'Machonachies Gym', and old sneakers. 'At least I chose blue – to match my eyes,' he said, catching her sceptical glance. 'Don't complain, Forster. It's hot tonight, and besides I'm tired.' He walked to the stove and checked the pasta. 'Speaking of tired, Doc, are those shadows I see under your eyes?'

'They only match those under yours,' she said, her chin jutting defensively. 'I just got off an eleven-hour flight from Paris. How the hell do you want me to look? At least I have an excuse.'

'Me too,' he said, 'but we won't go into it. Mmm, I thought for a minute there I might have to get jealous. Thought maybe you'd met another guy . . .'

She sighed, refusing to be goaded. 'Thanks for looking after Coco for me, Mahoney. I was wondering if you would mind having her again, just for a few days, this weekend.'

'Sure.' He didn't ask any questions, just poured her a glass of wine and began serving the pasta. They sat at the table and he passed her the chunk of parmesan cheese and the grater.

'Don't you want to know where I'm going?' she asked eager to tell him.

'Sure. Where are you going, Doc?' he asked, eating the food hungrily.

'Oh never mind,' she said perversely. She was suddenly angry with him. 'The pasta's good,' she admitted after a while.

'Sorry, no gourmet touches tonight. Straight ahead garlic and fresh parmesan.'

'And home-made tagliatelle.'

He shook his head. 'Forneau's deli. It's better than mine.

So, tell me about Bea. Sounds like the coincidence of a lifetime, her stumbling across the Villa Mimosa.'

'Don't you believe in fate, Mahoney?' she asked.

'Yeah. I do. And I also believe in coincidence. I might not catch too many killers if it were not for the coincidences. And you'd be astonished how many "coincidences" show up on the computer when you run the evidence through it. As Sir Thomas Browne once said in *Religio Medici*: "*Surely there are in everyone's life certain connections, twists and turns which pass awhile under the category of Chance, but at the last, well examined, prove to be the very Hand of God.*"' He grinned at her, 'You could say *coincidence* is a way of life with me, Doc.'

'I prefer to think of it as fate. Anyhow, here's another murder for you to think about.' She told him the story of Marie-Antoinette Leconte, and her husband, and what the old French journalist had seen.

Mahoney finished his pasta and leaned back in his chair, sipping his wine, looking at her. 'Y'know you're a very pretty woman,' he said inconsequentially.

'Mahoney.' Her sapphire eyes glared at him and he grinned back at her. 'Goddamn it, Mahoney, I'm telling you something *important*. About a *murder*.'

'Yeah,' he said wearily. 'But there's not much I can do about it now. It took place too long ago and besides, it's outside my area. More important is, what happened to the kid? Johnny?'

'The father came back for him five years later. To ensure getting his hands on the inheritance we think. Though he couldn't get his hands on it until the boy was eighteen.'

'Or unless the boy died first.'

She looked surprised at him. 'I hadn't thought of that.'

'Where did he take him?'

'To Hawaii. I'm not sure which island.'

Mahoney shrugged. 'That must have been before state-hood. They had their own laws, then, anything could have happened. What was the man's name?'

'He took on his wife's name, for inheritance purposes. Her father had made it a condition of his will. He was referred to mostly as the Foreigner. No one seems to know his real name.'

Mahoney sighed. 'Without a name, I don't have anything to check. There must be a hundred islands round Hawaii, as well as the main ones. He could have disappeared very easily, without any trace, especially in those days. And many did. But tell me, did the Foreigner ever claim the rest of the estate?'

'We don't know yet. Nick is working on it though.'

'Nick?' Mahoney raised his eyebrows and she laughed.

'I forgot to tell you, Bea has a boyfriend.' She described Nick and said how happy Bea was with him, though the mystery of the villa was getting to her.

'He sounds like good news to me,' Mahoney said finally. 'And at least it seems our killer is not on Bea's trail.'

'Do you think the two murders are connected, Franco?' she asked, frowning worriedly.

'Doc, I'm not clairvoyant. I don't have a single clue to go on, not even a name. In theory, and with the laws of coincidence, yes they could be connected. In truth, I don't know. But you had better keep me up to date on what else Nick and Bea uncover. Maybe somewhere in all the muddle I can find something that begins to make sense. But I wish it was not all so long ago. I deal in present day mysteries, Doc. Not the past.'

She nodded. 'It's odd about Hawaii,' she said. 'You can go for years without ever mentioning it, and suddenly it comes up twice in the same month. I met a guy who lives there,' she said smiling shyly at Mahoney. 'That's where

I'm going next week. He's invited me over, for a little vacation.'

'A guy huh? Am I gonna have to get jealous after all, Forster?'

She thought quickly of Brad's crazy jealousy, then she laughed as she looked at Mahoney. Mahoney was so straight ahead, he would just put all his problems on the table along with the pasta, to be discussed and sorted out. Not like Brad, who had undercurrents even she wasn't sure about.

'You met him in Paris, didn't you?' Mahoney said.

'As a matter of fact, no. I met him on the plane.'

'So, some Frenchman has swept you off your cool little feet?' He grinned mockingly at her and she blushed. 'Don't worry, Doc,' Mahoney said drily, 'I won't act the cop and ask questions.'

'There's nothing to hide,' she retorted defensively. 'Anyway he's an American. He has an apartment in Paris. His name is Brad Kane.'

'Brad Kane?' Mahoney looked thoughtful. 'Now where have I heard that name before.'

'You've probably heard about the Kanoi ranch. It's one of the biggest in the States.'

'He owns it, huh?'

She nodded. 'And I get to see it next week.'

'Lucky you,' Mahoney said, thinking of blue skies and beaches and sunlight bronzing her beautiful body. 'And maybe I am jealous after all.'

'I'll send you a postcard,' she promised, gathering up her purse and Coco. 'Oh, I forgot. I have a present for you.' She handed him a carrier bag filled with sacks of Herbes de Provence and jars of spices and condiments. 'From the Moulin de Mougins boutique,' she said. 'It was the nearest I got to eating there, we were just too busy. And don't ask me how I got past the sniffer dogs at the airport, I felt sure they were going to arrest me for illegal substances.'

'They can tell the difference,' he said, sniffing the sacks of fragrant herbs, pleased she had thought of him. 'Next time, I'll take you to the Moulin to eat,' he promised. 'Treat's on me.'

Phyl laughed as he walked her downstairs to her car. 'That's a longshot, Mahoney, if ever I heard one.'

'Don't you know by now I'm a guy who always plays the longshots?' he said, leaning into the car window, looking at her.

She reached across and kissed him lightly. 'Mahoney, you know what? You're sweet,' she said.

Mahoney could hear her laughing as she drove away. He heaved a sigh and glanced at his watch. Ten-thirty. So much for sleep. What the hell, he might as well show up early for the midnight shift.

CHAPTER 21

Brad's plane, a sleek Gulfstream IV, was waiting on the tarmac at San Francisco international with its engines already warmed up. Phyl was the only passenger and there was a crew of four to welcome her on board.

'Mr Kane sends his regrets that he couldn't be here, Ma'am,' the steward said. 'He enjoys piloting the aircraft himself, but today there were just too many business meetings.'

The plane was spacious with comfortable chairs set around small tables. There was a smaller cabin at the rear with seats that converted into a full-sized bed, and a small but perfectly-equipped bathroom. The steward presented Phyl with all of the latest magazines and a selection of the newest novels, offered her a glass of champagne and told her their flying time to Honolulu would be five hours. 'I hope you will find it a comfortable journey, Ma'am,' he said smiling. Phyl was sure she would.

When they arrived in Honolulu a Kanoi ranch helicopter was waiting to waft her to Brad's home. They flew low along Waikiki beach then soared up over the towering cliffs, giving her a breathtaking view of the black rocks and the pounding foam-flecked emerald ocean. They circled exclusive Diamond Head and came down low over the house. Phyl stared at it in amazement. She was only just starting to realise how seriously rich Brad was. The King mansion looked enormous from the sky, sprawling across acres of lush green palm-filled gardens to the very edge of the great cliffs.

Brad was waiting on the lawn. He broke into a run as the helicopter finally landed. His handsome face lit up with a thankful smile as he swept her into his arms.

'God, I've missed you,' he said, crushing her to him so tightly she laughed and begged him to stop.

'This is it,' he said with a proud wave of his arm, and she turned to look at the long low house, a series of Hawaiian-style pavilions linked by *lanaiis* and covered walkways. 'It's not that much different from Grandfather Archer's day,' Brad said, 'except I guess it grew a bit.'

They walked up the steps to the *lanaii*, out of the hot sun and into the cool shady rooms. The house was simply decorated in pale shades of cucumber and peppermint with simple floating white drapes and pale marble floors. Dark antique Hawaiian chests and massive tables mingled happily with the contemporary furnishings and bright abstract paintings.

The servants were Chinese; they wore white jackets and soft black slippers that made no noise on the marble floors, but as Brad escorted her through the house, Phyl noticed they did not smile and they averted their eyes when they served them drinks.

Brad took her first to see his three Hockneys, his pride and joy. And the huge Rothkos in the long gallery, and the delicate Monet waterlilies in the sitting room. There were Edward Hoppers, and O'Keefes and many more modern painters she did not recognise. Finally, Brad took her into the formal dining room and showed her the family portraits.

'This is Archer,' he said, stopping in front of a portrait of a very handsome man with yellow blond hair and hard blue eyes. He was sitting tall and very straight in a high-backed leather chair with his hands clasped tightly in front of him, and Phyl thought the portrait seemed to crackle with his tension.

'And this is Chantal, my grandmother,' he said.

Phyl stared at the portrait. She said, 'I haven't heard about her.'

'Chantal O'Higgins,' Brad said bitterly. 'Half-French, half-Irish. And you will.'

Phyl thought Chantal was beautiful, a silver blonde with a sulky mouth and a dissatisfied look in her eyes.

'Here's Jack, my father,' Brad said.

Jack's was not a formal portrait like the others. He sat astride a powerful-looking black stallion, there was a jaunty smile on his very handsome face and he looked the perfect picture of the rich arrogant young rancher.

'He wouldn't sit for the portrait,' Brad explained. 'The artist had to catch him on the move. That was his favourite horse, Volcano. The stallion lived up to his name, it killed at least one man I know about.'

'*Killed him?*'

'Yeah. Threw him off. There was a party and the guy was boasting he could ride anything, so Jack put him on Volcano.' Brad laughed carelessly. 'I guess he learned his lesson the hard way.'

Phyl shuddered, wondering what kind of man Jack was to have done such a thing, knowing the horse was dangerous.

'And here's my mother,' Brad said softly. 'Rebecca.'

It was a full-length portrait and Rebecca was as lovely as he had described: a smooth oval face, blue almond eyes and rippling black hair. She wore a fetching smile and a clinging Nile green chiffon gown with satin ribbons tied, Empire-style, under her generously-displayed breasts. She was holding a spray of cream lilies in one hand, and the other rested gracefully on the back of a brocade chair. There was something opulent and overwhelmingly sensual about Rebecca's portrait: the rich textures of chiffon, satin, brocade; the gleam of emeralds and diamonds, the very lustre of her skin. Phyl thought each passionate brush-stroke revealed the true nature of the woman beneath the conventional façade. It was as though the artist knew her too well, as though he was having a love-affair with her.

She said, 'Rebecca is very beautiful.'

Brad shrugged and turned away. 'Well, that's it. The whole family.'

'What? No more brothers and sisters?' she asked, teasing.

He frowned. 'None, that counted,' he said abruptly, walking out into the sunshine.

The temperature was soaring and the humidity was high and Phyl said she thought she was going to melt, so they went for a swim.

The swimming pool was sixty feet long and a deep marine blue, and it seemed to spill into infinity, over the edge of the cliff. She dived in and swam to what seemed the very edge of space, then floated on her back, staring at the clouds puffing up in the blue sky.

'Those are storm clouds,' Brad said, frowning. 'I hope it's fine tomorrow. I'd planned to take you to see the ranch.'

But he was right about the storm; by six o'clock lightning was flashing over the sea and the rain was battering the island. They lay entwined on his huge four-poster bed, carved from the magnificent glossy Hawaiian koa wood over forty years ago, for his mother. The linen sheets felt sexily smooth against Phyl's cool skin and Brad's mouth felt even sexier as he began to kiss her. The scent of frangipani and jungly green plants wafted in the open window and rain drummed insistently on the roofs, matching the thudding of her heart. It seemed so peaceful. And yet, this time when they made love, she felt the tension in him, the same crackle of tension she had sensed from his father's portrait. And she wondered why?

The next morning, they arose with the dawn to clear blue skies as innocent of clouds as if there had never been a storm. Brad piloted the small Cessna himself on the short flight to the Big Island while Phyl sat next to him enthralled at the vista below. The Pacific was a rippling patchwork of emerald and aquamarine with paler turquoise over the sandbanks, glittering under the hot sun with a million diamond points of light.

Then they were flying over the peak of the volcano at the centre of the island, swooping low over deep forests and canyons, and over endless miles of flat plains where Phyl could see *paniolos*, the cowboys, riding alongside the long slow-moving columns of prime Hereford cattle; more than sixty thousand of them, Brad told her proudly. They skimmed grassy meadows and the flat shore, ringed with black lava rock and studded with bright green banana trees, and lofty coconut palms and sprawling *kiawes*, on over the emerald golf courses and pink resort hotels.

Phyl thought apprehensively it was not gentle scenery: there was a brutality about the jagged black rocks, and the foaming sea hurling itself on them surging and sucking and swirling away again in a flurry of foam into unknown depths. The rugged peaks and deep darkly-forested ravines looked forbidding, and the miles of flat empty black volcanic rocks inhospitable. But this was Brad's home, his inheritance, his love.

Brad brought the tiny aircraft into land and as they taxied

down the short runway, he turned to look at her. 'Welcome to the Kanoi ranch,' he said, smiling proudly.

A Jeep drew up alongside the aircraft as they stepped out and a Hawaiian wearing a large white stetson, called out, 'Welcome back, Mr Kane.'

'Thank you, Charlie.' Brad shook hands with him. 'Dr Forster, this is Charlie Kalapaani, he runs the ranch. I'm giving Dr Forster the tour,' he said, climbing into the Jeep.

They drove from the airstrip along a dead straight road for ten minutes, then turned into a long avenue lined with huge old banyan trees. 'Planted by my grandfather sixty years ago,' Brad told her, as they sped towards the simple wooden ranch house. It was painted white and surrounded by covered verandahs and inside it was dark with polished koa wood and a treasure-trove of the history of the Kanoi ranch, with the original hand-hewn furnishings and arti-facts, and dozens of photographs of the ranch and its workers in the early days.

'Archer started out with fifty of the worst acres, full of gulches where his cattle could get lost, and within three years he owned three thousand prime acres,' Brad told her proudly. 'He increased his acreage every year, and so did my father, until the ranch is now more than three hundred thousand acres. And that's not counting the lands in Texas and Wyoming.'

Phyl studied the map he showed her and said, 'No more acres left for you to buy then.'

'Oh, I guess I did my share of adding to the Kane heritage, though maybe not in quite the same way. But those hotels and golf courses along the shore are on Kanoi land, and I expect tourism to add a lot of new revenue to the Kane family coffers.'

She smiled teasingly at him. 'So you're not just a pretty face then.'

'You would be a fool if you thought that,' he said, suddenly cold. 'My work is my life.'

He walked outside and stood shading his eyes, looking out at the fenced corrals.

'Can you ride a horse?' he asked.

Phyl laughed at the thought. 'Brad, I'm a city girl. There were no horses on the streets of Chicago. Except police horses.'

He grinned. 'Then we'll take the Jeep.'

His good mood returned as they jolted along dusty lanes and he told her there were over a thousand horses, Morgans and quarter-horses and Arabians, in two hundred paddocks and corrals. There were hundreds of miles of pipes feeding water into the many tanks and water troughs; and the lower ranges were planted with special grasses and legumes while the upper, more rainy slopes, were naturally lush with clovers and a mixture of nutritious grasses.

They watched the endless line of cattle being driven up the slopes towards fresh pastures while Brad explained how they regularly left land to 'rest' and rejuvenate itself, and that Kanoi had some of the finest beef cattle in the country because of this system.

Brad introduced her to some of his hundreds of employees, the ranch hands and the cowboys. 'But I'm the man in charge,' he said firmly. 'And I make sure nobody ever forgets that.'

Phyl told him it sounded like something his grandfather might have said.

'Of course he did. And my father. "*You are the boss*," my father told me. "And you had better remind them of it every day. You have to let every man know, from the lowest ranch hand to the highest manager that this land belongs to you. If a man steps out of line, he is out of a job."'

It was late afternoon when they took off again and Brad's spirits seemed to soar with the plane as they skimmed over the beaches and across the ocean.

The sun was setting in a fiery orange glow when Kalani appeared, its twin volcanic peaks silhouetted against the horizon, and its shore fringed with tall coconut palms.

A Chinese servant waited in an open-top Jeep and as they drove to the Lodge Brad proudly showed her his beloved island. She saw the crystal green ocean crashing onto the silver shore, and the lava that had flowed down the mountain centuries ago, cooling into rivers of polished black stone, dividing the forest into deep fern-filled gulches of a green so dense they seemed, to her dazzled eyes, to shimmer in the twilight.

Brad took her to see the immaculate white-railed paddocks with the fine Arabian horses he bred, and the prize cattle roaming his meadows, and the perfectly tended lush tropical gardens surrounding the Lodge. And Phyl marvelled at the beauty and perfection of what she saw. She finally understood Brad's passion for Kalani. It was a true paradise.

The Lodge itself was a simple sprawling structure that had obviously just grown over the years: the floors were of smooth dark wood, the walls were plain white. It was simply furnished with antiques from the islands and comfortable sofas covered in sand-colour linen.

Brad's own room was as plain as a monk's cell, without even a rug on its polished wooden floor. His big bed with the barley-twist posts was made from koa wood and draped with mosquito netting. The only other furniture was a Chinese wooden chair and a low ebony chest, with a framed black and white photograph of Rebecca, staring haughtily into the camera. Her long sleek hair was caught up at the back with a flower in it, and she was wearing a black velvet evening dress.

'She was about thirty years old then, I guess,' Brad said. 'It was before the divorce.'

Phyl threw him a surprised glance, he hadn't mentioned a divorce. But just then a houseboy appeared with their bags and Brad did not elaborate.

An enormous Doberman with burning red-brown eyes and a coat as black and glossy as wet lava rock, suddenly ran into the room. Phyl shrank back with a frightened cry but the dog ignored her, leaping at Brad with yelps of joy. Brad laughed as he caressed the dog, sleeking back its ears and speaking softly to it in Hawaiian. He told Phyl its name was Kanoi, the Hawaiian word for king, the same as the ranch.

He saw she was apprehensive and he said reassuringly, 'The Doberman's reputation is misleading. It's quite simple: one man – one dog. They pledge their allegiance to no other than their master.' He caressed the dog's massive head and it gazed devotedly up at him. 'See how docile he is? Gentle as a lamb.'

Phyl shivered as she looked warily at the powerful dog. Brad put his arm round her and Kanoi leapt immediately to its feet. It stared balefully at her, tense as a steel spring. She suddenly recalled Bea's terrible scars and she shivered; she knew a powerful dog like that could rip a man to pieces in minutes if he chose, but thankfully unless Brad touched her, it just ignored her.

While Brad went to talk to his stable manager, Phyl showered and changed into a simple long black silk jersey shift. She caught up her hair for coolness and tucked a red hibiscus flower into it. Then she added long crystal drop earrings and a splash of Bellodgia and wandered out onto the *lanaii* to wait for him.

The humid evening air clung to her skin, and the ceiling fans wafted welcome patches of coolness over her as she leaned on the *lanaii* rail, breathing in the different tropical scents of jungly greenness and night-blooming flowers, listening to the croak of the treefrogs and the chirruping of the crickets and the whirr of unseen wings, high in the treetops. She did not hear Brad coming, didn't know he was there, watching her, until he said, 'Do you have any idea how like my mother you look? With your hair caught up like that, and the flower in it, the way she used to wear it.'

His voice had that hard edge and Phyl turned to look at him, puzzled. 'Rebecca was lovely. I take that as a compliment.'

'I saw it right away, when we met on the plane. I noticed you at the airport. You even have Rebecca's same arrogant walk, the same long easy stride.'

She smiled, startled. 'Was that why you wanted to see me again? Because I looked like her?'

Brad laughed. He put his arms round her, 'God no. I never wanted to see that woman again. It was *you* I wanted to see again. The oh-so-clever-and-brilliant Dr Phyl, whose power over men is such I'm sure she could persuade a real king to part with his most intimate secrets.'

He crushed her to him, breathing in the scent of her. 'What secrets would you like me to tell you tonight?' he murmured in between kisses.

'About Rebecca?' she suggested, still curious. But he shook his head.

'First I should tell you about my grandmother. The one and only Chantal.' He laughed bitterly. 'My God, the Kane men really knew how to choose their women. Every one of them a first-class bitch.'

He let go of her and began to pace the tiled floor angrily, tagged by the dog who never left his side. Phyl leaned against the rail, watching him as he talked.

'It was the 1920s,' he said. 'Archer was still very young when he met Chantal. And she was even younger *and* with the unlikely, but oh-so-impressive name of O'Higgins. The O'Higgins name spelled money – big money – on two continents. Chantal was half-Irish, half-French, and she was the spoiled, wayward heiress to the O'Higgins cognac fortune.' He looked angrily at Phyl. 'You saw her portrait. You saw how beautiful she was. Pale blonde, with that sullen look in her blue eyes. She had skin like milk and a very tempting mouth, and Archer fell head over heels this time. And I guess so did she. After all he was a very handsome man and he wanted her as much as she wanted him.

'Chantal eloped with him to Honolulu and then Archer brought her back here, to Kalani. *And she hated it*. God how she hated it. She was shocked when she saw the primitive wooden Lodge; she loathed the bugs and lizards, and the wind that hurled the Pacific breakers against the rocks on stormy days. She complained that the heat and humidity made her skin feel like blotting paper. She said the servants were sloppy and lazy, and she swore some of the girls had more than just a master/servant relationship with her husband. She was probably right, but despite all her complaints. I guess she loved him, or at least she wanted him enough to stay.

'Archer's crops had never done well, his pineapples had withered and his sugar shrivelled and wild grasses covered most of his uncultivated acres. But he bought a herd of Hereford cattle and shipped in some better horses. They roamed the gulches on the western side of the island, tended by the *paniolos*. It was difficult but the cattle thrived, and suddenly Archer was struck by the new possibilities of his land.

'He told Chantal he wanted to expand, to buy more acreage on the main islands, and he would need her money. But Chantal was difficult. She was pregnant, she was bored out of her mind and sulky. Finally she agreed, after many wild arguments, but she eked out the money to him, bit by bit, driving him crazy. Still, he managed to buy his first thousand acres on the Big Island.

'Then Chantal gave birth to a son, Jack, and as soon as she could afterwards, she left both of them and took off for San Francisco. She said she didn't want anything to do with either of them, ever again. Not long after, Archer heard she had run off with someone else, and he divorced her.'

Brad stopped his pacing and smiled at Phyl. But his icy eyes were not smiling as he said with a shrug, 'And that was Chantal, *my dear grandmother*.'

'But what about her son, Jack? Did he ever see her again?'

'He did,' Brad said grimly. 'Many years later and in circumstances I'd rather not talk about right now.'

'So Archer brought Jack up alone, on the island?'

'Almost. He married again a short while later.' Brad laughed. 'He always said he had been forced into it. He needed the money to buy more acres on the Big Island. He needed a new, sturdier breed of cattle, better horses, good men. He said his island, his ranch and his son were his three passions. Women came last.

'You see, women were easy for a man like Archer. He never had to look for them, they were always there when he wanted them. And he said he preferred to buy them in Honolulu's brothels or in San Francisco, where they were less trouble and more fun.

'He went to Europe to look for new cattle, but being

Archer, he was also on the lookout for a wife. He was handsome and he could be charming, but he was a hard man and he was determined not to let anything stand in the way of what he wanted. And right then, he wanted a fortune.'

Brad laughed, admiringly. 'So he married one.' He shrugged, 'What else could a good-looking young guy with a glowing future but no money do?'

Phyl said puzzled, 'So what happened to her?'

'She couldn't last the course either. She took herself back home and that was that. Until years later, when Archer suddenly presented Jack with a half-brother he knew nothing about.'

'And . . . ?'

He shrugged again, uncaring. 'He soon left. I guess the half-brother just couldn't stand Kalani either.'

'Or maybe he couldn't stand Jack? After all, Jack was there first. And you Kanes are very territorial.'

'Jack hated him,' he said brusquely. 'And rightly so. But that's a long story, and not one I feel like talking about.'

He turned moodily away and dinner later was a silent meal, as though he felt he had already said too much. Afterwards, he left her at the door of her room with just a brief kiss. 'You must be tired,' he said abruptly. 'Get some sleep.'

He went off down the hall and she heard him call the dog to heel and stride down the steps into the night.

Phyl waited a few moments, then she walked barefoot onto the *lanaii*, looking after him, but he had already disappeared. The big moon bathed the island in a silvery light and it looked even more breathtakingly beautiful than before. But she scarcely noticed. She was thinking that beneath Brad's urbane charming façade, he was the most complex man she had ever met.

She wandered back through the silent house and paused outside Brad's room. The door stood open and a lamp was lit but she could see it was empty. Suddenly curious, she went in and tiptoed across to the ebony chest. She picked up Rebecca's photograph and stared fascinated at it. She could see Brad was right; she did resemble Rebecca; the same big, startled-looking eyes, the same wide mouth, the pale skin and long black hair. '*You even have her walk*,' he had said.

Was that the real reason he was attracted to her? she asked herself with a shiver of apprehension. And was that also why he felt he could bare his soul to her about the past?

She glanced nervously round. There was nothing else personal in his room, not even a book on the bedside table. The big walk-in closet was as neat and impersonal as his bedroom: everything in its place, jackets in rows, shirts stacked in glass-fronted drawers, shoes all in a line. She ran her hand along the row of hangers, burying her face in the soft tweed of his jacket suddenly longing for him, wanting the feel of him, the scent of him. As she pulled the jacket towards her, she noticed a crumpled green canvas bag pushed into the corner.

It looked old and oddly out of place amongst all that rich neatness. It certainly did not look the sort of bag Brad would ever use. She looked at it, hesitating, then curiosity got the better of her and she pulled it towards her. Inside she saw a jumble of feminine travel items, cosmetic bag, hairbrush, T-shirts, sweaters . . .

Hot with guilt, she zipped the bag up and pushed it back into the corner. She told herself quickly that of course Brad invited other women here. Why wouldn't he? He was an attractive man. Plenty of women would be happy to be his guest. Still, the contents of the green canvas bag were not the sophisticated items she might have expected the women in Brad Kane's life to possess. They were the casual, inexpensive sort of things a young girl might carry.

It was none of her business, Phyl told herself guiltily, as she hurried back to her room. She was trespassing on Brad's privacy and she should feel ashamed of herself. And she did. But still she wondered about the girl who had left her bag there.

She undressed and climbed naked under the sheet, then lay awake for a long time, listening for Brad's return, hoping he would come to her. But he did not, and as she finally drifted into sleep, she wondered again about Rebecca, and the past that troubled him so deeply, and about Jack and the half-brother who suddenly arrived out of the blue to almost ruin his life.

CHAPTER 22

Nick Lascelles returned to Antibes with the news that the London bank would tell him nothing about the Flora Beale Trust, other than it was administered by them, and that their instructions were to maintain the cottage exactly as it was, in perpetuity. There were more than sufficient funds to support it and they believed the donor's intention was to preserve the property as a museum, or even a sort of shrine. The banker said the names and details were confidential and he would certainly not reveal them. Unless the police were involved and it became official business, of course.

'So now we're back to square one,' Nick said gloomily to Bea and Millie over lunch at the hotel. 'The only other link we have is the key we found at the cottage.'

He took the small silver key from his pocket and put it on the table. They all stared at it. It was small, anonymous, just the same as any other key. 'Perhaps it fits a suitcase, or a trunk?' Bea suggested.

'The only trunk we found at the cottage was in the loft and it wasn't even locked.'

'Well, what about a cupboard?'

He shook his head slowly. 'No locked cupboards. Nanny Beale kept her only secrets under her mattress. Unless . . .' He thought for a minute. 'You remember how the document finished abruptly . . . almost in the middle. She didn't say what happened on the island, just that they arrived there. And that she was no match for the enemy – meaning Johnny's father. She hadn't concluded her story, she hadn't even written, "The End".'

'You mean you think this key opens the door to the place she kept the rest of her secrets?' Millie asked.

'I'd bet my boots on it.' Nick studied the key again. 'Look there's a number engraved on it.' He grinned cockily at Millie. 'Now you tell me where a nice law-abiding old lady would keep her secrets.'

'At her bank,' Millie said promptly.

He nodded, 'I'll bet this is the key to a safe deposit box. Our problem is which bank?'

Bea sighed, defeated. 'There must be hundreds here, along the coast.'

Nick grinned confidently at them. 'Then it's up to me to play detective and find the right one, isn't it?'

Immediately after lunch, Nick hurried off on his new mission, and Bea decided to check on the progress at the Villa Mimosa. The kitchen and several new bathrooms were in the process of being installed, and the place was swarming with carpenters and tilers, plasterers and painters. The villa was still hidden under a mass of scaffolding, but the new swimming pool was almost finished and a landscape gardener was working with his team restoring the grounds to their former glory.

Millie's designer had his new deadline and he intended to meet it, especially in view of the lavish bonus she had promised, and she was satisfied that though it might not be completely finished, at least in a couple of days, some of the furniture would be in place and it would be habitable.

Millie intended to go with Bea to the villa, but then she told her she felt unaccountably weary. 'I'll just let you go alone, dear girl,' she said, kissing her goodbye. 'You can bring me back the progress report.' She yelped with laughter as she added, 'More like lack of it I suppose.'

Millie waved Bea goodbye and strolled happily along the terrace to her favourite spot overlooking the sea.

She summoned a waiter and ordered a glass of brandy to perk her up, sighing with satisfaction as she gazed at the beautiful view of pines and olive trees and pink and purple bougainvillaea and silvery blue sea. She thought that of all the places in the world she had travelled, this was her favourite.

'Silly woman,' she told herself, smiling, 'you say that about every place you go. You know by now it's not just the place, it's the company you keep. In the old days, when you were young and giddy, it was always a man. And now that you are old, it's that dear girl Bea. You know she reminds you of yourself at her age, though of course *you* never let your loneliness and vulnerability show. Always too proud for that, always covered it up under a loud laugh and a devil-may-care attitude.'

She laughed, thinking it was too late to care about all that now. The children were arriving soon, and the Villa Mimosa was almost finished. She had laid her plans, made sure everything was the way she wished it to be.

Millie sipped her brandy happily, gazing out onto the Mediterranean. Seabirds wheeled noisily overhead, the sun was warm on her bare arms and a gentle breeze rustled the fronds of the palm trees. She heaved a sigh of pure contentment as she put down her glass and leaned comfortably back against the cushions and closed her eyes.

She was fast asleep when the pain gripped her heart as it had done so many times over the past few years. Only this time it was to be the last. She was smiling when she died.

'I don't believe it,' Bea screamed, when they told her. 'It's just not true, please, please, tell me it's not true.' Her own heart felt as though it would burst with the pain as she turned ashen-faced to Nick. 'Millie was my friend,' she whispered. 'She was good and kind and generous. When I was lost and frightened, she took me into her life and made me part of it.' She began to sob, great heaving ugly sobs that almost choked her, 'Oh Nick, why should this happen to her now? Why? It's just not fair.'

He held her trembling in his arms. He liked Millie, he had seen the goodness beneath the bluff exterior and he was shocked and sad that she was gone. But he was desolate for Bea; her fragile persona seemed to be disintegrating under this new blow. He tightened his arms around her, wanting to give her his strength, his support.

She was talking incoherently about Millie, saying she must call Phyl, that Phyl was Millie's friend. He told her gently not to worry, that he would call Phyl; he would call Millie's attorney in New York, he would take care of everything. But first he took Bea to her room and called the doctor to give her a sedative.

The attorney, John Hartley, arranged for the funeral to take place two days later. He told Nick he would be unable to attend, but that he would be arriving to settle Mrs Fenwick's affairs at the end of the week.

It was impossible to get hold of Phyl. Nick left messages every day on her answering machine, saying that he was calling about Millie Fenwick, that it was urgent, asking her to call him, but she did not reply.

'She must have gone away,' Bea said, desolate that Phyl would miss Millie's last big event.

The day of the funeral dawned, clear and blue and sunny. 'It's perfect,' Bea said sadly. 'It's just the way Millie would have wanted it.'

They were the only mourners, apart from a straggle of

black-coated waiters and hotel staff keeping discreetly in the background, paying their final respects to Millie Fenwick, not because she was a generous woman, but because, as she had hoped, they were genuinely fond of her.

Bea laid a sheaf of Millie's favourite pink roses and white lilies on the grave. She stood sadly for a moment, her head bowed. She put her fingers to her lips and blew her a farewell kiss, then, with Nick's comforting arm around her, walked slowly away.

Bea had not been able to bear the thought of the hotel without Millie and had decided instead to move into the Villa Mimosa, even though it still wasn't finished.

She leaned her head on Nick's shoulder as they drove home in the big black funeral car, thinking what a happy day this was meant to be for Millie. And for her. She was going to live in the house of her dreams, only now, without Millie's forceful presence, somehow it all seemed meaningless. The car turned in at the big iron gates and she opened her eyes as they drove silently up the gravel driveway of the Villa Mimosa.

And there, sitting on the steps, with airline identification tags still around their necks, looking lost and forlorn, were two small, pale, frightened-looking children.

'*It's Scott and Julie Fenwick*,' Bea gasped, horrified. She had completely forgotten they were arriving today. In fact she had forgotten all about them.

The distraught Air France representative rushed towards them, relieved to finally hand over her charges. She told them that when nobody had met them at the airport, she had been worried. The airlines had the address of the Villa Mimosa and so she had brought them here. Her responsibility over, she left hurriedly before they could change their minds.

Bea looked sadly at the children and then at Nick. 'What do we do now?' she whispered.

The two children looked back at them, big-eyed, scared, and alike as two peas. The same round face and freckles, the same blue eyes; same ragged fringe of shiny conker-brown hair, hers in a ponytail with the ribbon sliding off it. The boy took his sister's hand, saying nothing, waiting apprehensively for what might happen to them next.

Scotty Fenwick felt the lump sticking in his throat again that meant he had to fight not to cry. He swallowed hard, staring back at the girl and the man staring at them as though they had never seen two kids before. He felt Julie's small hot hand grip his even more tightly and he knew he had to be brave for her sake. Hadn't they told him after Mom and Dad's funeral, that he had to be a man now and look after his sister. And he knew it was true. It was just the two of them now against the world. But the world was suddenly so much bigger than the small town they had always lived in, where they knew everybody and everybody knew them. These strangers were looking at them as though they had never even heard of them. And this girl couldn't be his Aunt Millie, wasn't she supposed to be old?

He slid his arm protectively round Julie's shoulders, waiting for them to do something. That's all that ever happened now, people did things to them, or for them: sent them places to live, gave them food, smiled a lot at them with that special pitying look in their eyes. Lucky you, they had said, having a rich auntie in the sunny South of France. Lucky you going to live in a grand villa. Oh sure, he had mumbled bitterly, lucky us.

The red-haired girl was looking at him now, with that same special look everyone gave them, and he gripped Julie's thin shoulders tighter, staring up at her.

'Welcome to the Villa Mimosa, Scott and Julie,' the girl

said warmly. 'Boy, are we glad to see you. Poor kids, you look exhausted. Come on inside and let me show you your rooms. Millie had them all fixed up specially for you.'

Scott glanced down at Julie. Her expression was blank, as it usually was these days. As though she had put her emotions into neutral. Julie hadn't cried once since the funeral, though she had cried buckets before. And so had he, howling like a wolf sometimes, letting out his pain. And his anger, because boy was he angry. Angry at whoever had caused his mom and dad to die; anger at them for dying; anger at himself for not being big and strong enough to take care of Julie. Anger at not being able to turn the clock back and make everything the way it used to be, the four of them in the little yellow split-level ranch house with the pepper trees surrounding it, dropping endless leaves onto the lawn. He had even promised God he would never complain again about clearing up those leaves, if only he would bring Mom and Dad back. But it seemed God wasn't one for bargains.

And now here he was, with Julie, in a foreign country called France where they all spoke stuff he couldn't understand, with two strangers, in an enormous house called the Villa Mimosa that looked like something in the movies. Because even though they smiled at him, they were still strangers. And the truth was he was scared. And homesick.

'Are you my Aunt Millie?' Julie said suddenly, looking suspiciously at the girl.

Scott gave her a quick nudge with his elbow; hadn't he warned her not to say anything, not to ask any questions. He had told her to let him take care of it all, that they wouldn't stay here. Leave it to him, he had said, and they would soon be home again. 'But Scotty, where is home?' Julie had asked plaintively, and that awful lump had come back in his throat again. He had no answer, he didn't know. He didn't know anything any more. He was only nine years old and he didn't want to be a man yet. He just wanted life to be the way it had always been.

'I'm Bea French,' the girl said, hunkering down and giving Julie a kiss on the cheek. She leaned towards him too, but he drew back. He didn't want any kisses from any more strangers.

'And I'm Nick Lascelles.' The man held out his hand and Scott took it reluctantly. 'We're friends of your Aunt Millie,' he said. 'Come on inside, let's show you around.'

Scott took Julie's hand again as they followed them indoors. He stared round the big empty hall, surprised. There was no furniture, no muddy boots kicked into a corner, no coats hanging on a peg like at home.

'This place looks like nobody lives here,' he said in his funny gravelly voice that used to make his dad laugh.

'Your Aunt Millie was having the villa redone specially for you,' Bea said reassuringly. 'She wanted it to be finished when you got here, but there's still not much furniture. Just in the kitchen and the bedrooms.'

'And there's the swimming pool,' Nick said. 'Don't forget that.'

'There's a pool?' Scott's tired eyes lit with a flash of interest.

'Sure there's a pool,' Bea said quickly. 'And there's a beach nearby, and lots of boats for fishing.'

'Yeah,' Scott shrugged his thin shoulders tiredly, glaring at Julie as she ran to Nick and slid her hand trustingly into his.

She looked up at him and lisped plaintively, 'Whereth my Aunt Millie?'

Bea shot Nick an apprehensive look that said she thought the truth was just too harsh for these poor emotionally battered children right now ... 'I just told you, sweetie,' she said, 'Aunt Millie couldn't be here today.'

Julie stared at her. 'She's dead, ithant she?' She turned her sad gaze on Nick. 'That's what they told uth when my mommy and daddy died. They said they couldn't be with uth any more.'

Oh God, Scotty thought, fighting that lump in his throat again. Julie's right, that's what they told us. Oh God, what will become of us now? They said she was our only relative ... now we have nobody ... nobody ... we are orphans ... in a foreign country ... with strangers ...

Nick said gently, 'I'm sorry, Julie, but everything's still okay. Bea and I will take care of you.'

'*I'll* take care of her,' Scotty muttered, 'she's my sister.'

'Bea, my hairth metthy,' Julie said, her lisp coming to the fore the way it did when she was tired or upset. 'And I need to go to the bathroom.'

She yawned wearily as they followed Bea upstairs, still holding tightly to Scott's hand and he squeezed it encouragingly. 'Remember, don't say anything,' he warned, as Bea flung open the door and showed them a pink ruffled bower, fit for a princess.

'Millie knew you liked pink, Julie,' Bea said as the little girl gave a delighted cry and ran towards the menagerie of stuffed animals awaiting her on the windowseat. 'And that your favourite colour is green, Scott,' she said including him in her smile.

'I don't care,' Scott muttered, with an indifferent shrug of his shoulders. He turned away, ignoring his sister exclaiming over the beautiful big doll awaiting her in the middle of the brass four-poster.

It was suddenly all too much, he couldn't keep that lump away; tears threatened, and he ran from the room.

He stood in the hallway, his shoulders hunched, his

clenched fists thrust into his pockets. Even from the back, Nick knew he was crying and that he didn't want anyone to see.

He said, 'It's all right to cry if you feel like it, Scott. A lot of sad things have happened to you. First your mom and dad, and now your Aunt Millie.'

'What did *she* care,' he said in a tight, choked little voice. 'She didn't even *know* us.'

'It's true Millie had never met you, but she knew all about you. And what she knew made her care. She was an old lady you know, but she told us she had never been a mother and now she could be. She was really looking forward to it, Scott. To being with you and Julie, taking care of you, and caring about you.'

He patted Scott's tense shoulder. 'You've had a long journey, old son. You're tired and I'll bet you're hungry. How about you and I go down to the kitchen and rustle up some food, maybe go and check out that pool?'

Scott sniffed back his tears noisily. He still didn't look at Nick but he followed him downstairs. He went and sat at the kitchen table, his head lowered as Nick checked the refrigerator and the freezer.

Nick gave an amazed whistle. He took out a couple of packages. 'Good old Aunt Millie,' he said with a grin. 'She knew what her two American kids would like all right. Hot dogs and french fries.'

Scott's eyed lifted interestedly but he didn't say anything. Then Julie ran into the kitchen and climbed onto a chair next to him. She cradled a green plush frog in her arms, watching silently as Nick and Bea prepared the food.

They kept up a stream of jolly chatter as they grilled hot dogs and fixed the fries, but still nothing lifted the children out of their silence. At last they carried their plates out onto the terrace and everyone sat round the table, trying to force down the food, but they were all choked up, and even Nick ran out of jolly anecdotes. Scott and Julie stared at their plates in silence.

Nick threw Bea a despairing glance and saw there were tears in her eyes. He knew she was on the brink of breaking down, it was all too much: Millie; the funeral; the orphaned children.

'Look!' Julie suddenly yelled. She pointed. 'Over there.'

A big dog crept from the bushes at the edge of the lawn, and stood, sniffing the air hopefully, watching them.

The dog was long-legged and curly-coated, shaggy, unkempt – and hungry. After a moment hunger got the better of his caution and he gathered his tattered courage and sidled towards them, crouching low until he was almost on his belly, anticipating a thrown stone, a blow, a curse. He lay down at Scott's feet, put his nose carefully between his paws and raised big soulful brown eyes to him.

Scotty stared at the dog. He thought the expression in its eyes was like the one he saw in his own eyes in the mirror. He suddenly wanted that dog with every fibre of his being, more than he had ever wanted anything in his life before. *Except to be able to turn the clock back*. But the dog was a stray, he knew these people wouldn't want it in their fancy villa. The dog could never be his and that's why he couldn't touch it.

Looking at the dog, Bea thought it had a lot in common with her and with Millie's two little orphans. They didn't say a word but she saw the longing in their blue eyes and knew she had found at least one way to break the ice around their hearts.

'All right, mutt,' she said, 'you're in.'

Scott pushed back his chair with a whoop of delight. He

flung his arms around the dog. The lump in his throat was magically gone and as the dog licked his hand and he caught himself in mid-laugh, I'm laughing, he thought, astonished, I'm laughing again. And he punched Julie on the arm and said, 'He's gonna sleep on my bed.'

'No, mine.'

'Mine.'

'You can share him,' Bea said quickly.

'What shall we call him?' Julie demanded excitedly, watching Scott feed him their hot dogs. The dog hoovered them and sat, one battered ear askew, happily begging for more.

'He's such a mutt,' Bea said, laughing. 'How about Poochie?'

They were finally acting like kids again instead of emotionally-exhausted midgets and she thanked heaven for the dog. She glanced at Nick and she knew the same thought was going through his mind. *What next? What would happen to Scott and Julie Fenwick, now that Millie had gone?*

Millie's attorney, John Hartley, arrived from New York two days later to settle matters. He was an older man, white-haired and stiffly pompous, and he had been Millie's legal advisor for decades.

'Mrs Fenwick had suffered from a heart complaint for several years,' he told Bea. 'Everything that could be done for her had already been done. She knew she might die at any time. That's why she refused to give up the cigarettes she enjoyed, even though she knew they were bad for her.'

Bea suddenly recalled her first meeting with Millie, at the Fifth Avenue apartment that rainy day ... 'It's not alcohol that will kill me,' she had said, 'it's these blasted ciggies ...'

'She wrote this letter for you,' Hartley said, handing her an envelope and sitting back, hands folded patiently, while Bea read it.

I know I might not have long to live and that's why I lived my life to the hilt, dear girl. I thought I was a lucky woman, I had everything I wanted. And then, like a blessing from God, you came into my life and I cannot tell you how you brightened it. You were the granddaughter I never had, the perfect companion, someone young to laugh with me and be my friend. Someone I could indulge and pamper a little. Someone who listened to my endless silly chatter and laughed along with me at my own foolishness. You made my days complete and I would have been a lonelier woman without you.

I wanted to help you find yourself again, even though I knew it would mean you would leave me. I wanted to keep you with me always, but even I am not that selfish, and when you found the Villa Mimosa and its link with the past, I thought I knew how to help you. Then my poor little orphans came along and completed the picture, because I knew then that even if I could not give you back your past, I could give you a future.

I enjoyed my life, dear Bea, so do not mourn me too long. Now I want you to enjoy yours. My attorney will take care of everything for you . . .

Your dear friend and surrogate grandmother,
*   Millie Fenwick*

Bea looked sadly at the attorney. 'She was so good,' she said quietly. 'A true friend.'

'She was indeed a good woman,' Hartley agreed. 'Most people only saw her frivolous façade, they never knew how many charities benefited from her generosity – and always anonymously. But now, Miss French, to the contents of Mrs Fenwick's will.'

He cleared his throat, looking at her over the top of his half-spectacles as he said, 'Mrs Fenwick wanted you to have the Villa Mimosa. She did not leave it to you in her will, she had already purchased it in your name. She made it clear from the very beginning that she wanted this house to be yours and yours alone. She says here, that she hopes it will bring you everything you ever hoped it would, including happiness.'

Bea's eyes widened with shock. She was too astonished to say anything.

'Mrs Fenwick also left you the sum of five million dollars, because, as she said – she wants you to have a future, since you have no past.'

'*Five million dollars*.'

'Exactly. But there is a condition: Mrs Fenwick wants you to take responsibility for the children. She asked that you bring them up as if they were your own. She felt that by doing so she was *ensuring* you had a future. You would have a home, a family and sufficient money to provide for your lifestyle. After further substantial bequests to universities and hospitals and various charities, and of items of jewellery – both to you and to Dr Forster, the remainder of Mrs Fenwick's fortune, amounting to around two hundred and fifty million dollars, is to be placed in trust for the children. Scott and Julie Fenwick.'

Later that day, after the attorney had left, Bea told Nick her news. 'Millie was sorry for me, not having a past,' she said tearfully. 'So she tried to give me a future. And now look at me, the chatelaine of the Villa Mimosa, "mother" to two kids who barely know me.'

'And a *millionaire*,' Nick said, stunned. '*And* you are the "mother" of two *extremely rich* little kids.'

'My God, Nick. What shall I do?' she asked, as the facts finally penetrated her aching head.

Nick put his hand under her chin. He lifted her face, smiling encouragingly at her. 'Do what you always do,' he said, 'call Phyl.' Despite her sadness Bea laughed. 'After that,' he continued, 'I suggest we crack open a bottle of champagne and drink a toast to your dear good friend and surrogate grandmother, Millie Fenwick.'

Bea tried calling Phyl's number endlessly, but still only got the answering machine. Worried, she placed a call to the San Francisco Police Department and asked to speak to Detective Mahoney.

Mahoney picked up his phone on the first ring. 'Yeah?' he said, sipping his third cup of coffee in half an hour. He propped his feet on his cluttered desk, and tilted his chair, teetering back and forth lazily. 'Jesus, *Bea French*. How the hell are ya? And *where* the hell are ya? This line's so good I swear you're down the hall.'

'I'm still here, in France,' she said. 'At the Villa Mimosa. Oh, Detective Mahoney,' she wailed suddenly, 'Millie's dead and she's left me all this money and two children and I don't know what to do . . . I've been calling and calling Phyl and she's not there and I'm so worried . . .'

Mahoney sat up suddenly alert. 'Okay, honey, take it easy. You just tell me all about it, and then we'll see what to do.'

She spilled out her story and said finally, 'Then I couldn't get hold of Phyl to tell her, and she missed the funeral and now I still can't reach her and, oh Mahoney I'm so worried . . .'

'Fine. Okay, Bea. First thing is don't worry about Phyl. I

happen to know she's with some guy she's crazy about. I guess she forgot to tell you about Mr Hawaii huh? This little vacation was a spur of the moment thing and she just stayed on a bit longer than she'd planned. And second, like you, she's gonna be heartbroken about Millie, and about missing the funeral. That's a tough break, and Phyl not being there made it harder for you.'

'Nick was with me,' Bea said, sounding calmer now. 'He helped.'

'Yeah. Good for Nick. You like him, huh Bea?'

'He's a nice guy,' she said a touch defensively and he laughed.

'Now where have I heard that before? Listen to me, young Bea French. Millie must have loved you a lot to do what she did. Trusting you with those two orphaned kids. She figured it was three of you against the world now, instead of just one. And from the vibes I'm catching about Nick, maybe it's even four. Those sound like pretty good numbers to me. So take it on the chin, babe. Be glad you had Millie's friendship and love.' He grinned and added, 'And after those words of wisdom, I'd better give you the Doc's number in Hawaii. You can call her for the professional answers.'

'Thanks, Detective Mahoney,' she said, sounding relieved.

'*Franco*, please,' he said, smiling. 'I thought we were friends now? After all we've been through together?'

'*Best friends*,' she said fervently.

He grinned. 'Call me if you need me, babe,' he said. 'And maybe I'll get out there to see you all, one of these days.'

Mahoney put down the phone and glanced at the clock. It said seven, straight up. He picked up the receiver again and dialled the Hawaiian number.

'Kalani. Good evening.' An Asian-accented voice responded immediately.

'Yeah, good evening to you. I'd like to speak to Dr Phyl Forster.'

'Yes, sir. And who shall I say is calling her?'

'Tell her it's Franco Mahoney.'

He propped his feet on the desk again and leaned back, smiling, anticipating her surprised voice.

'Who is this?' a man's voice demanded crisply.

He guessed it was Mr Hawaii in person and he jerked upright, interested. 'My name is Franco Mahoney. I wish to speak with Dr Forster.'

'The doctor cannot come to the phone. Do you want to leave a message?'

'Yeah. I do.' Franco raised a quizzical eyebrow. Mr Hawaii sounded like an arrogant bastard. 'Tell her Mahoney called. That's M-A-H-O-N-E-Y,' he spelled slowly.

'It's a common name, Mr Mahoney. I know how to spell it.'

There was acid in his smooth voice and Franco frowned. He was more than an arrogant bastard. He sounded like a first class jerk. 'Great,' he said abruptly. 'Then if you would just ask the lady to call me, any time day or night. It's urgent. And she has my number. Okay?'

'I'll give her the message,' the man said coldly, and then the line went dead.

Mahoney slammed down the receiver. 'Jesus,' he said, astonished. 'The Doc surely knows how to choose 'em.'

He stalked down the hall to the coffee machine, hands thrust in his pockets, staring at the floor, puzzling over his icy exchange of words. 'That is some jealous guy,' he concluded, grabbing his fourth cup of coffee since six-fifteen. And it was still only seven-ten. He had the feeling it would be a long night.

He was right. The first call came almost immediately: an arson attack in the Tenderloin district: the fire was still raging out of control and so far two bodies had been recovered.

He and Benedetti got down there fast, with Benedetti at the wheel of the Chevvy from the police pool, lights flashing and siren blazing. 'I dunno,' Benedetti grinned, satisfied, as the traffic parted for them, 'sometimes it's okay being a cop.'

Mahoney winced as they took yet another red light and swung round the corner with a screech of brakes. 'Yeah. Except maybe y'should consider going back to driving school. Jesus man, look out, will ya!'

Benedetti's grin became even wider as he glanced at his partner. 'What's the matter? You scared, Detective?'

'You betcha I am. With a maniac like you at the wheel. Remind me to ask for a different partner when I get back to the squad room. That way I might live longer.'

They saw the flames four blocks away and screeched to a stop just as the roof caved in in a flurry of sparks and glowing debris. 'God help them, I hope all the Fire Services guys are out of there,' Mahoney muttered.

'It's all over but the shouting,' the Fire Chief told him. 'Two dead so far, and all my men are accounted for. There's no doubt it's arson, there are gasoline-soaked rags all over the place.' He held out a piece of cloth for Mahoney to see.

Mahoney said, 'Put it in the plastic, Benedetti. We'll have it checked.' He scanned the crowd of watchers with narrowed eyes; arsonists almost invariably came to watch their own fires. That was their high. He didn't know what they thought about the people they had just killed, and he didn't care. He just wanted to put them away for as long as possible. But tonight he was unlucky. His famous sixth-sense seemed to have deserted him, and no one he got next to even had the faintest guilty whiff of gasoline on them.

'Strike one,' he said to Benedetti, heading back later, just as the next call crackled over the car radio: a stabbing outside a bar. 'Hey, any messages for me?' Mahoney demanded as they careened off again.

'Nah, nothing,' the Duty Officer said over the radio.

'Just let me know if a Dr Phyl Forster calls, okay,' Mahoney said. 'It's important.'

'Will do. Ten-four,' the Duty Officer signed off.

'You got a new girlfriend?' Benedetti said interestedly. 'I thought it was serious with the Italian chick . . . whats-her-name . . .'

Mahoney sighed. 'For your information women have not been called "chicks" for at least a decade. And the young lady you are referring to still deigns to see me occasionally. When I have the free time.'

'Yeah, you're right, that's the problem. Time. They get tired of waiting for ya, find themselves a guy with more sociable hours. Still, some of the guys manage it to the altar. You going to Connor's nuptials Saturday?'

'Wouldn't miss it,' Mahoney said, as they screeched to a halt again outside the Hot Trash Bar.

The body was lying face-down in the alley surrounded by a crowd of ghoulish onlookers, held back by a couple of uniformed cops. The victim had been mugged coming out of the bar and dragged into the alley where he had been stabbed and his wallet removed. Several witnesses had seen the culprit take off out of the alley and they had a description, but no one was willing to say he had seen the killing. Nobody wanted to get involved.

'Par for the course,' Mahoney sighed. And it was. By midnight the body count from the arson attack, the stabbing and assorted other homicides totalled four, plus one 'almost' hovering between here and eternity in intensive care in the SF General. And the total of suspects behind bars amounted to zero.

He was morosely typing up his reports on the IBM, sipping coffee and munching a cinnamon Danish when the phone rang.

'Yeah?' he snarled tiredly.

'Mahoney? Is that you?'

'Doc.' He dropped the Danish and tucked the receiver under his chin, leaning back, smiling. 'Sure it's me. Who else were you expecting?'

'You sounded so . . . tired.'

'You don't sound too great yourself, for a lady on a vacation.' He thought she sounded subdued and he wondered if arrogant Mr Hawaii was in the room, listening to her conversation.

'I'm fine,' she said a little too briskly. 'I got your message.'

'I'm surprised. The boyfriend didn't seem to like the idea of another guy calling you. A tad possessive, huh?'

'You said it was urgent,' she replied, ignoring his jibe.

'It is. Look, you had better sit down for this one, Doc. It's about your friend Millie.' He told her about Bea calling and about Millie, and what had happened.

He thought Phyl sounded tearful as she said she would never forgive herself for not being there. She told him she would return to San Francisco tomorrow and she would call him when she got back.

Mahoney put the phone down thoughtfully. For a cool, collected lady, she sure sounded uptight. Just like Mr Hawaii.

CHAPTER 23

Phyl put down the phone and looked at Brad sitting across the room from her. He was smoking a cigarette and drinking brandy. The Doberman, still tense as a coiled spring, was sprawled, as always, at his feet.

'Trouble?' he asked lightly, meeting her accusing blue eyes.

'Why didn't you give me the message that Mahoney had called? If I hadn't seen his name written on the pad I would never have known.'

He shrugged. 'I guess it slipped my mind.'

She looked levelly at him. 'I know you better than that. Nothing ever slips your mind. You remember every detail of the family history.'

'That's different,' he said curtly. 'That's important.'

'And telling me that someone wanted to speak to me urgently, was not important?'

He looked challengingly at her. 'Well, was it?'

'You didn't tell me because it was a man calling.'

'I don't like *anyone* calling you here. You should have respected my privacy. You should not have given him this number.'

She stared, unbelieving, at him. 'I can't just disappear. I have patients, things happen . . .'

Brad suddenly stabbed out the cigarette and leapt to his feet. The dog followed, bristling. He grabbed her by the shoulders, thrusting his face into hers. He said angrily, 'I told you before, *nothing* is more important than you and me. *You just don't listen.*' She heard the dog growl softly in the background as he added, 'When you are with *me*, Phyl, I expect total devotion. *No one else matters.* Why don't you understand that?'

'You're crazy,' she retorted, pushing him angrily away.

He grabbed her by the arm, spinning her round to face him. 'Is that all I mean to you? You think I'm *crazy*.' His laugh was bitter. 'I'm probably the most *rational* person you know, Doctor. At least I know what I want from life and I go all out to get it.' His expression changed and he smiled, suddenly gentle, running his hand along her cheek. 'And I want you, my beautiful Phyl,' he murmured, 'my muse, my confessor. Only you.'

Phyl glanced warily up at him; this was more than a lovers' tiff, Brad was crazy with jealousy. 'I have to leave first thing in the morning,' she said coldly, pulling away from him.

'But Phyl, why?' He shook his head, looking boyishly bewildered. 'We were so happy here together. Please, don't spoil it. Don't leave me. You see,' he added, almost pathetically, '*I need you.*'

Phyl hesitated; he had done one of those sudden about-changes and he was his old charming self again. Then she remembered poor Millie. 'A friend of mine has died suddenly,' she said in a shaky voice. 'I have to go back.'

'Phyl.' He looked shocked. 'I'm so sorry. I didn't realise.'

'Well, now you do.'

She left him and walked to her room. She heard him following her and the Doberman following him.

He stood in the doorway with the dog crouched next to him, watching her pack. Tears for Millie were spilling down her face. 'I'll fly you back myself,' he said penitently. 'I'll go with you to the funeral. You can come back here, to get over it.'

'It's too late, Brad. The funeral is already over.'

'Then why do you need to go?'

She sighed, exasperated. 'It's complicated. There is a patient involved. I have to talk to her. She needs me.'

'I told you, so do I. *Need you.*'

Phyl stopped folding clothes into the suitcase and looked at him standing in the doorway. There was a wild, desperate look in Brad's eyes as they met hers, and she knew he meant it. She sighed, he was obviously sorry. She guessed a little jealousy was okay, but his still bordered on the unreasonable. She went over to him and put her hands on his shoulders, looking deep into his eyes. 'You're a fool to be so jealous,' she said softly. 'You know I would stay if I could.'

'I guess so,' he said reluctantly. He pulled her to him. 'Who is this Mahoney whose number you know so well?'

'Just a friend,' she replied, sighing.

Brad clamped his arms round her, holding her so tight she cried out. 'I don't want you to have any friends,' he whispered in her ear. 'I don't want you to have anyone but me in your life.' A foreboding shiver ran up her spine. From the icy tone of his voice, she was sure he meant it.

In bed later, she watched Brad sleeping. He lay on his back, his arms and legs flung wide. With his bronzed, firm-muscled body and silky blond hair, she thought he looked like a statue of a young Greek god. Beautiful, but somehow defenceless. She remembered their fight and his menacing face close to hers; he had looked so different then from the innocently sleeping man beside her. Phyl shivered again, frightened, thinking about it. She leaned on her elbow, staring into his face, and for the first time in their relationship, the professional part of her began to wonder about him.

Phyl unlocked the door of her apartment and kicked it shut behind her. She threw her bags onto the floor, and hurled herself onto the sofa. Then she stretched wearily.

She thought that only a few months ago this apartment had seemed like her fortress, her refuge against the world. It had been tranquil, silent, orderly. Her life had a calm routine, a pattern that she enjoyed. Well, maybe *enjoyed* was not exactly true, but at least she had been in charge of her own emotions, even if she hadn't allowed them to surface much.

Then she had gone and let her guard down and now look at her: involved with a crazily-jealous man whose troubles she suspected ran even deeper than mere jealousy. Her good friend had died and she hadn't even made it to the funeral. And her patient and protégée had been forced to face a crisis alone, when she had given her word she would be there for her.

Phyl sighed angrily. Her carefully controlled world was crumbling at the edges and she knew it. It was time she pulled herself together.

She picked up the phone and called Bea. To her surprise she sounded cheerful and relaxed.

'I called you in Hawaii, but I couldn't get through,' Bea said. 'I spoke with Franco though, and he was a great help. He's such a nice guy, Phyl, so straight ahead. He helped me sort out my priorities.'

'I'm just sorry I let you down,' Phyl said. 'And I'm desperately sad that I missed saying goodbye to Millie. How could I have been so stupid as to not let you know where I was . . .'

'It's okay, I understand, and I'm sure Millie would, too.

Besides, Nick helped me. He's been like a rock, Phyl. Someone to lean on. I don't know how I would have coped without him. He's here now, helping me with the kids. Scott and Julie,' she added.

They talked about the inheritance and the children, and Phyl said it was typical of Millie. She offered to fly out to be with her but Bea said she had Nick and for the moment she was okay.

'Just don't forget my promise,' Phyl told her as they said goodbye. 'When you need me, I'll be there. You can count on it.'

Feeling a little better, she wandered into the bedroom, stripping off her clothes as she went, then she stood under the shower, letting the hot water wash away her fatigue. *And her sins*, she thought, wondering what she was going to do about Brad.

He had flown her, silent and grim-faced, from Kalani to Honolulu but she had insisted on taking a commercial flight to San Francisco.

'Why?' he had demanded angrily. She had not told him, but she knew the reason: it was because she had to start picking up the threads of her old independence again. Before things went too far and she lost all control. She could not allow Brad Kane to dominate her life.

At the airport she had reached up to kiss him, but he had stepped angrily back, and she had turned quickly away and hurried through the gate. She felt his eyes burning into her, but she had not looked back. If that was the way Brad wanted things, then she wasn't playing.

She stepped from the shower and wrapped herself in an oversized white terry robe, then wandered into the kitchen, wondering why the apartment seemed so empty. She smiled, wondering how she could have forgotten. Of course. The cat.

She dialled Mahoney's home number but there was no reply, so she called him at the precinct. 'I'm back,' she said, unexpectedly eager for the sound of his reassuring voice.

'So you are,' he agreed.

'I spoke with Bea,' she said. 'I think I straightened things out. About not being there for her when I said I would.'

'Right,' he said coolly.

Phyl held the receiver away from her, staring at it, frowning. What the hell was wrong with Mahoney. 'Are you okay?' she asked.

'Sure. It's just been one of those weeks. You want me to drop off Coco? Or maybe you're planning another vacation?'

'Hey, Mahoney,' she said, startled, 'what's wrong? I thought we were friends.'

There was a long silence, then he said, 'I thought Mr Hawaii might be there with you, that's all.'

She laughed, relieved. 'Well, he's not. He's home. Alone. On his island.'

'Great. So what are you doing tonight? You got a hot date with someone else?'

'No, I do not have a hot date. And I'm not doing anything. Unless of course, you were intending to invite me somewhere?' She suddenly wanted to see him. 'Mahoney,' she said into the strained silence, 'the treat's on me. All you have to do is name the time and place.'

'My place,' he said suddenly. 'Eight o'clock. And wear something fancy. It's a wedding.'

'You're not getting married?'

'Not unless you're asking me, Doc. No, it's a colleague. I couldn't make the ceremony, but this is an Irish-Italian wedding and there's gonna be dancing and carousing and a hell of a lot of drinking, all night long. See you at eight.'

She wore a new red lace dress, short and clinging, with a

wide neckline that left her shoulders bare. She swept up her hair and since she had no fresh flowers, she tucked a big red silk rose into it. She thrust her suntanned feet into high-heeled red sandals and flung a black silk shawl around her shoulders, then looked, satisfied at herself in the mirror. Her spirits suddenly soared. She didn't know any more what she felt about Brad and his crazy jealousy. All she knew was, she was glad it was Mahoney she was dressing up for tonight, and not him.

'Well, look at you,' Mahoney marvelled, opening the door to her. 'You look like my high school prom date.'

'I should have known better than to bother,' Phyl sighed resignedly, walking up the stairs.

'I see you took my advice on the colour,' he added mockingly. 'And on you red looks good. In fact,' he said, eyeing her long suntanned legs and smooth shoulders appreciatively as she slipped off her shawl, 'on you it looks terrific.'

She twirled for him, smiling. 'Am I really okay? You said dressy but I wasn't sure.'

He shook his head admiringly. 'Doc, let me tell you Connors just got married today. But when that hot Irishman sets eyes on my scarlet woman, you may find you've caused the quickest divorce in history.'

She laughed. 'You look pretty fancy yourself tonight, Mahoney.' She fingered the satin lapels of his tuxedo. 'Like a late-night talk show host. Or maybe a political candidate? Or perhaps the next Mayor . . . ?'

'Not this week, babe. It's been a toughie. It must be the summer madness. It happens every year about this time. There's a mini-heatwave and people go crazy and start killing each other. There are more bodies stacked in the city morgue than you or I would care to think about. And not one of them in the "solved" account.'

He took a couple of glasses from the cupboard and a bottle of champagne out of the refrigerator. She watched him, under her lashes, enjoying his panther walk and the way he looked in his tuxedo.

'Talking of butts,' she said, with a cheeky grin, 'yours is looking pretty good, Mahoney.'

'So I've been told,' he said coolly, pouring the wine.

She caught sight of the champagne label and said, impressed, 'You went to all this expense just for me?'

'Nothing but the best,' he replied, lifting his glass in a mock toast. 'Oh, by the way, Coco is asleep on my bed. You've been away so long she's almost forgotten you.'

'Well, I haven't forgotten her,' she said, rattled.

'So? What's with Mr Hawaii?'

She lowered her eyes, embarrassed. 'I haven't come here to discuss my private life.'

'Why not? You got something to hide?'

'Mahoney!' she glared at him, exasperated.

'You want *me* to talk about him then? I thought he was cold – *icy* – in fact. I also thought he was rude, arrogant and possessive. I thought he was just too fuckin' jealous for his own good.' He looked at her and added, 'Or yours.'

'Mahoney!' she exclaimed again, her blue eyes blazing.

He shrugged. 'Well, you asked me . . .'

'No I did not!' Their eyes met and she began to laugh. 'Oh hell, you're right about him,' she admitted finally. 'He is possessive and he is jealous.' Her smile was replaced by a worried look. 'In fact, Mahoney, sometimes he scares me, he's so jealous.'

'Does he have any reason to be?'

She shook her head. 'You know what's really worrying me? He thinks I look like his mother. *And I do*.'

Mahoney shrugged, not understanding. 'So what's wrong with that?'

'It's a bit creepy that's all. He hated her. He told me all these horror stories, about how promiscuous she was, how she flaunted her affairs. He said everyone knew about her. She even drove one guy to kill himself...'

Mahoney whistled, impressed. 'It doesn't take a top psychiatrist to figure that one out, Doc.'

'It's not like that,' she said defensively. 'Most of the time he's charming, warm and sensitive. He's handsome, urbane, a respected businessman, his ranch is his life...'

'He just hates his mother that's all,' Mahoney wasn't smiling now. 'Look Phyl, if you *feel* there is something wrong, then believe me there *is*. Trust that old gut instinct.'

'You mean he's really thinking about his mother when he's in bed with me?' she asked in a small frightened voice.

'Why didn't you ask *him* that?'

She shook her head. 'I did, almost. I asked if he wanted me because I looked like Rebecca and he just laughed. He said it wasn't true. I have to believe that, Mahoney.'

He nodded. He understood. Phyl was a woman who did not give her favours lightly. Even though she was a psychiatrist, the woman in her was unable to accept that Brad might have some perverted reason for wanting her in his bed.

'Anyway, I left him. At the airport,' she shrugged. 'He was mad because I wouldn't let him fly me home. So I guess it's goodbye.'

Mahoney grinned. 'Then there's no need to worry.' She was still frowning and he said, 'Okay, tell me your next problem.'

She said sadly, 'Oh, Mahoney, I wasn't there for Bea.'

'True. But she has come to terms with that. It was just circumstances.'

'It was *unforgivable*. Besides being my friend, she's my patient. I behaved irresponsibly.'

'Hey, we're all human.'

'*I'm a doctor!*' she yelled, still angry with herself. '*I should have been there.*'

'Listen, it worked out,' he said soothingly. 'Everything's okay. No more breast-beating, all right?'

Phyl raised tearful blue eyes to him. 'I missed Millie's funeral.'

He sat beside her and put his arm round her shoulders. She nestled her head in the crook of his arm and he heard her sniffing back the tears. 'Go ahead, babe,' he said, sighing exaggeratedly. 'Let it all out. You'll feel better.'

He heard her giggle through the tears and she said, 'Oh stop it, Mahoney,' pushing him away.

'Your mascara's running,' he said looking critically at her.

'Ohh, oh damn.'

'A good curseword like *damn* can surely relieve your feelings,' he said mockingly.

'Prick,' she retorted.

He laughed. 'That's my girl. Come on, Doc. Fix your face. We've got a wedding to go to.'

The celebrations had begun at four-thirty that afternoon at the Hibernian Banqueting Rooms and by the time Mahoney and Phyl arrived, around nine, the place was jumping. The band, augmented by several members of the SFPD were blasting Beach Boys' hits, and half the room was singing along. The dance-floor was crowded and the bar was five deep, and fresh supplies of Italian goodies were being ferried across to the buffet that ran the length of one wall. Irish and Italian flags celebrating the union hung like banners from the ceiling and swags of red roses were intertwined with shamrocks. The bride, gorgeous in white silk and lace and ten yards of sequin-scattered veil was sitting with her new husband and their families at the top table, and Mahoney pulled Phyl through the crowd to pay their respects.

'Connors, you old bastard, she finally made you an honest man,' he said, hugging his colleague. He looked admiringly at the bride, 'I always told Connors you were too good for an old mick like him. You look wonderful, baby. A beautiful bride.'

They laughed, and he took Phyl's hand and introduced her. 'This is Phyllida Forster, known as Phyl,' he said. She threw him a quick amazed glance, wondering how he had known her proper name, and suddenly found herself engulfed in a bearhug from the bridegroom.

'Jeez Mahoney,' he said admiringly. 'Where'd you find her? I tell ya, she's too classy for an old mick like yourself.'

'But you're *Dr* Phyl,' the bride, Sandra, exclaimed.

'Not tonight,' Phyl assured her. 'Tonight I'm just this old mick's date.'

They laughed and Connors said, 'Save me a dance for later, Dr Phyl. I'll let you analyse me any time.'

Most of Mahoney's shift were propping up the bar. Benedetti saw them coming. He nudged the guy next to him and said, awed, 'Look what Mahoney has caught himself.' They turned as one man to look and appreciative grins appeared on their faces.

'Whaddya have to do to get her here, Mahoney,' somebody yelled, 'put the cuffs on her?'

'Okay, wise-ass,' Mahoney said, 'we all understand you don't know how to behave in front of a lady, but we'd appreciate it if you would try. Allow me to introduce Phyl Forster.'

'The Doc,' Benedetti said reverently. 'Can I ask ya one question, ma'am? What the hell are you doing with a jerk like Mahoney? There's half the SFPD here tonight be happy to take over from him, any time you say.'

'Thank you, guys,' Phyl said demurely, accepting a barstool at the counter and a host of compliments and banter from Mahoney's colleagues.

'She's one of us tonight,' somebody said, pinning one of the mock SFPD detective badges that decorated the tables on her. 'Clinton,' he yelled to the barman, 'a drink for Detective Forster.'

'So,' Benedetti said, moving closer, beer-belly bulging over a turquoise cummerbund, 'tell us how you happened to meet Mahoney.'

'It's a long story,' Mahoney said, 'and too racy for your delicate ears.'

'How about a dance, Doc?' someone else said, whirling her onto the floor to the beat of 'La Bamba', until someone else tapped him on the shoulder and took over.

Half an hour later Phyl finally made it back to the bar. She sipped a glass of water, fanning her hot face with her hand.

'All right you guys, enough is enough,' Mahoney warned. 'The lady needs food.'

He took her hand and led her through the crowd, stopping every couple of minutes to introduce her to his friends.

The buffet tables were laden with every kind of seafood, as well as enormous lasagnas, and cheese gnocchi, pâté-stuffed ravioli, eggplant parmigiana and stuffed tomatoes, enormous salads and half a dozen different kinds of breads, and bottles of red wine. That was on the Italian side. The Irish had poached salmon and Galway oysters, colcannon and soda bread, and Guinness and Paddys. The tables were decorated with flags and shamrocks and roses, and the hospitality seemed never-ending.

Mahoney piled Phyl's plate with goodies, grabbed a bottle of wine and led her to a quiet corner. 'I'll bet you haven't eaten today,' he said, sliding an oyster into his mouth.

'You're right,' she said, contentedly doing the same.

They ate hungrily for a few minutes and then she said, 'I like your friends.'

'Yeah, they're good guys.' He grinned at her. 'I guess they're right though. What is a girl like you doing with a beat-up old cop like me?'

Her eyes met his and she said, 'First, you're not old. Or if you are then that makes me old too and I refuse to accept that. Second, you're surely not beat-up, Mahoney.' She reached out and ran her fingers lightly over his face. 'You must be the department pin-up.'

'Yeah, well anything seems good after Benedetti and his beer belly.'

'And third, you are a good cop, Mahoney. I know that.'

'Thanks for the compliments, lady.' Their eyes locked. 'Just hold on there for a sec,' he said finally. He stood up and threaded his way through the crowd to the bandstand.

When he got back minutes later, the band swung into 'Lady In Red'.

'They're playing our song,' he said, holding out his hand to her.

The lights dimmed and couples smooched round under the flickering old-fashioned mirrored ball in the centre of the ceiling. Mahoney wrapped his arms tighter around her and Phyl gave a happy little sigh. 'You're right,' she murmured in his ear, 'this is like the high school prom. I haven't slow-danced like this for years.'

'Then you don't know what you're missing,' he whispered back.

'Your friends are watching us,' she said.

'Let's give the lecherous old buzzards something to talk about.' He pulled her even closer. She tilted her head back to look at him, laughing.

'Mahoney . . .'

'*Franco*, please. After all this is an intimate moment . . .'

'That's just what I was going to mention . . . I mean I was wondering if the old Mae West saying was right . . . "Is that a bunch of keys in your pocket or are you just pleased to see me?"'

Mahoney unclamped one arm from around her. He grinned as he removed the handcuffs from his pants pocket. 'Sorry to disappoint you, Doc. But if that's what you want, I'd be happy to oblige.'

'Oh, Mahoney,' she said laughing, wrapping her arms round his neck. 'I haven't had this kind of silly fun since . . . well it's so long ago I don't even remember.'

'Me, too,' he said tenderly, looking down at her smooth dark head. 'Has anyone ever told you you're a damn pretty woman, Phyllida Forster?'

'How ever did you find out my name?' she demanded. 'I never tell anyone.'

'You forget, I'm a cop. I have access to such things as names and dates and addresses and telephone numbers.' He grinned. 'It's on your driver's licence.'

They danced for a long time until there was a tap on his shoulder and the bridegroom, Connors, took over. Mahoney whirled away with the bride and Phyl didn't see him again for another hour, while she danced her feet off with young Irish cops and tarantellad with old Italian poppas. Back at the bar again she laughed at the jokes and banter and stories, queening it from her barstool surrounded by her admirers. And she was having such a good time she didn't even think of Brad Kane.

Just before midnight the detectives decided to shift base to Hanran's, their local hangout near the Hall of Justice. Phyl swept into Hanran's flanked by San Francisco's finest, and the outgoing midnight shift, propping up the bar, turned to whistle and stare. 'Here babe, sit by me.' 'Come on honey, you don't know what you're missing.' 'Drop Mahoney, lady, I can do it better,' they yelled, making way for her.

'Normally,' Phyl said cocking her chin mockingly at them, 'normally, fellas, I would say you are the biggest bunch of sexist pigs I have ever met.' They yelled and stomped and she held up her hand for silence. 'But,' she said with a smile in her voice, 'tonight I think you're paying me the greatest compliment a man can pay a woman. And I want you to know I appreciate it.'

'Yeah, Doc,' they yelled, applauding and signalling the bartender to put up more of whatever she was drinking.

It was three in the morning when Mahoney finally drove her home. Her head was on his shoulder and she was grumbling contentedly about the discomfort of such a position in a Mustang. 'For Crissakes, Mahoney, can't you get a proper car?' she asked sleepily.

'You are talking about my pride and joy,' he said in a hurt tone.

'I know all about your pride and joy,' she murmured. 'Don't try and pretend those were really the handcuffs, Mahoney.'

He laughed as he parked outside her apartment building. 'I should never have let you near those guys,' he said. 'They're coarsening you.'

'Maybe that's what I need,' she sighed, straightening up. 'A little coarseness.'

'Just for flavour,' he agreed.

'Like oregano, or rosemary . . .' she murmured as he held

the door open. She swung her legs out and wriggled forward, holding up her hands. 'Help?' she said, smiling at him.

He took her hands, then slid his arm around her waist as they walked up the steps. She turned her face up to him, eyes closed, and said dreamily, 'A good night kiss, Mahoney?' He laughed and put his lips lingeringly on hers. 'Mmmm,' she said, 'very very nice.'

'I'd better see you to your apartment, Doc,' he said as she yawned and leaned against him. 'It's been a long night.'

'So it has,' she agreed. And then with a sunny smile, 'And such a fun one. I haven't had such a good time in years.'

'I'm glad,' he said, taking her keys and unlocking the door.

Brad Kane's Porsche was parked half a block further up the street. He leaned forward, watching, his eyes boring into them as they walked together into the building.

He took a Gitane from the almost-empty pack and lit it, dragging deeply on it. He knew which her apartment was, and he watched her windows, groaning with despair as the lights finally came on. He stubbed the cigarette out viciously. He had seen Rebecca behave just that way, so many times. Giddy, flirtatious, leading men on. She was just like his mother after all. She was Rebecca.

His eyes fixed on her window, he leaned forward, tensely, watching, waiting.

Phyl kicked off her shoes and walked towards the kitchen. 'Coffee?'

Mahoney shook his head. 'Why not just have a glass of water, Doc, and then go to bed. You'll feel a new woman in the morning.'

She heaved a happy sigh, 'I kind of like the woman I am right now, Mahoney.'

'Good.' He walked over and dropped a kiss on her cheek. 'You know what?' he said seriously.

'What?' Her eyes were very blue and innocent.

'You really are a very pretty woman,' he said, smiling as he turned and walked to the door.

'Thanks, Mahoney,' she called after him. 'For tonight.' He waved as he closed the door behind him.

She was smiling as she sauntered into her bedroom, shedding her clothes as she went. And she was still smiling as she fell instantly asleep. With her make-up on. Something else she hadn't done in years.

Mahoney had noticed the black Porsche 938 parked half a block away when he had driven past earlier. The cop reflex had noted that it was the only car on the no-parking street and there was a man in it, and he had wondered automatically what he was up to. It was still there, and as he climbed into the Mustang and switched on the ignition he saw the Porsche's lights go on. He waited for the guy to take off and pass him so he could grab his number and run a check on him, just in case he was up to mischief, but instead the Porsche backed up another half-block and made a quick right down a side street.

Mahoney shrugged; he was off-duty and besides he wasn't really up to tackling villains in expensive Porsches tonight. The guy was probably some pricey private detective making a packet staking out an erring wife or husband. What the hell, it was none of his business anyway.

CHAPTER 24

Julie hurled herself into the swimming pool after Scott, sending an avalanche of water over Poochie, prancing along the edge, barking warnings at them.

'Silly old dog,' she yelled scooping more water over him, shrieking with delight as he shook himself in a wild flurry of droplets. And shrieking some more as Scotty hauled himself out of the pool and then jumped back in again almost on top of her.

She went under and came up laughing and choking, searching for Scotty to get her revenge. She waved eagerly at Bea, sitting by the pool, watching them. She thought Bea was the prettiest girl ever, and she had already decided she wanted to be just like her when she grew up.

Bea had laughed when she had told her. 'I'm not sure that's possible, sweetheart,' she had said – she always called her sweetheart and Julie liked that. And Nick called her Jules and she liked that, too. 'I think from the photographs I've seen you are going to look just like your mom. And that's a compliment, Miss Julie, if ever there was one, because your mommy was a very pretty lady.'

Oh and she was, Julie thought fervently, leaning her chin on the curved edge of the pool and letting her legs float out behind her. Mom was just the prettiest of all. She thought how much her mommy would have loved it here, the blue skies and sunshine. Her mother had hated those cold grey

Ohio winters and, come to think of it, shovelling snow had not been one of her own favourite pastimes. She loved it here, and she knew Scotty did, too. The only thing was he kept reminding her that it was only temporary, 'like a vacation', he said. 'One day they'll send us back to Ohio and you'll see we'll end up in that orphanage after all.'

'No they won't,' Julie had said, stubbornly, but still she was scared.

Scotty had said, ''Course they will, they are not our relatives. We are nothing to them, Julie. Just a couple of kids they are looking after. Guardians, that's all they are.'

But she still didn't want to believe it. And she didn't want to go back home because there was no home any more. And besides, she didn't want to leave Bea.

Something told her Bea was different. She was hurting too, she sensed it. And she liked that little sneaky feeling of warmth creeping into her own heart again, into her life. Sometimes hours went by without her thinking of what had happened.

Julie fastened her eyes on Bea, watching her. She didn't ever want to let go of her.

Bea thought Millie must have known her better than she knew herself, she had fallen so neatly into her new role. She was watching the children hurling themselves tirelessly in and out of the water. They had been doing it for hours and the dog, Poochie, ran anxiously along the edge, barking worriedly. Every now and then they turned and splashed him, making him dance on his hind legs with excitement and bark even louder.

The whine of a lawnmower came from somewhere in front of the villa, and the new Portuguese housekeeper's shrill voice fought with the squawk of the green African parrot Scotty had begged Nick to buy last week when they had gone to the pet store to look for a couple of parakeets.

The man in the store had said it was a talker and that it knew half a dozen songs, but it had remained stubbornly silent for the first five days. Until the dog barked and it suddenly cursed in fluent French.

The Villa Mimosa had come back to life and she only wished Millie could be there to see it. The old brooding feeling had disappeared and now it was filled with light and the sound of children's laughter and squabbles, with music, squawking parrots and barking dogs. There were roller-blades on the terraces and bicycles in the hall and a scatter of toys and T-shirts and beach towels, as well as the aroma of something good cooking in the kitchen.

Scotty and Julie Fenwick were behaving more like normal kids again, though there were nights when she would go in to tuck them up, and she would find them huddled together in Scott's bed, with the tracks of tears on their innocent sleeping faces. She would carry Julie back to her own bed, and the exhausted child would lift her heavy eyelids and give her a direct searching gaze that struck to her very soul. She knew Julie was looking to see if it was her mother kissing her goodnight.

'It's only me,' she would whisper and the little girl would sigh deeply, half-choking on a sob as she stuck her thumb comfortingly in her mouth. She gripped Bea's hand tightly and Bea would stroke back her damp hair and sit quietly until the child finally slept the deep sleep of exhaustion.

Scott never cried in front of her, but sometimes she would watch him, disappearing up the hill towards the grotto. She would see his small crouched figure, perched on the rocks, staring out to sea, and she guessed he had sought solitude to cry away his pain.

She and Nick were doing their best to make life normal for them. They had established a routine with a French tutor for an hour each morning. Then they would go to the market in Cannes or Nice or Antibes and maybe have lunch in one of the cafés. Later, after a rest, they would go to the beach, or swim at the pool, or Nick might take them out in the little boat he had bought, putt-putting round the harbour.

In the fall, they would begin school, and by then, she hoped, maybe they would be more able to put the past behind them and become normal kids again. Meanwhile, they were still fragile from shock and grief, and unsure of their new way of life.

Bea felt a world away from sudden death in a ravine, from murder and a lost past, from no-person to someone with an identity. And she thanked Millie every day for her new life. But the terror of not knowing who she was and why someone had wanted her dead still haunted her. She would wake from some troubled dream that she was falling, down in to that never-ending dark tunnel and almost think she had the answer. But when she blinked herself awake, sweating with fright, it was gone.

Poochie pranced over to her, backside and tail wiggling enthusiastically. She thought Poochie had been a godsend, the kids adored him. The dog looked at her, its intelligent brown eyes shining with joy at the surprise of still being alive. 'We're survivors, you and me, old boy,' she said, rubbing his curly head affectionately.

She thought of Nick, out searching for the elusive bank vault with Nanny Beale's secrets, and she almost hoped he wouldn't find it. At this peaceful moment, life seemed perfect just as it was. She had her home, the children, and she had Nick. She was afraid of the past. She did not want to know about that other girl that was her. She felt safe as Bea French. He could never find her here and finish the job he had failed at before. It was only on those long restless lonely nights she wasn't so sure.

The children called for her to come on in the pool, yelling with delight when Poochie leapt in after her, paddling round with a bewildered grin on his funny face.

They were playing a wild game of water-volley-ball, shrieking with laughter when the telephone rang. Bea climbed from the pool to answer it.

'Nick?' she said, smiling.

'How did you know it was me?'

'It's simple. Nobody else calls. At least not at this time of day. Are you coming over for supper?'

'I'll be there about seven. Can we have dinner alone tonight? Without the kids, I mean. I need to talk to you.'

'Sure. They eat at six anyway. They're always starving by then. But what do you want to talk about?'

'I found it, Bea. Nanny Beale's safe deposit. We were right, there were other documents. I'm bringing them with me. I want you to read them.'

As she put down the phone Bea thought he had sounded ominously quiet, not the least bit triumphant at his find. She wondered worriedly what was wrong.

When Nick arrived the children swarmed all over him, begging him to go for a bike ride or rollerblade with them along the terraces, or run down the hill to the sea.

'Let's go fishing,' Scotty yelled excitedly.

'No, let's ride our bikes to the very top of the hill and then we can coast all the way down,' Julie shouted louder.

'Not tonight, guys,' Nick ruffled Scott's shaggy hair and gave Julie a bearhug and shooed them affectionately from the room. 'I've got to talk to Bea about something.'

They ran off to chat to Jacinta in the kitchen and he looked at Bea.

'It wasn't easy to get hold of this,' he said, taking several manilla envelopes from his briefcase. 'I must have conned

267

my way through fifty banks, pretending I'd made a mistake every time they looked suspiciously at me because the key didn't belong to them. I gave them this phony laugh and said, "Silly old me, I've got so many of these, I always forget where I've put things."'

Bea smiled. 'Until the final one.'

'Until I finally have what we were searching for.' He put the papers in front of her. 'This is Marie-Antoinette's letter to her son Johnny. And I can tell you it makes harrowing reading.'

Bea looked doubtfully at him, 'Do you really think we should be doing this?' She felt as though they were intruding into a dead woman's secrets, into private things she might never have wanted other eyes to see.

'I certainly do. For your sake and mine. You believe there is a link somewhere here with your past. And I want to solve this mystery for my book. It all happened long ago, Bea. We're not hurting anyone reading this.'

'I suppose you're right,' she agreed, but she was scared. 'Only Nick, I don't really want to know about my past any more. Let's forget about the past, let's leave it alone. I'm happy the way things are.'

Nick gripped her hand comfortingly. 'You must have a family somewhere, Bea. Relatives who are looking for you, wondering about you. You had a life before this and you have to find it, even if you decide never to go back to it. You have a responsibility to yourself and to your family.'

Bea sighed as she reluctantly began to read Marie-Antoinette Leconte's letter. She knew he was right.

My beloved son, Jean,

It is my dearest wish that you will never read this letter, because then it means I will never know you, I will not be there to hold my baby in my arms, to watch you grow, to count your birthdays and help you climb the rocky path of life. But if I cannot be there, then when you are old enough, I want you to know the truth, about myself and about your father, Archer Kane.

First I will tell you about myself, so you may know your mother a little better. Gossip will tell you that I was not a pretty woman. I know their mocking name for me – la Célibataire – and though I always pretended not to care, I was hurt. I yearned to be pretty and glamorous, like the smart beauties I used to see at dinner and at the casinos and in the cafés, but they never even spoke to me. How can I explain that inside I felt beautiful? But to them I was just the plain, rich woman who never belonged. And I was lonely.

Archer Kane recognised my loneliness. He was a handsome man, as fair and golden as I was dark and sallow. He looked like a young Greek god to me, the lonely Célibataire.

He was a man who felt completely at home in the new laissez-faire atmosphere of the Riviera; there was a loucheness that suited him; plenty of easy women, drink and money. But, even I knew there were as many fortune-hunters looking for women as there were women looking for lovers, and to capture a rich good-looking woman was not easy. These women were older and worldly-wise and they knew a fortune-hunter when they saw one. For them an affair meant fun, a few gifts, a whiff of passion – and on to the next.

I noticed him of course, how could I not? He was the handsome young American, always at the centre of the crowd lunching on the terrace of the Hôtel de Paris, or in the cafés, or at the casino. I saw him watching me, I caught his eye every now and then and he would always smile politely and bow his head, acknowledging my presence.

I know now, that he was stalking me, that I was already marked out as his victim. He was twenty-seven years old and I was forty-one. I was uneasy with people, shy and plain. He was handsome and in with the social set, and they said he had a big cattle ranch in Hawaii.

I knew all about him, but I had never met him, or any of his acquaintances, until he spoke to me that day. I was sitting at a café table in Cannes, alone as always. I was wearing a wide-brimmed hat to keep the sun from my face, but also to hide my plainness. How can I make you understand how ashamed I was of the way I looked? The Riviera was thronged with beautiful people, all so young and slender and chic, wearing the fashionable new styles that on me looked merely clumsy and stupid.

I remember wondering how Archer had even recognised me, I was so hidden behind my big hat, but I confess I was pleased that he had. More, I was thrilled when this handsome young man introduced himself and asked if he could sit with me for a while. We drank lemonade while he told me about his ranch, chatting sociably. I noticed people glance at us and I blushed with pride that he had singled me out for his attention.

I think he knew from that first blush, that I was his, but nevertheless he courted me assiduously. He invited me to dinners at the best hotels, to lunches at the beach and dancing at the Hôtel de Paris. Though I already owned the silver Rolls, he encouraged me to buy the very latest automobile, an open-topped scarlet Bugatti with dove-grey leather interior that I knew everyone envied as I drove by.

He escorted me to the fashionable shops and salons I had always been too shy to enter, afraid they would make fun of my stocky, full-bosomed figure because all the other women were reed-slim and fashionably breastless. He took me to have my hair bobbed in the new style, encouraged me to try make-up, massages, perfume. Archer Kane made me feel good about myself for the first time in my life. And he knew how to make me feel like a woman.

He was charming, sociable, handsome. The perfect suitor. When we got married a few weeks later, it was a nine-day scandal. I knew what the gossips said – that 'he was just another fortune-hunter who got lucky – but at what a price, because lord knows la Célibataire had been around a long time.' But I didn't care. I was in love and I thought he loved me.

I was prepared to be happy anywhere with him, even on the primitive island he took me to. And even when I saw the famous ranch was nothing much more than a few wild acres. But this was to be my new home, my new life with my handsome adoring husband, and I willingly gave him money so that he could buy more acres and more cattle, and expand the Lodge on Kalani. And also – unknown to me then – to indulge his male lust in Honolulu. Because, as he told me cruelly when I found out and confronted him, he found his own wife old and ugly and unappealing.

The blue eyes that had once gazed so adoringly at me now raked me with contempt; the caresses had become cruel blows, and I soon realised that when he was 'nice' to me it was only because he wanted money. And then I found out I was pregnant.

It was like a miracle for me, a woman of forty-one, having her first child and it brought me the first true happiness I had felt since I had come to Kalani. I did not tell Archer. I waited to see what would happen next.

He finally came to me with some legal documents that he wanted me to sign. He said they gave me an equal share in his ranch, but I saw that they really gave him control over my fortune. I refused to sign them and I was finally forced to face the truth.

Sick and disillusioned and heavy with child, I left him. I returned here, to my old home, the Villa Mimosa, that my beloved father had built for me when I was still his 'little princess', long ago when I still believed – because he told me so often – that I was a pretty girl and that the world was mine. He had built the silver aviary, so that I would always hear the sound of the songbirds that I loved, and the grotto on the hill with the stream, and the fountains so I would hear the music of the water. And he had filled the exquisite gardens with my favourite mimosas whose scent marked my birthday every spring. It was my home and now it became my refuge, I would have my baby there and bring him up in its peace and security. I never wanted to see Archer Kane again.

And then suddenly he arrived. He told me that because of me he was deeply in debt, he would be forced to mortgage his lands. He stood to lose everything: his cattle, his ranch, even his island, unless I give him the money. He promised to go away so I gave it to him, but by now it was obvious I was pregnant. He said he had decided to stay after all. He wanted to be with me, to help me. After all, he said, it was his child, too.

I'm ashamed to confess that, at first, a part of me wanted to believe him. But I could not allow myself to trust him. I wanted nothing to do with him, but he was my husband and there was nothing I could do. I refused to let him near me, I would not go out with him, though he tried to cajole me because, I know now, he wanted us to appear together as the happy couple. At the Villa Mimosa he was always the perfect gentleman, the adoring young husband with the older pregnant wife. He played his cards well: he never even looked at another woman the whole time. And then you were born, my dear son.

You looked so fragile and small, lying there in the crib I had arranged myself, purchasing the soft voile and the lace and ribbons to make it beautiful for you. I had longed for you so much, and now here you were. And I loved you with a mother's devotion.

It had not been an easy birth, remember I was older, and I was still shaken and quite ill, when your father came to see you the next day. He looked at you in your crib and I allowed myself to think for one fleeting moment, that maybe he would love his son and that there was some hope for our happiness. But then I saw from his face that he felt nothing for you. He said you did not even look like him. You were a Leconte not a Kane.

And now, my son, as I write this letter, you are one week old. Today I think you smiled at me, even though Nanny Beale said it was not a real smile yet. You mean everything to me and Archer knows it. There is something in the air here, a crackle of tension permeating the house, though he is still playing the role of the charming husband. I do not trust him, and next week when I am stronger and can go downstairs I intend to confront him. I shall tell him that I mean to divorce him on the grounds of his numerous adulteries. I will tell him that he will not receive another cent from me. And that you, dear little Jean, will inherit everything.

And that is the reason I am writing this letter, which I hope Nanny Beale will never have to give to you.

Archer is a dangerous man. He is ruthless and uncaring. I want you to understand that if anything bad happens to me, no matter what he claims or says, it will not have been an accident. And nor would I ever kill myself. You are too important to me for that. I am hoping, always *hoping my dear son, that I will be here to watch you grow up and to share your life. And I want you to know that I love you . . . your devoted mother . . .*

'So the Foreigner really did kill her,' Bea said shocked, looking at Nick.

'And he got away with it,' Nick said. 'At least now we know his name. Archer Kane. Still, it all happened too long ago for retribution.' He shuffled the other papers, looking at her. 'I want you to read this later. It's written by Johnny Leconte. It's his own story, telling what happened.' He hesitated. 'I thought you might prefer to read it when you are alone, without all the distractions of the children, and dogs and parrots and supper.'

He put the papers back into the envelope and took her hand. 'Let's take the kids for a walk,' he said smiling, trying to cheer her up. 'Buy them some ice cream.'

'*Ice cream!*'

The children hurtled through the door and Bea laughed at them, 'You must have invisible antennae tuned to words like ice cream, and french fries and Nintendo . . .'

'Can Poochie come too?' Julie said.

'Sure he can.' Bea looked at the pair of them, in their grubby T-shirts and shorts with the new shine of happiness on their faces, and she felt sorry for Marie-Antoinette Leconte who never had the chance to give her son Johnny a dog and take him for ice cream. 'Wash your hands and faces and put on clean shirts,' she said, smiling as she envisaged the clean shirts soon to be liberally daubed with ice cream.

'You know what,' Nick said with a grin. 'You make a great mom.'

Bea looked at him, at his almost-good-looking face, at his nice grey eyes that always held a hint of a smile, and his good lean body. Nick had shared all her problems about

274

her mysterious past; he had shared her sorrow over Millie's death, and he had helped her with the children. Their friendship had grown deeper and she was aware that was the other reason he wanted her to find the truth about her past: because he needed to know if there was somebody else in her life, someone who mattered, a lover, or a husband. When she was the real person she used to be and not Bea French.

She smiled as she kissed him. 'That's to say thank you,' she said as he slid his arm round her, 'for everything.'

'Hey, no smooching,' Scotty yelled from the doorway and they turned, laughing, to chase him down the marble steps where little Johnny Leconte had had his fatal meeting with his father so many years before.

CHAPTER 25

Phyl opened the package that had just been delivered by special Brinks van and stared amazed at its contents. A necklace of pearls the size of quails' eggs with a pavé diamond clasp, a pair of pearl and diamond drop earrings and a matching ring. There was a card: '*To remember me by*,' it said in Millie's handwriting.

She held the card against her cheek, smiling as she thought of Millie resplendent in shocking pink and the very same pearls at the opera last year. How could she ever forget her.

The phone rang and she answered it absently.

'I have to see you,' Brad said.

His voice sounded tense and she bit her lip, hesitating. 'Brad, I think it's better if we don't see each other again,' she decided finally.

'Please, Phyl. Please. It can't just end like this because of a silly quarrel. At least let's discuss it. Give me a chance to apologise.'

'Where are you?'

'Here in San Francisco. At the Fairmont.'

Phyl still hesitated: she knew it was more than just a silly quarrel, but she still felt that old allure. Brad could be so sweet, so charming, maybe she was being a bit hard on him after all. She sighed as she caught a glimpse of herself in the mirror, she looked a wreck after last night's shenanigans with Mahoney and his colleagues. But she guessed Brad was right, she owed him a chance to explain himself.

'Give me an hour,' she said. 'You had better come over here.'

'I know where you live,' he said, sounding elated. 'I'll be there.'

Phyl smiled as she showered, remembering Mahoney and the wedding party. It had been years since she had had that kind of careless fun, without strings, without responsibilities. Just nice people having a good time. Somehow it helped put Brad and her problems in proportion. She could handle it now, she thought confidently, dressing quickly in black jeans and a white linen shirt, cinching them together with the belt from Tucson with the silver and turquoise buckle. She brushed back her hair and tied it firmly into a knot, smoothed on her signature red lipstick and then, for Millie, she put on the extravagant pearls.

She paced the room nervously, waiting for Brad. Her footsteps seemed to echo in the silence and she wished she had the cat to keep her company, but it was still with Mahoney. She would call him later and arrange to pick it up.

She was remembering slow-dancing with Mahoney the previous night, when the doorbell rang. When she answered it Brad held out an armload of calla lilies.

'For you,' he said, looking penitent.

She smiled ruefully at him. 'You're not a man who does things by halves, are you Brad?' she said, taking the enormous sheaf of flowers into the kitchen.

He glanced curiously round, following her. 'So this is your lair,' he said. 'I wondered what it would be like.'

'And?' She faced him, arms folded defensively across her chest.

'It's exactly you. Cool, clever, cultured. And beautiful.'

'Thanks.' She watched him, prowling her home. He was wearing jeans and a blue workshirt and with his outdoors tan and rangy stride, he looked as out of place in her glossy urban apartment as a thoroughbred at the local ponyshow.

'Today you look like a cowboy,' she said.

'After all, that's what I am,' he said, studying the paintings. 'A rancher.'

'And proud of it. Maybe too proud, Brad.'

'What do you mean?' He looked genuinely puzzled. 'Don't I have a right to be proud of my family and their achievements?'

Phyl thought about that; after all, hadn't most of America's great fortunes been made by the robber barons, and weren't they all now American legends? 'I guess you're right,' she admitted. 'In a way.'

'I like this,' he said, standing in front of a small oil by David Oxtoby of a green English lawn and a clipped yew hedge. 'And this,' he was looking at a tempera by Tindle of a wooden chair standing by an open window, the muslin curtain blowing in a breeze. It was bleached-looking and other-worldly and it was one of her favourites.

He turned to face her. 'I'm not used to saying sorry,' he said stiffly. 'I find it very difficult.' She looked at him, saying nothing. 'Do you want me to go on my knees to you?' he demanded penitently. 'Were the flowers not enough?'

'The flowers are beautiful, Brad. It was a nice thought. But do you really expect me to forgive you for the way you behaved? Without even an apology.'

'You are right it was unforgivable.' He gripped her shoulders and pulled her towards him. 'The truth is, Phyl, I did it because I'm in love with you. I'm so damned crazy about you, I just can't bear the idea of anyone taking you away from me.'

'But no one was taking me away from you. It was an urgent call from a friend . . .'

'Was that the same friend you were out with last night?'

She pushed away, staring astonished at him. 'How do *you* know who I was with last night?' she exclaimed angrily.

'I called you for hours and you weren't here . . . I just guessed you were with someone else . . .'

'It's none of your goddamn business who I was with, Brad Kane. Not any more.'

'Don't say that. Please.'

She shrugged, undecided, torn between the old lure of him and her newly reasserted independence. 'Oh Brad,' she said wearily. 'It was all so beautiful, so special . . .'

'It can be again.' He caught her in his arms, holding her so close she could feel the muscles of his chest hard against her breasts, and the strong wiry length of his body against hers. He sounded desperate as he said, 'I'm sorry, Phyl. I'm really sorry. There, I've said it. Now *please*, tell me you forgive me.'

She felt herself capitulating, falling under his overwhelming sexual spell. 'I'm a busy woman,' she said quickly. 'My work takes up most of my time. I've been irresponsible, playing when I should have been working. I have to get back to my own life, Brad.'

'*Don't abandon me.*' His handsome face was contorted with agony, it was a cry from his heart and she recognised it. But Mahoney's handsome smiling face came suddenly into her mind. Her body remembered the feel of him, his arms round her, their steps fitting perfectly as they slow-danced. Like they were joined at the hip. Mahoney, the joker, the tease, the good friend. Mahoney, the dedicated cop, the poet, the opera-buff. And handsome, rich, overly-proud Brad Kane and all his problems seemed somehow less enticing.

She breathed a sigh of relief as she realised it was over. She was out from Brad Kane's dangerous spell, from his troubled life. But looking at his despairing face, she knew she had to let him down gently.

'I promise I'll see you when I have time. But on my terms.'

'I'll take anything I can get,' he murmured, 'the crumbs from your plate, a kiss on the hem of your garment, a glance from your jewelled eyes . . .' He dropped a gentle kiss on her forehead and she laughed, remembering how it used to be, how much she had enjoyed him. Perhaps it would be all right after all, and they could be friends. She could help him with his problems, because he surely had plenty. She was certain of that.

'In that case you can take me to lunch,' she said briskly.

'Anywhere,' he said eagerly, his anxious look disappearing. 'The moon, Mars, Venus.'

'Il Fornaio, round the corner,' she said laughing with him despite herself. 'For pizza. I'm starving.'

They had a corner table by the long windows and when they had ordered Brad eyed her necklace and said coldly, 'Who gave you the pearls?'

She heard the warning note of jealousy in his voice again and she said exasperatedly, 'Brad, these were left to me by my friend. The one whose funeral I missed.'

He played with the cutlery, not looking at her. 'She must have thought a lot of you, to leave you such an expensive necklace.'

'Millie also left me the matching earrings and ring. They're really too fancy for daytime but I felt like wearing her pearls. Somehow it makes me feel closer to her. I can remember the last time I saw her wearing them, at the opera last year. We saw *Carmen* and Millie even dressed for the part, in shocking pink flounces.'

'They must be worth a small fortune,' Brad persisted.

'Millie was a very rich woman. Though perhaps not quite as rich as you,' she said with a coaxing smile. 'And she was free with her money, she spread it around. She always wanted to help other people and she was a sucker for any sob story. That's why she took on my patient as her social secretary. The one I told you about in France. With the lost memory. Anyway, Millie has left her millions in her will, as well as two orphaned children that she has to take care of. She said she was giving the girl with no past a future. And I guess she was right because Bea seems happy enough now.'

'The woman sounds a typical misguided philanthropist and I would say that girl got very lucky,' Brad said savagely.

'Millie Fenwick was not misguided,' Phyl said angrily. 'She knew exactly what she wanted to do, and she had the means to do it.'

He looked up from the pizza, his eyes suddenly alert. 'Fenwick?'

'Yes, Millicent Fenwick.'

'I've heard that name somewhere else recently.'

'You've probably read about her in the society columns. Or maybe in the obits. Anyway she bought this villa in the South of France and she gave it to Bea. The Villa Mimosa.'

'*The Villa Mimosa?*'

'Yes. It's a beautiful place though Bea is convinced it has a mysterious past. Anyway, now it's hers and she's living there with the two children, Scott and Julie Fenwick, aged nine and seven. So I guess she has her hands full.'

'You said Bea was your patient? What exactly is wrong with her?' Brad took a gulp of his red wine and glanced at her with hooded blue eyes.

'I told you, she had an accident and lost her memory. She doesn't remember anything about it. It's just one of those strange things.'

'And will her memory ever return?'

Phyl sighed, regretfully. 'Who knows? I hope so, for her sake.'

'You are too involved with your patients,' Brad said, suddenly tender. 'You take on all their problems.'

She smiled, 'Including yours.'

'Do you mind me talking to you about my family?'

'I think it's probably very good for you.'

He leaned across the table and gripped her hand. 'Phyl, come back with me to Hawaii. Please, just for this weekend. I need you there. *I need to talk to you.*'

There was a note of such total despair in his voice and a look of such emptiness in his hooded eyes, that she knew he meant it. She wondered, panicked, what he might do to himself if she said no. But it still wasn't right of him to put her in this position . . . 'I don't know if I can . . . there's so much to do . . .' she hesitated.

'It's easy,' he said pleadingly. 'I'll fly you to Honolulu myself. *Please*, Phyl. I need you.' He gripped her hands tightly. 'I've never said those words to anyone else in my life. But I'm saying them to you now. Come with me Phyl, I promise faithfully to have you back in San Francisco on Monday morning.'

How could she resist such a plea for help. She knew only too well how it felt to be alone with only despair in your heart. 'Oh . . . all right, but no strings,' she agreed, hoping she was doing the right thing.

She could tell Mahoney didn't like it when she called and told him she was returning to Hawaii. 'Are you sure about this?' he asked worriedly. 'After what you told me about him?'

'He says he's a reformed character, Mahoney. What can I do? I really feel he needs to talk and that's the only reason I'm going. Brad needs me.'

Mahoney sighed. 'Sounds like a ploy to me.'

'I had such a great time last night, Franco,' she said softly. 'You're a terrific dancer.'

'It's only one of my talents,' he replied morosely. 'I didn't get to show you the rest.'

She laughed. 'Don't tell me you'll miss me?'

'Who the hell said I would?' he demanded, grinning. Then suddenly serious he added, 'Look Phyl, take care will you. This guy sounds a bit unstable to me.'

'Don't worry, he's as sane as you and I, whatever that means. Will you hang on to Coco for me? I'll call you when I get back on Monday.'

'Sure.' He was about to ring off when he thought of something. 'Doc,' he said, 'what kind of auto does Mr Hawaii drive?'

'A Porsche 938. Black. Why do you want to know?'

'Just wondered,' he replied, and then she said she had to hurry and pack and she would call when she got back.

'Well, well,' he said to himself, striding down the hall to the coffee machine, 'the hunch paid off. Jealous old Mr Hawaii *was* spying on her last night.' He remembered Phyl leaning affectionately against him as they walked up the steps into her building, and him putting his arm around her, kissing her. He gave a dismayed whistle as he thought about Mr Hawaii's unreasonable jealousy. He sure hoped Phyl knew what she was doing. And maybe in the meantime he would do a little quiet checking on Mr Brad Kane.

CHAPTER 26

The children were bathed and in bed. There had been no sound from them for the past half-hour, and Bea assumed, as thankfully as any mother, that they were finally asleep.

It was ten o'clock and she was alone. She covered the parrot's cage with a blanket, listening to its muttering as it settled sleepily on its perch. Then she took the ominous manilla envelope containing the Leconte family secrets with her into the kitchen, fixed herself a cup of tea and sat at the big pine table. She stared at the envelope. For some reason, now she had the answer she was reluctant to face it.

Poochie lapped noisily at his bowl then he flopped at her feet. The kitchen clock ticked the slow minutes away. The soft night breeze filtered in through the open window and somewhere in the distance she heard the faint sweet sound of birdsong. Was it a blackbird, she wondered? Or perhaps a nightingale? She sat, listening to the usual summer night sounds of crickets and frogs as the villa settled deeper into its own silence.

When she could put it off no longer, she removed the sheaf of papers from the envelope. They were written by Jean Leconte himself. 'Johnny' as Nanny Beale had called him.

Her heart sank like a stone in her chest as she began unwillingly to read.

* * *

I am writing about events which are better forgotten. And I am writing them only because Flora Beale has urged me to. 'For posterity', she says, meaning for any future Lecontes who shall come after me and wish to claim their inheritance.

For myself, I no longer care, but Nanny Beale insists it is their right. Since I am twenty-seven years old and unmarried, it seems a remote possibility, but I have to admit she has a point. And in that case, so that my mythical future descendants should know the truth, I shall do as she asks. I shall begin, therefore, at the beginning, which for me, meant the Villa Mimosa and Nanny Beale.

Bea shivered with foreboding. It was just like before. Even as she read it, she knew she heard the same story in her head ... someone was telling it to her, so vividly that it seemed engraved there. It only needed Johnny Leconte's own words to unlock her memories.

When you are a small child, it is not always the faces of people that you remember, it is the way they sound, or walk, or the smell of them. Nanny Beale was the first person I really knew, the first woman I ever loved. She was my mother and my friend, my helper and my fierce gardienne all rolled into one. And the fresh starchy smell of her white apron is my first memory.

She was small and round with a ramrod straight back and I remember watching her prepare for our daily walks. She would put on her hat, navy felt in winter, pale-straw in summer and she would say solemnly, 'Remember Johnny, a lady always wears a hat.' Then she would skewer it fiercely with a terrifying sharp steel pin surmounted by a blue glass ball. I would wait for her to yell because she had stuck it in her head, but Nanny was an expert and that never happened.

In summer, she wore sturdy lace-up shoes with 'sensible' heels. She had a chalky paste to keep them white and sometimes she would let me help her clean them. I remember that when the shoes dried, they would exude fascinating small puffs of white dust with every step she took.

I suppose she must have been in her fifties then, but to me she seemed ageless. Of course, I had little to compare her with, except the maids and they seemed closer to my age than hers. She was a sweet-faced woman but she could act very aloof when we were out on our drives in our big silver Rolls, nodding like a Countess to the hoi polloi along the Croisette or the Promenade des Anglais. I suspect the truth was she never recognised anybody because she was so near-sighted she couldn't see two feet in front of her nose, and she refused to wear her spectacles in the street. What mysterious creatures women are: even Nanny Beale had her small vanities.

But she was an Englishwoman to the core, and she never let her standards slip. I was dressed as her version of a prince, in silk and lace, and the nursery was devoid of animals, in case they got fleas and spread germs. So woolly old black and white Fido was my pretend dog and I can still remember how I loved him, and how later I mourned his loss.

I remember the nursery with her old Windsor rocker, always planted firmly in front of the firegrate in winter because, when the mistral blew, she complained its chill got into her bones. And her little round tortoiseshell spectacles always marking the open page of the book she was reading. I remember the smell of the toast we made over the glowing red coals of the fire, and tea with honey and ginger-biscuits. For a French child, it was a very English upbringing, but I knew no other children so I never knew if I was missing anything. I was happy at the Villa Mimosa, with Nanny

Beale and my dog Fido, and the gardeners who taught me all about the plants, and the parakeets and canaries in the silver aviary. I wanted nothing else. My world was complete.

Until the day my father returned for me, and sent me in exile, to Kalani.

He was a frightening man, though now I understand that he was handsome in a hard way. And I was a puny disappointing child, small and thin and as sallow as a beeswax candle. I had no idea what 'a father' meant, since I had never had one. I had never even met one. But I could tell from Nanny's terrified voice and his harsh one, that his return was not a welcome event.

I was quite relieved when we did not see much of him on our long journey to Kalani, and I thought travel a fascinating occupation, and a lot more interesting than the daily sameness of the Villa Mimosa. Little did I know how I would long for that safe daily routine later, and the haven of the villa.

When Nanny got sick on the liner in the middle of the Atlantic, I roamed the big ship alone. We were in a stifling little hole of a cabin on the very lowest layer and it was filled with fumes from the boilers and smells from the kitchens. I didn't even know that my father was aboard. I certainly never saw him, and he never came inquiring, from his first class stateroom, about the small son he had banished to the bowels of the ship. But I enjoyed my freedom and I made many new friends amongst the sailors, something I had never done before. I confess I was enjoying myself and I thought that if this was what life with a father was like, it wasn't bad.

Standing on the lower deck, clinging to Nanny's hand, I gaped at New York's famous skyline and almost before I knew it we were on an enormous steamtrain, heading west.

To San Francisco, Nanny said, but it might as well have been Timbuktoo for all I knew about the world and geography.

At first the train journey was fine. We changed at Chicago into another steaming monster and my father disappeared to his smart comfortable private carriage, while I spent many hours running up and down long swaying corridors, making a nuisance of myself, as Nanny said. But it was a long and tedious journey with no couchettes for us, and she was willing to let me run off my energy so I could sleep more soundly, stretched out along the hard plush seat.

We were heartily sick of that train by the time we arrived in San Francisco and drove to a big hotel. I remember staring up at this blond silent stranger who called himself my father and who had changed my life so drastically, as he glanced scornfully at us from the sidewalk, and then slammed the door on us.

'Stay in the car,' he commanded in the tone I used to Fido when he was bad. 'You are going to take the boat immediately to Honolulu.'

And so we were sent off to the docks, another fascinating place for a small boy, and the motor vessel the *Hyperion II*. God knows what the *Hyperion I* must have looked like, because even a child like me could see this one had seen better days. Flakes of paint clung like scabs to its rusting hull and small wiry foreign-looking men that Nanny called 'orientals', were swarming all over it, making ready for departure.

'Heathen Chinese,' Nanny breathed in my ear, as we walked up the gangplank as if to our doom. I didn't know what she meant but my heart sank at her ominous tone, and I clutched her hand, watching them warily. Her fears were groundless of course, though she refused to eat their 'heathen' food, and we ate only plain boiled rice. And then we were almost drowned in a storm.

I had never seen waves like that in the little Mediterranean; huge, glassy and green, racing at us and hurling gallons of icy water into our miserable cabin, until everything was awash. It was a relief when we finally made it safely into Honolulu harbour. Only to be sent immediately off again, in another rustbucket. This time to Maui.

I remember looking wistfully back at Honolulu's busy waterfront and the long white strand of Waikiki and wishing I could stay, but it was not to be. And two days later when we arrived at Maui, there was a small motor launch waiting to take us to our final destination. Kalani.

The stretch of water between Maui and Kalani was a glassy green swell that slid the little motor boat up one side of the wave and down the other with a sickening stomach-churning lurch. Nanny's back was firmly straight, and she held a black umbrella aloft to keep off the sun. Her face was as yellow as her straw hat but there was a determined look in her eyes. 'We shall not be sick,' she told me firmly, gritting her teeth together, and I nodded in agreement because, in truth, I did not feel ill. I was quite enjoying my boatride.

The rocky outline of Kalani appeared on the horizon, and as we drew nearer I saw the tall coconut palms and the tangled jungly vegetation fringing a strip of white sand. I remembered my daily routine at the Villa Mimosa and the uneventful days, each one the same as the last, and I thought Kalani looked different, exciting. I thought maybe the man who was my father was waiting there for me, to show me round my new home. I stared eagerly at the island, clutching Fido to my heart.

As the motor launch with the silent Chinese at the helm approached, the wind brought the scent of the island: spicy, rich, pungent. Quite different from the fresh rosemary-clean perfume of the Riviera. Nanny clutched my hand tightly in hers. 'Remember your home is the Villa Mimosa,' she said grimly. 'Never forget it, Johnny. And one day you will go home again.'

I was an obedient child and I looked solemnly at her, sealing those memories in my brain for future comfort. Suddenly I was infected with her fear. We were approaching the unknown. 'Pray, Master Johnny, pray for us,' she whispered as we glided closer.

I narrowed my eyes against the setting sun and saw a short sun-bleached wooden dock. And on it, dripping water, his blond hair sleeked back to his finely-shaped skull, his narrow loins wrapped in a skimpy piece of cotton that clung to him like a second skin, stood an older boy. Waiting for us.

Nanny Beale's face turned an outraged scarlet as the boat slid alongside the dock. 'Naked as the day he was born, or near enough as makes no difference,' she exclaimed loudly, glaring at him. 'Have you no shame, young man?'

The boy threw her a contemptuous glance. Then looked at me. I flinched as his narrow blue eyes flicked me derisively up and then down. His jaw set angrily and his well-shaped mouth turned down in a sneer as he took me in, in all my silken finery.

'A monkey,' he exclaimed contemptuously. 'You're nothing but a wizened fancy-dressed little monkey.'

And for ever after, that was how I was known on the island of Kalani. The Monkey. *It was my half-brother Jack who gave me that name and he never let me forget that I was the lowest creature on God's earth.*

CHAPTER 27

Phyl was sitting under a shade tree by the pool at the Diamond Head mansion. Brad was behaving perfectly, she told herself. He was the perfect host, the perfect gentleman. Then why, she asked, did she feel this tension between them?

She stared round, lazily admiring the avenue of blazing red royal poincianas in full bloom, the fragrant pink plumerias, and the vivid yellow blossoms of the leafless gold tree that more than lived up to its name. Nature had made no mistakes in Hawaii, it mixed and matched its colours with tropical abandon to create a harmony mere man could never achieve.

She looked at Brad, swimming long easy laps in the marine blue pool that stretched into infinity to the very edge of the cliff. The sun was dipping into the blue horizon and the silent Chinese servants were already setting the table on the terrace for dinner.

It was a scene of perfect beauty, peace and contentment. Then why, Phyl asked herself again, did she feel so uneasy?

They had arrived at Diamond Head last night and Brad had kept his word; he had looked after her and he had not attempted to make love to her. Her room was filled with white orchids; the fine linen sheets were delicately scented with lavender from Provence, and her bathroom was stocked with expensive soaps and lotions.

293

He had taken her to Michel's for dinner, an elegant restaurant overlooking the ocean and he had talked entertainingly about the ranch and Paris, and about flying and horse-breeding, and he had not asked a single question about her life. She knew he was making an effort not to pry and not to act jealous and she began to relax, enjoying his company. But she was glad when he said a brief goodnight at her door, and walked quickly away, without kissing her.

She had woken in the middle of the night with the uneasy feeling something was wrong. Then she saw Brad's shadowy figure by the window and the glow of his cigarette. She watched him silently, afraid to move. After a while he crushed out the cigarette and walked to the bed. Without thinking, she had closed her eyes and lain perfectly still, pretending to be asleep, but even so she could feel his gaze burning into her. Then she heard him groan. She peeked under her lashes as he strode quickly onto the terrace. The dog ran to his side, and then the two of them had disappeared into the night.

She had sat up, shivering with fright. She thought of locking her door, but then she had told herself she was being ridiculous. Brad meant her no harm. He loved her and wanted her, and she was denying him that. And Brad was not a man who was used to rejection.

This morning he had been sunny and smiling, and he had not mentioned his secret visit to her room. He had suggested an excursion to the volcano crater, or a drive round the island, anything to amuse her. 'All I want is for you to be happy,' he'd said warmly. And she could swear he meant it.

But she felt a new element in their relationship. She was still attracted to him, but there were undercurrents that made her apprehensive. And she was sure it all had to do with the past and his childhood.

Brad climbed from the pool and came towards her, shaking water from his blond head, sleeking it back, smiling at her with his father's hard blue eyes. Phyl wondered for the first time if the resemblance was more than skin deep.

'Tell me about Jack,' she suggested after dinner. They were in the sitting room. It was a sultry night with flashes of silvery-blue lightning over the ocean, and the occasional faint crackle of thunder. The night air moved sluggishly under the ceiling fans, fluttering her long hair and flattening her chiffon shirt coolly against her breasts. A Bach cantata played softly on the stereo and there was a distant roar of surf from the rocks at the foot of the cliffs.

She kicked off her sandals and stretched out on the pale mint linen sofa, looking at Brad. He leaned forward, his hands linked in front of him. She thought she had never seen a more handsome man, but it was an abstract thought, and lacking in passion. She told herself handsome was not the right adjective. Brad was beautiful, in the way a perfect animal possesses beauty. Lithe, sleek-muscled, bronzed. He was a man in the peak of physical condition, and he was also a man with a troubled past. And that was why she was there to help him.

'Jack was just like Archer,' he said. 'For them, the old saying, "Like father like son," was true. Archer taught Jack about life and that the best man always won. Regardless of what it took to do it. Archer had no morals and neither did Jack.'

'And is that what Jack taught you?' Phyl asked carefully.

He laughed. 'I'm my own man, Dr Phyl. And what I am has nothing to do with Jack and Archer.'

'Don't you believe it,' she replied coolly. 'Parents and families are at the root of most psychological problems today.'

'Are you planning on analysing me then?'

His tone was suddenly cold and she said smoothly, 'No I am not going to analyse you. I'm not here on business, Brad. But I am here to help you. And besides, I'm curious about your family. It's not often one gets to hear first hand about the rise of a dynasty such as yours.'

'They were no angels, it's true. They just did what they felt they had to do. It all seemed logical to them, and of course it was. Or there would be no Kane ranch today. And the one person who could have taken it away from us became Jack's mortal enemy.

'Jack was nine years old when his father told him he had a half-brother. Archer had never even mentioned another son before. Jack had simply not known. He went wild with jealousy and rage. He said he would kill his half-brother but Archer just laughed. He ruffled his hair and said indulgently, "Not yet, Jack. Not until Johnny's eighteen and comes into his inheritance. It's a fortune, young Jack. And make no mistake, we shall need it."

'Jack said he brooded all night about what his father had said and he realised there was nothing he could do about the half-brother. Archer's French wife had died and left him a lot of money and he had spent it. Now he was broke. True he had spent some of it on things that mattered: he had bought thousands of acres of ranchland on the Big Island and the best breeds of imported cattle, the finest horses. He had bought the Diamond Head mansion, expanded the Lodge on Kalani, and started breeding the thoroughbred Arabians. But he also had a retinue of forty servants here at the mansion, and more at the Lodge. He bought speedboats, a hundred-foot yacht, and a fleet of cars. He threw lavish parties and filled his swimming pool with French champagne. He bestowed diamond bracelets on beautiful and willing women, and he lived life to the hilt.

Archer Kane's reputation for high living and wild women spread as far as San Francisco and beyond.

'Jack had seen it all: the drinking, the women, the lavish lifestyle of a Kane. Archer never bothered to hide anything from him. Jack was a wild outdoorsy boy who liked nothing more than riding the range with the *paniolos*, but when he was seven his father decided to send him away to school in San Francisco. "We've got to civilise you, boy," he told him. But no school could hold Jack O'Higgins Kane for long. After he had run away a few times, Archer brought him home again.

'"Like father like son," he said proudly. "There's no institution strong enough to hold down my boy." Then he asked Jack if he didn't want an education, what did he want from life?

'"I'm like you, Dad," Jack said. "I want Kalani and the Kanoi ranch. And one day it will all be mine."'

Brad lifted his head and smiled at Phyl. 'Even at that young age, Jack had his priorities straight, though he did manage to get an education, of sorts, later. There was a series of unsuitable tutors here at Diamond Head, but they never seemed to work out and for a few years Jack was allowed to run wild on "his" island, or to spend weeks at the ranch, living with the *paniolos*, roping cattle and riding the range with them.

'Jack had always been king of his castle on Kalani. He was his father's only son and heir. There was no mother to boss him around, no one to tell him what to do. And he was a wild, turbulent, headstrong nine-year-old when the half-brother arrived to live with them on "*his* island".'

'Trouble?' Phyl asked, smiling.

Brad shrugged carelessly. 'It was just a boyish feud. Sure Jack hated the half-brother. He was the interloper. Jack was used to total authority on his island and he threatened that.

'Archer told him not to worry, he said the boy was a bit "soft in the head". He would stay on the island. He would never set foot in Diamond Head or the ranch or in Honolulu. And that's what happened. Of course people knew about him, but over the years he was forgotten, and those who did recall would just say, "Oh yes, I believe there was another son. A bit crazy," they said. "Archer Kane kept him on Kalani for his own good."'

A shiver ran down Phyl's spine as she listened to the heartless story. She thought Archer Kane was a monster. She said. 'What happened to the boy?'

'Oh, Jack said he was a weird little kid, only five years old, undersized and thin and sort of wizened-looking. He said he looked just like a monkey. And that's what he called him.' Brad laughed, enjoying the joke. '*The Monkey*. Jack said he made his life hell for a few years, and then there was some trouble on the island and the kid just disappeared. No one knew where. They thought he'd taken a boat out and drowned in a storm.'

'Like Lahilahi,' Phyl said, shocked.

'That's a ridiculous connection,' Brad said angrily. 'The boy did something stupid. The Pacific is a big ocean and treacherous. He should have known better.'

'What if he didn't drown? What if he were still alive? What would you do, Brad, if he suddenly appeared to claim his half-share of the Kane ranch?'

'You are talking nonsense,' Brad said distantly. 'He will not reappear. I can assure you of that.'

'How can you be so sure?' she persisted.

'There are strong currents round Kalani. Many boats have come to grief in those waters. The bodies are usually swept out to sea.'

But Phyl thought there was something in his eyes, deep down, as he looked at her. A wariness, as though he were hiding something. He poured himself his nightly brandy, then prowled to the window, the faithful Doberman, Kanoi, at his heels. He stared at the flickering stormy sky, and said moodily, 'It's all so long ago. The past is the past. What does it matter now? Archer and Jack were what they were. They knew what they wanted and they took it.'

'And do you know what you want, Brad?' Phyl asked, suddenly curious.

His hooded gaze met hers. 'Yes,' he said. 'I want you.'

CHAPTER 28

The Lodge on Kalani was made of wood, raised on posts from the ground – a barrier against the voracious termites, I learned later [Johnny Leconte said in the document Bea was reading long into the night]. *A wooden verandah, called a* lanaii *encircled it and the roof was made from palm thatch. To me it looked like a house from a fairytale. But it was soon to become the scene of my worst nightmares.*

My half-brother Jack O'Higgins Kane was nine years old and much bigger and stronger than I. He was tall and very good-looking, with his shaggy mane of yellow blond hair and his contemptuous hard blue eyes, like his father. He was a natural athlete and he could do all the things I had never learned. He could swim like a porpoise and gallop a horse bareback. He could climb the tallest palm trees, scaling them like the monkey he called me, deliberately sending the iron-hard fruits crashing down where I was standing so I had to jump out of the way to avoid being killed. He could shoot a hunting rifle and knock tin cans off a wall fifty yards away. He strode barefoot around the island never heeding the stones in his path. He shouted at the servants and they were forced to jump to his bidding. Whatever Jack wanted he got.

It took me only one day and one night, to realise that Jack Kane, my half-brother, was my rival, and my mortal enemy. He frightened me, with his shouting, his contempt, his showing off. But I had Nanny Beale and I knew with her I was safe. Then a few days later, the motor boat returned and with it, my father Archer Kane.

We watched him come ashore, Nanny and I, standing back a little way from the dock. Jack rushed past us. He jumped up and down waving excitedly, then he dived smoothly into the water without even a splash and we could see him, swimming to the boat, sleek as a seal, to meet his father. As the boat slowed, he clambered agilely aboard. We saw him gesture angrily toward us and my stomach clenched in sudden fear because I knew he was telling his father bad things about Nanny and me.

The boat docked and Jack leapt out first. He waited for Archer and then the two of them walked past us towards the Lodge without so much as a glance our way.

'Mr Kane, ' Nanny Beale called after them, angrily. 'I need to speak to you about the conditions here. They are not suitable for a young child.'

My father turned and looked at us and for the first time I understood what 'cold' eyes meant. His froze me on the spot. 'The conditions here are good enough for my other son, Miss Beale,' he said in an equally icy voice. 'I do not see any reason to make any changes.' He thought for a moment and then said. 'I will speak to you in my office in half an hour.'

Nanny clutched my hand even tighter as we approached the office at the appointed time. I could hear her breath coming quickly as it always did when she was agitated, and I clutched Fido to my chest, wishing I could think of something to say to comfort her. I said, 'Nanny, why don't we just go home? Back to the Villa Mimosa. I don't like it here.'

'That's just what I intend to tell Mr Archer Kane,' she declared firmly.

But Archer had beaten her to it. 'Miss Beale,' he said, lifting his eyes indifferently from a newspaper he was reading. '*You will pack your things immediately. The motor launch will take you to the Big Island and from there you will take the regular cattle boat to Honolulu. Your passage has been booked to San Francisco, and your return tickets to France will be waiting for you.*'

I heard her gasp with relief as he turned back to his newspaper. '*Then we are going home,*' she said and my heart rose hopefully along with hers.

'*You are going home, Miss Beale,*' my father said from behind the paper. '*The boy stays.*'

'*I will not leave without Johnny,*' Nanny cried heatedly. '*He cannot live here, he is not used to such wild places. His mother wanted him brought up at the Villa Mimosa, she entrusted me to take care of him. I insist he comes with me.*' And astonishingly she banged her fist on his desk to grab his attention.

'*I think you forget, Miss Beale, that his mother is dead,*' Archer said, suddenly angry. '*And that he is my son. Go pack your things and be down at the dock in an hour.*' He glanced at me and said decisively, '*There will be no lingering goodbyes. The boy will stay here until you have gone.*'

'*Nanny,*' I wailed, clinging to her. But she was beaten and she knew it.

'*Be a brave boy, Johnny,*' she whispered tearfully. '*Eat all your meals and grow big and strong. When things seem bad, remember I am thinking about you, and that the lord is on the side of the good. Don't forget me, Johnny,*' she said finally, kissing my cheek. '*I shall be there, at the Villa Mimosa, waiting for you, when you come home again.*'

But my heart sank into my smart little doeskin boots as I watched her go. I knew it would be a long time, if ever, before I saw her again.

Jack Kane set out to make my life hell. But it wasn't until

later that I learned why he hated me so much. My jealous half-brother knew more about me than I knew myself.

He started in a modest way, putting huge hairy spiders in my bed and forcing me to eat wriggling mealy grubs, and daubing me with red paint, like an Indian. He grinned wickedly at me because there was nothing on the island to remove the paint and he knew I would have to live with my red face until it finally wore off with ferocious scrubbing.

He fed my dinner to the pigs, so I was half-starved; he set trip lines across the paths and sent me running innocently up them, laughing as I fell. He took me into the forest where he had dug a trap, shrieking with joy as I tumbled into it and keeping me a terrified prisoner there until dusk, when Maluhia came looking for me. He crept into my room at night and I opened my eyes and found him grinning at me, holding a knife at my throat. 'I'll kill you one day, Monkey,' he whispered menacingly, sticking the point in, nicking my flesh. I felt the hot trickle of blood and I believed him.

I grew impervious to his taunts about my thinness and my looks, and instead I lived in dread of what new torture he might dream up for me. He was consumed with a jealous rage. He was king of his castle and he intended to keep it that way.

When Nanny Beale left I had thought I was alone, that there was no one who would even care about me. But there was a servant girl on the island, Maluhia, who my father, Archer, favoured. She was a beautiful mix of Chinese and Polynesian, exotic, gentle, soft-spoken and kind. Her name Maluhia, meant 'Peaceful' and she told me it had been given to her by her mother, a poor woman already burdened with too many girl children, in the hope this child's life might live up to her name. Sadly, it had not. Through various family disasters she ended up alone and homeless, aged thirteen.

Maluhia's skin had a warm golden sheen to it and she

walked with the fluid grace of a Hawaiian woman. She wore creamy plumeria blossoms in her long glossy black hair and she smelled of lilies and sweet fresh air. She was twenty years old and Archer had bought her when she was fourteen from the Honolulu waterfront brothel where he had discovered her. Now she was his 'personal servant', and she was grateful to him for being rescued from the squalid life she had led. She had a sweet oval face and luminous almond eyes of a light brown colour and a soft rosebud mouth. She was ignorant, uneducated, beautiful and kind. And too good for a man like Archer Kane.

I knew that, like me, she was afraid of him, though he did not treat her badly, only indifferently. She was there for his use when he wanted her. In Honolulu, Archer lived the life of a rich society gentleman with his fleet of cars and his yacht and his speedboats, his Diamond Head mansion and his grand parties and grand friends. But on Kalani, he was the old-fashioned 'Master' with a master's rights.

Maluhia was witness to Jack's daily cruelties. Maluhia overheard when he told me that his father despised me, that no one cared whether I lived or died. Jack said I was an interloper and this was his territory; that I was sponging on his father; taking things that didn't belong to me. 'Even the food you eat belongs to me, Monkey,' he snarled, and though Maluhia glanced sympathetically at me, she dare not say anything. But late at night when she heard my stifled sobs, she came and sat on my bed and held me close.

'Poor Johnny,' she whispered in her soft lilting island voice. 'Poor poor little Johnny. It is not true. You know I care about you. And Nanny Beale still cares about you. And look, Fido cares about you too.' And she put the little toy dog in my arms and tucked the white sheet tightly round me and whispered, 'Do not be afraid, Johnny, I will not let anything bad happen to you.'

Maluhia took me under her wing, a mother-bird to my wounded waif of a sparrow. But alas she too was an endangered species. I heard her telling my father that Jack was taunting me and leading me into dangerous games where I got hurt. 'Johnny is only a little boy,' she pleaded.

I peeked through the door and saw Archer push her roughly aside. He would not hear a word against Jack and she saw that he did not care. That Jack had the freedom to torture me as and when he wished.

Jack dared me on, knowing I could not compete. And poor foolish child that I was, I fell for every one of his ploys. 'Be brave,' Nanny Beale had said when she left me, and 'brave' was what I was going to be.

Jack dared me to climb the forty-foot coconut palm, not even explaining the special way it is done, laughing when I ripped my hands and skinned my shins, skidding down from the meagre height I had managed to achieve. He dared me to jump from high rocks that were easy for a nine-year-old like him, but impossible for a small boy like myself, and when I closed my eyes and hurled myself from the top, his mocking laughter rang in my ears. And he laughed even harder as I lay on my bed later, moaning with the pain of the sprains I had suffered, lucky not to have broken my neck.

One morning I awoke in my usual haze of misery, dully anticipating the day's tortures. I reached out, as I always did, for my old friend, Fido. I sat up and felt under the sheet for him. I leaned over and searched under the bed.

I heard Jack outside on the lanaii, laughing, and I guessed he had taken my dog. Fear mingled with anger inside me as I ran out, still in my nightshirt, to confront him. He was sitting on the lanaii rail, tossing Fido high into the air, catching him casually by a foot or an ear, grinning mockingly at me. 'Want him back?' he demanded. 'Then come and get him.'

I charged madly at him but he vaulted over the lanaii rail

and started walking backwards, away from me. I clambered over the rail after him and he began to run. 'If you can catch me, Monkey, you can have him back,' he yelled, waving Fido teasingly aloft.

I stumbled after him, too distraught even to be aware of where I was going, tripping over stones and scratching my face on the bushes. The dog was the only thing from the past I possessed. To me, he symbolised the security of the Villa Mimosa, of Nanny Beale and my sweet, ordered existence. Fido belonged to the time before I knew about fear and evil. Before I had had to learn to be 'brave' and live by my wits. And I loved Fido desperately.

When I finally caught up to Jack, he was standing on the rocks at the edge of the ocean, still holding Fido over his head.

'You are nothing, Monkey,' he yelled triumphantly. 'They wouldn't even give you a real dog because you were too stupid to know how to look after one. So Nanny gave her goddamn namby pamby pissy-pants little pansyboy a stuffed one. And you were dumb enough to think it was the real thing.'

I lunged at him and he kicked out at me, catching me in the chest and sending me sprawling back onto the rocks, smacking my head. Crazy with pain and anger I leapt to my feet and at him again, pummelling him and reaching desperately for the dog.

He leapt nimbly away from me onto another rock. His blue eyes raked me mockingly up and down as he held Fido out over the water. 'Okay, let's see how brave you are now, Monkey,' he yelled, laughing at me. 'If you love your stupid little woolly dog so much, go and get him.' And he tossed Fido into the ocean.

And poor sap that I was, afraid if I did, and afraid if I didn't, I jumped in after Fido.

Jack knew I could not swim and that Fido was lost. A few minutes later, he fished me from the surf, choking and retching seawater. Because you see my lithe, strong, murderous half-brother had remembered, just in time, that he could not let me die. Not yet.

He knew that he could not let me die for another thirteen years, when he and his father would have their hands on my inheritance. Those thirteen years yawned in front of me, a terrifying chasm of hatred and survival.

Suddenly there came an unexpected reprieve. Archer decided that Jack must return to school. 'There's more to running Kanoi ranch than riding a range,' I heard him snarl angrily to a sullen Jack. 'We employ paniolos to do that. How the hell do you expect to be able to run this place, after I'm gone, if you don't learn? You'll go back to school, Jack and then to college and you'll be a credit to me.' And when Jack said stubbornly he was damned if he'd go back to school, he yelled, 'You'll do as I say, son, or I'll give the goddamn ranch to the Monkey.'

There were no more protests after that. Jack knew his father was capable of anything, especially after he had been drinking, and I guess he knew he was right about running the ranch. And if anything in the world ever meant anything to Jack Kane, it was the Kanoi ranch. I knew he ached to possess it with every fibre in his body. I would have said 'with all his heart' but by then I knew, Jack had no heart. Jack went off to school in Honolulu and I was left in peace with Maluhia and the servants.

I was almost six years old now, and still puny, undernourished and thin. Then Maluhia took me to meet Kahanu, the young Hawaiian in charge of the thoroughbred horses, who also oversaw the prize herd of pedigree Herefords kept specially on the island for breeding.

Kahanu was around thirty years old and solidly muscular, with a broad Hawaiian face, shiny copper-brown skin, a shock of thick black hair and narrow amber eyes. Maluhia told me she thought he was the handsomest man she had ever met. She had no one else to confide in on the island, so she told me her secret: that she was in love with Kahanu but she was afraid to say so because of Archer. I too was afraid of Archer so I did not question this, but I understand now that she was afraid because she was Archer's concubine, his possession, and the oriental in her accepted that.

Maluhia begged Kahanu to help me. 'Make Johnny strong, like you, Kahanu,' she pleaded. 'Teach him all that you know, because if you do not I am sure he will die.' And she looked sadly at me, because she understood the inner death of a broken heart when she saw one.

Kahanu put me on a piebald pony, bareback. I clung desperately to its mane, afraid, not knowing what to do. 'Sit up straight,' he yelled at me. 'Grip with your knees.' I gripped and straightened up as the pony paced slowly round the corral. After a while I stopped being so afraid and began to look around me, enjoying myself. Sitting straight-backed I waved to Kahanu and Maluhia and they laughed and waved back. And for the first time, on the back of that little dapple pony, I felt a thrill of achievement.

Kahanu let me help around the stables and every morning when the sun woke me, I rushed there, working shirtless alongside him, currying the horses, mucking out the stables, hosing down the yards. I adored my new friend, and I hung breathless with admiration over the corral fence, watching as he broke a new colt.

I followed him everywhere. He let me eat with the men, squatting on the ground scooping poi and sweet baked meats from a banana leaf with my fingers the way they did. And later, exhausted, I would fall sweetly asleep in my own secret place in the hayloft.

Months passed and still Jack did not return to the island. Maluhia told me that Archer had sent him to boarding school in America. He was behind in his studies and he would not be allowed back on Kalani until he had done better: I cheered when she told me, whooping and hollering like a normal little kid as I danced over to Kahanu's room in the stables to tell him the good news.

'Then you are not gonna waste your time neither, Johnny,' he told me. 'Don't think you're just gonna loaf away your days doing nothing but currycomb a horse and ride a little pony round the island. No sir, I'm gonna teach you to be a man, so when that little bastard Jack comes home again, you can take him on. And win.'

And so I began my crash course in body building and physical skills. Kahanu taught me to climb trees, to chop wood, to box, to paddle a canoe, to fish. The Chinese cook taught me the martial arts, and Maluhia taught me to swim. And, gliding naked with her under the crystal-green water with tiny jewelled fish darting around us, I was happy again.

Three years passed in this fashion and I was beginning to believe that life would always be as serene and beautiful as this. Kahanu had even given me a new Hawaiian name Ikaikakukane, meaning 'the One of Manly Strength', to commemorate my new prowess.

And then, when I was eight, Jack returned and the torture began all over again.

The Hawaiians had given me a new name, but they also had one for Jack. Lauohomelemele, the Yellow-haired One. He took it as a compliment to his superior 'white-man' status, but the Hawaiians knew better and it was always said with a subtle veneer of contempt.

Everyone on the island, the stable hands, the paniolos, *the Chinese servants hated the Yellow-haired One. He treated them all like dirt, throwing orders around and kicking the little servants out of his way when they didn't move fast enough. He threw dishes at the Chinese cook when he didn't like the food, and he even had grown men fired and banished from the island when he complained to his father about their work, or their slowness or their 'bad attitude'. Archer gave him full power. 'It's good training for when you run the ranch,' he said approvingly.*

Jack was arrogant with Kahanu, but secretly he was afraid of him. Archer said Kahanu was the best man on the island; he was clever and a good worker and he was brilliant with the thoroughbred horses. Kahanu was valuable and therefore Jack did not have power over him, and Kahanu knew it. The Hawaiian ignored him and went about his work, whistling carelessly while Jack hung around, hoping he would ask him to help, and when he did not he would ride angrily off in search of another prey. Usually me.

He was twelve when he came home again for the school vacation and I was eight. We eyed each other warily and I saw his eyes widen as he looked me up and down. I was no longer the small wizened little Monkey. I had shot up five inches and my thin arms and legs were filling out with new muscles. But he had grown too; he was always a good athlete and now his body had bulked out. He was becoming a man and he was ready to follow in his father's masculine footsteps.

Jack had always treated Maluhia with the scorn he felt she deserved, as the lowest of women, his father's whore. But now he began to look differently at her.

Whenever Archer was home, Maluhia would serve at the dinner table. She would put on a colourful sarong and fasten her black hair into a fat glossy braid and she walked barefoot so as to make no noise as she carried the dishes of rice and pork and shrimp to the table and offered them to her master.

That first night they came home, Archer and Jack were seated at the table and Maluhia was serving them, as usual. I, of course, was supposed to take my food in the kitchen, but mostly I ate with Kahanu and the paniolos in the stables. I lay on my stomach in the jungly garden, hidden from sight, watching the quick green lizards dart up and down the wall and keeping a wary eye on Jack and his father at the dining table on the lanaii. Ours was a war of surprise attacks, and I needed to know where Jack was at all times so I could prepare my defences. Only this time, I was not the one on Jack's mind.

I watched Maluhia serve Archer and then offer the dish to Jack, bending forward politely. Jack glanced at her and then said something to his father that I didn't catch, but they both laughed coarsely. And then Jack reached suddenly forward and put his hands on Maluhia's breasts.

She leapt back, dropping the dish, clutching her sarong to her breasts as she stepped quickly away from him. Jack said something to Archer and they both roared with laughter. I saw Maluhia's head droop in shame, and I wanted to run to defend her. But I was no match for the two of them.

In the days after that Jack became even bolder, slapping Maluhia's behind as she walked by him, and cupping his hand slyly over her breasts, and Archer only laughed. Maluhia said nothing, but I seethed helplessly with the shared shame and anger I knew she was feeling.

'Come here, let's have a look at you, Monkey,' Archer called, a few days later. I had been keeping out of their sight as much as I could, spending my days with Kahanu. I hoped they had forgotten me, but I was wrong. I walked reluctantly *out of the stable towards them. Archer pushed back his stetson and put his hands on his hips, assessing me like a prize steer.*

'Well damn me, if the Monkey isn't growing up,' he finally said, astonished. 'He's bigger and stronger. Maybe there's some Kane genes in there after all. How old are you now, boy?'

'I am eight years old, sir.'

'Eight huh.' He glanced at Jack and said with a grin, 'How many years does that leave us, Jack?' Then laughing uproariously, he turned away. 'Kahanu,' he yelled over his shoulder. 'Put this boy to work. If we have to put up with him for ten more years, he might as well earn his keep.'

'Yes sir, Mr Archer.' Kahanu saluted respectfully.

I kept my distance from them, sticking close to Kahanu, riding the canyons looking for lost cattle. Sometimes we would take his little boat out fishing for grouper, and afterwards we would bake the fish over a driftwood fire, miles away from that evil Lodge. So it wasn't until Archer had left for Honolulu and Jack was at a loose end, that he came looking for me.

'Hey, Monkey,' he called, striding towards me and slapping me on the shoulder. 'Why don't you and I go fishing?'

'I have work to do,' I replied, stiff with fright despite myself.

'Aw come on, Monkey,' he said cajolingly. 'Let's forget our differences. You're older now, and stronger. We're more like equals now, I'd say.'

I looked into his smiling face and warning signals flickered up my spine. I did not trust him.

'I'm busy,' I replied curtly, turning away.

'Come on, Monkey.' *He followed me, throwing a friendly*

arm across my shoulders. I froze and turned my head to look to him. The only other times Jack had ever touched me was to punch me or kick me. 'Come on, fella,' he said tauntingly, 'don't tell me you're afraid?'

I never learned. I rose to his taunt, just like he knew I would. I remembered my new fishing prowess, earned in my expeditions with Kahanu, and the fact that now I could swim and knew how to handle a boat.

'Okay,' I agreed cockily. 'You're on.'

I followed Jack along the sun-bleached wooden jetty and we climbed into his little boat. He untied the painter and jerked the outboard into action and we chugged off, heading to a place where he said he knew shoals of grouper were to be found. It seemed a long way to me and after a while Jack's jolly bantering tone dissolved into silence.

After about half an hour I was becoming uneasy. 'Why do we have to go this far to find grouper?' I asked him. 'There's plenty to be found right off Keeper's Point.'

'These are better,' he said, curtly, shading his eyes with his hand and staring at the small island we were approaching.

I stared at it interestedly. It was the only other place I had seen since I came to Kalani more than three years before. Archer had made sure I never left the island, and I didn't even know what a 'town' or a 'school' was. I was as ignorant of the world and its ways and of culture and 'education' as I had been when I was five years old. I was excited to see this new place and when the little boat crunched onto the sand, I leapt out and pulled it into the shallows while Jack held the anchor ready.

I waded confidently onto the shore and turned to look for him. He was in the water, pushing the little boat back out to sea. I ran after him, but he leapt quickly into the boat and bent down, frantically jerking the outboard motor. It growled into life and I stood chest-deep in the water, watching as the boat sped away from me. Good swimmer though I was, I knew I could never catch it.

Jack was standing in the centre of the boat, his legs straddled, watching me. I saw him punch his fist triumphantly in the air and heard him laughing, 'Now let's see how much you've learned in three years, Monkey,' he yelled, as he sped away, leaving me alone on the deserted island.

He would come back, I told myself confidently. He couldn't just leave me there. Alone.

I looked at the dense mangroves behind me, sniffing their fetid swampy smell. They looked dark and dangerous and I walked hurriedly away down the shingly beach, searching for shade. A stunted bush was all I found and I crouched in its meagre shadow, waiting.

Hours passed. I watched the sun dipping lower in the sky until finally the glowing red ball touched the horizon and then, with tropical suddenness, it was gone, leaving an otherworldly greenish afterglow. It was then I knew for certain Jack was not coming back to get me. I was alone on a deserted island and I was afraid.

I had thought I would die of the heat, but now I was cold. And thirsty. There was no water anywhere near the beach and I had not dared roam further away in case Jack returned and I missed him. I paced around in the half-light, but found nothing. I crouched on my rock again, clasping my arms around my hunched knees, staring vainly out to sea. The greenish afterglow slid gently into midnight blue, and then almost imperceptibly into darkness. There was no moon. It was just black.

I told myself it would be all right. Jack would return in the morning. Maluhia would miss me, and Kahanu. But morning was a long way off and from the blackness behind me I heard fearsome rustling sounds, like animals on the prowl. I imagined alligators crawling towards me, ready to rip me limb from limb and crunch me up. In my head I heard tigers and lions breathing close to me, and the hissing of snakes ready to strike. In the blackness, I thought I saw scorpions, and giant toads and venomous spiders. My new courage disappeared beneath a thousand imaginary fears as I huddled on the cold shingle beach, waiting for Jack to return and get me.

I breathed a huge sigh of relief when the fearful night ended, planning how, when Jack arrived, I would swagger towards him, pretending I didn't care about spending a night alone on a deserted island. I would tell him of the fruit I had found to eat, and the crystal spring of water behind the mangroves, and how I had seen a twenty-foot alligator back there and not been the least bit scared. I would pretend I was a regular little Robinson Crusoe, whose story I knew because it had been one of Nanny's favourite books.

The sun lifted higher in the sky and still Jack did not come. I was dying from hunger and thirst and was finally forced to search around for a stream or fruit, all the things I had planned so confidently to tell Jack I had done. But I was no Robinson Crusoe and there was no fresh water, only the brackish evil-smelling swamp, and no fresh fruits hanging conveniently from a tree.

I finally found a coconut washed up by the tide into a rock pool, and I pounced thankfully on it. Then I realised I had no machete to open it. I smashed it onto the rocks, again and again, sobbing with frustration. I could almost taste its cool juices trickling down my parched throat. But when it finally cracked most of the milk spilled out before I could catch it. Sobbing with fear and frustration, I licked up what was left of the precious juices.

I sought the shade of the scrubby little bush again, and sat sombrely watching the sun's burning passage through the sky. Every now and again I dipped into the ocean to cool myself but the salt water crusted on my skin as it dried and the sun burned me even more.

As the sun began to set again, I stumbled along the beach, dizzy from the heat and weak from hunger and dehydration. Surely Jack would come now, before darkness. But when the green afterglow filled the sky again and then turned gradually to midnight blue, I realised that he was not coming. Jack was never coming back. He had left me here to die.

I knew that by now he must have made up some story about my falling overboard and how he hadn't noticed until it was too late. 'Poor Monkey's drowned,' I imagined him saying with a triumphant gleam in his eyes and a mock-sorrowful look on his face.

I lay spread-eagled on the shingle, too weak to care any more about alligators and snakes and lions. I closed my eyes and a feeling of tranquillity came over me. It would be so easy just to fall asleep and as Maluhia would have said, 'Let the lord take me.'

I was unconscious when Kahanu arrived with the dawn, and carried me tenderly back to his boat and to Kalani. Maluhia bathed my sun-blistered flesh with cold cloths, and made potions from aromatic leaves to bring down my raging fever.

'The Yellow-haired One is the true son of the father,' Kahanu said ominously. 'Evil passes from one generation to another . . .'

Later Maluhia told me that when she had told Kahanu I was missing, he had gone straight to Jack and asked him where I was. Jack had denied ever seeing me, and so they had searched the island.

'He must have fallen off the cliff and drowned,' Jack had said casually, but Kahanu knew by then he was lying and he exploded with anger. I had been gone a long time. He knew they were talking life and death now.

He grabbed Jack's arm and twisted it behind his back, jerking it up harder with each question. 'Where is he, you little yellow-haired bastard?' he demanded, and Jack screamed and said he would tell his father; that Kahanu would be whipped, he would lose his job and be sent from the island.

Kahanu inched his arm up even further and Jack screamed louder. Then Maluhia whispered in Kahanu's ear the secret reason Archer wanted me alive. 'If the Monkey dies,' Kahanu said softly to Jack, 'it is you who will get the whipping. Mr Archer will whip you until you are dead too, and you know it.'

Jack sobbed into the silence, brought suddenly back to his senses. He knew Archer would kill him if he had ruined their chance of getting my fortune. So he told them where I was; he said I had leapt off the boat and swum to the island and refused to come back. He said I had told him I never wanted to see Kalani again, I would manage on my own . . .

'Evil lying little bastard,' Kahanu snarled, jerking Jack's arm upwards until it snapped with a sound like a pistol shot. He screamed in agony. 'Murderer,' Kahanu whispered in his ear. 'You fell from a tree and broke your arm. Remember? Just the way the Monkey never left Kalani.'

Despite his pain, Jack recognised that a deal had been made and that Kahanu would not tell his father. He nodded his acceptance. The next day he was taken by boat to the doctor in Maui to get his broken arm set, and then he went back to Honolulu for the rest of his vacation, and then back to school.

I had won and Kalani was mine again. For the time being.

The years drifted slowly past and I was happy in a fashion, though my restless dreams were still filled with images of the villa, and I longed to see Nanny Beale again, and for the scent of the mimosa blossoms in springtime and the sound of the songbirds in their silver aviary. But Kalani was my reality.

Maluhia had taught me to read and I devoured all the books in the house, even those whose pages were half-eaten by the termites. And every now and then Archer would send a lazy, drunken, half-baked 'tutor' over to the island, to keep up the pretence to his social friends that he was doing the right thing, and poor Johnny was being educated, despite being 'soft in the head'. And one of them, a gaunt young Englishman already more than halfway down the fuzzy path of the alcoholic, brought water colours and oil paints and an easel. Whisky was his tipple but when that was not available, rum made a good enough substitute, or beer or wine or in extremity, turpentine or rubbing alcohol.

He was usually too hung over to do much teaching, but, when his hand was steady enough he painted well. I would stand on the rocks next to him, watching him magically recreate the seascape and the great swoop of the cliff and my own hand itched to emulate him.

He showed me the paints, explaining the different textured papers for the watercolours, and how to treat them first with a clear wash, and then how to apply the colours. He showed me how to go about mixing pigments to make my own oils, and gave me charcoal and taught me to sketch.

I was transported into a new creative world. I stopped

riding the gulches with Kahanu and instead began to draw and paint. I was obsessed with it. It took me over completely. And again, I was happy.

Jack never returned to Kalani in those years before he went to college. I don't know whether Archer got wind of his murderous intentions towards me before my allotted time was up, but he was kept out of the way and life was peaceful. When my drunken art tutor had to be deported back to Honolulu with a severe attack of delirium tremens, Archer made sure that I had a stock of art supplies. He wanted me kept quiet and happy enough not to cause trouble.

In that peaceful period, before I was fifteen, I painted my memories of the Villa Mimosa. I painted Nanny Beale as I remembered her, and the nursery with Fido on my bed and Nanny's rocking chair by the fire. I painted Kalani's lush green gorges spanned by rainbows, and the showy red cardinal bird who came to sit on the lanaii rail every evening, hoping for tidbits. I painted Maluhia combing her long silken black hair, and the beauty of a broken hibiscus blossom; I painted Kahanu on a galloping mare. Everything I saw offered a new perspective, a new detail, a new way to use colour.

'You have a special way of seeing things,' Maluhia told me, because when she looked at her portrait, it was not exactly the girl she saw in the mirror. She knew that instead, I had captured something of the girl she was in her heart.

I was left pretty much to my own devices in those long fallow years on Kalani, until I became fifteen. Kahanu had taught me well and though I was still thin, I possessed a deceptive wiry strength. I could ride any horse and rope cattle as good as any paniolo, and, after being kept a virtual prisoner on the island for the past ten years, I was a rough country boy, uneducated and unused to life in a normal society. I ate peasant meals from a banana leaf and wore ragged shorts and slept mostly in the stable loft. Maluhia saw to it that I kept myself clean and such clothes as I had were laundered. And she insisted that I did not use the island patois but spoke 'properly', and without the sweet Hawaiian lilt. Still, I was an island boy. I was a young ignorant savage.

Then Archer came to the island and this time he brought Jack with him. Jack was nineteen and I was fifteen. There were ten long years of hatred between us as we looked at each other. Lauohomelemele and Ikaikakukane – the Yellow-haired One and the One of Manly Strength.

Archer was drinking heavily by then. He ordered dinner to be served and insisted that I sit with them. He was always smart in his custom-tailored white sharkskin suits, his Panama hats, and hand-made shirts, and even though the night was hot he was wearing an elegant dark blue flowered shirt of Chinese silk. And Jack was the perfect suave young college man in an immaculate white linen shirt and linen pants.

Archer was still a handsome man, though the liquor was beginning to show in the puffiness under his eyes, and the tremor that afflicted his right hand after he had downed a few shots of his favourite Scotch whisky. And Jack was handsome all right. Tall, blond and strong-jawed, with hard blue eyes, a hard body and a hard head.

Those hard blue eyes simmered with hate as he looked at me in my old shirt, faded by the sun and many washings from blue to a soft grey, and the rough denim shorts that had once been his and were now worn to a smooth and I thought pleasing pale blue. Thanks to Maluhia they were immaculately clean and I was freshly showered and saw nothing wrong in my appearance. Until I looked at the two of them in their finery.

Archer was on his fourth or fifth Scotch. His hand shook

with a fine insistent tremor as he pointed at me and guffawed. 'Put that wild boy in a roomful of civilised folk in Honolulu or San Francisco,' he yelled, 'and they'll say, "You know what? Archer Kane was right. That boy is a savage. He must be soft in the head."'

'For Chrissakes get out of here,' Jack snarled, looking at me as though I were a leper. 'You're not fit to be in our company.'

'No, no. Sit down, boy.' Archer grinned genially at me. 'Tell me, what are you up to these days?'

'I help Kahanu with the thoroughbreds. I ride with the paniolos. I fish for food for the table,' I said.

Archer threw back his head in another great guffaw. 'There, what did I tell you,' he chortled. 'Wasn't I right about him? Well, kid, I guess you had better go back to the stables and the paniolos where you're comfortable. They say every man seeks his own level in life and I see that you have found yours.'

With that, he turned his back on me and snapped his fingers for Maluhia to bring his food.

I glared resentfully at him over my shoulder as I made my way back to the stables. I hated the disparaging way he treated Maluhia almost more than I hated his cruel cynical attitude towards myself. But I could do nothing about either. 'Get out of here you hick,' Jack yelled viciously after me. 'You're an ignorant pig, an eyesore in your hand-me-down shorts. You're not fit to sit at the table with civilised men.'

I knew Archer and Jack sat late on the lanaii, discussing business and drinking. Nevertheless they were at the stables early the next morning, where Kahanu had their horses saddled up and waiting. I lurked inside the stalls, hoping not to be noticed, and they soon went off with Kahanu to inspect the cattle.

For the next few days, I managed to keep out of their way

and they did not ask for me. I rode out early with the paniolos and often slept out with them, under the stars on a grassy hillside. Life was simple and sweet, away from the plotting and sophisticated corruption of the Kanes, and I thought that if I had no more than this, I could be happy.

Then Archer went back to Honolulu and Jack was alone again. So of course, he came looking for me.

It was late evening as I rode back with the men, sweat-soaked and smelling like a steer from a long hot day spent branding the new cattle. There were only a dozen paniolos on Kalani, and they were older men who had been sent over from the Kanoi ranch on the Big Island and given the easier job of caring for Archer Kane's prize herd. Archer's philosophy was that it was no use wasting the cowboys' lifetime-earned skills by putting them out to pasture themselves and wasting money on pensions. He figured they were still able to work and so work they did, and Archer got his money's worth instead of paying them a retirement pension, and, as he said, watching his money go down the drain.

I'll say this for Archer Kane, he was a good rancher. He understood his business and he understood his men. Those old guys would have withered and died without their jobs to go to, and Archer understood they would rather work and make an honest week's pay doing the only thing they knew, than be turfed off the ranch, living in some broken-down shanty-village talking about the old days. They hated him all right, everybody did, but he gave them what they wanted and in return they worked hard and kept their mouths shut.

Now, when they saw Jack, waiting for me, they turned their eyes away, concentrating on their horses, giving them buckets of fresh water and throwing blankets over them, allowing them to cool off before feeding them.

Jack was leaning back with his elbows hooked over the corral fence, one foot propped on the rail, smiling a sinister little smile. 'Hey, Monkey,' he called. 'Come over here. I want to talk to you.'

I walked slowly towards him. Out of the corner of my eye I saw the paniolos sidling away into the stables. Jack and I were alone. Then, with a thrill of my own power, I realised that for the first time I was not afraid of him.

'What's all this I hear about you painting?' he said coldly.

I took a step closer. I stood with my legs apart, my arms folded. 'What about it?' I demanded, looking him squarely in the eye.

'You are here to work not to paint,' he snarled. He tilted his arrogant chin pushing his cowboy hat to a better angle, looking down his nose at me. I measured him up: he was six-one to my five-seven and around one hundred and ninety pounds of solid muscle to my thin wiry one-thirty. His jaw jutted aggressively and the urge to hit him almost over-whelmed me. I hid my bunched fists and said instead, 'Archer knows about the painting. Who do you think supplies the paints?'

'Well, no longer,' he said. He pointed triumphantly to a pile of rubble lying in the corner of the yard. 'There'll be no more "painting" on this island, you fuckin' little pansyboy. You'll earn your keep just like the rest of the paniolos.' His nostrils flared as he sniffed the air. 'You smell just like a half-breed anyway, you might as well be one of them.'

He strode across to the pile of rubble and I stared after him puzzled, as he pulled a box of matches from his pocket. 'Watch this, Monkey,' he called, striking a match and setting light to the rubble. 'That's all your fuckin' pansy paintings going up in smoke.'

He jumped back as the oil paints and the turps exploded in a sudden whoosh of flames, and I watched numbly as the *only thing I had to show for the past ten forgotten years went up in a pall of noxious blue smoke. They were my memories of the times I had felt happy on Kalani. Jack was burning Maluhia and Kahanu, and Fido; he was burning the fish freshly caught from the crystal ocean; the paniolos sitting around their fires; the numb-eyed cattle as they were seared by the branding iron. He was burning the red cardinal bird and the green lizards and the dapple pony on which I first rode proudly round the paddock.*

Jack Kane was burning my life and I launched myself at him like a hot-branded steer exploding from the pen. 'I'll kill you, you bastard,' I heard myself screaming. 'Kill you, kill you.'

My speed took him by surprise and I had him on his back with the wind knocked out of him. My hands were on his throat as he rolled over, kicking out at me, gasping for breath. I had learned the martial arts from the Chinese cook and I knew how to kill a man: I raised my rigid hand and brought it sideways across his windpipe and he gagged, unable even to scream with the pain, searching desperately for breath.

'I'll kill you,' I said, and even as I said it I realised I was enjoying myself. The urge to savour the pleasure of killing him was so great it shocked me back to my senses. I was frightened by the depths of my hatred and by the power of my anger.

I straddled his chest, staring down at his purple face. And then I glanced up and saw Maluhia standing at the edge of the yard, watching us. Her hands flew to her face in horror as our eyes met and I knew I could not do it. If I killed Jack Kane then I would be a murderer. And he was not worth it.

I climbed off him and stood watching as he struggled to regain his breath. After a while he sat up, rubbing his throat, staring malevolently at me through bruised, puffed-up eyes.

'You're soft in the brain all right,' he called hoarsely after me as I turned and strode away. 'A mental retard like your fuckin' mother. Nobody wants to know you. Nobody cares if you live or die.' He clambered to his feet and stood, arrogant again, hands on his hips. 'Coward,' he yelled mockingly. 'Afraid to finish the job?'

I stopped in my tracks, burning like my paintings reduced now to mere flakes of ash, floating across the yard in the wind. My fists were balled in readiness, and for a moment he almost had me, just like in the old days. But this time the poor sap that I used to be had learned better. I ignored his taunt and stalked back to the corral, climbed bareback on my horse and galloped away.

I rode to the north-eastern tip of the island, pushing the horse to go faster; all the way to the very edge of the cliff where it fell, two hundred sheer feet into the rocky Pacific.

The horse dug in its hooves, whinnying with fear. I leapt off and stood there, gazing down at the powerful ocean hurling itself in a solid wall over the jagged rocks, then dissolving into a curtain of foam and spray, surging and roiling, sucking bits of driftwood and flotsam into its infinite depths. I stood poised on the edge, no longer caring. I told myself there was nothing to live for, that anything, even the nothingness of death was better than this.

I stood for a long time, until the sun began to set and I finally lifted my eyes from the rocks and the boiling sea and looked at the beauty around me, illuminated in a golden-red glow. And I sank to my knees and howled like an animal, crying for the first time since I was eight years old.

I slept under the stars that night, on my windy clifftop, communing with myself, asking myself what I would do. There was only one answer. I had to leave Kalani. But how? Kahanu was in charge of the motor launch that was the only *boat big enough to safely make the crossing to Maui. I could not ask him to help me because Archer would surely find out and then Kahanu would lose his job. And I knew Archer's vengeance was such he would make sure Kahanu never got employment again on the islands. The supply boats came to Kalani once a month, and occasionally a cattle barge to transport the animals to the ranch on the Big Island, but all these men were in Archer's pay and they would no more think of helping me escape than they would of cutting their own throats.*

The only answer was Jack's own little outboard motor boat. It was small, a mere seven feet in length with a shallow centreboard. It was meant for put-putting in the shallows and for fishing, not for the twenty miles of treacherous channel that lay between Kalani and Maui. The channel had notorious currents and the winds could blow up the weather in less than an hour, bringing fierce squalls and thunderstorms. It was a risk, but one I knew I would have to take.

I lay on my back, watching the passage of the stars across the tropical night sky, with Venus glittering as bright as a diamond, looking so close I felt I could reach out and grab it. And as shooting stars catapulted across the heavens like celebratory fireworks, I planned my escape and wondered what I would do with my new freedom.

I rode slowly back before dawn, looking around for the last time at the landscape I knew as well as I knew my own face. The long grass was pearled with dew and the birds were beginning their morning chorus, and my country boy's alert ears heard the rustle of a thousand small creatures stirring. I loved Kalani and its beauty would always be a part of me, just as would the evil at its heart.

I had planned to steal cans of fuel from the storeroom and stash them in the undergrowth behind the dock. Jack's boat was beached nearby and it would be easy, under cover of darkness to load on the fuel and some food, and glide silently out into the darkness, letting the current take the boat until I was far enough away that they wouldn't hear, and I could start the little motor. After that, steering by the stars, I would have to put my trust in my own skills and in God.

I wiped the sweat from my horse, then with a final affectionate slap on her hindquarters I set her galloping across the paddock. I watched the mare wistfully for a while, savouring my last sight of her, kicking up her heels and whinnying with the sheer delight of being free. I hoped soon I would feel the same way.

I skulked back to the Lodge, keeping an eye out for Jack, but it was still early, barely dawn and no one was around. Except Maluhia.

She was on the verandah outside the kitchen. She was crouched in a fetal ball with her knees hunched under her chin, staring into space. She stared dully at me with blank golden eyes and I looked, shocked, at her swollen mouth and bruised face.

'Maluhia,' I gasped, sinking to my knees beside her. 'What happened?' But even as I asked, I knew. I had observed Jack, often enough, sitting at the table, sipping whisky with his father, coveting her, noting the rhythm of her walk, the movement of her supple body, the firm upwards thrust of her breasts under the sarong. Jack had gone to her room and Maluhia had rejected his advances. When she screamed he beat her into silence and submission.

This time I knew I would kill him. I stalked livid-faced with rage towards his room but Maluhia cried out and stopped me. 'He is not worth it, Johnny,' she sobbed. 'After all, I am only a bought woman. What else can I expect?'

But my anger only grew as I listened to her telling me she was worthless, when I knew she had more integrity and *dignity than the man who had bought her. I strode off, looking for Jack, and Maluhia ran to get Kahanu.*

I found Jack snoozing in a hammock slung between two palms where the lawns sloped down to the sea. I took the knife from my belt and slashed the rope, spilling him onto the grass. Jack scrambled quickly to his feet, then crouched low in a boxing stance. He raised his fists, grinning.

'I guess you found out I took what you've always wanted, last night,' he taunted, circling round me. 'Funny, I thought Maluhia was a mother-figure to you. But then, you're not beyond a little mother-fucking, are you, brother?' He laughed as he said, 'Just for the record, she wasn't worth it. It's a myth, what they say about Chinese women. Maluhia's not woman enough for a man of my appetites and dimensions.' He laughed again, circling closer, 'Though I'm sure she would suit a little Monkey like you just fine. As for me, I'll take a good warm-blooded white woman any day . . .'

I lunged at him with the knife, catching him on the shoulder as he dodged backwards and I stumbled and almost fell. I saw him put his hand to his shoulder then hold it out looking at his bloody fingers. And at that moment he forgot all about the inheritance and needing to keep me alive for three more years.

I was desperately regaining my balance when he jumped me. He grabbed my hand and twisted it behind my back until I let go of the knife. He bent to grab it and I drop-kicked him, but his rage had given him lightning speed and he got the knife and slashed out at me. I heard a faint hiss as the flesh of my cheek opened to the bone and I tasted the warm metallic flavour of my own blood.

I kicked and fought in my oriental style but I was no match for his extra height and weight and the sheer power of his rage. He slashed at my neck, at my chest, my groin. I put up my arms to protect myself, screaming not with fear but with an anger that matched his. At that moment I did not care if I lived or died. I loved gentle Maluhia and I wanted to see Jack dead for what he had done to her.

Strong arms finally forced Jack off me. Kahanu punched him to the ground. He snatched the knife and towered murderously over him.

'No no, Kahanu,' I heard Maluhia scream, 'I am not worthy of such an act of retribution. I am only a kawhaini, a concubine.'

A tremor ran through Kahanu's massive torso as he looked from her to Jack, and then he strode to the water's edge and tossed the bloody knife into the ocean.

Jack sat up, rubbing his jaw, wiping the blood from his face. He was laughing. 'I hope you die, you motherfucking little Monkey,' he yelled, clambering to his feet. 'I'll get you yet. When you're not hiding behind Maluhia's skirts and Kahanu is not around to protect you...' He was still laughing as he walked away.

Kahanu picked me up and carried me back to the stables. He laid me on the sweet fresh straw and Maluhia bathed my wounds, but I was bleeding badly and she could not staunch the flow.

Kahanu looked worriedly at Maluhia, he knew I needed medical help. He said that when it was dark, he would take me by boat to Maui where his family lived. The doctor would stitch me up and his family would hide me and look after me until I was better.

Maluhia was the eyes and ears of the household, she knew everything, and now she told me that Archer was planning to kill me when I was eighteen and take 'my inheritance'.

I didn't know what she was talking about. 'What inheritance?' I asked, because as far as I knew I was penniless. She shook her head, she didn't know. But she knew Jack could no longer be trusted, he wanted me dead. Now.

'*I won't go away without you,*' I said stubbornly, realising that I was leaving her at Jack's mercy.

She said, '*You are only a boy. You must go at once, to Maui. When you are strong enough you must go far away, where they will never find you.*' And then she pressed her life-savings, forty dollars, into my hand.

'*Never come back, Johnny,*' she whispered, bending to kiss me goodbye.

I told myself I would remember her sweet chaste kiss for ever, and the scent of the plumeria blossom in her hair, the cool smoothness of her lips, and her soft dark eyes shining with love and unshed tears. I knew I would never see Maluhia again and the wrench in my heart was more painful than my wounds. As the boat slipped away from the dock into the darkness, I sat in the bow, staring sadly back at the now invisible island, holding her in my memory.

'*Go back where you came from,*' Kahanu urged me as the boat lifted over the waves. '*Tell no one who you are, or they will surely find you. Make a new life for yourself. You are being thrust into manhood, my friend. The gods are telling you to take the opportunity of a new life.*'

I watched the handsome bronze giant guiding his boat across the channel, and I thought how strange it was that Jack Kane should be the one who had finally given me my boatride to freedom.

I wondered what I would do with such a prize. I had not left Kalani for ten years. I was rough, ignorant and uneducated. I had never seen a town or a city. I had never even been to Honolulu or Maui. I thought with a sinking heart, that Archer had been right. I was a savage. And I did not know how to behave in a civilised society.

I sat in the bow of the boat, staring across the waves to Maui. I had Maluhia's forty dollars in my pocket and the bundle of clean clothes she had sent with me. And I was free.

CHAPTER 29

I knew Kahanu had planned to tell Archer I had made my escape on Jack's little boat, as I originally had intended. He said he would scuttle the boat and tell them that I must have been lost at sea. I don't know whether they believed him or not, but no one came looking for me. Kahanu's family cared for me as they would their own son, and I envied their slow island way of life; the gentleness of it, each day blending sweetly into the next.

They were happy people and I still remember them gathering on the lanaii of their small frame house on the long warm evenings, greeting friends and neighbours who always stopped by for a chat or to share their meal. Someone would be strumming a ukelele and they would sing the lovely old chants and songs, and the women would dance; even the old ones were still caught up in the rhythms and the joy of their island life. I envied it, but I was apprehensive and anxious to move on.

Five weeks later, with many farewell leis and alohas, I was on a slow boat heading for Honolulu.

The island of Maui and Kahanu's family had been an easy transition for me: I understood them and their way of life. After all, I was more like them than my own so-called family. But Honolulu was a sprawling crowded city, hard-edged and fast-paced for an island boy like myself. And when I saw the famous Kane name emblazoned on the wharves and on ships, and even a Kane Street, I knew I was in enemy territory. I wasted no time: I gave myself a new name, John Jones and got a job on the first cattle boat I came across, plying between Honolulu and San Francisco. Ironically, it turned out to be a Kanoi ranch boat, but no one knew me. After all, no one had ever seen Johnny Leconte. I could handle cattle and that was all anyone was interested in.

I had been awed by Honolulu, but I was terrified by San Francisco. I had never seen such tall buildings, so many automobiles, such throngs of people, such crowded sidewalks, such shouting and bustle and noise. I hesitated to cross the roads, not knowing which way to look, I did not know what to order in the cheap café I went to, nor how to pay. People looked strangely at me in the street, staring over their shoulders at the ragamuffin I was, and I went ashamed into a store and bought the first pair of real pants I had ever owned. I bought two shirts and had my hair cut at the barber's and when I saw myself in the mirror, I saw a different person. But I knew I was still the rawest country lad: a wild boy in the big city.

I counted my money and found I had five dollars left. I would have to get a job and the only thing I knew was cattle. I was wondering what to do when a young fellow, not much older than myself, standing in line at a hotdog stand on Market Street, spoke to me. He was wearing a smart uniform of short red jacket and black pants and he told me he worked as a bellhop at one of the big hotels. He looked me up and down in a friendly style, and I guess I looked needy all right so he told me there was a job going, if I was interested. Now I had kept to myself on the cattle boat, barely exchanging more than a few words with the other men and this fellow was the first real person I had encountered outside of the islands.

His name was Augustus Stevens. 'Call me Gus,' he said

cheerfully as we walked back together to the hotel. He was smaller than I and just as thin. He said he was from the east coast and had come out west to 'seek his fortune'. He was sixteen years old at that time, and many years later I was to see his name again, as the president of a famous oil company: so I guess he finally made that fortune. But then he was struggling to hold it all together, just as I was, and it formed an instant bond between us.

That afternoon I became a bus boy with my name 'Johnny' written on a badge pinned to my smart red jacket, running errands, opening doors and hefting baggage at one of the city's smart hotels. The pay was poor but Gus had said that the tips evened it up and with caution he could manage, and he was right. I found myself a small cheap bare room in the Chinese quarter and by eating mainly rice and beansprouts in the local cafés, I found I too could manage.

I had gravitated to the Chinese quarter. I felt safe there. I understood their customs better than those of the brash hard-eyed men I worked with. But there was still not enough distance between me and the islands. I knew Archer and Jack often came over to San Francisco and I was constantly on the alert, looking over my shoulder in the streets and keeping a watchful eye out at the hotel. I needed to put hundreds of thousands of miles between the Kanes and myself before I could begin to feel that I had really escaped them.

I hoarded what few dollars I could with the vague notion of somehow making my way back to France, and the Villa Mimosa. I wondered if Nanny Beale was still there? And if she would remember the boy she had left on Kalani all those years ago? But when I read in the newspapers about the war raging in Europe and that France was occupied by the Germans, I knew that Nanny and the villa were just a dream.

The year was 1941. I had settled anonymously into my job at the hotel, keeping myself smart and taking pride in my quick service, smiling my thanks for the tips I received. And on my days off I explored the city with the eyes of a man seeing the pyramids for the first time. I travelled on the clanging tramcars, and on the ferries that took me across the bay to the woods and hills, and occasionally I visited a movie theatre with Gus, mostly Westerns where I enjoyed the horses and the action.

And then, on 7 December, the Japanese attacked Pearl Harbor and America was at war. I thought horrified, of Oahu, that peaceful island and the waterfront and all the wonderful ships I had seen, now devoured by flames, and of the many lives lost. And filled with anger I went immediately with Gus to enlist in the navy.

'How old are ya, kid?' the recruiting sergeant asked me, with a twinkle in his eye.

'Eighteen, sir,' I replied hopefully, just the way Gus had told me to.

He just laughed and said kindly, 'You've got the right sentiment, son, but you need a few more years growing before you can stand up for your country.'

I was bitterly disappointed, and I admit that at the back of my mind had been the hope that I might be sent to Europe. Gus was luckier, somehow his streetwise confidence got him through and he walked from that store-front recruiting office a signed-up member of the US Navy.

Gus wasn't the only one to leave the hotel; men were drafted and sent immediately for training and with help at the hotel in short supply, I found myself suddenly promoted to waiter. I was observant, I learned quickly, watching the others to see how they behaved, but underneath I still did not know the rules of life. I was still the wild boy from the islands, learning as I went.

Two years passed. San Francisco bustled with navy personnel; they occupied all the hotels and their girlfriends and wives flocked into the city to be near them. I was seventeen. One more year, I told myself, then I could legitimately enlist in the navy. I followed the war news, still with the vague hope that I would be sent to the Mediterranean sector. Meanwhile I got myself a new job.

The St Francis was a grand hotel with a smart clientele: the men were officers, the women classy, chic, rich. One of them, whom I served regularly, kept a suite there on a permanent basis. She said her husband, an officer, was 'down in the sticks' at Camp Pendleton, the marine base near San Diego and she refused to go anywhere near it.

'It's the back of beyond,' I overheard her complain to her friends, drinking their usual six o'clock cocktails while they assessed the evening's action and amusements.

She was fortyish, attractive and flirtatious, with blue eyes and a pale, almost translucent skin. Her hair was a natural silvery blonde worn in a fashionable pageboy, and her wide predatory mouth was the colour of the cardinal bird that used to come to sit on the lanaii rail on Kalani in the evenings.

I noticed her because she was pretty and she was always gay, always laughing and joking with her friends and the officers they went out with. But there was a restless quality about her. I noticed her eyes searching the room all the while she was talking and I wondered what she was looking for. And, sometimes, I would feel her eyes resting speculatively on me.

I blushed as I felt her look me up and down from across the room. I was young and innocent, I had hardly even spoken to a girl. I was tall now, and wiry and muscular and I thought she was mocking the way I looked in my tight black pants and short red brass-buttoned jacket.

She watched my face as I put the martini carefully on the table in front of her, and I turned away from her smiling gaze because I knew I was not exactly handsome. My face was too thin, my features too strong and, thanks to Jack, a scar ran in a deep groove from beneath my left eye almost to my chin. But Mrs DeSoto seemed to find me interesting.

She said, 'I can see you are a good waiter, Johnny. I shall have to make sure I get you when I call room service. They are always so slow and then there's always a mistake, somebody always forgets something.' She sighed. 'It's bad enough there's a war going on without the room service waiters making our lives hell.'

And she smiled at me again, her cardinal-red lips stretching over her beautiful even white teeth. Like pearls, I thought, dazzled.

'Thank you, Johnny,' she said, giving me a generous tip along with an intimate glance that made me blush again.

After that I served her often in the bar and she always tipped me well, always gave me that smile and let her hand touch mine as she slipped a dollar into my palm, making me feel hot and uncomfortable. She always knew how to make me blush and I would hear her laughing and feel her eyes on me as I walked away.

A few weeks later I was on room service duty. It was late, after midnight. No one liked the 'graveyard shift' because they got all the drunks and somehow I, as the youngest, always ended up with it. Mrs DeSoto called down: she wanted a bottle of gin and a bottle of vermouth and ice sent up right away.

'I'm glad it's you, Johnny,' she said, flinging open the door and smiling at me.

I walked past her into the room and placed the tray on the side table. I looked at her. She was wearing a long slinky red evening dress, gathered at the hip, and a diamond and ruby *pendant nestled in the low 'V' neckline, just above the white curve of her breasts.*

'Open the bottles for me, Johnny, would you,' she said, sinking onto the sofa. 'And then pour me a drink. Wait, I'd better show you exactly how I like it.' She glanced up at me through her lashes and gave me that smile again. 'So you'll know for next time.'

The room was lamplit and smelled of her perfume, rich and musky. I handed her the drink with a trembling hand and she leaned towards me and put the glass to my lips. 'Taste it, Johnny,' she murmured, 'then you'll know exactly how I like it.'

I took a discreet swallow and the alcohol caught at the back of my throat. I began to cough and she stood with her hands on her hips, laughing at me. 'I bet you've never even taken a drink before,' she marvelled. She sat on the sofa again and patted the cushion next to her. 'Come and sit here, Johnny, beside me, and tell me what else you have never done before. So I know what else to teach you.'

I sat next to her, hypnotised by her knowing blue eyes and her sexy red mouth. 'Look at you,' she said, running a finger down the length of the scar on my face, 'you're like a young buck, on the way to becoming a stag.' She gave me that special smile again and I wanted to grab hold of her, to kiss her. 'Such an attractive young innocent,' she said thoughtfully, holding the drink to my lips again.

She stood up and put a dance record on the Victrola. It was Glenn Miller playing 'Moonlight Serenade' and I gulped down the martini, watching as she drifted round the room in time with the music.

'It's my favourite,' she said as it finished. She shook her hair free from the net snood she was wearing, stretching her arms luxuriously above her head. 'Don't you like it, Johnny?' she asked, fixing two more martinis.

'Sure,' I mumbled, watching her swaying hips as she glided across the floor and put the record on again. She turned and looked at me. Then she drank the martini down and tossed the glass into the fireplace. And she began to dance again. Only this time she also began unbuttoning her dress, swaying closer until she stood before me. And then she let it slide to the floor.

She was a blonde vision in a red satin slip and high heels and I was lost. She sat next to me and began slowly to remove my clothes, everything except my tie. 'Now what shall we do with this, I wonder?' she asked, playfully pulling me towards her. She smelled of rich perfume and gin and her own flesh and I was drowning in the scent of her, the softness of her, the sheer lavish femaleness of her. I couldn't wait.

The first time I was too quick, but then she taught me control, how to make love to a woman. 'You're a good learner, Johnny,' she told me. 'I shall remember you. Except I still don't know your name.'

And, my senses blurred with alcohol and perfume and sex, I blurted out my real name. 'Johnny Leconte.'

She stared wide-eyed at me for a long moment. Then she threw back her head and laughed, her long white throat rippling, her cardinal-red mouth stretched over her beautiful pearly teeth. I looked at her, puzzled.

'Isn't that amusing,' she gasped at last. 'It's just too good to be mere coincidence. I mean how often do you hear the name Leconte? I knew Archer Kane had changed his name when he married the French woman and that he had a son. It is you, isn't it? Johnny Leconte?'

My heart sank as I stared at her, still not comprehending. 'Of course,' she exclaimed, still laughing, 'you don't know who I am. Why, my dear young buck, I am Chantal O'Higgins. I was Archer's second wife. The mother of his goddamn son Jack.'

I threw on my clothes as fast as I could and ran for the door, not daring to look at her. She was still laughing as though it was the best joke in the world as I ran.

I left the hotel that same night and the next morning I faked my age and successfully enlisted in the navy. But somehow I knew that one day, that fateful encounter with Chantal O'Higgins DeSoto would come back to haunt me.

CHAPTER 30

I learned a lot in the US Navy, but my education was more about men and war, and life and death, than book-learning. I did two and a half years service on a destroyer, mostly in the South Pacific, and I had regretfully to let go of my dream of ever ending up in the Mediterranean.

It wasn't difficult for me to adjust to war conditions, after all I had spent most of my life in a state of siege. I already had that extra sixth sense that warned of danger, and my formative years in Hawaii had also made a sailor out of me. I was used to the ocean and its ways and I was not afraid of it.

That does not mean I was never afraid: I would have been a fool not to be. And whenever I manned my turret gun, and faced the enemy across a few hundred yards of grey water, that old metallic taste of fear was in my mouth. War was a bitter and thankless business, but as recompense I had the camaraderie of my fellow-sailors, my colleagues in arms. I learned at last how to live with my fellow-men, how to accept friendship and offer it in return. I finally became civilised, if not quite a man-of-the-world. I doubted, even if I lived through the interminable war, I would ever become that. The psychologists say that one's personality is formed in the years before puberty, and mine was battle-scarred.

Still, despite living on the knife-edge of war, dodging torpedos and suicidal aircraft on bombing raids, I was almost happy. At last there were the right number of miles between me and the Kanes. My eighteenth birthday had been and gone and I knew, had I still been on Kalani, I would already have suffered the planned 'fatal accident'. Death in the service of my country was preferable; at least that would be honourable.

I was even tempted to stay on and pursue a naval career when the war finally ended in 1945, but I lacked the education to become an officer and my prospects were limited. Besides, I had the old urge to paint again. I had taken to sketching the sailors, playing cards in their undershirts and steel helmets, or sprawling exhaustedly on their bunks after a long night on watch, or reading mail from home, and I captured the longing expression in their eyes as they thought of their wives and children. From memory I sketched battle scenes of warships blasting the hell out of each other, of fire and mayhem and bloody broken bodies. And convoys slipping silently across the horizon while we kept watch, the vigilantes of the South Pacific.

The captain saw my sketches and he praised them and had them hung in the wardroom. When the long war finally ended he submitted some to the Chief of the Naval Department, and they were framed and hung proudly in the Department's lofty corridors in Washington.

I felt sad the day I became a free man for the second time in my life. The US Navy had taken the rough boy I was and moulded me into a man and I missed the camaraderie and the discipline. Now I had to think for myself again.

I knew only one thing: I wanted to paint. I had a bit of money I had managed to save, plus the financial sweetener the War Office gave us men to ease our way back into civvy street, but I knew it would not last long, and I also knew I could not go back to the west coast, or to Hawaii.

My life became a series of odd jobs, working the summer season as a waiter at the east coast mountain resorts to make enough money so I could spend the winters painting. I had no idea if my art was 'good'. It was just something I felt compelled to do, the single driving force in my life. That, and the need to return to France again some day, to see my old home and to find Nanny Beale.

There were girlfriends in those days, sweet young things who I loved for a while, and models who fell for the romantic scarred young artist in his icy 'garret' – actually a loft over a hardware store in a little seaside town in Maine. I could never be far from the sea, it lured me back, just the way my paints and brushes did. But I fell in and out of love along with the seasons and my only true love was my art.

The years drifted slowly past, the way they do when one is young. Occasionally I would sell a painting and the wrench was terrible when I had to let it go. I wanted to keep them all because they were my memories of the people I met and the places I had been, and the girls I had loved. As always, I was painting my life. But I never painted Kalani or anything to do with my childhood. I had hidden it away at the bottom of my mind and it lurked there, like an unexploded torpedo, biding its time until it detonated with the past.

By the early 1950s my paintings began to be noticed. I was offered an exhibition at a small but exclusive New York gallery, and I sorted through my canvases carefully, reluctantly parting with those I considered my best. I bought myself a new suit for the occasion and shaved off my winter beard, and stood around in the gallery, clutching a glass of champagne in my hand, feeling foolish and out of place as I eavesdropped on their comments. To my surprise they were mostly praise, and soon a row of little red stickers adorned my works. I was a minor success, but at least now I was a working artist: one whose works had sold. And on the strength of that I received a commission from a man of power and high finance to paint a portrait of his wife.

She was a simple woman, quite plain but with dramatic bones that lent her great dignity. She had married her husband when she was eighteen and had stuck with him through all the hardships, living in garden apartments on Long Island and tenement apartments in New Jersey, until he had finally struck it big in the life assurance business. Mergers were followed by acquisitions and over the years he had become a renowned if rather dubious financier, a multi-millionaire. And now he lived like a lord. He was seen at every charity function and every fancy dinner and he was a close friend of those in high places in Washington.

The only thing was his wife was never seen with him. Sometimes his daughter accompanied him, but more often it was a stunning blonde less than half his age, ablaze with diamonds and couture.

I knew the portrait was a ploy on his part to make his wife feel he still cared. And to keep her quiet, I thought as I looked at her the first time we met. I also knew the reason he had chosen me as the artist was because I was cheaper than the more well-known ones, and he thought his wife wouldn't know the difference anyway.

She was a sweet woman with a gentle kind of charm, a genuine goodness of heart that refused, against all odds, to see bad in anyone. I liked her and I despised him and I gave that portrait everything I'd got.

I dressed her in bronze-green velvet, like a medieval princess, with her hair upswept showing off those dramatic cheekbones and her Nefertiti nose. I hung her with gold and emeralds and she lifted her chin proudly, standing tall and straight as a woman who values herself should. And, peeking from all this pride and arrogance, were her wonderful dark eyes, filled with warmth and a kind of innocence that we rarely see.

That portrait became the cornerstone of my success, even

though I was never in essence, a portrait painter. It went on loan to various museums and the name of John L. Jones began to be heard around and I even read about myself in the newspapers and in Time *magazine. I received more commissions, but I put them all on hold because I finally had enough money for that trip to Europe.*

I travelled across the Atlantic by ship, the way I had come, only this time I had a decent cabin in second class. I could not yet afford first, but it was of no account. I was going home. I lingered a while in Paris, stretching out the blissful moment of my return, and drinking in the sights that even a war had not been able to destroy. I saw the museums and the paintings and I sipped red wine in boulevard cafés and watched the world go by.

When I finally boarded the sleeper train to the south, I was like a lover held too long at arm's length by his amoureuse. I needed it.

Though I could not remember it exactly, the Côte d'Azur was somehow, magically, as I had always imagined it: the way the light fell on the green hills, the sandy white lanes, the umbrella pines and the tall cedars pointing like needles into a sky so blue I thought nothing could be bluer. Until I saw the Mediterranean and I knew the true meaning of 'azure'. I was trembling with delight, it was an artist's dream and the light an inspiration.

I checked into a small auberge on the coast run by a couple of sturdy peasants, mother and daughter. The father was a fisherman who went out with his nets at night and returned with the dawn with samples of his catch that later adorned our dinner table. They were a charming family, simple and courteous to the stranger in their midst, and they were intrigued when they saw my easel and realised I was an artist and I intended to paint them. And I was delirious with this new-old way of life, the freshness and the still-unsullied beauty of it, and the quality of it: the food, the wine and slow pace that belonged to a Mediterranean climate.

But having arrived, I nervously put off my search for the past. I told myself it was because I wanted to paint, but the truth was that now I was here, I was afraid of what I would find. I was afraid Nanny Beale was dead, perhaps killed in the war, or maybe she had disappeared back to her home-land, England. I was afraid the Villa Mimosa belonged to someone else and that I would be forbidden entry to it, and my dreams would have to stay mere dreams. And most of all, I was afraid I would find Jack and Archer Kane there, lording it over my old home.

But I had to do it. I had to find out about my past. About Nanny Beale, and the truth about my mother.

I found the Villa Mimosa right away, of course, like a cat taken and dropped hundreds of miles away can find its way home. I cycled along the sandy road leading up the hill and past the crumbling pink stucco wall, half-hidden under its burden of bougainvillaea and roses. My heart was pounding like a rider in the Tour de France as I leaned my bike against the wall and rang the bell, peering through the rusting iron gates up the gravel drive, as far as the curve that hid the villa from sight.

The *gardien*, a pleasant fellow in blue work overalls who said he was also the gardener, answered my ring and told me no one was there.

'I used to know someone who lived here,' I told him, fishing for a response. 'The Leconte family.'

His face lit up, and I could see he was pleased to hear the name mentioned again.

'They are long gone, M'sieur,' he told me. 'Madame is dead and her husband, the Foreigner, and the son live far away on some tropical island. I heard they returned once, after the war, to claim the boy's fortune, but they never came here to see the villa. The boy's old home, M'sieur. The very place he was born. It would have broken Madame Leconte's heart to know her son cared so little for the place she loved best.'

I realised that Maluhia had been right. There was an inheritance, and the Kanes had got their hands on it after all. I guessed that Jack had posed as me, pretending he was Jean Leconte and claiming my fortune. I shrugged uncaring, I didn't give a damn about the money. I was alive and free, and I was happy in my own way. I wanted nothing more.

The gardien saw my interest in the house and he offered to show me around. As we crunched up the gravel path and the beautiful pink-washed villa came into sight, I remembered with total recall the day my father came to get me. I remembered the small boy that was myself sitting on the marble step, so cool against my bare legs, with the morning sun on my face and my beloved Fido clutched in my arms. And I felt again the terror when my father's eyes met mine with such blank indifference and he said, 'Pack him up. I'm taking him with me.' And then the black cloud that settled over me, blotting the sunshine out of my life, for ever.

I knew the villa: I remembered every detail, the marble floors, the great curving staircase with the koa wood banister that Archer had installed to replace the one made of ordinary oak, as a present to my mother when they married. I hesitated at the door of my old nursery: looking at the empty room that had been Nanny's domain.

The old firegrate still had the big brass club fender with the leather seat, but her high-backed rocking chair was gone and the big toy cupboards were empty. I opened the door to my bedroom and saw that my little cherrywood bed was still there, with my initials JL scratched with a pin, and I ran my fingers over the place, smiling as I recalled Nanny's furious face when she had seen what I had done.

I walked slowly through my mother's empty room, imagining her looking out at the view of the sloping lawns and the fountain sparkling in the sun, past the cypresses to the sea. I thought of her being woken by the melodious chirping of her gay little canaries and songbirds in the silver aviary that the gardien *told me had been destroyed in a storm long ago.*

I stood by her window, wishing I had known her, thinking that the Villa Mimosa was my rightful inheritance. I could legitimately claim my fortune; I could live here in this wonderful house, be free to paint knowing I would never have to spend another summer season as a waiter in the Catskill Mountains again. But I knew I would not.

I thanked the gardien *for his courtesy and asked hesitantly about Nanny Beale. I feared the worst, remembering how old she must be and expecting to hear him say he knew nothing, or that she had gone home to England to die. But instead he told me she was living in a little cottage, just down the hill.*

'She stayed here right through the war,' he told me proudly, 'though many times the Germans threatened to intern her because she was English and they suspected her of being a spy.' He gave an insouciant Gallic shrug and said, 'We were all involved in the Resistance in some way around here, channelling the escaped prisoners and the English airmen along the coast to Spain and then Portugal. Our little boats played host to more than just fishes in those awful years, M'sieur,' he added with a sly grin.

I cycled at top speed to the bottom of the hill and down a sandy white lane curving round the little peninsula to where there were a few scattered houses. I knew which one must be hers: it was tiny and whitewashed, with a plume of smoke curling from the chimney, even though the day was warm. And the garden was a riot of English roses and delphiniums, and big white daisies and lavender. And there, bending over her herbaceous border, wearing a large straw hat and sensible white lace-up shoes, was an old lady.

My heart jumped as I leaned on the gate watching her, absorbed in her task of snipping the finest blooms, placing them in the wooden garden trug beside her. Her back was stooped and I noticed that arthritis had twisted her hands into grotesque shapes. I was shocked to see how tiny she really was, when in my childish memories she had been tall and stately.

She lifted her head, suddenly aware of being watched. Our eyes met and it was as though time stood still. Each saw before us the person that now existed – and the one that used to be. I saw the strong-boned face that was indelibly imprinted on my memory, crumpled now and crisscrossed by a network of fine lines and the marks of pain of her crippling arthritis, and her faded patient eyes that told me she bore it with all her old fortitude.

And she saw the boy she used to know in the tall young man, his frailness gone, his stick-like limbs sleeked out with muscle and a face that had finally grown into its features. She told me proudly afterwards, it was the face of an interesting-looking man. Not handsome, but a face no one would forget. Especially with the evil-looking scar running along the cheekbone.

'You haven't changed that much, Johnny,' she said quietly, her eyes smiling at me. 'I still recognise you.'

'And I you, Nanny Beale.'

I leapt the garden gate and clasped her to me. Tears were running down both our faces, but I felt her frailness and knew that now I was the strong one and she the weak.

'I thought you were dead,' she murmured, her voice trembling with emotion. 'Then they told me you had returned and claimed your inheritance. I said it couldn't be

you, that you would have come here to the Villa Mimosa, that you would have found me. All these years I've thought about you, and every night I said a prayer for your safety. And every birthday that passed I wondered if you were still there to enjoy it, because I knew the man who took you was evil and capable of anything.'

I took her arm and we went inside and she smiled at me through her tears. 'I bet you never thought you would see your old Nanny cry,' she said, 'but these are tears of joy.'

She bustled about, fixing tea and we sat by the fire, she in her rocker and me on a straight-back wooden chair, balancing plates properly on our laps. We had proper starched white damask napkins and old-fashioned ginger cake taken from the special red tin she kept in the larder, but we were too busy talking and re-kindling our love for each other to eat it. She poured tea from an old brown pot, though I noticed she was forced to use both hands to lift its weight and the cup trembled noisily on its saucer along with the trembling of her hand as she passed it to me.

I had come home again and I sighed with the sheer glorious happiness of it. I looked round her room, seeing her things just the way I remembered and I said, 'I shall never leave you again, Nanny. I'm here now and I shall look after you.'

I told her briefly about my years on Kalani, and my life after. I did not want to distress her, and I said I was happy with my life.

'But you must fight for what is yours, Johnny,' she said, looking worriedly at me over the tops of her round tortoiseshell spectacles. 'When I heard that Archer Kane had been here with his supposed "son", I went to the notaires and said it could not be you. They described the man who claimed he was Jean Leconte: they said he was tall, blond, blue-eyed, a young giant. I told them you were dark-haired

and dark-eyed like your mother, but they said time changes a person. Of course I knew they were wrong. I guessed it was Jack Kane. And all my hopes for you disappeared, Johnny. I felt sure they had killed you too.'

'Too?' I asked, puzzled.

And then she told me about my mother.

The teacup shuddered noisily in its saucer again, only this time it was my own trembling hand as I put it down. Nanny handed me the letter written to me by my mother before she died and I read it numbly. I thought about the pain my unknown mother had gone through: the plain little rich girl growing up and finally being forced to acknowledge her lack of beauty; the solitude imposed on her by her father deepening into isolation after he died; and finally the poor Célibataire living in lonely splendour at the Villa Mimosa, falling head-over-heels for a man she thought saw her as she really was, with the inner beauty she knew she possessed.

But Archer Kane never saw the beauty of my mother's nature, he never cared about her soul. All he wanted was her money and now he had got it.

'You must fight for what is rightfully yours,' Nanny said firmly again. 'Go tell them what has happened, claim your inheritance.'

I shook my head miserably. My mother's fortune had blighted my life. I would rather be poor and free and happy.

'But when you marry,' Nanny urged, 'what then? You cannot deny your children the right to claim their grandmother's fortune. It is what she wanted. The Kanes have stolen it, just the way they stole your childhood from you.'

I remained adamant about not wanting the money. I told her all I wanted to do was to paint, and that now I felt I had found my spiritual home. When she finally saw I would not change my mind, she persuaded me to write my story down 'for the next generation'. She said she would take it, with my birth certificate and her own 'document' telling the story, as she knew it, along with my mother's tragic letter and place them all in a safety deposit box at the bank. She would put the key to the safety deposit in her bureau drawer and a copy of the 'document' under her mattress for safe-keeping, just in case she wished to add anything to it. And then, she said, she would finally be content.

Flora Beale had kept her promise to Marie-Antoinette Leconte. She had done what she could to protect her son, and also her future grandchildren. 'When they are old enough,' she told me, satisfied, 'they will make their own choice.'

And as for me? I too have made my choice, and I am happier for it. I have no wish to possess the Villa Mimosa, with all its sad memories, though it is probably the place I love best in the world. I have no need of my dear mother's fortune because I have seen how money and greed can destroy a man. And I have learned how to live on my own terms. I have my painting and I am back in my homeland, and I have found my old mentor and friend Flora Beale, and a man could wish for no more. I am finally happy.

CHAPTER 31

Bea was still curled up on the green wicker sofa on the terrace when the sun came up the next morning. She clutched the papers telling Johnny Leconte's story to her chest, watching the glow spreading over the sky turning the Mediterranean into a lake of gleaming gold.

She stretched the weariness from her bones and walked back along the terrace, and into the hall. She stood looking at the place at the foot of the stairs where Marie-Antoinette Leconte's body had been found and she ran her hand along the smooth koa wood banister, as Marie must have done so many times before.

'I'm so sorry,' she whispered. 'I'm sorry for what happened, and I'm sorry I never knew you.'

She went to her room and called Nick. She told him that she had read Johnny Leconte's story, and asked him to come over right away.

She was waiting on the steps for him when he drove up half an hour later.

They sat together, hand in hand, on the front steps. 'Just like Johnny used to sit,' she said with a sad half-smile. 'Of course it was he who told me the story, I remember it so well. I can't think how I ever forgot. He was such a vivid raconteur, and the way he wrote it was exactly the way he told it to me. Now I remember everything and I'll continue where he left off.

'He told me that in 1954 he rented a little stone house in St Paul de Vence, a tiny village up in the hills behind the coast. He said it was an enclave of artists, writers and musicians; like-minded souls who gathered in the cafés in the square of an evening to share a meal and a glass of wine, and sometimes afterwards a game of pétanque. The hill villages then were still the way they had been for centuries, with the same families, the same simple way of life. He said it was like stepping back in time to a more innocent era.

'He told me he had finally unfettered himself from the past and he painted with a new freedom. He painted a hundred pictures of Nanny Beale, bending over her roses in her garden, pouring tea from her old brown pot, dozing on the vine-shaded terrace. I remember him showing them to me and explaining that they were not portraits as such; they were never photographic reproductions of a set of features. They had a subtle dream-like quality and as Maluhia once said, they captured the person she was in her own heart.

'He showed me the paintings he did of the village women with their lined weather-burned faces, their sharp eyes crinkled against the strong light, with black scarves covering their hair and white aprons over their black dresses, and their large peasant feet thrust into clumsy black shoes. Somehow, with the magic of his brush, he captured the gentle bovine innocence of their children, and the stooped backs of the men who had worked half a century in the fields. He painted the owner of the café, his bulk propped against his zinc bar, his sharp eyes for ever scanning the little saucers on each table, assessing who had paid and who had not. He painted the priest sitting on an old wooden upright chair outside his little white church. His arms were folded across his ample stomach, his legs outstretched, his hat tilted over his eyes and his black *soutane* blowing in the mistral, as he dozed.

'And he had painted a dozen pictures of Maluhia. His colour palette changed from the clear sunbaked Riviera tones and his paintings became more dreamlike, more exotic; outlines of shape and form half-hidden beneath a veil of colour: Maluhia combing her long black hair, like a silken screen hiding her face, the plumeria *lei* around her neck covering her breasts, a mere hint of an image. He painted the slender naked girl swimming under a crystal green ocean, as at home in her watery environment as the jewel-coloured fish he remembered so well.'

She looked at Nick and he nodded, he knew those paintings; everyone did. They hung in some of the most famous museums and galleries in the world.

'He put his heart into those paintings of Maluhia,' Bea said softly. 'He told me he would never forget her. He said her love had made his life on Kalani tolerable and that he had wondered if he would ever love anyone like that again.

'Then one day he met Severigne Jadot. She was visiting from Paris where she lived with her mother. He was sketching the village men at their evening game of pétanque and she stopped to admire his work. She was as tall as he was, and she had fiery red hair and a piquante face with a dusting of freckles, and expressive green eyes. He followed her into the café and they began to talk.'

Bea smiled as she thought of them meeting for the first time, imagining them when they were young and passionate. 'They fell in love,' she said softly to Nick, 'and instead of going back to Paris, Severigne moved in with him. He was crazy about her and of course he took her to meet Nanny Beale.

'He said the old lady put on her hoity-toity-Countess expression because in her opinion no woman was good enough for her Johnny. She served them tea and ginger cake and he could tell she was watching Severigne's manners and assessing her upbringing, but Severigne was the model of French politeness and *bon genre*. Despite her flaming hair and mischievous eyes, even Nanny Beale couldn't fault her.

' "Marry her," she whispered to him as they left. "It will be the best thing you have ever done."

'He said he just laughed; he knew she was right, and anyway he had already asked Severigne to marry him. Nanny was a witness at their wedding a month later, conducted by the same village priest whose portrait he had painted, in the same simple village church. The wedding party was held at the café and all the locals came, and all the other artists and the writers and the musicians. He said there was music and dancing until late into the night and it was the best party they ever had.

'It was the early 1960s then. He was in his thirties I guess, and Severigne would have been in her late twenties. They lived a simple life in their little stone house in St Paul de Vence, but things were changing on the Riviera. It was growing up. He said it was taking on a new kind of sophistication and that tourists were beginning to penetrate their little stronghold.

'Nanny Beale didn't live to see the changes though. One spring evening she was reading a passage from her favourite Charles Dickens. She put her spectacles down on the open page as she always did, to mark it. And then she just fell asleep and passed peacefully into another world.

'That's why her cottage looks the way it does. Johnny said it shouldn't only be the rich and famous who are remembered. He wanted it kept exactly as she left it. He said it was to be like a museum commemorating Flora Beale's unselfish life of service to others, her dignity and simplicity, and her goodness.

'After she died, he and Severigne moved further away

into the hills of Provence. They bought an old farm near Bonnieux, overlooking the fields of lavender and poppies and they were happy there. He only wanted to paint, he had no business head and no time for art dealers. If it had been up to him, he would never have wandered further from home than Avignon or Aix. So it was Severigne who took his paintings to Paris and arranged an exhibition at a major gallery. It had been a long time since his first portrait had caused such a stir, but he had not been forgotten. And those years of seclusion had given him the time to develop his talent. The paintings of Maluhia and Nanny Beale caused a sensation.

'After the success, he was restless. He said he couldn't paint, he needed a change of scenery. There was to be an exhibition in Manhattan and they went there and stayed a while and found they liked it. But he could never live in a city so they bought an old mill in upstate New York, in the Berkshires.'

Bea's golden velvet eyes were filled with the warmth of her memories as she looked at Nick. 'And that's where I was born,' she said softly. 'On July 28th, 1968.

'They named me Marie for my grandmother Leconte, and Laure because it was pretty. I was like my dad, a skinny waif of a child, with my mother's red hair and his dreamy brown eyes. We spent every summer at Les Cerisiers, the farm in Provence, and I grew up speaking French as easily as English.

'And then, when I was fourteen and he knew I was old enough to understand what he had to say, my father took me to see Nanny Beale's cottage. And the Villa Mimosa.'

She dropped Nick's hand as she said, 'My father and I sat on these very steps, gazing at this same magical view, while he told me the terrible story of his life. We were so close, so in tune with each other's emotions, I was devastated with the pain of what he had gone through. I felt it so deeply it was almost as if it had happened to me. As if I were the innocent happy child on the cool marble steps, listening to the songbirds and clutching Fido to my heart. As if I were the one whose small safe world ended that day, with the great black cloud shutting out the sun for ever.'

Tears coursed down her cheeks and Nick put his arms round her. 'It's all right, Bea,' he said. 'It's all right now, love.'

She nodded, letting her tears fall. 'He said he was telling me because Nanny had been right. He said one day, when I was older, I would have the right to claim my grandmother's fortune. If that was what I wished.

'I told him I didn't want anything to do with it. I didn't care about the money. But I thought he should have the villa. "It should be yours," I said to him. "It's the place you loved, where you were happy. And Grandmère Marie would have wanted us to be here."

'He just smiled and said it wasn't possible. "Let the sleeping dogs lie," he told me, "in case they turn round and bite you again."'

Bea wiped away her tears and said wearily, 'So that was that. He never lived at the Villa Mimosa again. Life went happily on. I was the child of an artist, but still it was a normal sort of life, and I was a normal sort of kid. You know, I did all the usual things, sleep-overs, and local high school, and then college.' She smiled thinking about it. 'They never sent me away to a smart prep school because Dad said he couldn't bear to part with me. "The only day you're going to leave home is the day you marry," he said, laughing at me. And Maman really had to work on him to let me go to college. Vassar. Not too far away, so I could come home weekends. And how I loved coming home, it was the best place in the world. My father loved his solitude, he needed it in order to paint, and our house was a sort of haven of tranquillity. It always seemed miles away from the harsher realities of life.

'I guess they didn't have any real close friends, there was just never time for them. They were complete you see; the perfect couple. They didn't need anyone else.

'It was just a normal loving childhood,' Bea said. 'I didn't even realise my father was famous until my teacher in high school told me. I remember feeling surprised. After all, he was just my dad.'

She fell silent. She took her hand from Nick's and hugged her knees under her chin. Her eyes were closed and her face tight with emotion as she said in a strangled voice, 'I can't talk about the rest.'

Nick put his arms round her and held her, stroking her short springy hair, waiting for the trembling to stop.

He knew the story. It had been in all the papers. Johnny and Severigne Jones were on their way to the opening of an exhibition of his latest works at a gallery in Washington when their car had skidded in the rain and gone off the road. It was four hours before the police emergency services had been able to cut them from the wreck. They were both dead.

'I wish I could help,' he said quietly.

She shook her head. 'Not even you can bring them back.'

'What did you do? Afterwards?' Nick asked.

'I came here for a while, to the farm in Provence. Then I went home again.'

She fell silent again. 'And?' he prompted.

She lifted her head and looked at him, anguished. 'I don't know,' she said. '*I still don't know what happened at Mitchell's Ravine.*'

The children came running into the room, their bare feet pattering on the tiles with the dog skittering behind them. They stopped with a jolt, staring at Bea's tearful face with big frightened eyes.

'What's the matter?' Scotty said gruffly, fear catching in his throat. It couldn't be happening again, he thought panicked. Bea wasn't leaving them was she?

Julie ran to her. She flung her arms round Bea's neck. 'Don't cry, please don't cry, Bea,' she wailed, tears spurting from her own eyes. 'I'll do anything, I'll be good, I'll tidy my room, I'll clean up after Poochie. Only please, please don't cry. I love you, Bea,' she sobbed, all her new fears surfacing. 'Don't cry, don't leave me. I want to stay with you for ever . . .'

Scotty ran to join her, entwining his thin brown arms tightly round Bea's. The two of them clung to her like limpets and Bea managed a smile. 'I love you too,' she whispered. 'But now I want to tell you about my own mother and father, about why I'm crying. And why I understand so well what happened to you.'

Holding them close, she whispered the story in their ears, of how her own mother and father had been killed in an automobile accident, just the way their parents had.

'I was grown up, of course,' she said quietly, looking at Nick as she spoke. 'I was supposed to be able to cope with grief. But I just couldn't face seeing anybody. I wanted to be in the place where we had all been so happy together. The home my parents loved best. Their farm in Provence, Les Cerisiers. I needed to do my crying alone.'

'We cried too,' Scotty whispered, sniffing back his tears. 'We cried and cried, Bea, but it didn't bring them back.'

She ran her hand through his rough hair, 'No darling, crying doesn't bring them back,' she said. 'It's just our way of saying we loved them and we shall always miss them. Crying is a good thing, Scotty, remember that.'

'It made me feel better,' Julie volunteered, gazing up at Bea. 'But I still wanted my mom and dad.'

'Me too, baby,' Bea said, kissing her upturned face. 'But

now look at us. How lucky we are to have found each other. Now we are a whole new family. Of course I know I'll never take the place of your real mother and father, that's only right and proper. But now we have each other and that makes me very happy.'

'Then you won't cry any more?' Scotty said anxiously.

'Oh, I don't know, maybe I will cry now and then. Just like you do,' she added, smiling at him. 'But remember, that's a good thing to do. It makes us feel a bit better, a bit closer to them. One day, as time passes, we shall be able to remember them without crying, we'll remember all the good things and the happy times we spent with them. And that is good too.'

'How long will it take, Bea?' Julie asked wistfully, wiping a tear away with a grubby finger.

'A little while, baby, a little while. You'll see, one day you will smile as you remember something your mommy said to you.'

'I can tell you that's true,' Nick said from the background. He looked at Bea and she thought his glance was almost as wistful as Scotty's. She smiled, including him in the new family.

'What ever would I do without you?' she said.

He shook his head, still wistful. 'I was hoping you would never have to try.'

Scotty darted a quick glance at him then at Bea. His brown eyes narrowed as he looked shrewdly at them. 'Are you two going to get married?' he said with a grin.

'Oh yes, yes.' Julie danced over to Nick, her tears blending into a sunny smile. 'Please, please, Nick. Then we'll have a proper mommy and daddy again.'

'This is the damnedest proposal of marriage I've ever heard,' Nick said, holding Bea's eyes.

'You mean I should wait for you to go down on your knees?' she said smiling.

He grinned as Scotty tugged at him. 'On your knees, quick,' Scotty said urgently. Nick knelt and the two children knelt down next to him.

'Darling Bea French, Marie-Laure Leconte. Will you do me the honour of becoming my wife?' Nick said, as humbly as he could manage.

'Oh please become his wife. Say yes, say yes, yes, yes . . .' the children chanted.

Bea's eyes brimmed with love as she looked at them. 'How could I possibly say no?' she marvelled.

Julie threw her a worried glance. 'Does that mean yes?' she asked suspiciously.

'It means yes,' Bea said.

'With all your heart?' Scotty said, making sure.

'With all my heart,' she promised.

'Are we yours for ever now?' Julie asked still anxious.

They laughed. 'For ever,' they promised.

'It's for ever, Julie,' Scotty said, solemnly catching her hands in his.

'For ever, Scotty,' she whispered back.

'Yeah yeah,' they yelled suddenly cavorting round the room, turning cartwheels and leap-frogging over chairs as the dog danced madly after them, barking its head off.

'I wasn't joking,' Nick said seriously, taking her hand.

'Nor was I.'

'I love you, Bea Marie-Laure,' he said, bending to kiss her lips.

'And I love you,' she whispered back.

'They're kissing, they are kissing . . . uugggh,' Julie yelled, laughing with joy.

'That's our new mom and pop,' Scotty yelled back, skidding across the polished floor, heading for the kitchen to tell Jacinta.

CHAPTER 32

The sky was black and moonless without even the suggestion of a breeze. Phyl sat on the sofa in the beautiful summer room at Brad's Diamond Head mansion, watching him as he prowled the floor, still talking. It was four in the morning and she was tired, but fascination with what he was revealing kept her there. '*I want you*,' he had said, looking broodingly at her, but instead of the thrill she would have felt just a few weeks ago, this time the shiver that ran up her spine was fear.

She asked herself why? She told herself he was still the same good-looking sexy more-than-eligible man she had fallen for in Paris. The difference was that now she was seeing him with professional eyes. He was revealing a dark, troubled underside to his character that interested her technically, but at the same time repelled her.

As she listened to him, she knew she had never been in love with Brad. She didn't even know him. It had been one of those strangers in the night, flash-heat all-consuming affairs that was doomed to self-combustion. She wished she had never come to Hawaii, now she saw how disturbed he was. But the man was searching his soul, baring his emotions and his life to her. She owed it to him to listen. To help him.

'I lied to you about the Monkey,' he said. 'The reason he ran away from the island was because he was responsible

365

for the death of a servant. Her name was Maluhia. She was young and pretty. He raped her and so she threw herself over a cliff. But somehow the Monkey escaped in Jack's little boat. My father never believed he had drowned. He always said one day he would come back to haunt him.

'Archer was drinking heavily by then and the responsibility for Kanoi was falling on Jack's shoulders. He had found out their financial affairs were in chaos, and the ranch was in dire need of an influx of capital. Archer spent money like there was no tomorrow. But Jack was different.'

Brad's eyes met Phyl's, and there was a quiet desperation in them that touched her.

'You see, to Jack the Kanoi ranch was his identity, his reason for being. He valued it above everything. Above morals, above his own life. Even above his father's life.

'Jack was in Honolulu the day the Japanese bombed Pearl Harbor. He said when he saw what they had done he was filled with murderous rage. He just wanted to get in there and kill the bastards with his bare hands. America was at war and supplies were at a priority. The ranch got a financial reprieve thanks to the government, and Jack joined the Marines.'

Brad laughed, his mood changing as he said, 'God, he was a tough fighter,' he said proudly. 'He earned himself a couple of medals for valour, won, he told me because of his total uncompromising hatred of the enemy. "*No one hates quite like Jack Kane*," his fellow-marines used to say. "*All he wants to do is kill*."

'Archer had been given the rank of Major in the army and a desk job supervising the Japanese interned on the island, which allowed him plenty of time to run the ranch.

'Then the war was over and the need for money raised its ugly head again. Archer figured out a plan. The whole of

Europe was in chaos; many years had passed since his French wife's death and by now the Monkey would have been of an age to inherit. But he had no proof that the Monkey was dead and anyway he knew it would have been too difficult to take his claim through the French courts. So he took Jack to France and passed him off as Marie's son.

'He said it was easy. The old lawyers and bankers who knew about La Célibataire were all dead, and the legal papers had been lost in the chaos of war. He just gave them the birth certificate and Jack signed his half-brother's name and they handed over the inheritance.

'You see,' he said, spreading his hands wide and looking appealingly at Phyl, 'to them the ranch had to come first. It may not have been strictly legal, but Jack said it was the right thing to do.'

'And did you agree with that?' Phyl asked quietly.

'Of course I did,' he said astonished. 'I would have done the same myself.' He shrugged her question impatiently away as though it scarcely mattered. 'The money should have been Archer's by rights anyway if it were not for the French legal system.'

He began pacing the floor nervously again. The dog crouched near the door, watching him, waiting for a command, but for once Brad was not even aware of it.

'They were in Paris,' he said abruptly, 'and Jack told me Archer was drunk with triumph.

'"La Célibataire's fortune is finally ours," he said. "No one can ever take it away from us. Now we have enough for everything, Jack. For Diamond Head, the ranch, whatever you want it's yours."

'Jack was around twenty-four years old then, I guess, but he knew he had to take control of the ranch before Archer threw all that money away on booze and women and high living, just the way he had before.

'They were in the Ritz bar drinking champagne and congratulating themselves when Jack noticed a blonde expensively-dressed woman across the room, staring at them. She was smiling, an odd, knowing little smile. She was older, but still very attractive and smart-looking, and there was something eerily familiar about her. She caught his eye and then she got up from her table and walked over to them.

'"Surprise, surprise," she said, kissing Archer on the cheek. He just stared up at her, a stunned look on his face, and then she turned to Jack and said, "The last time I saw you, you were a squalling red-faced infant. I have to admit you have improved since then." She blew him a kiss, throwing back her head and laughing as Jack just stared at her.

'"Don't you know me?" she said, still laughing. "I'm your mother. Chantal O'Higgins."

'Jack said he felt the same sudden hard rush of hate towards Chantal as he had the Japanese after Pearl Harbor. He could have killed her with his bare hands right there in the Ritz bar. He had never seen her before, but he'd read plenty of dirt about her in the gossip columns.'

Brad stopped his pacing for a minute. He glared at Phyl and said bitterly, 'Didn't I tell you the Kane men really knew how to pick their women? Well Chantal was a true bitch. "*Surprise, surprise,*" she'd said to them, as though she had seen her son just last week.

'She told them she was in France to check her properties in the Charente. She said, "Fortunately the Germans liked cognac and they had left them in good shape. Lucky for me the family trust is in Switzerland huh?" she said, "I get to keep it all."

'She stood looking at them, mocking them with her eyes

368

and her smile. Then she said, "I heard your third wife left millions, and most of it went to your son. By the way," she added casually, throwing out her bombshell, "did I tell you I met Johnny? Of course he's not nearly as handsome as you, Jack. But I want to tell you, *he is something else in bed*." Her peals of mocking laughter rang in their ears as she turned and walked away.

'Jack leapt up to go after her, he would have killed her there and then, but Archer held him back. "Sit down, you fool," he said angrily. "Don't give her the satisfaction of thinking you believe her."

'But Jack did believe her. He knew it wasn't the kind of thing Chantal could have invented on the spur of the moment to just rile them. *His goddamn half-brother was still alive. And he had screwed his mother*. He burned with humiliation and he said to Archer, "One day I'll find that little bastard Monkey. And then I'll kill him."

'"You'd better," Archer replied, ordering up a Scotch. "Or else he'll be back to claim the money. And where will the Kanoi ranch be then?"'

Brad poured himself a brandy. He swirled the amber liquid, staring blankly down into the glass. Phyl thought it was almost as if he had forgotten she was there, he was so caught up in the story of the past.

Finally he tossed back the drink and said, 'Jack knew Archer was capable of running through the second fortune even faster than he had the first. But this time the money was in Jack's name. All Jack wanted was the ranch. He gave Archer enough money to live out his rich man's life and then he began to build up the business again.

'He put everything he had into the ranch, it consumed his life. And he did anything he had to, to make it a success again. But he told me that he never forgot that the Monkey was out there somewhere, and that one day he might return to claim back his fortune.

'Jack worked hard those years, and he played hard. There were plenty of women in his life, they liked him all right. They always had. Then he met Rebecca Bradley at a party in San Francisco. Even afterwards, when he hated her, he always said she was the most beautiful woman he had ever seen.

'Rebecca was rich and spoiled and very social and she looked down her nose at the young rancher. "A wild man", she called him mockingly when they were introduced, and Jack said he laughed, remembering the Monkey and thinking how ironic it was that now he was the one being called "wild".

'He said Rebecca was elegant and proper but underneath he sensed a like spirit. She was just as wild and wicked as he was and he loved it. He told me the first time she let him make love to her was in the back of her father's chauffeured limousine.

'They were driving home from a party out in the hills somewhere, and it was dark. The chauffeur kept his back discreetly turned, but Rebecca knew he was aware of what was going on and she liked it. She always liked that sense of danger, Jack told me. She enjoyed the feeling that she might be caught out. She wanted to do it in hotel elevators, in bathrooms at crowded parties, up against an alley wall, like a cheap hooker.'

Brad turned his pale ravaged eyes on Phyl. 'That was Rebecca,' he said bitterly. 'And she never changed.'

His hand shook as he poured another brandy. 'But Jack was giving her what she wanted and Rebecca decided she couldn't live without him, so they got married a couple of months later. It was the wedding of the year in San Francisco. Her father was a Hawaiian sugar baron and there was mixed blood in there somewhere, you could see it in her long black hair and the shape of her eyes, but her mother was an old guard socialite and the cream of the society crop attended their nuptials.'

Brad stopped his pacing and looked at Phyl. 'Wait here,' he suddenly commanded, holding up his hand. He strode off into the hall and the dog trotted quickly after him, its claws clicking on the wooden floor.

Phyl shuddered, thinking about what he had just told her. She knew she was finally getting the truth about Brad, and she was afraid of what he was going to say. She wished they were in her office; that Brad was just a patient and she the cool, aloof doctor. She looked nervously at him as he strode back into the room, clutching a silver-framed photograph.

'Here,' he said, pointing with a trembling finger at the couple standing outside a church in their wedding finery, smiling for the cameras. 'That's my father. And that, goddamn her, is Rebecca.' He groaned like a man in pain, then suddenly hurled the photograph across the room.

Phyl gasped, horrified as it hit the wall and the glass shattered into a thousand fragments. The dog ran towards it, sniffing and growling softly.

'Oh God,' Brad cried anguished. He knelt in the debris, and picked up the scarred photograph

'Why did I do that?' he demanded, frowning with anger, flourishing the scarred photograph under Phyl's nose. She drew back, alarmed. 'I know why,' he cried angrily. 'My mother was no good. She was a cheap lay. She was insatiable. Anyone was fair game to her. Her husband's friends, her own friends, a casual acquaintance. Even after I was born she just kept on doing it, taking what she wanted.'

He sank into a chair and put his head in his hands. 'I was the façade of innocence she used for her assignations,' he whispered through his fingers. 'She used to take me along with her. After all, who would suspect a woman of screwing around when her child was with her? But she did. She made me a witness, an accomplice to her dirty little game.

'My father was away at the ranch a lot of the time, and she would take me to San Francisco. We would set off and I would think maybe this time it will be fun, just the two of us together. Maybe this time it will be all right. But I hardly saw her, except when she dragged me along to her "social events" as she called them. She would give me toys and books and tell me to be a good boy. She said she and her friend were going into the other room and I was not to disturb them, they had a lot to talk about.'

Brad lifted his head and looked bleakly at Phyl. 'And I never did,' he said. 'I was the good boy, the model son. I wanted to please her and I did as she asked. Until the day she kept me waiting so long – two hours, three, four even – that I got frightened. I put my ear to the door of their room but there was no sound. I was afraid she had forgotten me, that she had gone off and left me, I thought maybe she had died ... I pushed open the door and peeked inside. The curtains were drawn and a lamp was lit on her side of the bed. I saw her clothes, scattered on the floor and I breathed a sigh of relief. I knew she could not have gone away and left me without her clothes.

'I slid through the door, peering into the darkness. And then I saw them. She was lying there naked, her black hair flung across the pillows. His head was on her breast and he was sleeping. She turned and looked at me. Our eyes met. Then, still looking at me, with a smile of terrible complicity, she took his genitals in her hand and began stroking them.

372

'I heard him groan and he began to stir and I ran, terrified from the room. Her mocking laugh followed me as I closed the door.'

Brad was looking at Phyl but she doubted he even saw her. His head was full of Rebecca as he said, 'Her laughter has haunted me ever since. I hear it in my dreams, waking and sleeping. And that smile. It was not the smile of a mother for her son.' He shook his head despairingly. 'She was so beautiful.

'Afterwards we went shopping and she bought herself a new hat, red with little feathers in it. And then for tea at some grand hotel she liked. She met her friends there. "Look at me, what a good mother I am," she said laughing with them, "taking my son out to tea." And she gave me that knowing smile again. "He's a boy who knows how to keep a woman's secrets," she said, and they all laughed.'

Brad lapsed into a deep silence, his head in his hands. Phyl waited, almost afraid to breathe in case she triggered off another dangerous memory.

He sighed deeply and he said, 'Years later, after they were divorced, I asked my father why he had put up with her. He just shrugged his shoulders and said he took his own pleasures where he could. Besides, she was part of the great Kane image: the beautiful society heiress, the glamorous wife and mother. In an odd sort of way I guess they suited each other. She took what she wanted and so did he. And he told me that women meant nothing to him. He said the only thing that mattered in our lives was the Kanoi ranch. "Never forget that, son," he said to me.' Brad's blank pale eyes met Phyl's as he said quietly, 'And I never have.

'My father told me the history of the ranch, how Archer had started it, and their financial difficulties over the years, trying to hold it together. And about the fortune that should have been theirs years ago if it were not for that half-brother.

'Jack told me, "That goddamn wizened little Monkey tried to steal our birthright from us, Brad, and don't you ever forget that. If it hadn't been for your grandfather Archer's cleverness he would have done it, and you and I would not be sitting here, looking out at one of the biggest cattle ranches in America." He said bitterly to me, "I should have killed the Monkey when I had the chance because I know in my bones he is still out there somewhere, like a coiled rattlesnake waiting to strike. He will try to take that fortune from us one day, son. He will want to take everything the Kane family have worked for all these years: our sweat and toil, our land, our heritage. *Our name*. Make no mistake, he will come to claim his fortune, and when he does we must be ready to act. Quickly and without mercy."'

Brad looked calmly at Phyl and said quietly, 'I have been waiting for that moment all my life.'

Phyl perched warily on the edge of her chair. Brad's mood swings from anger and violence to icy calm presaged trouble, she was sure of it. 'And do you think it will ever come?' she asked softly.

He stood up and poured himself more brandy, gulping it down. 'Not now,' he said coldly. 'Not any more.'

That fateful icy shiver ran down Phyl's spine again. Did he mean that the Monkey had returned? And that he had killed him? She was afraid to ask. Suddenly she was afraid even to be here alone with him.

'Jack almost killed Rebecca you know, before she left,' Brad said, almost conversationally. 'He said she had flaunted her affairs once too often and something in him just snapped. He grabbed a rifle and threatened to shoot her, but she just laughed and walked away. She knew all about him, and all about the Kane family. "Like father, like son," she said contemptuously, daring him on.'

'Oh God,' Phyl whispered, afraid to ask what happened.

Brad said moodily, 'He should have, but he didn't. He just beat her up a bit. It was what she deserved. I was watching from the doorway and I was glad. I was glad when she went away and it was just my father and I, alone. They got divorced and we got on with our lives, running the ranch. He sent me away to school and college but I couldn't wait to get back.'

He began pacing again, backwards and forwards, his hands in his pockets, his head down. 'I never saw my mother again. Archer had died several years before and then we heard Rebecca had had a stroke. She lingered on for a couple of years, but nobody ever saw her. They said one side of her face was paralysed, dragged down into unspeakable grotesqueness, and the other half was almost normal, the same beautiful Rebecca. But she couldn't speak and she couldn't walk. She died a couple of years later.

'Jack was drowned in a boating accident the year after I got out of college. They said he was drunk, but I didn't believe them. He was a good sailor and he was just caught in one of those sudden storms. I knew he would have made it through if he could. He wouldn't have left me alone.

'I inherited everything. The ranch, the houses, the island.' He laughed bitterly. 'And the ever-present threat of the Monkey. The rattlesnake at the heart of the Kane family, waiting to strike.'

Phyl looked at him, debating whether she dare ask the fateful question. But she had to know. 'What did you do about it?' she whispered.

Brad came to stand in front of her. He looked deep into her frightened eyes. He leaned forward and tenderly stroked her cloudy black hair from her frightened face. 'Why, I took care of it of course,' he said gently.

Phyl stared up into his handsome, gently smiling face, into his beautiful mad eyes. She thought of Mahoney saying: *'You get so you can feel who the villains are, even when they are cloaked in normality. Straight decent-seeming folks, just like you and me. But you must know better than anyone what goes on in people's minds, in those deep dark recesses. Things that are hidden behind good-looks and charm and expensive clothes. The wife-beaters, the child-abusers, the murderers. They are all just folk, like you and me.'*

He had been describing the man she was looking at. Brad was a textbook sociopath and she, the clever psychiatrist, had failed to see it.

Phyl flinched, as she felt his hands on her shoulders; with an effort she stopped herself from running from him. She dropped her head quickly, afraid he would see the panic in her eyes. She had to stay calm, humour him. She had to get out of here . . .

He said in that gentle concerned voice she knew so well. 'My poor Phyl. I've kept you talking all night. Look, the sun is already up. Go to bed, my love. Get some rest.' He glanced at his watch and added lightly, as if the long soul-searching confessional night had never happened, 'I almost forgot. I'm due at a meeting at the ranch first thing this morning. I'll fly over there now.'

She closed her eyes, trying not to flinch as he dropped a quick kiss on her forehead. 'I'll be back later,' he promised, sounding just like his old self. 'I want you to wait here for me. Don't go out. Don't leave this house. Promise me?'

She nodded, numbly. 'I promise.'

'Good.' He smiled, satisfied. 'I shall trust you this once then.'

Phyl watched him walk to the door. He whistled for the dog. The long night and the drinking had left no marks on him. His face was smooth, smiling. In his expensive shirt and well-pressed jeans, he looked every inch the rich urbane man of the world.

He turned to smile goodbye at her. 'Wait for me, Rebecca,' he said as he closed the door.

CHAPTER 33

Phyl listened for the sound of his car leaving, then she ran to her room and began frantically throwing her things into her bag. She telephoned the airport and booked a seat on the next flight out, then she called a cab, pacing the floor nervously until it arrived. A silent Chinese servant appeared from nowhere to carry the bag for her and she wondered, surprised how he had known. He must have overheard, she decided, wondering what else the servants overheard in this house of secrets.

She hesitated at the door, thinking what Brad would do when he found her gone without an explanation. She decided to write him a note. *'Brad, it's better if we do not see each other again. There is nothing I can do to help you.'*

She gave it to the servant and climbed quickly into the cab, looking over her shoulder through the rear window, half-expecting to see him come tearing down the road after her with that vicious Doberman at his heels.

The United flight was already boarding and she took her seat, breathing a sigh of relief when the doors were finally closed. She almost wept realising how frightened she had been. She didn't even want to think about the implications of Brad confusing her with Rebecca. All she wanted was to sleep until she woke up five hours later in San Francisco. And then she wanted to see Mahoney. She shivered with fright. *Oh God*, she thought, *I really need Mahoney*.

* * *

It was a slow Sunday night on the four to midnight shift. Mahoney figured the clock must have stuck a couple of hours ago, and he sighed. He guessed he should be glad the drug dealers and the armed robbers and the domestics were giving him a break and not killing themselves on his shift, but time was surely dragging.

He fiddled with the computer until Brad Kane's name came up again. He had replayed the details endlessly because there was still something about Mr Hawaii that bothered him. And here he had confirmation that the man was violent.

The first incident had taken place in college. He had attacked another guy in a bar. Nothing unusual you might say for college kids with too much beer inside them. Except this had been a particularly vicious attack: a broken glass shoved in the other guy's face. Mr Hawaii had gotten reprieved on that one because his father had hired him a smart lawyer. An undisclosed amount of damages had been paid to the victim, Brad Kane had gotten two months suspended, and nothing more was said.

A couple of years later he had been arrested for possession of an offensive weapon. A knife. He hadn't used it but the victim said he had threatened to, and this time the victim was a woman. A hooker, in fact. In Honolulu. Again money changed hands and a warning was issued, and nothing more was said.

The third was more recent. A few months ago a servant in the Kane household had been killed. The report said that one of Brad Kane's dogs, a Doberman, had suddenly gone wild and attacked him. Brad Kane had shot the dog himself, then he had called the police. He told them he was devastated; the victim was an old man who had been employed by the Kane family for more than fifty years. He said he had to leave on urgent business but he would answer any questions on his return. And he had. A month later when he came back from Paris. By then the old man was buried, at Kane's expense, and the incident was just a matter of formality. A sworn statement, an expression of regret, and that was it.

Mahoney sighed as he shut down the computer. One incident of youthful violence after drinking might be condonable. Two certainly was not. And a third, inexplicable one, was just too much in any man's life.

He considered calling Phyl in Hawaii and telling her what he had found, telling her he didn't like it and to get the hell out of there. He sighed again as the phone rang.

It was Phyl. There was a booming noise over her voice and she said, 'I'm calling from the plane. I need to see you, Mahoney.'

She sounded desperate and he said quickly, 'What's wrong? Did he harm you?'

'No,' she said, shakily he thought. 'I'm okay. My flight gets in at six-thirty.'

'Why don't you come round to my place? I'll leave a message on your machine if I get hung up here.'

'I need you, Mahoney,' she said quietly.

'Glad to hear it, Doc,' he said, smiling. 'After all, we are here to serve.' But he knew she meant it.

The phone rang again immediately and an English voice said, 'This is Nick Lascelles. I'm a friend of Bea French and Phyl Forster.'

'How ya doin', Nick,' Mahoney replied breezily. 'I've heard a lot about you from Bea. And I wanna tell you all of it was complimentary.'

Nick said, 'I can't get hold of Phyl, so I thought I'd better call you. We were doing some research, finding out about the villa. I guess Bea told you about it. Well, we found out the connection. She remembered the little boy in her dream was her father. He lived in that house until he was five years old. He took her back there when she was fourteen, and told her the whole story. She's really upset, Detective Mahoney, because she also remembered her parents were killed in a car crash last year. He was the artist, John Jones.'

Mahoney gave an amazed whistle, he knew and admired Jones's work. 'I remember reading about it in the newspapers,' he said. 'It's a tough break. But what about the rest of her family?'

'There is none. She was left alone.'

Mahoney wondered if that was one of the reasons she had lost her memory. It was surely a big enough trauma. 'What about Mitchell's Ravine?'

'That's just it. She still doesn't know who tried to kill her. Or why. It's driving her crazy. She was terribly upset, but the children helped her and she seems better now. Still, I thought I had better call you and let you know. Bea says you're a friend.'

'Yeah. We're best buddies. Bea didn't seem to have too many friends when this happened, though. And it sounds as though they are a bit thin on the ground even now. What the hell, the girl is the daughter of a famous artist. Surely somebody would have missed her?'

'She said she had just dropped out for a while, after the funeral. She came back here to their farm in Provence. She wanted to be alone. I guess people respected that and so no one bothered her. Eventually she went back to the States, to their house in the Berkshires, and she doesn't remember anything else after that.'

'Right. Give me her full name, Nick, and I'll get to work on it.'

'It's Marie-Laure Leconte Jones. She was born in 1968, and the family's main home was the Old Mill, Faversham, Mass. They spent their summers at their farm, Les Cerisiers, near Bonnieux in Provence.'

Mahoney nodded. 'Thanks for being there for her, Nick. Stick with her, she needs all the help she can get.'

He put down the receiver, switched on the computer and drummed up the long list of names of women flying from warm countries into San Francisco International the week Bea had been attacked. He scanned quickly through them. They were all accounted for. He glanced through the long list again until he caught it. It had been marked checked and he scowled. He had a love-hate relationship with computers but the goddamn things were not infallible. They made mistakes just like men did.

'M.L.L. Jones,' it said. 'United Flight 511 from Honolulu. Dept: 18:00 hrs. Arr. 23:00 hrs.'

Hawaii! Again. He whistled, surprised. Again. Maybe lightning did strike twice in the same place after all. As he placed a call to the Honolulu Police Department, he wondered what the hell the young recently-bereaved Marie-Laure had been doing in Hawaii. He told himself it was probably just that she had needed a vacation. Still it was worth following up, and he asked his colleagues in Honolulu to find out when she had arrived, what hotel she had stayed at, and anything else they considered relevant. Then he shrugged on his jacket and signed off his shift and went home to meet Phyl.

She was waiting for him, sitting nervously on the edge of the sofa, clutching the cat to her breast for comfort. She had no makeup on and there were deep shadows beneath her famous blue eyes.

'You look like hell,' Mahoney greeted her.

'That's the way I feel.'

She fell into his arms and he held her, surprised. 'Hey Doc, what's going on?' he said gently. 'I know I'm a great-looking guy, but I didn't think I rated anywhere near as high as Mr Hawaii.'

She clutched her arms tighter round his neck. 'Don't even mention his name,' she said in a muffled voice, her face buried in his chest.

'That bad huh?'

'That bad,' she agreed with a shiver.

'I don't want to be the one to say I told you so. I already gave you my opinion.'

'I know. And you told me not to see him again.' She sighed, releasing him. 'I should have believed you.'

'You should have believed yourself. Your gut and your head told you something was wrong. You just didn't want to acknowledge it.'

She sank into a chair. 'I admit it,' she said, looking up repentantly at him. 'How could I, of all people, have been so stupid, Mahoney?'

He shrugged. 'It's easy. You just believed what Brad wanted you to believe. That's the art of a conman.'

'He's more than that. He's very seriously mentally disturbed.'

'Is that right?' He walked into the kitchen and began fixing coffee. 'It might interest you to know that I've been doing a little research on Brad Kane myself. I can't say I was totally surprised to find he had a record.' She looked at him, alarmed. 'Oh nothing too serious,' he said. 'Just cutting up a kid with a broken beer glass in college, and threatening a hooker with a knife. Nothing really truly bad. Yet.'

'He scared me, Mahoney,' she said.

'What happened?' He poured thick rich espresso into

small cups and put them on a tray with a bowl of brown sugar.

'He called me Rebecca.'

He glanced sharply at her, then he grinned. 'The mother?'

'It's not funny,' she said defensively.

He shook his head. 'You're damn right it's not. It's sicko, baby, that's what it is.'

'He terrified me,' she wailed. 'He talked right through the night, pacing the floor like . . . like a caged animal. He told me everything, about his wicked grandfather, and Jack and Rebecca.'

She grabbed Mahoney's hand. 'Oh God, Mahoney,' she wailed, 'I think he's killed someone.'

He handed her the cup of espresso. 'Sugar?' he asked politely. She spooned some in, looking numbly at him. 'Okay,' he said, 'first drink the coffee. Then tell me everything he said. From the beginning.'

Phyl did as she was told, and for once Mahoney listened in silence. 'So you think he killed this guy Monkey?' he said at the end.

She nodded. 'What else could I think?'

'And you thought maybe he was going to kill you?'

She shook her head and said helplessly, 'I don't know. He veered between manic and gentleness. I was afraid. You know, that gut feeling, the one you tell me I should listen to. I couldn't believe it. I looked at him, so nice-looking, so successful and . . . oh I don't know. He's a man who has it all, I guess. And then I remembered what you'd told me. About murderers and the child-abusers looking like regular folk, hiding their sins behind expensive clothes and a façade of normality.'

'As a psychiatrist I understood what had happened had damaged him. I understood about Rebecca. And I knew

Jack was a bullying father, a man without a scrap of moral sense. I felt almost sorry for him, for a while. And then I realised it was too late. He had gone over the edge into his fantasy. Oh, he was able to keep up a perfect façade. No one would have ever guessed. And that's when I was afraid, because I knew he was capable of anything.'

'You think he has confused you in his mind with Rebecca?'

'He has,' she agreed quietly. 'He swings between love and hate for her. But I know that the hate is winning.'

'We've got ourselves a problem,' Mahoney said. 'Where is Mr Hawaii right now?'

She looked at Mahoney and said, astonished, 'After this night of madness, of letting it all out – something I swear he has never done before – he calmly says he has a meeting at the ranch. He'll fly there and be back later. The ranch comes first, whatever else is happening!' She shuddered and the cup rattled. 'Thank God he remembered, or I . . . I don't know what he might have done . . .'

'So he's still in Hawaii?'

'Yes.'

Mahoney grinned. 'Pity. I thought I could ask you to stay the night here. For safety purposes of course, just in case he showed up.'

She laughed, despite herself. 'Even you can't pull that one off.'

Mahoney headed for the kitchen again. He took a chicken out of the refrigerator and began hacking it up with a cleaver. Phyl shuddered again and he grinned at her. 'Don't worry. I'm just fixing us some soup. Meanwhile, just so you don't think things are all bad, here's a bit of good news. Bea has got her memory back.'

Phyl's jaw dropped. 'Oh God,' she cried. 'And I wasn't there to help her. Again.'

'She didn't need you,' Mahoney said, searing the chicken in a copper-bottomed sautée pan and throwing in a fistful of chopped vegetables. 'Nick was there.' He told her what Nick had said.

'So there it is,' he said finally. 'Bea is Marie-Laure Leconte Jones. And by some strange stroke of fate, she flew from Honolulu to San Francisco the night she was attacked.'

Phyl's eyes widened. 'Of course it's a coincidence,' she said.

'You know I'm a great believer in coincidence. Especially where crime is concerned.' He handed her a glass of red wine and she sipped it moodily.

'Poor Bea. Marie-Laure, I mean,' she said sadly. 'She loses her parents and then she's attacked by some madman. No wonder she blocked it all out of her memory.'

'No wonder,' he agreed, adding chicken stock.

'I'm going to France,' Phyl said, heading determinedly for the phone. 'I'm calling the airlines and getting the first flight out to Paris tomorrow.'

'Of course you are, Doc,' he said calmly. 'But first you eat, then you call the airlines. The soup will be ready in ten minutes and I bet you haven't eaten in twenty-four hours.'

He was right; she felt much better after she had eaten. Mahoney booked her a flight to Washington with a connecting flight to Nice and she thought, relieved, that the trip to see Bea would also put thousands of miles between her and Brad.

She looked at Mahoney. He was leaning against the window frame, looking out at the nightly panorama of brightly-lit vessels skimming across the bay and the bridges twinkling like garlands strung across the sky, dotted with the red pinpoints of tail lights. His arms were folded and he was humming along with a Mozart aria playing in the background. He looked relaxed, at ease with himself and his surroundings, and Phyl thought of the contrast with Brad, pacing her apartment like an enraged animal.

'What are we going to do about him?' Mahoney asked, reading her mind.

'Tomorrow I'll be gone,' she said firmly. 'I'll send him a letter and tell him I can't see him any more. I'll recommend a therapist in Hawaii. Perhaps by the time I get back he will have come to terms with it.'

Mahoney glanced sceptically at her. 'You really think so?'

She sighed wearily, reaching for her jacket. 'Let's hope.'

He drove her home in tired silence. 'I wish I were coming with you tomorrow,' he said as he dropped her off.

'Me too,' she said looking wistfully at him.

He said gently, 'Remember to take care of yourself – as well as Bea. I'm not sure which of you needs looking after most.' He kissed her lightly on either cheek, watching until she disappeared through the doors, then he gunned the Mustang down the empty street.

Riding up in the elevator Phyl wished she had the cat with her. She hated the idea of the empty apartment, but Coco was staying at Mahoney's until she got back from France. As she unlocked the door, she remembered how she used to treasure her privacy. Now she recognised her solitude as loneliness.

The apartment was in darkness and she hesitated. She could have sworn she left a lamp on. She always did. The hair on her neck bristled as she peered into the darkened foyer, sliding her hand along the wall to the light switch. And then her hand connected with someone else's warm flesh.

His arms were around her and one hand was clamped across her mouth as he kicked the door shut. 'You left me again, Rebecca,' Brad whispered harshly. 'Why did you do that? When you know how much I love you?'

He switched on the light. She spun round, staring horrified at him. 'How did you get in here?' she demanded.

He smiled coolly, holding up a key. 'I had yours copied when you were in Hawaii,' he said calmly. 'I wanted to make sure I could reach you, any time. Day or night.'

His eyes held hers like a stoat mesmerising a rabbit. He was immaculate in a blue cashmere blazer and chinos and tassled loafers. He was smiling at her, the perfect gentleman. Only behind the gold-rimmed glasses, his pale eyes were not smiling. They were icy and withdrawn, and she knew he was seeing the fantasy inside his head, not her.

'I'm sorry if I startled you,' he said. 'God, look at you, you're shaking.' He stepped towards her, his arms outstretched. Instinctively, she backed away from him. 'Oh come on, Rebecca,' he said with a sigh, 'you know I'm no good at saying I'm sorry. I came here to take you home, that's all. You know you're always happiest at Diamond Head. And I want you with me. I don't ever want you to leave me again.'

Phyl edged towards the bedroom. Her terrified eyes were fixed on his as he said with a puzzled smile, 'Don't walk away from me. You know you love me. I just want to hear you say it.'

She was almost at the bedroom door now. Her heart was pounding like a marathon runner's. If she were quick enough she could be in, she could shut the door, and lock him out. She thought longingly of the bedside telephone, and Mahoney . . .

'Say it, Rebecca,' Brad said, walking towards her. 'Say it, my darling. Say you love me. Tell me you will never leave me.'

Her limbs had turned to stone. She was frozen with fear

as he came closer. The smile had gone and his eyes were cold.

'Brad,' she said desperately, 'this is no good. Of course I care about you. You are my friend.' She took a quick step backwards, holding up her hands to ward him off. He was as tense as the Doberman, and she was afraid to say the wrong thing, afraid to trigger his madness.

'More than friends,' he said, as she took another cautious backward step towards the bedroom. 'A love like ours is for ever, Rebecca. You know that.'

She could see the door handle from the corner of her eye. One more step, she thought, just one and then I'm safe. Then I'll call Mahoney. She leapt suddenly for the door, slamming it behind her, sobbing with fear. But it would not close. She looked down and saw his foot in its expensive tassled loafer, and she heard him laugh as his hand came through the gap, then his shoulder.

The door flew open and she crumpled to the floor. She put her head in her hands, too frightened to look up at him, sobbing tearlessly in great tearing gasps.

She could feel his eyes on her, but he said nothing. Finally, she peeked through her fingers at him. He was looking at her, his arms were folded and his face expressionless. Suddenly he knelt on one knee next to her and took her hand. 'I can't let you reject me again, Rebecca,' he said gently. 'Not again.'

He pulled her to her feet, looking sadly at her. 'Poor girl,' he said softly, 'poor beautiful girl.' He smoothed her wild hair gently back from her face, gazing intently at her. Then he took both her hands in his.

'Brad,' she said desperately. 'You mustn't call me Rebecca. I'm Phyl. Remember? I'm the doctor. The one you like to talk to.'

He smiled. 'The witch-doctor,' he said. 'I remember.'

'Rebecca was your mother, Brad. You told me everything about her.'

'Not *everything*,' he said levelly, and his voice sent shivers down her spine.

She looked at him, so calm, so icy. He was still holding onto her hands. His grip was like a vice and she imagined his hands on her throat, squeezing the life out of her. *Killing Rebecca.* She fought back the wave of terror, fighting to keep her wits about her. The only way she could win was to try to talk him out of it.

'We have to talk about this, Brad,' she said speaking slowly, trying to keep the tremor out of her voice. She had to let him know she was in control. That she was the one who called the shots. It was her only chance.

'You told me I was your confessor and now I want you to tell me everything about Rebecca. I am here to help you, Brad, you know that.'

'You betrayed me,' he said, gripping her tighter. 'You promised you would stay. You know you should not have done that, Rebecca?' He bent his head and kissed her on the lips, drawing her passionately to him.

Phyl went limp in his arms; she trembled with the urge to scream, to push him away. He lifted his face from hers and stared into her eyes.

'Brad, please, I have to talk to you,' she said quickly. 'I'm just so tired . . . I feel so awful . . .'

He swung her into his arms and carried her to the bed. He laid her gently down and sat beside her. There was a puzzled frown between his brows as he picked up the pillow and turned to her.

She stared at the pillow in his hands and knew what he meant to do. Her eyes were dark with horror.

'Why do you look so frightened, Phyl?' he said, suddenly normal.

She gasped as she realised he had called her by her own name; he had remembered who she was. She cast around frantically for a way to get him out of the apartment. 'I'm so hungry, Brad,' she said quickly. 'Why don't we go out for a bite? You must be starving too. We could go to Il Fornaio. You know you like their tiramisu? We could talk this over sensibly. I want to help you, Brad. I promise I'll do everything I can.'

She saw the doubt in his eyes, 'You promise you won't leave me again?' he said, stroking her arm rhythmically.

'Yes, yes. I promise.' She stared breathlessly at him, waiting, praying for him to say yes.

The telephone shrilled suddenly, shattering the silence. Phyl's eyes fastened on the phone. Her lifeline. 'I'd better answer it,' she lied quickly. 'I was expecting someone to call. My . . . my colleague. If I don't answer, they'll wonder why.'

Brad held up his hand. He shook his head as he looked at the telephone, still ringing on her bedside table. She was dying inside from frustration and fear. She'd almost had him convinced, almost got him out of here . . . oh God who the hell was calling her . . . ?

The ringing stopped and they sat motionless in the deepening silence. Brad was still staring at the night table, and she wondered if he was going to pull the phone from the wall. Instead, he picked up the photograph of Bea. It was the one Phyl had taken before she left for New York, of Bea looking sweet and pretty, with her cropped head and wide scared eyes.

Brad held the photograph under the light, studying it for a long time. 'How do you know this girl?' he asked in that 'other' voice that sent the shudder through her again.

'She's my patient. The one I told you about, with the lost memory. I told you she had become a friend.'

'What is her name?'

His eyes were hooded, and she saw the tremor in his hand holding the picture. She said puzzled, 'Her name is Bea French.'

'French?' He glanced at the girl in the picture and then back at her. 'Are you sure?'

'Well . . . no. I forgot she just got her memory back. She's Marie-Laure Leconte Jones.' Phyl began to laugh hysterically, she knew she wasn't making sense . . .

Brad stood up. He put the photograph in his pocket and then he looked at her, lying on the bed, sobbing and laughing at the same time.

That remote look was back in his eyes as he said, 'Poor darling. You are overwrought and tired. Why don't you get some sleep now.'

She lay, frozen with fear as he strode to the door. He looked back at her and smiled, his old confident smile. 'There's something I have to do. Then I promise you everything will be all right. I'll be back in a couple of days. Why don't you plan on coming to Kalani with me this weekend? We can continue our discussion there. After all, Kalani is the centre of my life, the soul of the Kane family. And I want to share it with you, Phyl. I want to share my whole life with you.'

He was still smiling as he walked away. She heard his purposeful footsteps and then the click of the door latch. And then nothing.

Phyl lay still, too afraid to move. She strained her ears into the silence. Maybe he was trying to trick her. Maybe he was waiting for her behind the door, ready to grab her by the throat as she emerged . . . She swung her feet cautiously to the floor. She listened again.

She tiptoed barefoot across the room, then flattened herself against the wall, peering round the door. She slid

393

through, looking nervously round. He might still be hiding, waiting to grab her, waiting to kill her, finally. Her nerve suddenly cracked and she screamed, running like a madwoman from room to room, flinging open doors. 'You crazy bastard,' she yelled, 'come out, come out . . .'

Finally, she slid the bolts on the front door and sank sobbing to the floor. 'Oh dear God,' she sobbed, 'help me, help me . . .' She dialled Mahoney's number, clutching the phone to her ear. It rang and rang . . . 'Answer it goddamn it, Mahoney,' she groaned, 'answer, please, please answer.'

Mahoney swung the Mustang round the corner onto Phyl's street in a squeal of rubber, cursing as he saw the black Porsche speeding down the middle of the road towards him. He threw the Mustang quickly right, mounting the sidewalk and narrowly missing a fire hydrant.

'Jesus Christ man,' he snarled, staring angrily over his shoulder at the Porsche's disappearing tail-lights. Then he groaned as he realised he was looking at Brad Kane's car.

He leapt from the Mustang and ran across the road to Phyl's building. He put his thumb on the bell and left it there until the doorman, red-faced with anger, confronted him.

He flipped him his badge and said, 'Dr Forster. Is she home?'

'She is,' the doorman retorted. 'And one ring would have done.'

'Not tonight,' Mahoney said, striding across the soft carpet to the elevator.

'Wait, I have to tell her you're here,' the doorman yelled. 'It's the rules.'

'No rules tonight, fella,' Mahoney said. 'Don't you dare pick up that phone.'

He pushed the elevator button, waiting impatiently for the doors to slide shut. When he had called Phyl and she had not answered he had been worried. He knew she was home and he had let it ring. When she still didn't answer he wondered uneasily what was up? Something was wrong, he knew it. He wondered if Brad Kane had shown up but Phyl had said he had been on his way to the ranch. He should have been back on Diamond Head. Then he had remembered. Brad Kane had a Gulfstream IV. He could be anywhere he wanted before most of us had time to buy a ticket.

He strode from the elevator and rang Phyl's bell. He put his head to the door, listening. There was no sound and he banged on the door. 'Phyl,' he yelled. 'It's me, Mahoney. Open up.'

She flung it open and hurled herself, sobbing into his arms. 'Mahoney, oh thank God. Oh Franco . . .' she cried.

'Okay, okay. Take it easy, baby.' He led her gently inside. 'Was it Brad? Did he hurt you?'

Her shocked blue eyes met his. '*He was going to kill Rebecca*,' she said.

'What stopped him?'

'The phone rang. It sort of broke the spell, I think it brought him to his senses.' Phyl's legs suddenly turned to jelly and she sank helplessly onto the sofa. He looked at her white face, then he inspected her meagre stock of liquor and poured her a stiff bourbon.

'You look as though you need it,' he said. 'And I want you to answer some questions.' She nodded, sipping the bourbon, looking trustingly at him

'Did he actually assault you?'

She shook her head. 'I mean, he grabbed my arms and put his hand over my mouth, but he didn't hit me.'

'Did you let him into the apartment?'

'He was here when I got back. He took me by surprise.'

'Then how the hell did he get in?'

'He had my keys copied. He said he had taken them when I was in Hawaii.'

'What about the doorman?'

She shrugged. 'I don't know. Yes I do. You know the way Brad is. He looks as though he owns the place. He had been here before and I guess the doorman knew he was a friend. He probably told him I'd asked him to wait for me, that I had given him the keys ... I guess.'

She looked pleadingly at him. 'What are we going to do?'

He heaved a sigh. 'Nothing much we can do. He gained illegal entry to your apartment, but he can always claim you gave him the keys. After all you were friends. He can say it was just a lovers' tiff, a domestic argument. We see them all the time, though not usually in apartments as fancy as this.'

'But he's *crazy*, Mahoney. He thinks I am his mother. He's in love with *her* – not me!'

Mahoney knew it and that was what was worrying him. Crazy men were unpredictable, there was no way to know what Brad Kane's next move might be. 'You said he left when the phone rang? Do you mean he just got up and split?'

She shook her head. 'He had me on the bed. He took the pillow. I thought he was going to suffocate me ... I was trying to talk to him, to calm him. Suddenly he seemed to come to his senses, he remembered who I was. I wanted to get him out of here. I suggested we go and have something to eat, talk it over. Then the phone rang and we both jumped. We just looked at it, listening to it ring and ring ... and then it stopped. Brad was staring at the night table and I thought he was going to rip the phone out of the wall. But instead he picked up Bea's photograph.'

Phyl looked bewildered at Mahoney. 'He asked me who

it was. I had mentioned her to him once before and told him about her lost memory. I said her name was Bea French and then I got confused because she's not Bea French any more.

'And then Brad did something really strange. He put Bea's photo in his pocket. He said there was something he had to do, and he would be back later. He said why didn't I plan to go to Kalani with him this weekend, and we could talk some more. And then he left.'

'But why would he take Bea's photograph? Had he ever met her here?'

'Never. He never met Bea, I swear it.'

Mahoney prowled the floor, his hands clasped behind his back, asking himself what the hell Bea French had got to do with a crazy guy who had been in love with his own mother and had transferred that fixation to Phyl? He sighed, looking at her, sitting on the edge of the sofa, clutching the empty bourbon glass, with her knees together and her ankles buckled like a kid. He thought she looked terrible. Her face was colourless, unless you counted the shadows under her eyes, and every now and then a shudder ran through her.

'Come on, sweetheart,' he said, taking the glass from her. 'You're coming home with me.'

She smiled tremulously at him. 'For safe keeping?' she asked, remembering how they had laughed earlier about the idea.

'Damn right, baby,' he said, throwing her jacket over her shoulders. 'You can have my bed. Coco will curl up behind your knees for company, and I'll be in the next room, making sure nobody disturbs you.'

'Oh Mahoney,' she said, relieved, leaning against him as they wafted down in the elevator. 'Whatever would I do without you?'

* * *

Four hours later, Mahoney was still up. He was in his favourite place, leaning against the window frame, watching the fog rolling in great soft silent waves across the horizon until it finally blotted out the bridges and the landscape. The tabby's yellow eyes followed him as he began to pace the floor again. He wished he could put on some music, something sad and haunting and a bit kitsch, an aria by Puccini or Verdi. But Phyl was sleeping the sleep of the dead. Or *almost* dead, he amended. Thanks to his opportune telephone call.

The thing he didn't get was the Bea French connection. Why would Brad want her picture? Maybe he had another fixation? Maybe he had multiple fixations? They were not dealing with a 'normal' man here. And yet it was a fact that Bea had flown in from Hawaii that night. But that was the only link.

He sighed, putting Bea on the back burner. The important thing was what was he going to do to protect Phyl? Brad Kane would be back, and then he was not going to take no for an answer.

He sighed worriedly as he finally threw himself onto the sofa and closed his eyes. It had been a long day. He would think about it in the morning when his brain was functioning again. Tomorrow he would put Phyl on the plane to France. At least there she would be safe, and it would give him time to sort out Mr Hawaii.

CHAPTER 34

It was a beautiful morning in Cannes. A soft breeze rustled the palms, fluttering Bea's short hair as Nick drove the red Alfa convertible along the Croisette and then up through a maze of one-way streets.

'Where are we going?' Bea asked, but he just grinned and said, 'It's a surprise.'

He parked outside the City Art Gallery and she said, 'I think I know what the surprise is.'

'Betcha don't,' he said, taking her hand and running up the steps to the entrance.

He walked her quickly through the galleries. 'Close your eyes,' he ordered finally.

'It's going to be one of my father's paintings isn't it?' she smiled. 'Of Nanny Beale, I'll bet.'

'I told you, it's a surprise. Okay, now you can open them,' he said softly.

Bea stared at the full-length portrait of the plain dark-haired woman in an unsuitable yellow silk dress. Her features were large but she had a pleasant expression and her long hair was caught girlishly back with a ribbon, though she was no longer that young. Unsoftened by the artist's brush, all her uncertainty about herself was revealed in her sombre deep-set brown eyes.

'Marie-Antoinette Leconte,' Bea said quietly. 'My grandmother.'

'I found it quite by chance,' Nick said. 'I was hunting down pictures in the newspaper archives when I read about it. Isn't she exactly the way you imagined her? It was painted a few years before she met Archer Kane. Before he tried to make her over into his version of a twenties flapper with bobbed hair and short skirts.'

'The saddest thing must have been that he took her dignity away,' Bea sighed. 'I'm glad she was painted like this, the way she really was.'

They walked from the gallery with their arms round each other, still thinking about Marie Leconte, back to the car. Then they drove to a favourite café near the marketplace for lunch and afterwards to the jeweller's to buy her an engagement ring.

'I want Phyl to be the first to know,' she said, happily surveying the antique-set diamond. 'Let's keep it our secret until she gets here.'

Brad Kane drove the sleek black Ferrari up the curving gravel drive of the Villa Mimosa. He knew Bea was out, he had seen her leave. And shortly afterwards he had telephoned the housekeeper.

'My name is Johnny Leconte,' he lied. 'I am an old friend of Miss French from the States. I'm meeting her for lunch in Antibes. She asked me to pick up the children and bring them with me.' The housekeeper had hesitated and he had laughed with his reassuring easy charm. 'She said it will be a special treat. Their first taste of the famous bouillabaisse.'

He had felt her relax as she agreed to have the children ready in ten minutes.

They were waiting on the steps for him and he saw the boy's eyes widen as he looked at the car.

'Wow,' Scotty yelled, 'oh wow, a real Ferrari! Oh man!'

He almost fell down the steps in his hurry to inspect the gleaming black monster. He ran his hand along the paintwork, peering at the sleek leather and wood interior and the glittering instrument panel.

Brad grinned at him. 'Hop in, my friend,' he said easily. 'I'll show you how well she drives.'

Jacinta came towards him, holding Julie by the hand.

'Hi,' Brad said genially. 'I'm Johnny. And I know you are Julie because Bea told me all about you.'

She looked at him unsmiling. 'Where is Bea?' she asked suspiciously.

'Didn't I tell you, she's waiting for you at the restaurant,' Jacinta said, eyeing Brad and his expensive car approvingly. 'Now you just go with Mr Johnny, and have a good time.'

Scott clambered excitedly into the Ferrari with Julie after him.

'Don't worry, I won't speed,' Brad said, throwing Jacinta a charming smile. 'I'll take good care of them,' he promised as the powerful engine roared and he drove off in a spurt of gravel.

After a leisurely lunch, Nick dropped Bea off back at the villa. He knew she was still afraid of what she might remember about the night at Mitchell's Ravine and he hated to leave her alone, but there were things he had to do. He told her he would be back in an hour and then they would go together to meet Phyl at Nice airport.

'I'm glad I found you, Nick Lascelles,' Bea called after him as he drove off, and he beeped his horn cheerfully as he rounded the bend in the drive and disappeared.

Bea felt good as she walked up the steps into the villa. Into *her* villa, she reminded herself with a smile as she thought of Millie. There wasn't a single day that went by that she did not think of her, and the Villa Mimosa was the best memorial Millie could ever have had.

'Julie,' she called, striding through the silent hall, 'Scott.' But no one came running, beaming a welcome, and gladdening her bruised heart. She went out onto the back terrace, shading her eyes, looking across the lawn at the pool, but that too was empty. Surprised, she went into the kitchen and asked Jacinta where they were.

'But your friend picked them up, the way you asked him to,' Jacinta said surprised.

Bea stared at her. 'But Nick was with *me*.'

'Not Mr Nick. Your friend M'sieur Leconte came for them in his big black Ferrari.' Jacinta smiled. 'The children loved it. He told me you had sent him to collect them and they were meeting you for lunch at a café in Antibes.'

'Monsieur *Leconte*?' Bea's knees gave way and she sank weakly onto a chair. She stared, stunned, at the housekeeper.

'He said his name was Johnny Leconte,' Jacinta said, looking worried. 'Is something wrong, M'mselle?'

'*It's him*,' Bea whispered to herself. '*He finally came to get me*.' Panicked images flashed into her mind as she remembered with sudden awful clarity who the man calling himself Johnny Leconte was and what had happened. Her heart lurched sickeningly as she realised the past had finally caught up to her. Brad Kane wanted her dead and now he had taken Scott and Julie. She knew only too well that he was capable of murder and now he was using the children to get her.

The telephone rang and she ran to answer it, praying it was Nick. She would tell him everything, he would know what to do, he would help her. Jacinta watched anxiously as she picked up the phone.

'The children want to say hello to you, Marie-Laure,'

Brad said in that nice easy voice of his. 'Or do you prefer to be called Bea now?'

A violent rage swept through her as she realised what he had done.

'Where are they?' she screamed. 'Why have you taken them?' She heard him laugh, then Scotty came on the phone.

'Hi, Bea,' he yelled. 'Your friend has a terrific car and he even let me start it. When are you coming to meet us?'

'Soon, Scotty,' she replied, her voice trembling with relief, he sounded so normal.

Then Brad said, 'Here's Julie,' and she could almost see him smiling. But she heard the edge of uncertainty in Julie's sweet little voice as she said, 'Bea, why didn't you meet us for lunch like you said?'

'I ... Julie, Nick and I got held up. I'll see you soon though.'

Brad got on the phone again. He said, 'I told her you would be here for dinner, for certain.' He laughed lightly, easily. 'Though of course I did not mention what might happen if you are not.'

His voice had that remote freezing edge that she recognised and Bea suddenly knew without a shadow of doubt that this was the real Brad Kane she was talking to. The man with the mad obsession behind the normal handsome façade. A man crazy enough to kill.

Her heart felt like a lump of solid rock in her chest. She said, 'Where are you?'

'I'll give you directions, get a pen and write them down,' he said briskly. 'Take the A7 Autoroute du Soleil west, past Salon de Provence. Exit at Cavaillon and pick up the D2, then the N100 to Apt. Stop at the Café Saintons, three kilometres after the Gordes turn-off. Be there at six o'clock. Wait for my call.'

She wrote it down and said shakily, 'What are you going to do with the children?'

'My dear Bea,' he said, 'you know I have no interest in the children. They mean nothing to me. They are not part of this. Obviously you will tell no one about them – or us. You will not go to the police. That is part of our bargain. Otherwise, I agree it would be a pity for such nice little children not to enjoy a long and happy life.' He laughed softly. 'The decision is yours, Bea.'

'I'll be there,' she said quickly.

'Wait at the café for my call. And make no mistake, if you have told anyone, or brought anyone with you, I shall know.'

The phone went dead and she sat helplessly cradling it, wondering what to do. She thought of Nick coming back to collect her, and of Phyl arriving at Nice airport in a couple of hours. She remembered Scott happily telling her about the beautiful black Ferrari, and the wavering edge of uncertainty in Julie's voice. And she knew she could not tell anybody. She had to do as Brad said. And she had no time to lose.

She leapt to her feet, then she realised she was going to meet a madman, a killer, and she had not even got a weapon. There was no gun in the house, not even a hunting rifle. She saw the rack of sharp kitchen knives and quickly took one. Not too big, she thought, so she could hide it in her pocket. Then she realised, shocked, that she was thinking like a criminal. *Like a murderer.*

She read the scribbled directions again and she realised she knew exactly where Brad was. She had no need of directions. She crumpled the paper and threw it at the basket just as Poochie came gambolling in from the garden. He leapt enthusiastically at her, but she pushed him away. She put the knife in her purse then ran outside and got in the Mercedes. Poochie's claws skidded on the marble hall floor as he ran after her. He stood at the top of the steps, his big shaggy head cocked to one side, staring pleadingly at her. Bea hesitated. The thought of his company was comforting, and maybe it would be a good idea to have the dog there to comfort the children. Because she had no idea what might happen to her. Or them.

She opened the door and the dog leapt in beside her, barking joyously as they sped off down the gravel driveway. Bea had no need of the directions. The Leconte summer home was in Provence. She knew the roads as well as she knew her own face. And it was Marie-Laure Leconte who was setting off to meet her destiny, for the second time. Not Bea French.

At the San Francisco Police Department in the Hall of Justice, Mahoney grabbed his first cup of coffee of the day. He paced the corridors, thinking about Bea – aka Marie-Laure Leconte Jones – still troubled by the idea there was something he had missed. He grabbed another cup then checked the files once again . . . the flight manifestos . . . the private planes. And there it was. The Gulfstream IV from Hawaii to San Francisco, piloted by Brad Kane on the night of the attack.

Mahoney sat back in his chair, thinking about coincidences and telling himself that in this case one plus one surely added up to two. It proved Brad had been in San Francisco at the time of the crime. And the man was crazy enough to kill. There *had* to be a connection, he felt it in his bones.

He put through a call to the Villa Mimosa and Nick Lascelles answered. 'I'm glad I got you, Nick, instead of Bea,' Mahoney said. 'I wanted to ask her some questions, but it's tough over the phone because they are likely to upset her. I wanted to ask if she knew a man called Brad Kane?'

'Brad Kane? I don't know if she knows him personally, but she certainly knows about the Kane family.' He quickly filled Mahoney in on the story of Johnny Leconte and Archer Kane, and the Kanoi ranch on Hawaii.

Mahoney tilted his chair back and breathed a sigh of satisfaction; he finally had his motive. And his man.

Then Nick said, 'The thing is though, I just arrived at the villa. I arranged to meet Bea but she's not here. And nor are the children. The housekeeper said a friend of Bea's picked the children up earlier in a black Ferrari. And the weird thing is he told her his name was Johnny Leconte. She said when Bea got home the man calling himself Johnny Leconte telephoned her. Jacinta heard Bea speaking to the children on the phone and arranging to meet them somewhere.

'The fact is, Detective Mahoney, we were supposed to be picking Phyl up at Nice airport right around now. Bea wouldn't just forget that. Phyl coming here was important to her, she couldn't wait to see her. And who is this guy calling himself by Bea's father's name? I'm worried, sir, and I don't know what to do.'

'Don't do anything,' Mahoney almost yelled. 'Don't make a move. Especially do not call the police. Let me take care of it. Go and meet Phyl and warn her. Tell her the guy is Brad Kane. Tell her I'm on my way.'

Mahoney slammed the phone down on Nick. He contacted Interpol and alerted them to the situation, then he called the FBI. International kidnapping came under their jurisdiction. He didn't even want to think about murder. Within the hour, he was on a special flight heading for Washington, then Concorde to Paris where another plane would be waiting to fly them to Nice. He prayed to God they would make it in time.

Phyl paced the terrace of the Villa Mimosa distractedly. Nick had filled her in on what had happened on the way back from the airport, and fear and guilt dragged at her heart as she thought of Bea and the children, alone with Brad Kane.

Nick was leaning against a pillar, staring blankly across the lawns. He finally threw his hands in the air with frustration and said, 'I can't stand just *waiting*.'

Phyl stopped her pacing and looked at him. Their eyes met and she knew the same terrible thoughts were going round in his head.

'Why the hell didn't Bea leave a note?' she cried, distractedly. 'At least give herself a chance?'

'Because Brad Kane had the children and he told her not to. That's the power of the kidnapper – the threat of what he might do.' Nick didn't say it but they both knew that Brad Kane was not an ordinary kidnapper; the ransom he was demanding was Bea's life.

'But she knew it was dangerous,' Phyl cried. 'She must have remembered what happened to her at Mitchell's Ravine. Oh God Nick, what can we do? We can't just sit here and wait.'

'I'll ask Jacinta again, see if she remembers anything else,' he said, heading for the kitchen.

'Tell me again *exactly* what happened, Jacinta,' Nick said, keeping his voice gentle because the housekeeper was obviously distraught.

'I know now I should not have let the children go,' Jacinta wailed. 'But he was such a nice man, so friendly and so . . . so smart, and kind to the children. He did not look like a kidnapper . . .'

'Yes, Jacinta, I know that,' he said. 'Look, the police will be here soon to ask you some questions. But first I want you to tell me again *exactly* what happened.'

'He telephoned,' she said. 'M'mselle Bea answered. She spoke nicely to the children, it sounded normal to me. I heard her arrange to meet him. She wrote down some directions and I went back to my cooking because I thought now everything is all right . . . and then she left in the car. The dog jumped in beside her . . .'

'The directions, Jacinta,' Nick said quickly. 'Where did she write them?'

'On the pad, sir. By the telephone, here in the kitchen.'

Nick grabbed the pad: the top page had been ripped off. Of course Bea would have taken the directions with her . . . unless . . . He looked at the paper basket but it was empty. Then, on the floor behind it he spotted a small crumpled ball of paper. He pounced on it. 'Autoroute du Soleil,' he read. 'Exit at Cavaillon, D2 to N100 . . . 3 kls G. exit . . . Café Saintons . . .'

'My God, Phyl,' he yelled, 'I think we've got it.'

She said quickly, 'We must tell the police at once.'

'No . . . Mahoney said not to. He said to do nothing. Just wait for him.'

'At least let's leave a note for them,' she said. 'They have to know where we've gone.'

They wrote the note with the directions and told Jacinta to give it to the first policeman to arrive. Then they took off in the red Alfa, following Bea's directions to the café in the village in Provence.

CHAPTER 35

The Café Saintons was a typical roadside stop, set back a pace or two up a couple of steps. There was a tiny iron-railed terrace with a couple of plastic tables and chairs and faded umbrellas emblazoned with Kronenberg logos. Inside was the usual cheap grey-speckled floor and a zinc bar with a glass-covered plate of wilting commercial pastries and a couple of browning bananas.

The patron was leaning on the counter, reading a newspaper. He glanced briefly up as Bea walked in.

She looked quickly at the few customers, but none of them was Brad Kane.

Bea ordered a brandy and asked for a bowl of water for the dog. The surly patron served her without a word and without bothering to remove the cigarette stuck to his lower lip with an inch of ash trembling at the end.

Poochie slurped the water noisily then settled himself under the table, behaving for once like a proper well-brought-up French dog. Bea gulped the brandy, her eye on the telephone by the counter, willing it to ring. When it did, noisily, a minute later, she almost jumped out of her skin. The patron dropped ash over the wilting bananas as he answered it.

Bea got up from her chair, gazing anxiously at him, but he was talking animatedly, obviously to a friend. She sank back down and checked her watch. It was five minutes to six. She eyed the patron nervously; he was talking about the Marseilles football team, throwing his arms around. He looked as though he might talk for ever and the six o'clock deadline was fast approaching. She stared at him, willing him silently to please get off the phone.

He finally finished his conversation and she breathed again as he began to serve another customer. Her eyes were riveted on the silent phone. She heard the minutes ticking lethargically past on the big wallclock: six-one, six-two, three, four . . . on five it rang. And this time she got there first. '*Excusez-moi, Monsieur*,' she said quickly to the patron, snatching up the receiver, '*mais j'attends un coup de téléphone.*'

He shrugged, watching her as he wiped the zinc with an old rag, then lit another Gauloise from the butt of the one in the yellow Ricard ashtray.

'You were on time,' Brad said evenly. 'And alone. I'm pleased to see you accepted my terms.'

The sound of his voice sent fresh tremors of terror through her. She sank onto a barstool, clutching the phone with both hands.

'Where are the children?'

'They are here, with me.' There was that smile in his voice again as he said, 'I don't have to tell you where to meet me, do I? It's a place you know well.'

She knew he meant the Leconte farm. 'Les Cerisiers,' she said.

'Wait for me there. If you are alone, the children will be released unharmed. You have half an hour.'

Bea slammed down the phone. She flung money for the brandy on the counter and without waiting for her change, she ran down the steps and hurled herself into the car. Poochie barked excitedly as he leapt in beside her and she gunned the Mercedes, squealing onto the main highway almost under the wheels of a giant nine-wheeler truck. She scarcely even heard the long blast of its horn as she sped towards the Bonnieux turn-off.

Nick ignored the speed limits. It would normally take him a couple of hours to Cavaillon but tonight he cut thirty minutes off that. It was a silent drive; they were both too worried and too frightened to talk.

Besides, Phyl thought, staring out at the countryside, they had discussed it endlessly. What more was there to say?

They were cruising along the N100, searching for the Café Saintons and they almost drove past it in the deepening dusk, just an anonymous little roadside stop like a hundred others along the route. There were a couple of pick-up trucks parked outside and a blue Opel Rekord with German plates, but Bea's white Mercedes was not there. And nor was the black Ferrari.

The patron lifted his eyes from the sports section of his newspaper and looked sourly at them. '*Bonsoir M'sieur-Dame*,' he said, folding the paper and lighting another cigarette. The other customers flicked interested glances in their direction as Nick ordered two Kronenbergs and asked if he had seen a red-haired girl in here earlier.

The patron removed the beers from the refrigerator and slapped them onto the zinc with a couple of damp glasses. He shrugged indifferently. 'It's possible, M'sieur. Many people come in here, it is a popular café.'

Nick stared exasperatedly at him, 'A pretty girl, short red hair. She had a large brown dog . . .'

'Ah the dog. Of course, M'sieur, why did you not say so?' He ground out his cigarette and wiped the damp circles slowly off the bar with a wet rag. 'She was here,' he said. 'She was waiting for a telephone call. After it came,' he shrugged and looked at them, 'pfff, she was off like a rocket. "Out of here" as they say in the movies,' he added in a terrible approximation of an American accent.

'Do you know where she went?'

'How would I know?' he said disgruntled when his joke didn't raise a laugh. 'I'm no mind reader.'

Nick looked at Phyl. 'There's only one place we can try. The family's summer home was near Bonnieux.' He threw some money on the counter, grabbing Phyl's hand as they ran from the café.

The patron stared after them astonished. He looked at the two untouched beers and the money. He glanced at the other customers and shrugged again in disbelief. 'Mad foreigners,' he said, taking a swallow of the Kronenberg and returning to the sports page.

They almost missed the Bonnieux turn-off, a narrow little road leading through flat fields of vineyards, then snaking steeply up to the village perched on top of the hill. It was dark when they finally got there. The steep, cobblestoned streets were empty, and the medieval stone houses already shuttered for the night, but they found a couple of cafés open, and a gallery selling the works of local artists and craftsmen. And the proprietor knew where Johnny Leconte Jones had lived.

'Everyone does, of course,' he told Nick, regarding him suspiciously. 'But he was a very private man. He needed his solitude for his art, and we respected that privacy. No one round here would tell you where Monsieur Jones lived.'

'But it's urgent,' Phyl said desperately. 'His daughter, Marie-Laure, is a friend of mine. In fact she is my patient. She needs help, I've come all the way from San Francisco to help her . . . please, M'sieur . . .'

Bea sat on the terrace waiting for Brad. She had been here

an hour and there was still no sign of him. Now it was almost dark. Her stomach tied itself in a thousand knots and her heart thumped rapidly as a dozen different scenarios passed through her mind: the children bleeding, abandoned, shot ... or maybe pushed over a cliff, like her ... 'Dear God,' she prayed, 'just let him free the children, I'll do anything, just let them go unharmed ... I promise ...'

She remembered the first time Brad had called her, all those months ago. She had just returned home from France where she had gone alone after her parents' funeral. She hadn't yet contacted any friends to let them know she was back, and she was in the middle of unpacking in the sad silent house when he called.

'Hi, I'm Brad Kane,' he said. 'I don't know if you've heard about me, but I think I have some explaining to do. Some amends to make for the things my grandfather, Archer Kane did.'

She had recognised the name instantly of course, from her father's story, and she had been on her guard. 'How did you know about me?' she asked warily.

'I read your father's obituary in the *New York Times*, and I saw your photograph in a magazine, taken at the funeral. I can't tell you how sorry I am.'

He sounded so warm, so sincere, she felt herself wanting to believe him. Still, she asked herself, why was he calling now, after all these years? Her father had never wanted anything to do with the Kanes – 'Let sleeping dogs lie,' he had warned ...

'Look, maybe this is a bad time,' Brad said hesitantly, 'I don't want to upset you. In fact, quite the opposite. I've been learning a bit about my own family history. *Our* history, Marie-Laure. After all, we are related. In fact you may be my only living relative.'

And you may be mine, she thought, surprised.

'I have some explaining to do,' he said quickly. 'I need to get things off my mind, expiate my grandfather's sins. That's why I need to talk to you. Marie-Laure, the Kanoi ranch is one of America's largest. And half of it legitimately belongs to you. I'd like you to come out here to Hawaii and see it. See for yourself what your grandmother's money helped to create. I think, I hope, she would be proud of it, despite everything. And I'd like to think Johnny Leconte's daughter would be too.'

'My father didn't want any part of the ranch. He didn't want to know anything about the past,' she said passionately. 'He hated Jack Kane.'

'I know,' Brad said sadly. 'And with good reason. But I am not Jack. I am his son, and I have to live with the guilt. Please, for my sake as well as yours, Marie-Laure, won't you allow me to make amends?' He added persuasively, 'Don't let me go on feeling all this guilt. At least come and see the ranch. Maybe you'll even fall in love with it.'

He sounded so nice, as though he really wanted to see her. In her new loneliness the thought of Hawaii and the ranch was tempting. It would be fascinating to see the place where her father grew up. Perhaps Brad was right – together they could finally make up for all the past evil. She forgot her father's warnings, and she went.

A sleek Gulfstream IV was waiting at San Francisco to fly her to Honolulu, and then a small two-engined Cessna took her the short last hop to the ranch. Brad was waiting for her at the airstrip and she was surprised how handsome he was. She hadn't known quite what to expect, but she remembered her father had said the Kane men were blond and good-looking and she thought Brad must look like them. He was wearing jeans and a denim work-shirt and boots, and as she shook his hand, she told him, surprised, that he looked like a real working rancher.

'Of course I am,' he said, looking deep into her eyes. 'Your photograph did not do you justice,' he added. 'I didn't expect anyone as pretty as this.'

He was so easy and relaxed she felt instantly at home with him. They drove up the long avenue of banyans to the little ranch house built by Archer Kane and he showed her the flower gardens and the far-reaching acres with the pedigree herds of the finest cattle. He took her to see the little town built by the Kanes for the *paniolos* and their families; and the school and the medical facility and the church that Kane money had built.

'Just so you don't go on thinking we were all bad,' he said lightly, smiling at her. 'And so you'll know that your grandmother's money was put to good use.'

At the end of the long day they drove back to the airstrip. He said casually as they climbed back into the Cessna, 'And now I'm taking you to Kalani.'

Kalani. The beautiful, terrible island where her father had been kept prisoner for ten long years. Brad saw what she was thinking and he leaned over and took her hand. 'Marie-Laure,' he said gently. 'Let's both go and exorcise our ghosts.'

Brad piloted the little Cessna himself. He circled the island, pointing out the twin volcanic peaks, the great cliffs on the north-eastern tip and the forested gulches and the meadows with the contentedly grazing prize Herefords. When they landed and finally took the Jeep to the Lodge, Bea imagined the skinny little Monkey and his lonely life here. There had been happy times, her father had told her, when Jack and Archer were away, and he was left alone with Maluhia and Kahanu. And then he had discovered painting and that had completed his life, in a way.

415

The Lodge was a long, low white house with a palm-thatch roof. 'It doesn't look much different from when your father lived here,' Brad said easily, as a Chinese servant came running down the steps to collect her bag. 'In fact, I've put you in his old room. I thought you would like that.'

She threw him a grateful glance; he seemed to think of everything.

Her father's old room was small, there was just enough space for a narrow brass bed and a night table. A braided blue rug covered the dark wood floor and some old black and white photographs of Kalani hung on the walls. French doors led out onto the *lanaii* and the glorious view of the gardens and the ocean.

Bea lay down on the bed. She put her hands behind her head, staring out at the lawns and the palm trees and the ocean. Her father must have lain here, just the way she was, looking at the very same view, and praying that Jack Kane would not come back. How many mornings, she wondered, had the little five-year-old boy woken in that familiar haze of misery wondering what fresh torture Jack would have in store for him today? How many nights had he lain here, wondering how he could escape? *Wondering if he would ever escape.*

Yet, from all that madness, all that violence, Brad Kane had emerged unscathed. He was gentle, and good, and sympathetic. He understood that what Archer and Jack had done was wrong. She was smiling as she showered, anticipating the evening ahead, and it occurred to her that she hadn't felt like smiling since her parents died. Perhaps it was good that she had come to Kalani after all. She put on a simple cream silk shirt and long black skirt, and the new red Kelian sandals she had bought on an impulse in Avignon just last week. She hesitated at the door, looking back at her father's old house with a sudden flash of doubt, remembering his words of warning. She was looking forward to seeing Kalani, but she still did not want anything from Brad Kane.

He was standing on the *lanaii*, leaning against the rail with a drink in his hand, watching a pair of red cardinal birds greedily pecking scraps from a dish. Two enormous black Dobermans crouched either side of him, bristling, their burning eyes fixed on the birds.

'Don't worry,' he said seeing her horrified look. 'The dogs are well trained. They won't go near the cardinals. Unless I give them the word of course.'

'But you won't,' she said anxiously.

'Of course I won't. The birds come every night to be fed, just as they have done for decades. Your father would have known them well.'

He poured her a glass of champagne and said, 'I think this merits a toast. To the reunion, finally, of the Lecontes and the Kanes.' He raised his glass and touched it to hers. 'To us, my dear Marie-Laure. The survivors.'

'To us,' she repeated, wondering uneasily what her father would have thought.

Brad was the perfect host. The dogs sat docilely behind his chair as they ate the simple meal of freshly-caught Mahi Mahi and he talked to her about the history of the ranch, and about Kalani. He told her the story of Archer's Hawaiian first wife and how the island she had named Kalani – or Heaven – was their wedding gift, and that it became the cornerstone of the ranch and the Kane family fortune.

'And half of that fortune is now yours,' he said, holding her eyes with his own.

She could see he meant it and she was touched. She reached out and took his hand across the table. 'I don't need it, Brad,' she said. 'I don't want it. The past is the past. Kanoi ranch belongs to you. Besides, I can see how much you love it, and it means nothing to me.'

'You are very generous, Marie-Laure,' he said, with an odd little smile.

'It's not generosity. My father felt that his inheritance blighted his life. It was the cause of his unhappiness and he wanted nothing to do with it. And nor do I.' She hesitated, 'Except perhaps for the Villa Mimosa.'

Brad threw back his head and laughed, 'I offer you half the Kanoi ranch and you tell me all you want is the Villa Mimosa. Do you know, I've never even seen it.'

'I have. Just once,' she said. 'It's beautiful. Kalani is your place but the villa belongs to my family. It was my grandmother's house, my father was born there. He was happy there, for a while, until . . .' She didn't want to say any more. Brad Kane knew the story of Johnny Leconte's abduction from the Villa Mimosa just as well as she did.

'Then of course, it is yours,' he said suddenly abrupt. 'And now I'll say goodnight, Marie-Laure. I have some paperwork to do.'

'Goodnight, Brad,' she called after him, watching puzzled as he strode away. The two huge black dogs followed silently at his heels, like his shadow.

She slept soundly that night in her father's old room, in his narrow little bed, with the soft thud and slap of the waves hurling themselves onto the shore to lull her dreams. And when she woke and saw the pearly dawn sky and the flocks of brightly coloured birds chirruping outside her window, she smiled and thought that Lahilahi had named her island well. It was truly 'heaven'.

A Chinese servant brought a tray with hot coffee and rolls and sliced fresh fruits. Their tropical colours looked like a jewelled mosaic on the plate.

She asked him curiously how he had known she was awake.

He smiled mysteriously. 'We always know, Missie,' he said, busily setting out the dishes on the table on the *lanaii*.

He looked frail and thin as a reed in his white cotton mandarin jacket and black trousers and though his delicately-boned face had almost no lines, Bea knew he must be very old. She asked him how long he had worked for the family.

'For many years, Missie, since I was a young man,' he said clasping his hands and bowing his head courteously. 'First I worked a long time for Mr Jack at Diamond Head. Then after he died, for Mr Brad. And now, when I am an old man, I stay here mostly on Kalani. Mr Brad says it is easier here for me.' He smiled mischievously at her, 'He want me to retire, but I say no. No retire. Like your father, I work till I die.'

Bea laughed and asked him his name. He told her it was Wong. 'Is not my real Chinese name, Missie. Mr Jack gave it to me. He said he could not pronounce my real name. So now I am Wong.'

Bea suddenly realised that she was with someone who had actually known Jack Kane personally. Someone other than his son, that is. Didn't they say servants always knew everything. If anybody did, this old Chinese man would know the truth about her father's torturer.

She said, 'What was Mr Jack like, Wong? Was he a bad man?'

The old Chinese hesitated, his head bowed. 'Mr Jack was proud man. Missie,' he said finally. 'He very proud of the Kane name. Sometimes he good man, sometimes bad.' He sighed. 'Sometimes very bad. But I am only his servant. I see everything but I say nothing.' He looked up at her and said, 'I no speak bad of a dead man.'

He bowed again and she watched him walk slowly away.

'Wong,' she called after him. He turned and looked at her, his hands folded patiently. 'Did you ever know the boy they called the Monkey?'

He shook his head, 'No, Missie. I never did.'

Brad came striding towards them, the dogs, as always, following at his heels. 'Marie-Laure, good morning,' he called cheerfully. 'I hope you slept well.'

The dogs crouched obediently on their haunches as he smiled down at her. 'I'm sorry but something has come up. I have to return to Honolulu. I had hoped we could spend a couple of days here but I'm afraid it means we have to leave this morning.'

He shrugged irritatedly. 'It's business, otherwise I wouldn't do this to you. After all, you've only just arrived on Kalani. Never mind. At least you got to see it. And perhaps you'll find Diamond Head even more to your liking.'

Wong and one of the dogs, Makana, flew with them to Honolulu. The dog lay quietly at Wong's feet until the plane began its descent into Honolulu, then it began to howl loudly.

'Quiet, Makana,' Brad yelled from the cockpit. 'Wong, shut that dog up.'

Wong patted its big head and said something in Chinese and the dog stopped its howling though it was still trembling nervously.

'No matter how many times that animal flies with me he always howls when we're landing,' Brad said impatiently. 'Wong has spent as much time with the Dobermans as I have. He practically brought them up from being pups. He is the only other person they answer to besides me.'

Bea thought amused, that the tiny Chinese must weigh half what the Doberman did. One leap and he would have been flattened on the ground.

'You don't control a dog like that by force,' Brad told

her, reading her mind. 'The secret is in their training. They are ruled by commands.'

Bea thought of the exuberant joyous retrievers that had been her own family pets and she felt a pang of sympathy for Makana.

The Kane helicopter was waiting in Honolulu to waft them to Diamond Head, while Brad went downtown to his meeting. 'Wong will make sure you have everything you need,' he assured her, waving goodbye. 'Just make yourself at home.'

Bea stared down, amazed, as the helicopter hovered over the Diamond Head house. It was a dream mansion enfolded in tropical greenery, with fountains and flamboyant blossoms, and a cobalt blue pool that seemed to slide over the edge of the great black cliffs, into the huge green foam-flecked breakers combing the Pacific.

Wong escorted her to her room, but he looked so old and tired she would not allow him to carry her shabby green canvas bag. She followed him, glancing admiringly around at the paintings and works of art they passed.

'This was Mrs Kane's room,' Wong told her, flinging open a door. It was a big beautiful light-filled room with a view across the tree-studded lawns of the sea. Wong took her bag and put it in the biggest closet Bea had ever seen.

'Madame must have liked clothes,' she said, awed. 'Wong, do you mean Mrs Kane? Brad's mother?'

'Yes, Missie. Her name was Rebecca. She was very beautiful. There is a portrait of her in the dining room. And all the others. Mr Archer and his second wife, and Mr Jack.'

Bea couldn't wait to see them. Wong showed her around, proudly pointing out the family portraits, but he didn't need to tell her who they were. Her father had described that cruel arrogant face and that look of icy indifference so well, she would have known Archer Kane anywhere. She could understand why poor vulnerable la Célibataire had fallen for him though, he was certainly a handsome virile-looking bastard.

Jack Kane's blue eyes stared mockingly at her, just the way he must have looked at her father. 'You thought because you were a Kane you were king of everything,' she whispered to him. 'But you didn't win in the end, Jack. All you got was the money.'

Rebecca was even more beautiful than she had imagined, glamorous and glittering with emeralds and arrogance. It must have been a family trait, she thought amazed, even the wives had it. Chantal did too, the artist had caught the mocking curl of her lip, the impatient hauteur in her eyes, though Bea thought there was a hint of self-laughter in there somewhere.

Bea felt better as she turned away from those long-dead faces. It was good that she had come here and confronted the ghosts of her father's life. She believed he would have approved of that.

She went back to her room and found a maid unpacking her bag and she was forced to smile when she saw her T-shirts, a dress, a skirt and a couple of shirts, hanging forlornly in the vast closet. Her simple things were just not up to the grandeur of their surroundings. Rebecca's closet needed couture and hatboxes and Vuitton steamer trunks, not off-the-peg and an old green canvas duffle from L. L. Bean.

She put on a bathing suit and swam laps in the magnificent pool, then she lay on a beautiful bamboo chaise under a shady umbrella, sipping iced tea brought by another slippered Chinese servant, thinking about Brad.

He was acting really nice to her, she told herself. He couldn't be more hospitable, more sympathetic, more generous – offering her half the Kane ranch. Then why did she still have this sneaking feeling that something was wrong? *Why* was he being so nice? She kept remembering what her father had told her about all the Kanes: that the only thing that mattered in their lives was the Kanoi ranch and their name. Nothing else counted. They had even killed to keep it.

Then *why* would Brad Kane suddenly offer to give her half the Kane ranch? It was like offering her a half share in his heart.

She sipped the iced tea, suddenly uneasy. Brad Kane was a hard-headed businessman. He was not a philanthropist or a born-again Christian, or a madman. It just wasn't in character. He knew exactly what he was doing. If he wanted to give her back part of the ranch, he must want something in return.

Her father's words of warning repeated themselves endlessly in her head, she could hear his voice telling her, 'Let sleeping dogs lie, in case they come back and bite you . . .' Something was wrong. And she suddenly didn't want to stay around and find out what it was. She had to get out of here.

She ran back through the paradise gardens to Rebecca's room. She repacked her bag, took a shower, then put on a white T-shirt and jeans and her red sandals and went out onto the terrace to wait for Brad.

It was twelve-thirty when he returned. 'It's good to see a pretty girl waiting when I get home,' he said breezily, pouring himself a brandy.

He offered her one and she shook her head, wondering if she could be wrong, after all. He looked so great, so cool and handsome and suntanned and . . . rich. He looked as though he owned the world. Then why, that nagging little voice asked again, does he want to give half of it to you?

'You're very quiet, Marie-Laure,' he said, watching her.

'I'm tired. I did a lot of swimming . . . laps,' she replied evasively.

'I thought we would have lunch at the gazebo,' he said. She could see it, a pretty white wooden folly at the edge of the cliff. He took her hand and pulled her to her feet, sliding a friendly arm round her shoulders as they strolled towards it with the Doberman at their heels.

The gazebo was built like a Hawaiian pavilion, a white wooden octagon, open on all sides, with a curved thatched roof that came to a point at the top. Heavy canvas curtains were swagged back between the posts ready to shut out the wind, and the view was tremendous: straight down the steep black cliffs to the rocks and the great high-crested Pacific rollers gliding majestically towards them.

Wong was arranging dishes on a buffet but Brad dismissed him, saying they would serve themselves.

Looking at the beauty all around her, for a moment Bea was tempted to believe his offer. These lovely gardens filled with heavy-scented tropical blossoms, the emerald lawns, the rolling ocean view. All she had to do was say the word and half of this could be hers. But when she glanced at Brad she caught a strange expression on his face as he watched her. A distance and coldness that sent warning prickles up her spine.

'Come, let us eat,' he said, with a quick smile. His expression was neutral again, and she told herself she was just being silly, that she had just imagined that icy look.

She nibbled at a salad and Brad did not seem to be hungry. He sat silently, drinking brandy, watching her.

Black clouds appeared over the sea, blocking out the sun, and a sudden strong wind whipped the waves into dark foam-speckled mountains. She shivered, looking nervously at him in the deepening stormy dusk, wondering why he was so quiet. 'Brad, I think I should leave in the morning,' she said quickly. 'You have been a wonderful host. Thank you for showing me the Kanoi ranch and Kalani, and for your generous offer. But I cannot accept. I just don't want any part of it.'

He looked expressionlessly at her. Still he said nothing, and Bea felt those warning prickles again. She thought apprehensively that even though Brad was looking at her, he didn't seem to be seeing her.

She got up and walked nervously to the edge of the gazebo. She leaned against the rail, looking out at the ocean, wishing she could think of something to say to break his strange silence. She turned to speak to him, to apologise again for her sudden departure. And then she saw the shotgun, lying on the chair behind him. It was a handsome weapon with a polished wooden stock ornamented with silver.

'That's a beautiful gun,' she said, surprised she hadn't noticed it before. 'But what do you shoot here?'

'*Predators*,' he said viciously. 'Sit down, Marie-Laure Leconte.'

There was a sudden whiff of danger in the air, as tangible as the sweet aroma of the brandy. She froze, staring at him.

'*I said sit down.*'

There was an edge to his voice that made her obey. Her knees buckled and she sank into the chair opposite him. 'I'm sorry I can't stay any longer,' she said frightened, 'but it's better this way. My father was right. I should not have come here . . .'

'Be quiet,' he snapped impatiently, 'and listen to me, you silly girl.' Her brown eyes widened with shock and she stared, stunned, at him.

'Of course you are right,' he said in a remote voice. 'You should not have come here. And your father should not have come here. Archer Kane should have killed him at the Villa Mimosa when he killed his mother. It would have been the best thing for all of us.' He smiled coldly as he took another gulp of his brandy. 'And it would have saved me a lot of trouble.'

'What do you mean?' Bea pushed back the chair. She got to her feet, edging nervously away from him. The Doberman gave a low growl and she glanced at it. It glowered menacingly back.

'You were a stupid silly girl to think I would give you even the smallest fraction of the Kanoi ranch. You have seen it. You know that it belongs to the Kane family. That it was our hard work, our intelligence, our dedication – *our superiority* – that made this place. All Marie-Antoinette Leconte and her son contributed was money. Not another goddamn thing. They didn't build this house; they didn't create Kalani, they didn't plant the avenue of banyans and build that little ranch house, and the medical facility and the church and the houses for the workers. They did nothing, Marie-Laure.'

He fell silent again and she looked appeasingly at him. 'I know that, Brad,' she said quickly. 'You have done wonders . . .'

'Jack was right,' he said, as though she had never spoken. 'He said he should have killed the Monkey that night on the island when they had the fight. He should have stuck that knife into his heart and been done with it. He regretted it all his life. "Make no mistake, son," he said to me, "I know in my bones, Johnny Leconte is out there somewhere, like a coiled rattlesnake waiting to strike. He will try to take that fortune from us one day, son. Everything the Kane family have worked for all these years, our sweat, our toil, our land, our heritage. *Our name*. Make no mistake, he will come to claim his fortune and when he does we must be ready to act. Quickly and without mercy."'

Bea drew a sharp frightened breath as Brad slammed down the empty brandy glass. He stood up, towering over her.

'My father is dead,' she cried. 'He never wanted anything to do with Kalani and the Kanoi ranch. He never wanted to come back here. He didn't want anything from the Kane family.'

'But *you* are not dead, Marie-Laure. And one day *you* will get to thinking about things. About this rich ranch and this beautiful house, and Kalani and all that money. And you will go to a smart attorney with your story and your claim. You'll want more than half then, Marie-Laure. You will want it all. And you see, I cannot let that happen.'

'You're crazy,' she cried, stepping backwards away from him. 'I told you I don't want anything from you. I don't want the Leconte name ever to be associated with the Kanes. My father was right about you. You live above the law, you have no morals, your grandfather killed his wife to get his hands on her money, and he would have killed Johnny too, when he was eighteen. I should never have come here, I should not have listened to you. I should have trusted my father.'

Purple lightning zigzagged suddenly across the midnight-dark sky as Brad said, 'It's too late now.' He leaned against the rail with his arms folded, watching her through hooded eyes.

'I was going to leave tomorrow,' she said, edging towards the steps. 'But I think it's better if I go now.'

His cold bitter laugh followed her as she hurried down the steps, freezing the blood in her veins. She started to run. She heard Brad shout a command and she glanced over her shoulder. 'Kill,' he cried again. And then she saw the Doberman, a fleet black arrow in the stormy darkness, racing towards her. She screamed and flung up her arms as the powerful dog launched itself at her. She felt a searing pain as its jaws clamped down on her arm, then she heard Wong shout.

'Down, Makana,' he yelled at the dog, running towards her. 'Drop it. Down, you bastard dog.'

The dog let go on command and Wong flung himself between her and the animal.

'Kill,' Brad yelled again, running towards them through the dark and rain with the shotgun in his hands.

Just as the Doberman grabbed the old Chinese man by the throat and sank his teeth deep into him.

'Oh God, oh God,' Bea screamed, frozen with horror. The old man was on the ground and the dog was tearing his face to pieces. There was blood everywhere, spurting from the big artery in his neck. A shot rang out and the dog lifted its bloody mouth from the old man. It stared for a moment at her, then it gave a thin unearthly wail. Its burning red-brown eyes glazed over and its legs crumpled, and it slid in slow motion to the ground, beside the body of Wong.

Horror and fear lent wings to Bea's feet and she took off down the slippery-wet path, waiting for the shot that she knew would send her into eternity too. Nothing happened and she glanced back over her shoulder. Brad was standing in the pouring rain over the two bodies. She saw him throw the shotgun aside and kneel beside them. 'Oh God,' she heard his anguished cry, 'look what they have done now.' She thought she caught the glitter of tears on his face as he raised his head to the sky, howling his agony.

She fled down the path towards the house. She had to get out of here as fast as she could . . . she would go to the police

... tell them her story ... tell them he was a madman ... Even as she thought it, she knew it would not work. They would look at Brad Kane, the gentleman rancher who owned a good part of the islands, whose family had lived here for generations. And they would look at her, an hysterical young girl with some wild story about an attack, and she knew whose side they would take.

She started running down the drive to the gates, then she remembered: her money and her credit cards were in her room. She dithered helplessly, she could not get far without them.

She looked back towards the house and saw the servants running, heard their cries of distress and guessed she had a few minutes' grace. She ran to her room, grabbed her bag and fled back through the gardens down to the gates. The guard had heard the shot. He had run to see what the trouble was, leaving the gates unguarded. She pressed the electronic device that opened them and slid through. Then she began to run, down the hill, jogging steadily in the pouring rain, her heart thudding in her throat.

It seemed ages before she saw a gas station and she began to slow down. She checked her watch. She had been running for twenty minutes. He wouldn't dare come after her in a public place, she thought, fumbling in her bag for a dime.

She went to the payphone and called a cab, and then she went into the washroom and cleaned herself up. Her arm was bleeding and she washed it, then took off her T-shirt and wrapped it around the wound. She put on a fresh T-shirt and a light sweater over it to hold the improvised bandage in place. She rinsed her face with cold water and combed her wet hair and then went back outside to wait for the cab.

Her throat was parched from running and she got a Coke

from the machine and sipped it, watching the road, still trembling inside. She thought of Brad's grieving face as he had looked down at Wong, and his wild agonised howl and she wondered if those were really tears she had seen? Or was it just the rain? And she remembered the dying dog, its eyes glazing over, sliding in slow motion to the ground. She knew that Wong had saved her life, and because of him, Brad would not be coming after her. Not yet.

The cab circled into the forecourt and she ran towards it. She climbed thankfully in, leaning back against the cushions, feeling safer as they sped off to the airport.

The next United flight left in two hours. Two hours! It stretched in front of her like eternity. She bought a ticket and hurried from the counter, hiding herself in the crowd, watching, waiting. But there was still no sign of Brad Kane when at last her flight was called.

She breathed a sigh of relief when she finally boarded the plane and took her seat. Now she was safe.

And then she arrived in San Francisco. And Brad was there, waiting for her.

Now, sitting on the terrace of her family's beautiful old farm in Provence, Bea wondered how she could have ever thought she would be safe again. Brad Kane was obsessed with the Lecontes. He was crazy. She had not realised how fast he would act. And how silently. She had not known that he was in the Gulfstream and on his way to San Francisco before she had even boarded her United flight. She could not have known that he was a man who could buy anything he wanted; and that he would know where to go to get what he needed ... the syringe with the fast-acting anaesthetic that would safely put her out for hours. So he could kill her and make it look like an accident. And then the Kanoi ranch would finally be all his.

* * *

She felt his presence before she saw him. There had been no sound, he was just suddenly there, a deeper shadow against the blackness. She saw the glow of his cigarette as he put it to his lips.

'So, Marie-Laure,' he said in that quiet flat tone. 'We meet again.'

Poochie bristled and lurched to his feet. He growled and showed his teeth warningly.

Brad laughed. 'I hope you haven't brought that mutt here to defend you. Somehow I don't think he's the right breed.'

Bea said quickly, 'Where are the children?' She was amazed that her voice sounded so calm. Now that she was seeing her killer face-to-face, she felt a hatred so intense she was shocked by it. But she had to keep that veneer of calm if she were to win. She had to know he had kept his word and they were all right.

'I kept my promise,' he said. 'They are in a taxi en route to the Villa Mimosa.'

She peered warily into the dark, tracking his hand with the cigarette. 'How do I know that's true?'

He shrugged indifferently. 'I guess you will just have to trust me, Marie-Laure.'

She saw him crush out the cigarette and then he walked towards her. She put her hand in her pocket, gripping the sharp little kitchen knife. Her hair was stuck to her head with the sweat of fear and she trembled with hate for him, and for Jack and Archer. They had gotten away with their crimes, but she wasn't going to allow Brad to get away with his. Not again. She would kill him first. She sobbed, horrified, as she realised what she was thinking, what Brad Kane was turning her into. A killer. A murderer. No better than all the Kanes.

And then she saw the gun in his hand. Poochie gave another deeper growl. She could see his bared fangs gleaming and she gripped his collar tighter.

'We are going for a short ride, Marie-Laure,' Brad said, ignoring the dog. 'A little sight-seeing. Pity it's so dark, but then you must know these roads like the back of your hand.' He took her arm and marched her to her car. He held the door open and indicated with the gun for her to get into the driver's seat. Poochie leapt in next to her, whining, not understanding

Brad climbed into the back and said, 'Okay start driving. Make a left at the T-junction. You remember, where it begins to climb steeply.'

Bea sensed the gun levelled at her head. She started the car and did as he said. Of course she knew the place he meant. It was a lookout point where she had spent many a lazy afternoon, scanning the peaceful valley hundreds of feet below, watching the cars crawling like ants up the steep roads to the beautiful *village perché* on the opposite side; listening to the summer sounds of the birds and the crickets; feeling the sun-warmed rocks beneath her as she lay there, admiring the poppyfields spread like a red carpet that changed with the months to acres of lavender or sunflowers; and vines ripening under the hot sun, readying for the fall harvest. The lookout point was an even more precipitous drop than Mitchell's Ravine.

Her hands shook as she drove slowly up the hill, casting round wildly for a way to escape. She still had the knife, but it was no match for his gun. Goddamnit, she told herself savagely, she wasn't drugged this time, she would fight for her life . . . she was not just going to let him push her over the edge again . . . he would have to shoot her first . . .

It occurred suddenly to her that Brad could have shot her just now on the terrace, if he had wanted. She had been a sitting duck. He would have saved himself all this trouble. But he had not. *He didn't want to shoot her.* That's why he'd had the Doberman attack her, and why he had pushed her over Mitchell's Ravine. *Because he didn't want it to look like murder. He still wanted it to look like an accident.*

She stopped the car at the top of the road. 'Drive to the edge,' he commanded. She did as he said, then switched off the engine, waiting. Brad did not make a move, did not say a word. The silence was deafening. She imagined the gun pointing at her head, but now she was sure he did not want to use it. The familiar night sounds began to penetrate her consciousness: the croak of tree frogs, the scurrying of nocturnal animals; the startled whirr of disturbed birds. Somewhere, in the valley far below, she saw a car's headlights. She watched hopefully as they flickered, then disappeared. And then nothing. She was alone with Brad Kane.

She heard Poochie whining as Brad got out of the car. In the glimmering darkness she could just make out the outline of the gun, pointed at her.

'Why are you doing this?' she screamed, suddenly needing to understand. 'I told you I don't want the ranch. I don't want the money. I don't want anything you've got . . .'

'You still don't see it, do you,' he marvelled. 'That all his life Jack was waiting for the Monkey to come back and steal his land. To take his birthright from him. I'm only protecting my interests. Keeping Kanoi for the Kanes. I cannot allow you – or any future Lecontes to jeopardise that. It is, my dear Marie-Laure, time to redress the balance of things.

'I think this is the best way,' he said, and she could see he was smiling at her. 'We have to make sure this time, don't we?'

He opened the car door. He reached in and took off the

handbrake, started the engine and put it in gear. Brad held her back with one arm as he reached for the accelerator. With a terrified scream Bea suddenly wrenched herself free. She hurled herself out the other door and Poochie leapt out after her, barking frantically. She lay stunned on the rough stony grass, as the car lurched towards the precipice. It teetered for a few seconds on the edge, then slid gently over. She heard the terrible shattering of glass and the great rending of steel as it bounced from rock to rock down the steep slope. And then the huge explosion as it burst into flames. She would have been in that inferno if Brad had had his way.

Fear got her to her feet, but Brad grabbed her from behind. He locked his arms round her and forced her towards the edge of the precipice. She screamed, endless throat-tearing screams, digging in her heels, clinging to the thorny branches in their path, scrabbling for a foothold on the loose stones. She had to get the knife . . . it was her only chance . . . she had to kill him before he could kill her. She heard Poochie's wild snarl and saw his black silhouette against the red glow of the inferno as the big dog hurled himself snarling at her attacker, taking Brad by surprise and knocking both of them to the ground.

Bea rolled away and scrambled quickly to her feet. She saw Brad put the gun to the dog's side and she kicked it out of his hand. She reached down to grab it but he was too quick for her. He snatched it, then smashed it savagely down on the dog's head. Poochie gave a high-pitched yelp and fell back and Bea cried out with fear and anger as Brad grabbed her foot, dragging her once more towards the edge.

She kicked out at him, rolling away, but he was on top of her in a second, then he was banging her head against the stones. The pain was intense and she knew it was never going to stop. She was slipping away into unconsciousness and she fought against it. She couldn't let him win, she *would not* . . . Somewhere in the back of her brain, over the noise of her own screams, she became aware of a new sound . . . then suddenly there were lights and other people.

Brad was up on his feet in a minute, pulling her with him, holding her in front of him as a shield. Groggily, she made out the half-circle of gendarmes. Their guns were aimed at them and dimly she heard Nick's voice shouting to her to 'hold on'. And then she slid backwards down the familiar black tunnel into unconsciousness.

'*Brad.*' Phyl called softly, '*Brad, it's me.*'

He peered into the lights, puzzled. '*Rebecca,*' he said in a harsh whisper. 'What are you doing here? I thought you were waiting for me, in San Francisco. We were going to Kalani. Remember?'

Phyl's numb heart felt as though it were no longer part of her body as she looked at him. This was not the charming lover she had known. It was not the urbane man-of-the-world. The rich handsome rancher, who had it all. She was looking at a stranger.

Taking a deep breath, she walked into the circle of light created by the cars' headlamps. Brad was still holding Bea's limp body and she could not tell if she was dead or alive.

'Let her go, Brad,' she said softly, close to him.

His pale eyes searched hers as he said, 'I had to do it. You know that, don't you? You, of all people, must understand.'

'I do, Brad. I understand. But I think I know a better way.'

She was shaking with terror. All it would take was one quick thrust and Bea would be over the edge . . .

Brad looked at the surrounding gendarmes. He seemed

435

suddenly to come to reality. 'It's too late now, isn't it?' he said, looking searchingly at her.

She nodded, unable to speak. He was changing in front of her eyes, from the cold-blooded mad hunter with his prey, back to the easy charming man she had known.

'And too late for us.' He stared at her and added softly, 'If I hurt you, I'm sorry, Phyl. You were the only woman I might have loved.'

He pushed Marie-Laure towards her. Then he put the gun to his head. His wild mad eyes met Phyl's for a split-second. '*You traitor, Rebecca,*' he said viciously as he pulled the trigger.

Her own screams echoed in her ears as she knew they would in nightmares for ever after, as Brad's handsome blond head exploded into a thousand bloody fragments and he spun over the edge into the abyss.

CHAPTER 36

Mahoney arrived at the Villa Mimosa early the next morning. They were sitting on the terrace, sipping lemonade, looking out over the sloping lawns, at the towering cedars and the needle cypresses pointing into the clear blue sky; out to the tranquil view of the Mediterranean whose colour had once made Johnny Leconte redefine the word 'azure'.

Scott and Julie had been found frightened but unharmed, locked in the boot of Brad's car, though Mahoney had no doubt he would have killed them too. Brad would have wanted no witnesses.

Bea – or Marie-Laure as they must now learn to call her – had her poor head wrapped once more in bandages and she said wryly she was beginning to like the shaven-head look. She was badly cut and bruised, but it was all nothing compared with the relief in her heart, now that she knew who she was, and the fear was finally gone.

She was just glad she didn't have to wear the stiff white plastic collar like Poochie to stop him scratching the row of stitches on the back of his own poor shaven head. He was lying happily at her feet, sated with as much steak as a dog could eat. And Nick was holding her hand as she told them the story of what happened to her that day at Diamond Head, and how Brad had caught up with her at San Francisco airport.

'It's all over now,' Phyl said comfortingly, as they watched the children racing joyously across the lawn to the pool. 'You have to learn to forget. To go on with your life.'

Bea smiled affectionately at her. 'It's thanks to all of you I'm still alive. And I intend to stay that way.' She glanced round at her home, at her children, her man, her friends. 'After all,' she said, 'I've got a lot to live for.'

Phyl leaned back against the cushions. Her eyes were still swollen from the tears she had shed, and she looked pale and exhausted.

'You could surely use a touch of that red lipstick,' Mahoney said with a grin, pulling a chair companionably next to her, and pouring himself a glass of lemonade.

She glared at him but he thought it was a weak glare, none of her usual flashing-blue-eyed stuff.

'The American cavalry to the rescue,' she said sarcastically. 'Just a bit too late.'

'Yeah. Even Concorde wasn't fast enough. And they haven't yet found a way to beam us over, like Captain Spock. But the FBI and Interpol have those magic computers that keep us all in touch. So the cavalry did get there in time, after all.' He threw her a serious glance and added softly, 'Thank God.'

'But how did you find out it was Brad?'

'Two and two. I should have caught it earlier, when I heard Hawaii mentioned. A private plane piloted by Brad Kane came in from Hawaii that night.' He shrugged, 'I should have known.'

'No man is infallible,' Phyl said gently, not wanting him to feel guilty.

'And no woman,' he replied, meeting her eyes. 'Maybe you should remember that.'

He held her eyes for a long moment. She knew he meant what had happened to her baby, to Marie-Laure, to Brad.

She could not be all things to all people any more. She was not perfect. She just had to be Phyl Forster, a woman doing the best job she could. And getting on with her own life.

Mahoney leaned over and whispered in her ear, 'Guess what?'

She leaned back and looked at him. 'What?'

'I've made a reservation tonight at the Moulin de Mougins. Remember, I promised one day I'd take you there. See if their chicken is as good as mine?'

She put her head back and laughed, and then she kissed him. It was a happy kiss. 'Mr Longshot,' she said, remembering.

His eyes crinkled at the corners as he gave her that wide, mocking grin.

'That's me,' he agreed, taking her hand and kissing her back.